VICTOR NAMELESS

Gabriella Mautner

VICTOR NAMELESS

Torn Apart by War, Reunited by a Miracle,
Two Lovers Triumph Against All Odds

Gabriella Mautner

Published by Eva Michele Mautner

ISBN **978-0-578-58107-1**

Author photo: Nancy Alcott Photography

Praise for GABRIELLA MAUTNER

"Gabriella Mautner is a local treasure—an internationally recognized novelist and memoirist who has distinguished herself with literary work of a rare and high caliber."

—MICHAEL KRASNY, *KQED Radio, San Francisco*

Praise for VICTOR NAMELESS

"*Victor Nameless* is an impressive novel, suspenseful from beginning to end, a tale that will preoccupy my mind and heart for a long time. I accompanied Victor, deeply moved by his long path of suffering, which is also his path to maturity. The author almost off-handedly succeeds in writing a Bildungsroman in the German tradition of Goethe and Gottfried Keller. But her major literary accomplishment is that she does not attempt to present the Holocaust (which would be impossible, given its magnitude), but creates protagonists who are called to live their lives "face-to-face with the Shoa" (Paul Celan). In addition, it's a marvel that the author, at her advanced age, has written such a passionate and convincing love story."

—WOLFGANG EMMERICH, *professor emeritus of modern German literature at the University of Bremen, Germany*

"A spellbinding tale of love and resilience. Two people torn apart by the chaos of war and persecution, forced onto dangerous odysseys through Europe and the Soviet Union. Two lovers searching for freedom and for each other. An incredible true story of survival of the human spirit against all odds. *Victor Nameless* is written with deep feeling and a sense of humor about the cruel and absurd turns of fate—a humor that can only come from a German-Jewish author who has been a refugee and survivor herself. A wonderful book."

—KIM CHERNIN, PhD, *writer, poet, and spiritual consultant*

"Just when you think you've read every last account of the Holocaust, along comes *Victor Nameless*, a heartrending, beautifully narrated story about a survivor, relocating his identity and soul. Gabriella Mautner's riveting story is one of those inspiring tales that let the world know that there are still stories left to tell."

—JOAN GELFAND, *poet and author of* Fear to Shred, *a novel about a Silicon Valley startup*

"A deep, poetic portrayal of love and courage, told with imagination, humor, and integrity. The originality and resonance of Gabriella Mautner's voice takes us to the inner lives of her characters with nerve and compassion. She writes with a passion that is at times breathtaking, drawing us into a world beneath the obvious, inspiring us to examine the contradictions within the human spirit and the complexities of a journey that can lead to enduring love."

—TOM BENTLEY-FISHER, *theater director, acting teacher, writer*

"A story of love and survival during World War II—two lovers, two separate paths through terror and loneliness, written with a gentle hand and a warm heart. I was captivated."

—JOE M. COHEN, *inventor and musician*

"Gabriella Mautner's latest captivating book, *Victor Nameless*, reveals the depth of the author's anguished experiences from which the story springs. She writes with a poignant intimacy, reminding us of our capacity to be light bearers for each other, dispelling the blackness that oozes from the human soul."

—SUKI MUNSELL, *PhD*

"I loved this book! It's well-written, gripping, and tells of a Holocaust experience I'd never heard before."

—RUTH FLAXMAN, *editor*

Praise for OUT OF A SEASON

"Mrs. Mautner knows her Italian life and landscape like the back of her hand. Setting her gently understanding portrait of a quixotic thirteen-year-old girl evocatively against the dreamlike, soon-to-be-lost Italian summer days, she has produced a first novel that is nicely perceived."
—*Publisher's Weekly*

"This is an unusual, even haunting 'woman's' book. *Out of a Season* leaves no question that one more serious, dedicated writer is launched."
—*San Francisco Chronicle*

"*Out of a Season* has a simplicity, a young fervor, and a remarkable timelessness not unlike that of Radiguet's *Devil in the Flesh.*"
—**KAY BOYLE**, *author of* Monday Night and Generation Without Farewell

"A wise and beautiful tale about growing up through the agonies of love, many kinds of love, and the renunciations and forbearance they entail. Simply, clearly, and movingly told, too, for though its complications are many and subtle, they are the complications of life."
—**WALTER VAN TILBURG CLARK**, *author of* The Oxbow Incident

Praise for LOVERS AND FUGITIVES

"A taut, convincing story—each border crossing is as gripping as the last ... and the wartime life of shortages, rations and continuous fear is rendered with a fine eye for detail."
—*New York Times Book Review*

"This is a competent escape saga—with the built-in solidity of fiction that reflects real tales of courage no less extraordinary."
—*Kirkus Review*

"The perilous odyssey undertaken by some European Jews during World War II to avoid the doom awaiting them in concentration camps is depicted in this vivid, haunting novel."
—*Publisher's Weekly*

"You have been tenacious, you have been triumphant, you have carried *Lovers and Fugitives* through to this happy moment. You are a writer, come hell or high water, and I salute you with congratulations!"
—**WRIGHT MORRIS**, *author of* The Field of Vision and Plains Song

Praise for THE GOOD PLACE

"Her experiences are told from a child's viewpoint, but so appealingly that the reader may at times feel drawn into the story as a participant."
—**DAVID KOBLICK**, *reviewer/translator, Austria*

Praise for ADDIO POSITANO

"A gem of a novel, evoking another time and place in a truly refreshing way. Gabriella Mautner's descriptive skills make the Southern Italian people and landscapes come alive, like a musical sonata."
—**TOM SOLINGER**, *independent reviewer*

Other books by Gabriella Mautner

Out of a Season (1968)

Lovers and Fugitives (1985)

The Good Place (2006)

Addio Positano (2011)

For Ari,
My beloved grandson

Contents

World War II began on September 1, 1939 with the German invasion of Poland. The Poles' courageous resistance was soon crushed by the powerful forces of the enemy. A few weeks later, following a pact with the Nazis, the Soviets invaded the country from the east.

By the end of the month, another German-Russian agreement was signed in Moscow stating that the western provinces would remain under German command, while the eastern part of the country was assigned to Byelorussia and the Ukraine.

During the Nazi offensive the country was subjected to bombardment and plunder. Towns and villages were destroyed; people shot at random. Jews and resistance fighters faced relentless persecution.

PART 1

1.

FORSAKEN

Victor rushed to the countryside in desperate search of a refuge. Germany was expected to invade Poland at any moment. He had to find some farm or convent where he could hide his family, but his German accent was enough to make even nuns and priests slam the door on him.

When he returned to the town where he had left Sophie and little Hannah, there was no sign of them in the barren room. A cold dish of mush sat congealing on the kitchen table. He looked at the two wicker chairs turned upside down, their wooden legs stretched toward the ceiling like those of the dead horse he had passed on the road.

A neighbor looked in and told him that his wife and child had been swept away by the merciless broom of the enemy. Two days before, during the first German onslaught, the neighbor had been in the square in front of the church. He had seen Victor's family shot, along with the others.

The others? Victor could only think of Sophie and the baby. He ran out to the square, but the square was deserted and clean, without a sign of struggle or death. Everything was still. People had either left town or were hiding behind locked doors.

Stumbling back, sobbing helplessly, he almost collided with an elderly woman who carried a knapsack over her shoulder. He tried to tell her in his broken Polish that he could no longer find his wife and child. Was it true that people had been shot in front of the church?

"I'm afraid it's true," she said reluctantly.

"But there were no bodies—nothing in the square."

"They do quick work, the Germans." Seeing his tears, she added,

"Perhaps your wife tried to escape."

"But she was waiting for me." His own words convinced him that Sophie would never have tried to run without him.

Back in the kitchen, he noticed the broken mirror above the sink and stared at his stubbly face. In a trance, he rubbed his wet brush across a brown piece of soap. It turned into white foam on his skin. He shaved his left cheek with meticulous vertical stripes, cut himself, and cursed. He dropped the razor and wiped his face. He threw some dates into a knapsack, took his coat and scarf and rushed out.

Mindlessly, he ran toward the main road leading out of town, then followed a group of refugees who were moving as far as possible to the east in order to evade the German army. He went on that way for a long time, unaware that he was fleeing from the invading armies in the west toward the forces of the Soviet Union.

The band of refugees multiplied as they kept moving through a no-man's-land of shadows. In his madness and deadly fatigue, Victor wondered how many bristles were still sprouting on his right cheek and how many days it would take for a beard to grow back in even. One shoulder made him feel lopsided, thanks to the light weight of his knapsack. All he had left in his coat pocket was the miniature recorder he had purchased after losing his flute at the Polish border.

"What's that?" the border guard had asked, pointing at the black case in Victor's hand.

"A flute."

The man snatched the case, put it on the table beside him, and snapped it open. Victor stared in shock at his precious silver flute—his mother's last gift—as brutal hands tore it out of its bed of red velvet, like wrenching a child from its sleep.

"You don't need this anymore, dirty Jew." The guard locked the instrument back into its case. With the sweep of one hand, he threw it to the end of the table, pushing Sophie out of his way. She nearly fell with the baby in her arms. Victor caught her just in time.

Shivering with cold in spite of the warm September evening, he wrapped the red scarf, another of his mother's gifts, around his neck. She had died six months ago, shortly after his twenty-second birthday, and he had bitterly grieved the loss. Her heart had given out when they received the order from Gestapo headquarters: they had twenty-four hours to leave Stuttgart, the city where they had lived all their lives. The decree stated they must go to Poland because Victor's father, who had died seventeen years earlier, happened to be born in a Polish town near the German frontier.

No one had noticed Polish fighters caught between the two powerful invaders. On the second night, the fugitives came across fields full of the dead lit up by a harvest moon: people, horses, rabbits, birds. Victor turned to stone. The refugees slept on the ground or in ditches. The next morning they met with a reconnaissance patrol of the Red Army. The men looked as uncouth as the plough horses they were riding. After a huge display of militarism in the west, people expected dashing hussars with sparkling eyes and well-made uniforms. Victor watched one of the refugees empty his pockets of cigarettes and offer them as gifts to a ruddy fellow. One of the Russians gave him a heel of bread. Victor thanked him with a nod of his head. Devouring it in a daze, he searched his empty pockets for a token in return, but was unable to manage even so as much as a smile.

The Russians exchanged a few words and gestures with the refugees, then went on their way. Sudden rain poured from the sky, turning fields into muddy ponds. Dots of soldiers appeared on a distant hill. An enormous Soviet tractor smoothed out the mud and transformed it into a road. Tanks, cannons, and infantrymen began to glide down a slope as if skating across a polished floor.

An hour later, the refugees entered a town recently occupied by the Red Army. People were standing in line for bread. The rain had stopped. A theater was showing a film of the Soviets fighting White Russians. Victor went in. He stared at the screen, yearning for the touch of his baby. His wet clothes clung to his back. The movie ended with the triumphant victory of the Red Army. His shoes were clogged with mud.

Marching until his heels began to bleed, crossing abandoned villages where hungry wanderers rummaged for bits of food, he moved on, head bent, heeding no one. Polish words addressed to him remained unanswered. "The poor fellow must be deaf and dumb," he heard a woman say in Yiddish. Her words, close to German, were easier for him to understand.

As soon as darkness fell and the fugitives settled down for the night, Victor took out his miniature recorder. The wooden pipe comforted everyone except the disheartened piper; still, it sent him into brief, nightmarish spurts of slumber. When he opened his eyes, the woman offered him an apple.

"Understand Yiddish?" she asked.

"A little."

"So you can hear me?"

"A little."

"So you can speak?"

"A little."

She laughed. "Eat," she told him. "You earned it. Your beautiful music…"

***

Soon after the refugees crossed the river Prut, their march came to an end. They entered the city of Lvov, or Lemberg. Under the terms of the Molotov-Ribbentrop Pact, it had just been turned into the capital of the Ukraine.

Victor made no attempt to unravel the tangled threads of his predicament. A first encounter with the new regime taught him that a man without proper documents was like a hare surrounded by hunters. When ordered to present himself to the authorities, he was quick to learn that foreigners were despicable dogs, especially when unable to communicate in Russian. Effacing himself wasn't enough. He wished to be invisible. His wish was granted by an official who asked for his family name. Unable to understand Victor's answer, the official grew impatient, writing *"Nameless"* next to *"Victor"* into a ledger. He wrote it again on a temporary identification card.

"Where you from, Nameless?" he asked. Victor tried to tell him that he had just arrived from Poland. The official repeated a Russian word that sounded like "*Polish*", and then handed the card to Victor after writing the word on its last line.

***

After the ditches, bedding down in one of the city's doorways was a change for the better. It reminded Victor of the time when he was a child and had seen an old beggar. The poor man was asleep on a sidewalk. Staring at him in shock, he had asked his mother to take the man home.

"And where would we put him?"

He suggested the bed in the sewing room, where his friend Walter slept when he came over to spend the night. He had never forgotten the sight of that pitiful man. And now he was grateful for the portico that kept him dry on rainy nights. The city was overcrowded. Men and women slept wherever they could. Victor found his niche at a small distance from the Krakowski Hotel. In the morning, he walked along the stalls of the bazaar, gathering from shreds of Yiddish conversations that there had been no fighting during the Russian invasion of Lvov. A number of inhabitants were still hiding in the basements of their gabled houses. The city was swarming with Russians and refugees. Private trade was forbidden, in spite of a frantic demand for wares. Shopkeepers were forced to sell off their merchandise at prewar prices. Like wild herds seeking the last stubs of grass on an overgrazed meadow, people swarmed into shops, looking for clothes and fabrics.

Caught in a crowd, Victor was swept into a store. Without knowing what he was doing, he pointed at a roll of tan cotton material blooming with Forget Me Nots and put his last money on the table. The rosy-cheeked Ukrainian mama figured out how much of the cloth to cut. With cracked sausage fingers, she wrapped his purchase into old newspapers. He thanked her with a friendly gesture and went out.

A red soldier stopped him in the street, pointing at his parcel. Victor gasped. *Jail*, he thought, *Siberia*…"How much, comrade?", the soldier asked in Russian. He raised two fingers of one hand. Taking Victor's stunned silence for a no, he raised two fingers, then three. Realizing that he was to receive three times the amount he had paid, Victor dropped his parcel into the lad's hands. He returned to the shop a few minutes later, bought three times as much material, and tripled the price for the next customer. All transactions were performed in pantomime.

When he tried to buy himself a meal in the late afternoon, he learned that rubles were worthless. His trading hardly provided him with a loaf of bread. For the next few days, he managed to increase his bartering on the black market, watching the wares decrease until the shops were stripped naked.

Time to find other means of survival. The new administration was taking over. Victor was chased away when he offered his services in one of the better restaurants. Caviar and dry cod were served only to officers of the occupying army or to black marketers able to afford such luxuries.

Day after day, food was growing more costly and scarce. His money spent, Victor looked for work in the residential quarters of the city. Knocking on doors of respectable homes, he offered to carry out trash, clean cellars, prune bushes. More often than not, he was chased away by housewives or servants. Crossing the Zanuck Park, he walked bent with an old man's gait, hands clasped behind his back, climbing the steep *Kurkov Ulica* in the shadow of gabled houses, ringing bell after bell. At last, an elderly woman took pity on him with a plate of borscht. On the steps in front of her patrician home, he dipped his slice of coarse bread into the hot beet soup, unaware of the tears running down his cheeks. The woman kept stroking his hair, speaking to him in Polish. From her words, he gathered that his pleasing looks were the cause of his good fortune.

One late afternoon, after another fruitless search for work, Victor settled in front of his portico. Ignoring his hunger, he pulled the recorder from his coat pocket and dropped the red scarf onto his thighs. Eyes closed, he blew a wordless lament against the darkening sky. The song turned like a sunflower toward the last rays of the sun. As the music flowed from his body, he was transported into another world. The final notes reverberated through the limpid air to the sound of hands clapping.

When he opened his eyes, he saw that a small crowd had gathered in the street around him. A few kopeks had fallen into the nest of his red scarf. Men and women with haggard faces, natives and refugees, were looking at him appreciatively. They continued applauding, waiting for an encore. Heartened by this response, he played a few more tunes. An old woman with a black kerchief tied under her hairy chin dropped a wrinkled apple into his scarf. He thanked her with a birdlike trill. Others followed with small chunks of bread and more kopeks. Victor raised his hands and smiled at them in gratitude.

The manager of the apartment building, who had been watching and waiting for the end of Victor's performance, now told the crowd to leave. At his signal, Victor hastened to stuff the scarf with its treasures into the pocket of his coat and hurried up the stairs behind the man. Panting heavily from the climb, the manager opened an office door on the third floor. He ordered the young man to sit down on a bench and wait. Left alone, Victor glanced uneasily toward a dark hall, awaiting the verdict like a patient in a doctor's office.

After a long time, a squat Russian functionary appeared. He sat down at the table of the barren room and stared at Victor in silence.

"*Polish?*" he addressed him at last. Victor nodded. "*Sprichst Deutsch?*"

Victor shrugged. "Just a little...."

"I hear you play music down there?" the official said in German, gesturing toward the street. "Play something for me."

Victor pulled out his *sopranino* recorder, careful to keep the coins, the apple and dates concealed in his pocket. He remembered the tune of a Russian folksong. The functionary beamed at him in delight. "*Ah, die Wolgaschlepper!*" he said, listening attentively, then hummed the tune in a deep bass voice.

Victor waited in silence.

"You go to Cultural Chamber of district. Here," the official said unexpectedly, writing an address on a piece of paper. "They have work for you. Tell the director Comrade Tertloff sent you. You get room there, too."

"Thank you, comrade," Victor murmured. He couldn't believe his good luck. Work and a room at the Chamber of Culture! They might need a flautist for the opera or ballet…Lvov was well known for its cultural life. The new administration might reopen its symphony, opera house, and theaters in order to give the people work and education, just as it was beginning to open public cooperatives.

On his way to the Chamber of Culture, he saw a crowd forming in front of a new public cooperative. Even at night, people waited in line for wares supposed to be for sale. Victor learned from a passerby that supplies were scarce. Only the first ten people received anything. He fortified himself with a chunk of bread and the apple.

On reaching his destination, he was stopped by a guard at the entrance. "Director Malenkov," Victor said, producing the paper with Comrade Tertloff's name.

"Comrade Director Malenkov," the guard repeated respectfully. "Second floor to your left."

There were four doors on the second floor. He began knocking at the first. No answer. He found the director at a desk behind the third, a jovial man of medium height and age with a ruddy complexion and a scar across his left temple. After a moment of the usual linguistic confusion, Malenkov addressed him in flawless English, a foreign language Victor spoke with some skill. He briefly explained his situation, then expressed the hope that the work Comrade Tertloff had promised him might be of an artistic nature.

The director laughed heartily. "You must be dreaming. Your post will be that of janitor for our Cultural Chamber. There will be a small room for you in the attic. You ought to kiss the ground for your good fortune."

"Of course," Victor said quickly. "I'm grateful for any kind of work that gives me food and shelter."

"As to your salary," the director went on, "we have to consult with the chief office in Moscow. So you'll have to wait."

A pimply young official was called in to instruct Victor in the various duties expected of him. His function as a government employee without salary consisted of making a fire in the stove for the comrades at five o'clock each morning, bringing and receiving messages, and running errands, such as buying food, vodka, and cigarettes. He was to sweep the halls and rooms and be at everyone's beck and call.

Victor was quick to learn the needs and idiosyncrasies of the various officials. They soon depended on him for the luxuries they craved. As to his salary—since Moscow did not answer and probably never would—he had to do the next best thing: namely, take care of himself.

The attic room was crowded with officials' crates and cases, leaving barely enough space for his cot, but he had a cot to sleep on, and it was good. Since one of his tasks consisted of kindling the comrades' stove, coal and wood were under his control allowing him to barter a few of those precious items for an occasional meal.

During his daily walks, he observed that the members of the new administration occupied most of the city's apartments, while former tenants were crowded into one room with their families. The nearest bazaar was strewn with a hastily erected stall, which offered expensive soups, coffee, hot cabbage, or *piroshki* for sale. Most refugees survived on such meals. For a steep price, the more affluent spent the night under the tables of closed restaurants. Others had to squeeze into the overcrowded rooms of residents trying to earn a few extra rubles.

At seven o'clock in the morning, the marketplace reminded Victor of a fair. People streamed out of buildings. Women tried to sell their husbands' personal belongings. Among them were the wives of men imprisoned for their wealth and the wives of Polish high officials sent to Siberian camps. Soviet soldiers and officers with women on their arms shopped and strolled from stall to colorful stall. Distrusting the currency, the peasants refused to take money for their wares, but bartered firewood or victuals for clothing, shoes, shirts, or linen.

One morning, Director Malenkov asked Victor in a whisper to follow him into the toilet. Before obeying the comrade's request, Victor glanced uneasily down the empty hall.

"Lock the door!"

Victor stalled for time. He asked, "What can I do for you, Comrade Malenkov?"

The director pointed at the toilet seat. "Show me," he said impatiently, "how it's done."

"You sit on it," Victor said, averting his head to hide the grin on his face.

"A splendid idea!" Malenkov exclaimed in honest delight.

"But you stand, raise the cover, and aim into the bowl when you piss."

"This is great." Malenkov smacked his knee. "Some of those capitalist dogs are clever devils! They sit when they shit and they aim when they stand…"

"W.C. Water closet. When you are done, you pull the chain and flush. An English invention. You speak English so well, Comrade Director. I was under the impression that you lived abroad."

"Never left Mother Russia." Malenkov put his arm around Victor's shoulder as they walked out. "Had an English aunt. Taught me many tricks…" He winked significantly.

Used to latrines, the masters of the new cultural administration seemed baffled by toilet seats and flushing water. Since his work included cleaning the men's rooms, Victor had not failed to notice that his masters climbed on the seats and, trying to take aim in this unstable position, defiled everything around them. In addition, the gentlemen used thumb or index finger to blow their noses. Seeing that capitalists availed themselves of handkerchiefs, they rose to Western standards by using shreds of newspaper and throwing them on the floor or into the corners, expecting janitor Victor to sweep them away.

At last, word came from Moscow about his salary. Unfortunately, Malenkov explained, he had to send in papers and credentials.

"You said you had no passport. That means you can't prove your identity. Let sleeping dogs lie, the English say. I was told one of the theaters is going to be reopened. I know the man in charge. Maybe he can use you."

"Thank you, Comrade Director. I like nothing better than to play the flute. I could look for work in a symphony or opera and..."

"Wait, my impetuous Romeo. Did I say anything about music? If we had silent films, you could certainly do something with your good looks. But this is Russian theater..."

Victor was shocked at his own exuberance about the mere possibility of playing the flute. How could he forget his family's tragedy so quickly and yearn to improve his lot? How could he be so worthless and shallow? He deserved nothing better than cleaning latrines.

2.

MAESTRO BUBACHOFF

The ice covering the pond in Zanuck Park had melted and the acacia trees were in bloom. A windy spring followed that first hard winter of the war. Coal, as precious as gold during the cold season, was no longer in demand. Victor might have starved were it not for the help of Director Malenkov, who paid him a few rubles for his services.

The theater opened at last and Victor was hired as a stagehand. He slept in one of the dressing rooms. Most of the actors were Polish refugees with perfect command of Russian. They had no conception of the Soviet theater, nor of the kind of plays acceptable to members of the Communist Party. Friction and complaints abounded from the start because the Western actors and intellectuals felt superior to their administrators. The young Russian leader, fascinated by their new ideas, tried to comply with their wishes. This caused some comrades at the main office to file a complaint stating that their leader was treating those individualists with kid gloves. As a consequence, the party line was used to prepare a fat post for another man from whom the clique who had filed the complaint expected to reap rewards. One morning Victor found a stranger in the office, a man who introduced himself as the new leader. The former boss had vanished after being demoted to some obscure position.

The new leader had spent five years indoctrinating people in Siberia and was obviously ignorant of anything connected with the theater. All he could do was make life hard for everyone by using the bureaucratic methods he had applied in the Far East. His complaints about sabotage by capitalist actor dogs making fun of his incompetence fell on deaf ears, and he was promptly shipped off to indoctrinate fresh territories.

His post was taken over by a former Volga skipper, an imposing captain, expected to organize the theater along with the entire new cultural life of this great city of the Western Ukraine. He was a true giant whose tread made the stage planks sigh and whose voice shook the rafters. High Slavic cheekbones engulfed the slits of his lively black eyes. There was only a small division between his head and shoulders, and a watermelon's bulge above the belt of his sailor's shirt. A true sailor, he held onto the custom of drinking vodka from large glass vases. Victor learned that he used to entertain his crew as a remarkable accordion player. Enthusiastic mates spread the word about his gift at every harbor. As a consequence, their skipper had been sent to a conservatory of music to develop his skills. He succeeded so well that he was given the post of director of several larger orchestras. Since a good conductor was a man of culture, it was not surprising that such a person of note would be elected cultural leader of the Western Ukraine.

Yet the envy of colleagues succeeded in destroying his privileged position. State funds, they claimed, had allowed the Maestro to furnish his offices, but not his own apartment, with the most lavish leather sofas and chairs. As Victor learned later from the conductor's loyal friends, the rumors about his apartment were an outright lie; he had furnished his lodgings with his own private means. Yet the story turned into a major scandal. Comrade Bubachoff, oblivious to money and commerce and unable to prove his innocence, was demoted to conducting a minor orchestra in town.

The city received a new cultural stamp as soon as it reopened the opera house, some art galleries, and a major theater. At the same time, life in the streets changed its aspect. Along with the many refugees, Soviet officials could now be recognized by their civilian dress. Instead of party uniforms, they wore black suits, black coats, and black peaked caps.

Victor's work consisted of changing the scenery and furniture of various plays, which needed to be carried from basement to the stage each day and earned him the nickname of "culture-carrier". He quickly acquired the tricky skill of lowering the sky or a cave dwelling from the rigging loft and helped to build terraces and pavilions which were abruptly transformed into a forest or cemetery. He ran back and forth among heavily painted actors and actresses as they repeated their lines. At such close proximity, their colorful costumes and striking faces lost all glamour. But as soon as the curtain rose and Victor was watching from the wings, the magic of the spoken word carried him into a world of dreams. Although his Russian was improving, much of the dialogue escaped him, but the make-believe of a performance supplanted, at least for an evening, the dull routine of his days.

As the curtain fell, he gleaned from the actors' remarks that they were far from sharing his ardent involvement in the drama. While speaking their lines, they were dreaming of bread and meat.

Unable to grasp his current odd existence, Victor's past grew equally unreal. The new order allowed no time for idle thought or mourning. Panting under the weight of terraces, pavilions, and cloudy skies, he was hardly aware of his uprooted state and isolation. A stranger to himself, he observed his own actions as he watched those of others. He had become one of the people. Workmen kept yelling at actors who got in their way, venting their frustration with curses — one brute cursing another and wishing that the devil should get into his father's father, or that misery should befall his whore of a mother. Knowing that he was unable to respond in kind, Victor kept out of their way.

Each morning, he and the other stagehands were required to move last night's props to storage rooms behind the theater. Every piece of movable scenery carried the name of the play on its back. A Roman numeral marked the act, an Arabic one the order of succession in which the scenery or the pavilion had to be arranged. Each object had to be carried across the stage while another group brought in the pieces for the play to be performed that night. Everyone was in everyone's way. Particularly the electricians, who became targets for the wildest curses, thanks to the actors bumping into projectors and falling over their cables.

It seemed to Victor that one by one, fragment by splintering fragment, he was storing away the pieces of his life. Covered with mold, they would rust in some forgotten room or attic, their backs marked by

Roman or Arabic numbers, hieroglyphics he could no longer decipher.

If only he were given the comfort of music. A first flautist and child soloist in a youth orchestra in Stuttgart, he had meant to pursue a lifelong career, playing and writing his own compositions. Not even under the persecution of recent years, when his only outlet had shrunk into a secret ensemble of Jewish musicians, did he give up his cherished dream. But now, deprived of the exquisite flute the Nazi guard had torn from him at the Polish border, and with no opportunity to practice, he dared not look for an audition in any orchestra. His callused hands only made matters worse.

At night, he fell on his cot exhausted from the day's work. He tried a few times to acquire fabrics or shoes in a low-cost cooperative, then sell them at a higher price at the bazaar. More often than not, militiamen would catch and arrest both vendors and buyers, then confiscate all black-market goods in order to sell them. Bewildered by this maze of corruption, he feared to fall into the hands of the secret police and finally asked the director for a modest salary. To his relief, the director agreed without asking to see his passport and paid him just enough to keep him from starving.

Having lost his last name and identity, Victor felt at one with thousands of others equally uprooted. He was a pariah among refugees, in flight from battles or the hunters of the master race, without sharing their hope of returning home after the war. No home was waiting for him. And where could he find new roots, however modest?

The war was in full swing, and there were rumors that the Germans had suddenly turned against the Soviet Union and might start a spring offensive any day — all the more reason for Victor to keep to himself. With his German accent, anyone might denounce him as a Nazi spy. His loneliness and frequent misunderstanding of the galloping conversations between Polish and Russian actors made him feel like a deaf-mute. He had given up any hope that Sophie and their sweet baby might still be alive. He often wept bitterly about the loss of his family, but found some consolation from their being spared a future of endless suffering.

Forced to work ten hours each day, the actors were now divided into categories and paid according to their skills as first, second, or third-class performers. This caused a great deal of jealousy and was followed by the disintegration of a once harmonious collaboration. Each one tried to prove to the director that he was a better performer than his rival, documenting this with some extravagant gift. As a result, the director showed favor to certain people, thus giving rise to additional friction. All gossip was reported to him, the absolute ruler of the group. At theater meetings, he unfairly reprimanded a small number of individuals, singling them out for criticism. Such meetings took place once a week. They were part of a holiday serving to raise contributions for a fund meant to widen the goals of the Great New Order. Everyone had to be present or else be branded a rebel. The director would appear on stage, inciting everyone to work harder. "Literature and the arts shall be promoted to serve the people, to improve the consciousness as well as the labor enthusiasm of the people. Since now everything belongs to us, the more we work, the more we shall receive."

It was all in the spirit of *We the People*. Victor heard that such speeches were addressed to employees all over, in cooperatives and factories of the state.

After these meetings, most of his colleagues would continue going to the bazaars and look for certain black marketers or racketeers, in order to pave the way for a more lucrative *Me, the People*. As to the art of commerce, Victor knew that neither luck nor talent was on his side. Though tempted to play his recorder, hoping for a repeat performance of that early September evening which had unexpectedly improved his lot, he decided against it. The innocence and spontaneity of that incident could hardly be recaptured. This time it might make him feel like a beggar and erase his one good memory of Lvov.

Change was in the air. Government offices opened all over town enrolling people for work. Day after day, crowds stood in line to apply for labor in the territories of the Ukraine, the Don, or the Ural. Transports continually left the city. The authorities were handing out passports to people living at a stable address. Anyone able to prove his or her former occupation, including those of the applicant's mother and father, along with the proper documents, was not only entitled to a passport, but forced to take it. There were those without permanent job or domicile who had applied to return to their country of origin. Then there were others who, like Victor, feared any kind of contact with the authorities.

He hoped to be forgotten in his dark corner of a dressing room. He had no official work permit, no valid legal papers. Too poor to buy himself a document or to find proper witnesses at the bazaar, he feared being shipped off to some faraway territory.

A few workers managed to return from such places and reported that they were welcomed with music on arrival, told to take a shower, and sent to a canteen for a meal. One of the natives showed them a loaf and said, "See, this is bread," adding with pride how generously the government took care of its workers. "You eat in a canteen what everybody else eats. One group of people works for your comfort so that you may have a warm meal. In turn, you work for others. Each one works for the people, and we, the people, are working for you. Here you sleep in one room with twelve other comrades. The bed, linen, and covers belong to the factory. That is, us, the people. For recreation, we have films showing you how a factory or a coal mine looks, and how saboteurs, discovered by loyal comrades, are brought to justice. We also have performances of plays and comedies created by our own workers in the interest of our people. Comrade, give me that watch, you don't need it, and we don't have enough timepieces. You must concentrate on more important matters. Everything else will come later. Our sirens will wake you and blow the time for meals. Your dedication will earn you money and fame. A good worker will get into the paper you can read on the wall. And the money you won't need to spend will be kept in a savings bank of the state, again serving us, the people. Now go to work."

Victor had no knowledge of the state of the war or the German invasions of eastern and western countries. It was during those restless and fearful times that he ventured into the symphony hall one night after work to watch a rehearsal conducted by Maestro Bubachoff, the former Volga skipper. He had seen Bubachoff a few times at the theater during his brief and glorious leadership. The Maestro would relax in the state's soft leather chairs that were the color of the wilted cigar stump that was perennially glued to his moist red lips. Now the comrade wielded a delicate ivory baton in front of a scant orchestra of hungry musicians who seemed to be playing in their sleep. The tongue and stick of the maestro whipped them into sporadic action, so that the music swept across the hall in abrupt spurts.

Victor sat quietly in the back of the darkened hall. He was about to leave when Bubachoff turned and caught sight of him. He looked like an angry hippopotamus. Interrupting his work, he shouted at the intruder who had no right to be there, then made him step forward. Victor moved down the aisle. He stopped in front of the giant on the podium.

"Who are you?" Bubachoff snapped at him.

"A music lover."

The conductor raised his thick eyebrows with interest. "Sit down. Wait here."

"Yes, Comrade Maestro."

Victor settled into the front row of the orchestra, wondering why the man had asked him to stay. Hardly able to concentrate on the next piece, some overture from an opera by Mussorgsky, he was kept from falling asleep by the usual hunger pains. Face buried in his hands, he did not notice when the rehearsal ended, and the players left the stage. The conductor roused him from oblivion. He stood in front of Victor with a thin-lipped smile. "We must talk," he said, lowering his body to sit on two wooden chairs next to Victor's, half his bottom on each. "You strike me as a man with a true Russian soul. A music lover, eh? But you aren't Russian, do you understand me?"

Victor nodded in confusion.

"I can tell," Bubachoff added in a broken German, "where you come from. Nurtured at the bosoms of Beethoven and Mozart, loving our famous Russian authors. I won't mention any names for today they are in disgrace and tomorrow they'll be raised on a pedestal. And you, obviously a cultured young man, doubtless a German, last year turned friend from archenemy and now, again, deadly foe. Mark my word."

Victor raised both hands to protest any affiliation with present-day Germany, but the Maestro waved away what he was about to say.

"I know where you come from, music lover. Be careful of what you say to whom. I can recognize a good man with a wide-open nature. So let's talk soul to soul. Come with me, let's have a drink."

Stunned, Victor followed the conductor into the street. He would never have suspected a need for the company of a kindred fellow human behind the fleshy façade of this gargantuan official. To his surprise, he was led into a restaurant accessible only to dignitaries.

The drink turned into a banquet. Following caviar and vodka, Bubachoff ordered dish after tasty dish: borscht, *golubtsi*—cabbage rolls filled with ground meat—and a delicious apple tart for dessert. Victor marveled at his good luck. The vodka went to his head. He gulped down his food with the greed of a starving man.

"Poor devil," Bubachoff said, watching him eat. "You must be dying of hunger. The whole country is full of empty bellies. What kind of work can one expect from our people? Well, if they drop dead, there are always more and more to follow. Life is cheap. We have an endless reserve of slaves — our richest commodity."

Victor looked at him uneasily. He wished he would lower his voice. This was dangerous talk, but who was he to remind Bubachoff of his own warning to be careful what you say to whom? The man's daring and generosity matched his size. Victor asserted his faith in the spirit of the Russian people.

"Ah, my friend, I can see you're imbued with our literature. Remember the Serfs? Well, they've been liberated and then regrouped in masses. We are a nation of Slavs. Just insert an 'e' between the 'v' and 's'. The "*golubtsi*" are sweet and sour, some made with tomato sauce or chicken broth, but they are still cabbage rolls…"

Perhaps. But Victor didn't give up his cherished belief in the goodness of human beings. And the Maestro couldn't deny the spiritual hunger of his people. Bubachoff agreed, but asked if Victor had ever heard of indoctrination? Brother was taught to spy on brother; it had been bred in the bones for generations. "But let's drop the sad subject.

Tell me, music lover, who are your favorite composers?"

To Victor's relief, the subject turned to Bach, Mozart, and Schubert. He grew more and more excited to talk about music with a full stomach and a mind pleasantly clouded with drink. Politely refusing the offer of Bubachoff's expensive cigars, he accepted the pack of imported cigarettes the conductor thrust at him. Leaning back in his chair, slowly blowing the smoke from his lips, he was delighted to give the Maestro a shot lecture about the subtleties of the Goldberg Variations and *"Death and the Maiden* with each puff. He was amazed by Bubachoff's know-ledge. Eyes brimming from vodka and enthusiasm, he treasured every moment of their conversation.

"So tell me, what instrument do you play?"

"The flute."

"And now you have no way to…"

"Exactly. The Nazis killed every chance to do anything."

Bubachoff looked at him closely. "Then you must be a Jew. I never met a Jew in my life. Are they all as handsome as you?"

Victor looked at him quickly. "The Russians don't like us either."

"I certainly do, if the rest of them are like you. But don't worry. Just stick to your music - a universal tongue, a universal comforter. I want you to come to the concert hall for an audition." He fingered his glass of vodka. "If I like what I hear, I may have a job for you."

Victor looked at him, incredulous. "That would be wonderful… though I'm a bit rusty, and I don't have a flute." He pulled the miniature recorder from his pocket. "Nothing but this baby *sopranino*, as I call it."

"Don't worry, I'll lend you an instrument."

"You are too kind, Comrade Maestro. But the theater is short of stagehands and the director may not let me go."

"I still have friends there. I'll leave you a ticket for the concert on Saturday night and bring you the flute, so you can practice before the audition. I want to hear your story, music lover. You must promise to tell me all about your life."

3.

A PROMISE AND A PACT

Later that night, Victor tossed and turned on his cot in the dressing room. The chance of playing once more in an orchestra seemed too good to be true. His whole being was flooded with light at the thought that his passion for music might save him at last from the onslaught of grim reality. Now the seizure of his cherished flute reminded him of a severed limb, throbbing with pain long after its amputation. He had feared that the loss of his music might be as permanent as all those other deprivations.

What caused this supposedly corrupt giant to be capable of caring for a poor Jewish refugee? Renewed hope filled him with a gratitude that brought him close to tears. He wished to open his heart to this generous man who had entrusted him with remarks dangerous enough to get him shipped to some gulag in Siberia.

"How was I to jump over hurdles, with my legs tied by the threat of deportation and fatherhood?" He might ask his new friend that at their next meeting. "As children we used to play a game, hopping about with our feet and legs tied in a sack. I have been unable to take a single step forward for much too long. But now, thanks to you, Comrade Maestro, I might get out of that sack and move ahead."

The fragments of his life drew together like clouds, dissolved in the dark, drew together again. What should he let the maestro know about his past?

Here is Sophie, rushing to meet him in the park for lunch close to the Jewish department store where he works as a window dresser. She has come to reveal her dark secret. It closes a heavy door to the future. He, too, is pregnant, with fear of fatherhood and guilt about their clandestine meetings at home while his mother is at work. "Do the honorable thing," he hears his mother say. Of course he will. Sophie is crying; she refuses to be a hindrance to him or his musical career (pray, what career?) and will only marry him if he needs her, regardless of the baby. He assures her of his devotion. He has known her forever and loves her more than a sister. And yet, trapped within this huge German prison, how can they escape with an unborn child and an ailing mother?

Then there is Walter, his best friend. Ignorant of Victor's predicament, he wants them to flee together to France. He has found a guide who will take them across the border.

"I can't leave."

"And why not?"

"Because of my mother." Victor can't reveal the other reason. "I would feel like a rat…"

"Are you telling me that I'm a rat? What about leaving *my* parents? They are dying to know I'm free and safe. I'm sure your mother feels the same."

"She does. But you know that she has a bad heart. Suppose something happened to me. The shock might kill her."

"She's stronger than you think. Let me talk to her."

"If you do, I'll never speak to you again."

"She might die anyway, with or without you." Walter looks at him angrily.

"Thanks for telling me. What if they catch us at the border?"

"Coward! Defeatist!" Walter turns away in helpless frustration, without goodbye.

Victor moves in the opposite direction, nursing his wound. Walter has always been the stronger of the two and now misinterprets Victor's refusal to join him as an act of cowardice. A moment later, he is overcome by a vision of Walter hit by a bullet as he runs for his life.

Shot in flight. Each time Victor reads this announcement about fugitives in the daily papers, he chokes on the bitter bone of his premonition.

No, he can't tell the maestro about Walter's tragedy, or speak about poor Sophie and the baby. He will never know what happened during his fruitless search for a refuge from the enemy. He can't bear to think of it.

Next, he remembers the schoolboy crush during his second year at the gymnasium. For a long time, it felt like a bruise that would never heal. Dorle, in turn, had a crush on movie actor Willy Fritsch. She asked Victor to take her to one of his films. On leaving the theater, she told him that the girls in her class found Victor much more exciting and better looking than Willy Fritsch. But Victor felt neither handsome nor exciting when she let him know two days later that her friend Clara had called him a dirty Jew. "And I'll never go out again with a dirty Jew," Dorle declared unexpectedly. Guilt-ridden for having sneaked out with the blond-plaited girl behind his mother's back, he shunned any person disdaining him or his people or any other human being.

It was probably better not to burden the Maestro with fragments of his past. He might tell Bubachoff that his father had been a symphony player and his passion for music was passed on to his five-year-old son. He had taken Victor to a performance of Mozart's *Magic Flute,* and the boy fell in love with the sounds of Papageno's charming tune. Deaf to any suggestion of trying out other instruments, Victor insisted on playing the flute, nothing but the flute.

Two years later, after his father's premature death, his mother shunned no sacrifice to support and encourage her young Papageno. He appeared as a soloist in various youth orchestras. Her pride at his achievement was reflected in her eyes. Shared grief over their loss drew them closely together, while Victor concealed his growing anguish about her health.

How much could he tell the maestro about his life? Anything he would say might miss the right pitch. It was more important to concentrate on what to practice for his audition.

If only he could get hold of Mozart's B minor flute quartet and use the adagio he had played at the moment Tatyana entered the room. Their first encounter took place at a musical gathering at the home of Martha, his mother's best friend. During his solo, Victor heard the door open softly and from the corner of his eye, he saw her step across the threshold.

He had a glimpse of her short raven hair and high Slavic cheekbones.

After the concert, Martha introduced the girl to her other guests: Tatyana, her Yugoslavian niece, a student at the University of Zagreb, had just come for a short visit. Victor could still feel her firm handshake as he took in the warmth of her smile. He would never forget her dark velveteen eyes with pinpoints of light in the center. Immense, radiant eyes.

They hardly exchanged any words, but Victor basked in the melodious inflections of her voice as she spoke to others. The thought of her filled him with passionate longing. Since the disappearance of his family he hadn't allowed himself to think of her, but now the power of her memory made him forget everything else.

***

The day after the concert at Martha's home, during his lunch break in the public garden, he caught sight of Tatyana on the path. Sitting on a bench, he watched her come closer, tall and slender in a tan raincoat, with a camera in hand. She had stopped at a short distance in front of an SS man in uniform, and probably asked if he would allow her to take his picture. A moment later, Victor had seen him pose for her with angry impatience, then walk away without turning his head.

She returned the camera to its case and was about to go past Victor when he called her name. Startled, she stopped, then sat down beside him.

"What are you doing here?" Her eyes lit up as they met his.

"I should ask *you* that question. A Jewish girl taking pictures of a Nazi."

She remained silent.

"I work here," he said at last.

"Where?"

"Across the street, in the department store."

"Doing what?"

"Dressing windows."

"I just went by there. Did you dress those fashion dummies on the main floor?"

"Among other things, yes."

"But you are such a fine musician."

"My music doesn't put bread on the table. What on earth made you take a photo of that Nazi?"

"It's a class assignment for my university studies. I just came back from Munich, where I took pictures and was expected to write an article about my impressions of Hitler's Germany."

"What's your subject?"

"Photo journalism."

"Does Martha know? About the assignment?"

"Of course not. It would scare her to death."

"Suppose he had asked for your papers? He might have taken you for a spy and found out that you are Jewish."

"I'm a foreign visitor. We aren't at war yet. Though Yugoslavia won't be safe for long. Those fiends will spread their poison to the far corners of the world. We had better be prepared."

"But how can we?" Victor asked, trying to conceal his anguish.

"If we have to go, I'd rather go down fighting."

He listened in silence. She was raising her camera to take his picture.

"What are you doing?"

"Just another snapshot."

"For your 'assignment'?"

"To compare an ugly Nazi to a handsome Jew."

"Oh, Tatyana, you need to be more careful."

"Sorry. Of course, you are in a different situation," she said, putting down the camera.

"You are married, with a baby on the way, and must have felt like a prisoner for the last five years."

"It doesn't show yet. The baby, I mean. Did Martha tell you?"

"Yes. She's worried about you. Couldn't you get out of here?"

He shook his head. "We tried. Sophie's sister has recently become an American citizen and hopes to send us an affidavit. I'm afraid it's too late. What about you? Any family in Yugoslavia?"

"My parents and a sister. And a childhood friend, who proposed to me when I was eight and he was twelve."

"Is he still thinking about it?"

"Who knows?"

"If he isn't Jewish and you get married, he may be able to protect you, in case of an invasion."

"That's not a reason to get married. As I told you, I'd rather fight."

A wind was rising. It was time to get back to work. He felt unable to tear himself away.

"You are so brave." He looked at her with admiration. "Foolhardy, too, but that's probably the right way to be."

"Who knows? You don't seem to have much confidence in yourself. Maybe you don't know your own strength yet. But I could hear it in your music. Life will give you a chance to find out."

"That's the most encouraging thing anyone has said to me. How can you tell?"

Instead of answering his question, she got up to leave.

"I would love to see you again," he said.

"I don't know how, since I'm only staying for another day."

They shook hands as he rose in turn. Disheartened, he watched her walk up the path.

She waved at him, and then was swallowed by the gray November day.

The next afternoon, Victor was draping elegant dresses over mannequins in the front window of the department store. With the excuse of bringing Martha some sheet music she wanted to borrow, he hoped to see Tatyana again. But tonight of all nights, before the opening of the Christmas season, he was to work overtime.

After yesterday's encounter, he had tossed in bed beside Sophie, unable to sleep. Now, as he kept working, each mannequin sprang to life with Tatyana's slender body and stunning features above a dress of silk, velvet, or crêpe de chine.

About to pin a red rose to the shoulder of a dummy, he was startled by shouting voices. He saw men rounding the corner of the street: black boots, brown uniforms, and swastikas. As they hurled rocks at the Jewish store, Victor heard the windows break and shatter, heard the shouts and taunts from the uniformed, faceless robots.

The rose slipped from his fingers. A hand pulled him away.

"Come quickly," Tatyana whispered. She held his hand as they ran to the rear exit, then guided him through a back alley. They headed for the park, crossing the street in the darkness of the late afternoon. Beyond the park, the sky was aflame with burning houses. They ran all the way to Martha's apartment building, opened the portal, and flew up the stairs. Tatyana unlocked her aunt's flat. They slipped in and bolted the door.

"Is it you, Tatyana?" Martha called anxiously, coming out of the living room. "I was worried to death. What on earth were you doing out there?" Not waiting for an answer, she stared at Victor. "My God, what happened? Victor, are you all right?"

"He's all right now," Tatyana said. "But he shouldn't go out again."

"Absolutely not. It's much too dangerous. You can sleep on the couch."

Victor called Sophie. She and his mother were frantic with worry. They were relieved to hear he hadn't been beaten or arrested. They had just learned that Jewish stores and people had been attacked all over Germany.

Martha went into the kitchen to warm the dinner. Tatyana collapsed on the couch. Victor looked at her wan face. She was still wearing her coat with the camera slung over one shoulder.

He sat down beside her. "How can I ever thank you? You saved my life. But what were you doing in the store at that moment? How did you guess I was working at that time?"

"Just a hunch. I was trying to take pictures of those brutes, but it was too dark, which helped me stay invisible."

"I called you foolhardy. But you must be mad," he whispered.

"As an eyewitness, I was able to see their savagery firsthand," she went on. "They were rounding the corner of the building, about to break the main window, so I ran through some alley on the other side and found the back entrance. Thank God I was just in time..."

"You saved my life, risking your own!"

Martha called from the kitchen: "Come, children, have some soup."

Victor thought he might tell this part of the story to Bubachoff, who knew nothing about Jewish people. The conductor would be moved to hear how this exceptional girl had saved him, but Victor would never tell him that he had fallen hopelessly in love with her. They didn't know one another; but there she was, in his heart since time immemorial. What cruel god had brought her into his field of vision after his wedding to give him a glimpse of what might have been and could never be, its very beginning foretelling an ill-fated end? That night, sleepless on Martha's couch, he was overwhelmed with sorrow. Hearing light steps in the hall, the opening and closing of the bathroom door, he turned on the light and waited.

As soon as she came out, he called her name in a whisper. The next moment she stopped before him in a blue flannel nightgown.

"I couldn't sleep either." She sat down in Martha's wine-red armchair. "I know how worried you must be about Sophie and the baby, your mother, the future."

"Yes, but there's something I need to know." He hesitated. "When you rushed to get me out of that store, were you there because you meant to take pictures of Kristallnacht for your assignment? Or was it because you were worried about *me*?"

"Both."

"I don't understand."

"Never mind. It doesn't matter."

"But it does matter! Because…" He spoke quickly under his breath, surprised at his daring. "I never believed in such unexpected love. But now it has happened."

"How can you say that? You just got married. Don't you love Sophie?"

"It's a different kind of love. I had no idea that someone like you existed. I'll never let her down. But I want you to know, so you won't forget me."

"What a romantic boy you are!"

"And you are not?"

"I'm not a romantic boy." She laughed, fighting tears. "I don't really know who I am."

"So you came to save me because you too, that's what I had to find out."

"It makes no difference under the circumstances."

"It will give me hope and courage for life."

"Then it's a good thing and makes me glad. You must carry that hope and courage like a torch. Keep it burning no matter what happens."

"It's a promise--and a pact. Oh, Tatyana, if only we had met before it was too late."

"It was always too late. You here, with your family—and I, back in Zagreb…"

***

The sum of his life, of his past. This was the first time he had thought of it. The first time since the day Sophie and little Hannah had vanished. For eighteen months, he had kept his grief in abeyance. Since he could not properly mourn, he did not allow himself to think of Tatyana. It was not fair to the memory of Sophie. Only once, just once, did he relive the moment of their parting that same night. He had taken Tatyana into his arms and barely kissed her lips before tearing himself away. He did not allow himself to think of her, but kept the burning torch he had promised to carry in his heart. It symbolized everything Tatyana stood for: courage, freedom and self-reliance.

By Saturday, Bubachoff might have forgotten his request to hear Victor's story; but if he remembered, Victor would be unable to reveal his secret. It would be sacrilege to disclose their encounter to anyone, he thought drowsily, at last drifting into sleep.

4.

A LABOR CAMP NEAR THE WHITE SEA

To his shock, Victor was unable to keep his appointment with Bubachoff. Torn from a dream about Tatyana, he was roughly awakened by two policemen. By the end of the first week in June, 1941, just before the German invasion of Lvov, vagrants, refugees, and men without valid passports were arrested all over the city. They were gathered in vacant lots and the courtyards of empty school buildings, where they had to wait all day to be deported to some unknown destination.

At dusk, Victor was pushed into the stock car of a freight train with a crowd of fellow prisoners. It was hours before the train gave a sudden jolt and slowly moved out of the city. After venting their fears with curses and complaints, the men grew quiet and listless. Hours later, they were given some cabbage soup and bland-tasting mush, a heel of bread, and a drink of lukewarm water. This daily ration was repeated at noon, or whenever the train would stop in the open countryside for the men to relieve themselves under the watch of armed guards.

Victor could hardly keep track of time as they moved farther and farther east. There had been no way to send a message to Bubachoff. While swallowing his mush, he dreamt of the delicious cabbage rolls he had shared with the maestro. What was it the conductor had said about Slavs and slaves and the physical and spiritual hunger of the Russian people? Now it was Victor's turn to experience their misery. Back in Stuttgart, he had read Dostoevsky's *House of the Dead* in the luxurious warmth of his feather bed at night, relishing the bitter experiences of those long-suffering heroes. And now they were here again — not in books, not as heroes.

Poles, Ukrainians, and those Russian brothers for whom he had found such fine words at his dinner with the Maestro.

It occurred to him that during his stay in Lvov he had only thought of himself. Was life worth living without extending oneself to others? The careworn faces in the freight car mirrored his own; the faces of nameless and expendable men who seesawed between hope and despair. Perhaps fate was teaching him a painful lesson: to reach out, instead of shutting himself off.

Just then, an elderly man sitting upright in the opposite corner reminded him of the saintly servant Gerasim, a character in Tolstoy's *Death of Ivan Ilyich*. His kind face and patient bearing set him apart from the rest of the crowd.

Here I go again, Victor reproached himself, *with my useless literary mind.*

The sopranino. He pulled the miniature flute from his coat and put it to his lips. It quivered in his fingers as he played the first few notes. He began with tunes borrowed from Mozart, followed by Schubert's "Ave Maria" and songs by Schumann, adding melodies meant for other instruments. His companions applauded after each tune, some of them smiling, others weeping. Each time he stopped, his fellow travelers asked for more. Weakened by hunger, stiff and rusty from lack of practice, he went on playing, encouraged by their warm response. After days of loud complaints, everyone grew silent, listening intently to the soothing sounds rising above the rattling noise of the train.

As soon as Victor stopped playing, a bearded old fellow wished to examine his recorder. The instrument was passed from hand to hand. A few tried to blow as hard as they could. Victor showed them how to cover the holes with their fingertips. Only *Gerasim* was able to play a few coherent notes. Victor marveled at the men's genuine delight. They had suddenly come to life. Laughing, he raised his hands and shoulders to indicate that he didn't understand everything they were saying, but they kept pouring out excited words, at last breaking through their mute distrust of one another.

After the family's arrival in Krakow, Victor had repeatedly stopped to look at this piccolo recorder in the window of a music shop. Shortly before her death, his mother had wrapped some money for his birthday into the red scarf. Instead of buying himself a gift, he decided to hold on to it for a day of need. Ready to leave Krakow for a smaller town, he was about to buy provisions for little Hannah, but first stopped to look once more at the instrument.

The bowlegged owner hobbled to the window, picked up the recorder, and wrapped it ceremoniously into some tissue paper. He explained to Victor that he was about to be the lucky owner of a precious piece imported from Switzerland — the last of a family of recorders. Victor put the money on the counter. An instant later, he heard the bell of the register and the drawer snap shut, stealing away the money that could have kept the family in bread and meat for weeks. He walked out feeling remorseful, triumphant, and mad with joy.

Enlivened by the music, the prisoners discussed various possibilities for their final destination, concluding that they must be on the way to some labor camp near the White Sea. Taking turns, they tried to get a glimpse of the outside world through a tiny barred window at the upper end of the wagon. No one ever saw a town or a village. The train came to a halt in the afternoon and remained there for hours. The journey was not resumed until midnight.

***

At last the doors were opened at the station of Kotlas. The men were ordered to get out and form lines. Stiff-limbed and giddy from the onslaught of fresh air and light after their long confinement, they were given some watery soup and bread, then followed a command to march across a long, treeless plain.

They stopped by the bank of a river where boats were lined up along the shore. Armed with rifles, surrounded by police dogs, the guards prepared for the next stretch of the transport. Each boat was filled with twenty-five prisoners and two additional guards. As soon as they were settled, the last man would jump into the boat. The effort caused three prisoners to fall into the rushing stream. It took fellow captives some time to save them. They all struggled, drenched and shivering, cursing under their breaths.

They began to drift downriver. Less than half of Victor's group consisted of men he had met on the train. After ten days in oppressive darkness, everyone savored each breath of fresh air. Beneath sprouting beards, Victor detected smiles of relief on gaunt faces that seemed to have aged overnight.

For many hours, the current carried them down the ever-widening river. Additional boats appeared out of nowhere. Listening to the sound of faraway women's and children's voices, the men grew restless, asking, "*Where to? And how much longer?*"

But there was no answer. By late afternoon, the river meandered through a forest. Settlements appeared without a sign of human life. Now leaving the wooded area, they encountered open spaces and distant mountains. At dusk, they floated through an enchanted landscape that caused Victor to forget his hunger and misery. Topped by silver-rimmed clouds and bathing in the last rays of an early summer sunset, the deserted lowlands burned in a rosy-violet glow. Far away, a golden harvest moon separated itself from the silhouettes of the mountain peaks and rose up into the clouds.

It grew dark and bitterly cold. The boats with their cargo of captives moved more slowly, held up by long stretches of driftwood and clustered logs. Unfamiliar smells and unpredictable changes of weather and scenery added an alien atmosphere to the landscape, filling the disoriented men with new apprehension.

Hours later, the boat was intercepted by calls from the shore, and then guided by a barge to a settlement in a forest. Ordered to go ashore, the captives were marched to a dimly lit blockhouse where each man was given a drink of water, some bread, and a sausage. After the meal, they were taken to their quarters for the night. Victor immediately fell on his cot. Half asleep, he could hear the voices of men, women, and children arriving on other boats-entire families of prisoners who were guided to the empty huts he had seen across the road. His hand groped for his *sopranino* nestled in the pocket of his overcoat.

At five o'clock the next morning, a guard roused the sleep-drunken men and ordered them to wait in line outside the hut. Each was handed a document informing him about the task he had to perform. Victor was assigned to cut and saw trees. Once more, he found himself among strangers. Most of his companions from the train or boat were sent to other parts of the forest. Days later, one of his fellow workers confirmed his suspicion: comrades had been separated, since fraternizing was strictly forbidden for fear of insurgence.

At each sunrise, the prisoners were marched to the forest. Victor had never sawed a tree in his life. Weakened and half-starved after the journey, he followed the movements of a husky, good-natured peasant boy. The young fellow showed him how to attack a tree with deftness instead of force. Each time he was about to collapse, the boy gave him an encouraging smile or a helping hand.

At the end of the day, the workers dragged themselves two long miles back to the hut. Worn with fatigue, Victor was unable to sleep. Each morning he would devour the piece of bread he had saved from the previous night. Little by little, he grew accustomed to the new routine. He learned that these settlements had already existed under the czar's regime. For more than a century, people had been sent into exile here.

Bread and warm meals, consisting of soup or mush, could be obtained with food stamps; but stamps were only given to prisoners who fulfilled their daily quota of required labor. Women and older men were rowed downstream to work in the sawmills. Victor's team chopped down trees, another group cut them into chunks, and a third rolled the chunks to the river. From there, the water's current carried the logs downstream. Along the shore, small posts with single huts about 300 feet apart were occupied by two to three men. Those men freed the logs washed ashore and push them back into the current with long poles, making sure they were transported downstream to the saw mills.

It seemed to Victor that the entire country had been turned into one huge factory. Everything was accomplished on some primitive, in-visible running belt. In this huge territory inter- laced with a network of rivers, he gathered that thousands of people were condemned to slave labor. Escape was impossible. The nearest town with railroad connections was a hundred miles away.

Boats might be stopped by agents at a hundred different points. There were rumors soon verified—about more camps in the area where the men lived in barracks surrounded by barbed wire. These were criminals building canals under the vigilance of armed guards.

The prisoners were ordered to march to work in silence. In silence, they waited for meals brought to the woods on carts. In silence, they were to retire at night.

One evening, hoping to get a glimpse of family life, Victor managed to sneak into a couple of huts in which prisoners lived with their wives and children. It was painful to watch those tired, emaciated women in rags, despairing of keeping their children from illness and starvation. The women stared at him with mistrust and hostility. He saw that there was nothing he could do. Suppose Sophie and the baby…no, it would have been unbearable. He had at least been spared the torment of watching his family suffer this agony.

A few days later, he observed one of the fathers offering the camp's director a pair of shoes and some piece of clothing in exchange for a day's rest for his wife, hoping the director might accept the gift without depriving the man's wife of her food rations.

Guards and employees were treated as roughly as the prisoners by the director and the brigadier general. The women were addressed as whores, the men with sarcasm and vulgar curses. Aliens were despised as fascist bourgeois and enemies of the masses. Friendly feelings were expressed with curses.

One night the director handed an old man an ax and ordered him to cut firewood for the brigadier general. Having no idea how to use such a tool, the man gesticulated with only one hand, then clumsily chopped a small branch from a tree. The director towered over him while guards and fellow prisoners watched and jeered. "You son of a whore! How could you live so long without knowing how to build a fire!", the director shouted in Russian.

Victor rushed to the old man's aid. He took the ax, chopped several pieces of wood, and put the ax back into his trembling hands. A heavy fist hit his shoulder.

"Where did you learn to chop wood so efficiently, you intellectual pig?", the director asked in a surprisingly friendly tone.

"I have always worked with my hands, Comrade Director."

"So your files are telling me. Moving scenery in the theater, hoping to be some artist or actor, someone better than ordinary folk, eh!"

Victor remained silent.

"Looking down on honest labor, just like this old philosophy professor. And what did you profess?" He pointed derisively at the old man. "Can't make a fire with his philosophy. Much good it does you now. Don't just stand there gaping at me, old man! Go back to your flea-ridden bunk and thank your stars I don't beat the shit out of you!"

Victor wanted to protest that artists and intellectuals were friends, not enemies, of the workers, but the director turned to him and said he had heard sounds of music coming from his quarters at night.

"You know this is strictly forbidden."

"I didn't realize…"

Victor was amazed how much the director remembered about each of the stoic captives under his command. Although preferring to remain inconspicuous, he was glad to have diverted attention from the old man, who nodded at him gratefully and then was able to withdraw to his bunk.

"What's your instrument?" the director wanted to know.

"A recorder—a tiny flute."

"Take it to the office immediately." Victor looked at him, aghast. "I won't tolerate any defiance."

"I'm not trying to defy you, Comrade Director. Only to assure you that even a touch of music helps me do my best work."

"Take it to the office at once, or I'll break it in two for firewood."

During the months of July and August, heat and swarms of mosquitoes were a new plague. Deprived of his only comfort, Victor tried to replace his *sopranino* with tunes he composed in his head before finally falling asleep. Winter set in abruptly, ahead of its time. Soon the men went to work in subzero temperatures. Each laborer was given a dirty old overcoat with a white cotton lining turned yellow from wear and tear, a cap and trousers of the same material, and a pair of felt shoes, which quickly filled with rain or snow. All this added more weight than warmth, and each day Victor shivered with cold and disgust. For months, the captives sawed trunks, felled trees, cleaned branches, and rolled logs to the river which was now covered with ice. Their hearts were equally turning to ice while trees crashed to the ground, every now and then blotting out a life like a flickering light.

When you see trees all day and look up at the top of tall trunks threatening to dash you to pieces, you hear sawing in your uneasy sleep. You see the sky falling over you, and the crowns of trees covering your freezing limbs. You envision the wedding of bark against skin, trunk covering trunk, and you dread that embrace, even though you may welcome the end of all pain.

During days and nights of hallucination, Victor was hardly aware of the changing seasons. Another year passed, another winter was about to begin, prisoners collapsed or died, a number of new captives arrived to replace a crew recently transported to some other camp. No one had the strength to find out where that former group had landed. Captives were mere pawns on a chessboard. Newcomers were soon turned from white to black. As the old ones continued to vanish, Victor felt unable to reach out to men who shared his listlessness and depletion.

He kept asking himself, "*If I am only for myself, what am I? Yet, if I can't even be for myself, how can I extend my non-self to others?*"

One morning he was ordered to join a group of newly arrived prisoners. Bent over a large trunk, he straightened for a moment when he noticed the gigantic proportions of the worker assigned to fell the trees Victor was supposed to cut into chunks. The man's face was covered by a dense black beard. The trousers hanging loosely over his stomach barely covered his calves.

Feeling himself observed, the new prisoner watched Victor in turn. At last, the two of them stopped to stare at one another in disbelief.

"Comrade, Maestro!"

"Music lover!"

Dropping their tools, they embraced.

"How strong you've grown, my friend!" Bubachoff whispered. "Suntanned like a man on holidays! I hardly recognized you with that thick beard…"

"Dear God," Victor whispered, "this is the last place I expected to see you."

"Envy," Bubachoff explained, wiping his cheek with the back of his bluish-red hand. "They kept denouncing me, those sons of whores who wanted my position, my vodka and cigars…"

"How thin you have grown, Comrade Maestro!"

"No more Maestro. And no more caviar and cabbage rolls. Better for the waistline. This is the right life: fresh air, good exercise, and a diet that keeps you streamlined."

The guard, out of hearing distance, was looking in their direction. They went on working while Bubachoff conducted a staccato, whispered conversation. He expressed his regret that Victor hadn't had a chance to play in his orchestra. "It wouldn't have worked out anyway. You don't know your good luck. The barbarians invaded Mother Russia right after you left, and they immediately came to Lvov. Imagine what might have happened to you. Coming here may have saved your life. So don't give up hope. You are young. Someday you'll be able to go home again, back to your family and your music."

Victor did not tell the maestro that he had no home. "I have hardly anyone left in the world," he said sadly, an image of Tatyana rising to his mind, a lonely, distant yearning for an impossible dream.

"Can you imagine," Bubachoff continued, "I was arrested the day before the Huns got to Lvov. Sent to prison in the Soviet Union with a bunch of criminals. So I wouldn't have been able to meet you on that Saturday…"

"What an amazing coincidence!" Victor exclaimed. "That we both…"

Bubachoff began to cough fitfully. He confessed that his lungs were giving out and that he was suffering from a bad heart. "You ought to go to the infirmary," Victor suggested, but the conductor declared he preferred dying on his feet. More than anything, he missed his music.

"Look at those poor trees." He stopped and took a deep breath. "I feel sorry for them. Well, I, too, may soon come crashing down from a blow by that other Invisible Chopper."

"It may happen to any of us."

Bubachoff did not listen. "But at night, I conduct entire scores by Mozart or Beethoven in my head and, above all, Schubert's Unfinished Symphony. There are a few notes I don't know by heart, and those missing notes drive me out of my mind. I work on concerts with my heavenly musicians," he whispered, glancing at the guard, who was shouting at a fellow worker. "They play like angels. Because they are. And they fill the gaps not only in the music, but in everything else I have missed in my miserable life. And Schubert, think of Schubert. He died way before my age. I am fifty-four years old. Who am I to complain?"

"I, too, hear all kinds of music in my head," Victor said. "Ever since the director confiscated my recorder…tunes I make up or remember from concerts I played since I was a child. I was hoping to prepare the adagio from a Mozart flute quartet for your audition."

"Why on earth would that bastard rob you of your instrument?"

"Who knows? Spite, I suppose."

"People are jealous of artists and intellectuals they fear and don't understand."

Bubachoff's premonition came true on the nineteenth month of Victor's exile. The Maestro died the day the director rallied the prisoners under his command. "You devil-dogs are free to go," he declared. "Pick up your stuff and get your papers in my office." Thus captivity ended for them both at the same time. Victor was forced to leave at once and not allowed to stay for the burial. Filled with sorrow for the loss of his only friend, he was unable to enjoy his freedom and the return of his *sopranino*. With a group of liberated prisoners, he stepped into the motorboat waiting to take him back to the world, lonelier than ever.

5.

BUKHARA

After the German invasion of Russia, Polish exiles were expected to join the Red Army. They were released, gathered from labor camps and other settlements by decree, and hastily trained for battle. Civilian prisoners who were unable to join the army were forced to choose between moving to Siberia or into Asian territory.

Victor would have liked to sign up, if only to reach the allies in the west. But a Pole without a passport who did not speak Polish might be severely punished as an impostor. A number of people headed for cities beyond the Ural, for Novosibirsk and places he could not pronounce. Others chose more southern regions in Central Asia, such as Bukhara or Tashkent. Victor was given a ticket to Bukhara. Having heard that Bukhara and Tashkent were pelted by rain and mud storms during bitterly cold winters, he wondered whether he might not be better off in snow-buried Siberia.

Exhausted, too weak for work, he was forced to stop in a small town, whose name he couldn't remember, although he was treated with unaccustomed kindness at the hospital and the Polish center. Since the German invasion, the document declaring him Polish stood him in good stead as long as Poles were regarded as allies of the Soviet Union. He waited for the snow to melt and news of warmer weather in the south. After a few weeks, he joined a group that had been organized by the Russian-Polish committee for refugees and set out for Bukhara with fifty other men.

Bukhara, he learned, lay in an oasis west of Samarkand, among branches of the Zeravshan River. As soon as the travelers left the station, high towers, mosques, and portals came into view. They passed through ancient narrow streets winding like stony brooks between white walls. Heavy doors led to inner courtyards of houses, most of them topped by flat roofs.

A medieval site since the days of Tamerlane, Bukhara was an Eastern fairytale. In a time warp, Victor began to float through an ancient city where *"Arbas"*-- high two-wheel barrows drawn by donkeys—were the only means of transportation. The shouting of drivers was heard every time two *"arbas"* moved toward each other from either end of a narrow street. They yelled in a high falsetto, gesturing wildly and relishing their self-importance.

The refugees were received in an ancient mosque converted into offices by the Soviets. Still recovering from his labors near the river, Victor was assigned a place to sleep on the flat roof of the music school. His "domicile" consisted of a small space with four columns supporting a canopy that sheltered him from the sky. He slept on top of a blanket. The columns reminded him of a four-poster bed.

Once more he was alone. Accustomed by now to isolation, he quickly adjusted to his new environment. Powerful rays of sunlight hit his face like daggers each morning, rousing him from sleep. Sand flew incessantly through the air, inflaming his eyes and settling on his hair, his skin, and his clothes. Many people, Uzbeks in particular, were sensitive to the sun, wind, and flying particles of sand. One of the music teachers provided Victor with a pair of dark glasses.

During the day, he found refuge in an empty classroom. Made of clay, the insides of houses were pleasantly shady and cool. The music school was two stories high. Each of its many rooms was inhabited by one or two students, young city girls and boys clad in national costumes. The girls, their bare feet in rubber sandals, wore trousers under white dress-length shirts of homespun silk. The youths donned wide Turkish linen pants and white shirts open at the chest. The heads of the men were covered with the *tibetska*, a small black cap sometimes embroidered by the sweethearts of the men with arabesques or flowers.

Victor communicated with non-Russian students in sign language. The school taught singing and various instruments. Some of the instruments resembled banjos or guitars with small, wooden bodies, long necks, and three strings. They accompanied songs presented in falsetto or high nasal sounds. The songs were drawn from old folktales. Victor would listen and applaud, then play a tune on his *sopranino*. His music was as strange to their ears as theirs was to his, but they applauded each other in turn.

Thanks to his past experience in Lvov, he was sent to work at the theater. Again, he was to move scenery behind the stage at the lowest salary, for only three days a week. Soviet red tape reminded him of Germany's powerful bureaucracy. He hoped his free days might give him a chance to supplement his meager income.

Compared to the past harrowing years, his life in Bukhara, was almost easy, improving from day to day. His relative freedom and the shaving of his beard restored him to his former self. And yet, in spite of his friendly surroundings, he felt more alone than he did in the camp. Leisure gave him time to think and thinking brought home the grief he had been too exhausted to face. He tried to distract himself by watching musicals performed in the Uzbek language. Plays consisted of twelve to thirteen acts, usually lasting from seven to midnight. Most of them were based on ancient folktales he was unable to follow. Nightmares and the recollection of his losses woke him in terror.

He was quick to observe how the city thrived from a great deal of commerce. The bazaar was divided into produce and victuals on one side, various objects and clothes on the other. Immense and captivating, it was thoroughly oriental in character and seemed to embody the living heart of the city. Uzbek women, adorned with golden earrings and bracelets, sold their wares sitting on the ground in loose garments, legs crossed Turkish fashion, bargaining, screaming, and haggling. Men on donkeys brought dried figs, dates, apricots, and fresh fruit according to season.

Donkeys were essential to Uzbek households. At times an entire family could be seen riding on one: the man in front, poking the animal behind its ears with a stick, croaking, "*Kra, kra, kra,*" wife and children at his back, each tightly embracing the one in front. Two heavy sacks hung on either side of the donkey's flanks. Victor pitied the poor animal, expecting its skinny legs to cave at any instant.

He liked to watch people meeting one another. A Russian bystander explained to him that they addressed an old man as *Ata*, Father, a younger one as *Aka*, Brother. People met in the market for business and pleasure. Men pressed friends or acquaintances to their breast, speaking words of blessing from the Koran, wishing them well and voicing happiness at finding them in good health.

Having managed to get by in Russian, Victor now tried to learn the Uzbek language. Settling down near a market stall, he studied words from a small dictionary or sometimes pulled the recorder from his ragged summer coat and played some Western tune. Out of pity or politeness, the women smiled and applauded, and asked for an encore. Mamas enthroned behind tall fruit stands rewarded him with some dates or dried figs, delicacies he could not afford. To his chagrin, such small sowings never brought him the hoped-for harvest of some real work as a musician. Western music was apparently too strange to local ears.

One afternoon he entered a teahouse. It consisted of a large room with an elevated stage-like platform in its midst. Near the entrance stood the clay oven with its built-in kettles. Steaming water flowed from taps heated from outside. On a podium stretching along the wall, men sat wearing white chest-baring shirts with colorful sashes wound around their waists. Black mustaches emphasized the fierceness of their dark brown faces. Embroidered skullcaps sat on short-cropped hair or a shaven head. Their eyes followed each of the proprietor's stylized gestures as he presided over the tea ceremony.

Victor sat down at the other end of the podium to watch. Solemnly, the proprietor dropped small green leaves into a pot. Everyone looked on in silence as he slowly poured the boiling water. The first bowl was offered to the oldest patron, who cupped it in his hands, took one sip, murmured a blessing, bowed, and passed it to his neighbor.

Victor was the last in line. He followed everyone's example, bowing as he returned the cup to its owner. Some of the men looked like savages in starched white shirts. He could feel their eyes piercing him like daggers. What had made him hope that anyone would talk to him in such a place? And if so, what did he have to offer? These men were hostile, suspicious of strangers. The memory of their warm embraces faded for Victor as he caught sight of sheathed knives attached to their trousers.

After the tea ceremony, the place took on the activity of an office. Victor observed that the town's social and commercial life was unfolding within its walls. Contracts were made by handshakes and word of mouth. Now those silent men began gesticulating and talking in a confusion of tongues. No one paid attention to the light-skinned stranger.

Hungry and discouraged, Victor was about to leave when a man of striking good looks walked through the door. It was as though Abraham himself were stepping out of the Bible: tall and regal with emerald eyes, a white beard, and fair complexion. With each step, his long white hair rose from the shoulders of a white embroidered garment.

"Abduluh, *Ata!*" he said to the elderly Muslim at Victor's side, spreading his arms to embrace him.

"Hey, Ata Benjamin…"

Victor assumed the exchange of questions that followed between the two friends was about the well-being of their respective kin. A moment later, they settled down to a serious discussion about business.

Feeling the stranger's eyes on him, the patriarch turned to look at Victor. "And who are you?" he asked in Russian.

"An exile."

"Understand Yiddish?"

"If you speak slowly…"

"Then you must be a Jew?"

"I am."

The patriarch held up a hand. "Please wait till I finish my transaction. Then we will talk."

They talked on their way to the steam bath. It was Friday afternoon, and the old man asked Victor to join him in a cleansing for the Sabbath. Used to a stagnant well in the courtyard of the music school (where precious water was drawn from tiny canals whenever he wished to drink or wash his hands), Victor was delighted to join him. He was happy, above all, to exchange words with a kindred spirit.

On the way, he learned that the patriarch raised a special kind of sheep bred only in Bukhara. Karakul furs, or Persian lamb coats, were made of the short, curly hairs of two-day-old animals, killed for their pelts and succulent flesh. Benjamin raised and sold those lambs, he explained, keeping what was allotted to him after paying the lion's share to the state. Victor assumed that those transactions in the teahouse had to do with a bit of extracurricular black marketeering.

The bathhouse, like everywhere else, was affected by water shortage. After undressing in an anteroom, the men took a wooden pail and filled it with hot water from a basin. Sparingly, they poured it over their heads and shoulders. Most people lacked the luxury of soap, but the patriarch had brought a small, precious cake, which he now handed to Victor. After passing the soap back and forth in a ceremonial cleansing, the two of them entered the steam bath in the rear, where men poured boiling water over large stones. A thick fog spread through the room, muffling objects and sounds. They sat naked side by side, two ghostly shadows in the rising steam. Victor told the patriarch of his activity in the theater and his need for additional work, asking whether he might earn a little extra money by playing the recorder at weddings and other festive events.

"Are you a musician?"

Victor nodded. "I used to play the flute." Bubachoff, he thought. *Chopping trees.* "I can chop trees," he added, thinking, *I must have chopped a thousand.*

"For a start, you could play at a wedding on Sunday. It won't pay, but there'll be plenty of food."

"Suits me fine. Western music?"

"They'll love it. What else?" The patriarch smiled. "Real work, I mean."

What did he learn in that other life? Literature, English, window dressing, cleaning latrines.

"Any family?"

"All gone," Victor said, while a memory of Tatyana threatened to shake him.

"Thanks to the war?" Benjamin sighed as he nodded. Then, after

48

a moment, "What about helping me bring sheep to market, on your free days? For meals and pocket money."

"Meals are better than rubles," he said, shuddering at the thought of becoming an accomplice to the slaughter of two-day-old sheep.

"Good." Benjamin spoke before Victor could voice his scruples. "Come home with me. There's always extra food for a guest on holy days."

***

To Victor's amazement, many people in the Jewish quarter of Bukhara seemed to have stepped out of the Bible. Benjamin was no exception. Deported from Jerusalem after its defeat by Persia, the Jews had been enslaved and presented to the Emir of Bukhara by the Persian king. From those ancient times to the present day, they had preserved their language and religion.

Benjamin's house was a small, sparsely furnished clay building. Victor was introduced to the rest of the family: Benjamin's wife Rebecca, their lame daughter Rachel, two sons and daughters-in-law and four grandchildren. They spoke Yiddish and Victor answered in German. After the Friday night prayers, Benjamin broke the bread. To Victor's relief, dinner was served without delay. The main dish, pilaf and lamb, had been prepared by the men.

The family sat on the floor in Turkish fashion. They used their hands as utensils. Victor had never tasted such tender lamb. He relished each bite, too famished to worry about man's cruelty to animals. He was reminded of his outing at the restaurant with Bubachoff, followed by the constant, nagging hunger in the labor camp. It seemed inconceivable that more than two years had passed since his departure from Lvov.

During the meal, the women were silent. The sons ignored Victor. They laughed and talked in a Yiddish jargon he did not understand. The lame girl kept looking at him with ancient, knowing eyes. He felt engulfed by that gaze. It aroused memories and feelings he wished to leave untouched.

"Be here for dinner at seven sharp tomorrow and every night of the week," Benjamin told him. Victor began to suspect that Benjamin's hospitality might have an ulterior motive: while helping him with the sheep and becoming part of the clan for supper, he might be considered husband material for Rachel. He was hardly the first young stranger to be invited for the Sabbath meal.

Thinking of the girl on the way back to the music school, he was touched by her handicap and her fine narrow face. She had her father's emerald eyes. Victor sensed that he must brace himself, be on guard. An odd twist of circumstance had brought him to this Jewish home. Was he wrong to surmise that Benjamin expected him to settle down in Bukhara and tend sheep seven years for his daughter Rachel?

Benjamin had invited him to play his recorder at a friend's Jewish wedding, in the hope that this might bring him engagements for other occasions. But Victor feared his music would sound too foreign to unaccustomed ears. The night before the wedding, he dreamt of Bubachoff conducting a small orchestra for such an occasion. In his dream, Rachel was the bride, waiting for him in a garden full of red hibiscus. Her face was covered by a heavy white veil, which she lifted to kiss him. But when he bent over her face, he said, "I can't be your bridegroom. Tatyana is waiting for me." A hand pulled him out of the garden, a voice—was it Bubachoff's? — said, "Let's get out of here; your American visa is waiting. One more tree to fell, and we'll ride to the States." "On a donkey?" Victor asked. "Yes, a donkey," the voice said. "A carpet, anything. Come along, hurry up."

The next morning Victor wrote to the American consulate in Moscow applying for a visa, adding the address of Sophie's sister Lisa, which he had committed to memory. Before leaving Stuttgart, Sophie had let her sister know about their marriage and the imminent birth of the baby. Victor was sure she would try to help him. By now she might be an American citizen, and in a position to do so.

Since communications had failed before, Lisa might not have any idea about her sister's tragedy. Unable to count on an answer, he posted the letter, if only to remind himself not to succumb to the lure of Benjamin's bucolic idyll.

The wedding took place in the home of the bride's family. The veiled bride had to walk around the groom seven times. After the ceremony, the guests sat cross-legged on the floor of an empty living room, encircling a myriad of colorful dishes. Victor noticed that utensils were kept in built-in niches, along with all other precious patrimony, such as oriental tapestries and carpets. An exquisite hand-wrought chest of imported wood contained treasures for the bride and other members of the household. Benjamin told him that all Jewish homes in Bukhara were similar in character. The most treasured object consisted of a large tray, hand-carved in gold or silver, which was passed from generation to generation. Always in fear of persecution, the Jews were poised for a nomadic existence. Should the war spread to Uzbekistan, they hoped their movable possessions could be carried away on carts and mules.

The wedding feast, prepared by the host, consisted mainly of pilaf and lamb, the staple food of the region. Various other dishes brimmed over with exotic fruit, figs, dates, and sweets. Victor could not believe his luck and gratefully savored the respite in this land of milk and honey.

He was still unaware of how much two years of hard labor and learning to overcome hunger, deprivations, and loneliness had strengthened and matured him. What would his mother say if she saw him now? He glanced at Rachel. She sat by his side in an exquisite cream-colored shirtdress of pure silk, soft brown locks flowing over narrow shoulders. Her emerald eyes kept drawing him close with genuine frankness. To Victor, she looked the picture of innocence. After a while, he rose to join the musicians. Everyone helped clear the room. The dance was about to begin.

Bride and bridegroom were followed by family and guests. Like the Uzbeks, whose folk dances Victor had watched in the music school, the Jewish pairs faced one another. Tambourines and the blows from a high, shrill whistle shaped like a long nail were added to the sounds of three-stringed guitars. Young men and women stamped the ground with small dancing steps, arms moving in rhythm with their feet. All at once, everyone began to sing, elders surrounded young couples in a circle. As the rhythm of the tambourines grew faster and faster, the dancers followed at breathtaking speed. Arms, hands, and bodies whirled in circles, feet stamped more and more forcefully. The watching audience drove everyone frantic with their clapping and shouting.

The music stopped abruptly. Breathless girls ran back to their friends, now bashful and subdued. Their partners joined the other men who slapped their backs and praised their skill.

During the lull that followed, Victor hesitantly blew a few notes on his recorder. He began with an excerpt from "The Marriage of Figaro." Most of the guests complied with Benjamin's request for silence. Victor was unable to tell whether they liked the sounds of Western music. Being out of practice and having forgotten much of his repertoire, he ventured into a few lieder, improvising as he went along. Bowing modestly, he applauded the guests for listening and was applauded in turn. Then he invited them all to resume their dance.

Rachel joined him and told him how much she had enjoyed his playing.

"It must sound strange to you..."

She shook her head. "No, not strange."

"Perhaps you are familiar with Western music?"

"Not really—but I like *your* music." She looked up at him. "You are so beautiful. Inside and out."

He felt the blood rise to his head. Had he misunderstood her words?

"That's what I should say to you, Rachel."

"To a cripple? Never. I want no pity."

"I mean it. You *are* beautiful. And you mustn't say such things about yourself."

"Why not? It's the truth." She looked straight at him. "I can say anything, because I've no hope."

"Oh, Rachel...you have every reason to..."

"You don't allow me to say anything—but I do. I say what I like to say."

"I'm sorry. Of course you may say anything you like. But you must never give up. Sometimes our best dreams go underground, like hidden springs, but they may come back. Take it from me."

"What do you mean, 'from you'?"

"I have no reason to hope against hope. I have no family. No country. No identity. I'm a non-person. And yet, as long as there's life..."

"You are right." She was smiling. "Now I know why you are beautiful."

"What do you mean?"

"I work with cloth. I can see what cloth you're made of."

He shook his head. "I no longer know who or what I am. These are terrible times…" His voice quivered. She had breached his defenses, yet he was not embarrassed to open his heart to her.

She looked at him warmly. "I told you the truth about yourself. And now you are weeping for me."

"For you, Rachel, yes." Victor took a deep breath. "For all of us."

"At last, we are breaking bread…together."

"Exactly." He pressed her hand. "You are an exceptional girl."

"And you don't know much Yiddish, but you understand things most other men don't. Someday you will find what you are looking for…" She paused for a moment. "Though I can't hope for myself, I shall never stop hoping for you."

That night, sleepless on his roof, Victor was overcome by the darkness that had continued to gather in his soul since he first set foot on alien soil. He felt a strong compassion for Rachel, who had probably never wept with self-pity. He mourned for Sophie and sweet little Hannah. At last, they would find rest in his heart. *But no,* he thought grievously, *not my little one.* Her unlived life would always hover there, in abeyance. He recalled one night lying in their small bed in Krakow. He and Sophie had taken turns carrying the sick, crying infant back and forth through the narrow room. When she finally quieted down and he had gone back to bed, Sophie was weeping into her pillow. He stroked her hair, but his caress only unleashed her sorrow. Asking her to tell him what was wrong, he took her into his arms.

"Everything's wrong, Victor. It's all my fault. If it weren't for me, you could have fled, could've had a life before getting stuck with this burden on your back."

"What life?" He reminded her that Walter had been shot in flight. He didn't allow himself to think of Tatyana.

She kept shaking her head. As she sobbed herself to sleep, Victor knew it was his turn to weep, not for his life, but for Sophie's.

The following day he went to the market with Benjamin. Their agreement would only last until the moment of any reply from the American consulate. Meanwhile, Victor pictured himself in the patriarch's home with the lame, lovely Rachel, begetting heroic sons destined for great future deeds—a devoted shepherd husband recycling a legend from the Bible.

But knowing that Victor would lay at her side yearning for another place, another time, perhaps another woman, Rachel would never allow herself the folly of such dreaming. Each evening he met with the family after helping the patriarch with anything but killing lambs, though he sometimes shared their tender meat for dinner. Rachel spent long days at a factory sewing men's shirts. At night, she would help the family earn some extra money by embroidering women's blouses.

Benjamin observed the bond between the two young people, unaware that it was a bond of mutual encouragement and renunciation.

After several weeks, the reply from the American consulate arrived from Kuybyshev. Since the German army had penetrated the Soviet Union, foreign consulates had been moved there. The letter confirmed that an affidavit and other papers had been sent for Victor to the consulate, presumably by Sophie's sister, Lisa. Regretfully, the Soviet government was refusing all exit permits, and therefore the Americans could not give him a visa. There was a short postscript telling him that one of the headquarters of the new Polish army was in Yangiyul, a short distance from Bukhara.

Victor imagined leaving the Soviet Union with the Polish army. He had heard that some divisions were moved through Iran and Palestine to the African front. It was a slim chance, but unless he left Bukhara, he would never find a route of escape.

When he mentioned his plans to Benjamin, the old man turned to him with genuine sadness. "I was hoping you would put down your tent, be one of us. You and Rachel…"

"It wouldn't be fair to her. I have nothing to offer."

"Of course you do."

"Please understand, *Ata* Benjamin. I can't be the man I want to be until I am free."

"I respect that." Benjamin sighed. "We are a free people, a proud people. But we are at the mercy of the dictates of the state."

"You have been more than good to me. I shall always remember you with gratitude." "Take Rachel with you."

"How could I? If the army accepts me, where would she be? And if all fails, would you like to see her sleep in the street or in some teahouse or be arrested and sent to forced labor?"

"Such a fate may be ordained for any of us." Benjamin lowered his head. "But you are right. Go with God."

That night, Victor took his leave from the family. He would have liked to disappear without farewell, but considered it an act of cowardice. Rachel walked beside him for a stretch, then stopped for a silent goodbye. He ran back to the music school, waving at her in the dark without turning his head. Later, lying for the last time on his terrace with the four-poster bed, he realized that he had renounced all comfort in his search for freedom and Tatyana.

PART TWO

6.

TATYANA

Nothing will ever be the same.

Zagreb, July 1940

Nothing had changed after my short journey to Stuttgart; but now, after eighteen months, I feel that nothing will ever be the same. Victor is still in my heart and mind, and I miss him sorely. I haven't mentioned our encounter to anyone—not even to Mama, my best friend and confidante. Europe is in the grip of war and persecution and any day Yugoslavia may be the next victim.

My grief began about six months before the outbreak of World War II. Aunt Martha wrote me that Victor's mother, shocked by an order to move to Poland with the whole family in less than twenty-four hours, had died of a heart attack. Victor, Sophie, and their baby girl had been forced to leave Stuttgart after her hurried funeral. Weeks later, Martha received a short note from Victor, telling her that he, Sophie and the baby had spent some time in Krakow, but were now moving to a smaller town.

I was devastated. Martha had told me about Victor's close relationship with his mother. Now my fear for him and his young family is stronger than the bleak prospect of never seeing him again. After the invasion of Poland I wanted to sleep, not to feel, to forget all that anguish. I buried myself in my studies. In the meantime, most of Western Europe has been invaded, and I'm afraid Yugoslavia will be next.

***

When Bogdan asked me to marry him, I told him I was too young to settle down. I've known Bogdan as long as I can remember. He would look after Leila and me each time our parents went out. From the time he was eight and I four, my parents regarded him as my protector. I knew that he would overwhelm me with questions, had I told him that I loved another man. Cocksure that I would change my mind, he said he was going to wait for me.

I have been working incessantly for my diploma, trying not to think about the horror Victor and his family must have endured after the invasion of Poland. While country after country was falling into the hands of the Germans, I completed my studies and exams after my twenty-second birthday, much sooner than anticipated. Then Bogdan proposed to me again. I told him that I was worried about my family's safety. The Jews would be in great danger and I could think of nothing more crucial than finding a hideout ahead of time. He promised to help. He has friends who will be willing and able to give us shelter. I was relieved when he agreed that we had better not rush into marriage.

May 1941.

I'm writing these notes, so that I won't forget what is happening in all of this confusion. A few weeks ago, Yugoslavia was attacked by Hungary, Bulgaria and Romania. Italy and Germany have carved up Slovenia between them. Armed resistance began in Bosnia, where Croatian fascists started the massacre of Serbs. Now Serbs from all over have joined the resistance, and the daily papers are full of deadly threats against the Jews. Bogdan called to tell me he was about to leave on a long journey. I realized that he was joining the partisans. "You were right," he said. "Under the circumstances, we had better postpone our plans."

Our plans?

Dad decided at the last minute to leave with Bogdan and other comrades. I begged him to take me along. He refused, saying it was much too dangerous. I felt rejected, arguing that staying home was just as risky, but he wanted me to take care of Mama and Leila instead of exposing myself to additional dangers and hardships.

Now that he is gone, the three of us live in constant apprehension. We miss him sorely. My diploma is gathering dust in the drawer. I can't find work—any work. Sometimes I hide with my camera behind doors or windows and take snapshots of the Nazis, trying to collect evidence of their brutalities. Fear spreads like a lethal gas over the city; food is disappearing from the stores. There is more hunger every day. It's hard to tell enemy from friend. As time goes by, I am stagnating at home, getting more and more worried about our safety.

Bogdan hasn't kept his promise to find us a hideout. Perhaps he forgot.

September 1941.

One of my former fellow students came by to tell me he had joined Bogdan's and my father's partisan group in the hills. I asked him to give Dad my photos along with a letter containing our news. Since it's not possible to stay in touch, I was glad for this opportunity. Dad would appreciate my desire to contribute to the struggle, but I'm itching to do more, to be with him, fighting.

1943.

I can hardly believe that eighteen months have passed since my last few notes. Constant worries about my family made me lose the desire to write. But here, at last, is my first chance to sort out the latest events: everything changed when the student who took my photos and letter to Dad came back to see me. I introduced him to Mama as an old friend. We went to a café around the corner where he asked me in a whisper if I would take pictures of certain buildings now occupied by the enemy. I agreed at once.

A few minutes later, I squatted beside the back seat of the young man's car to hide myself from view, snapping pictures while he drove slowly through the streets of Zagreb. I wanted to know if he worked with Bogdan, and he said yes. In fact, it was Bogdan who had asked him to get in touch with me. He had seen the portfolio I sent to Dad and wanted more photographs.

I took pictures of German secret police headquarters and a number of other strategic places. These were more daring acts than I had anticipated. At one point, I was under the impression that a German car was following us. Soon all grew quiet, however, and the car disappeared at a corner behind us. My companion pocketed the film I gave him, and I got out of his car a few steps from our apartment building.

In the middle of the night, someone was throwing pebbles at my window. I went down and carefully opened the door. A stranger slipped in, introducing himself as Stefan, one of my father's partisan friends. He told me my fellow student was missing. He must have been caught, or managed to escape. In any case, Stefan had promised to bring me to my father. I wondered in panic if the German car might have turned back and followed us once more.

Since leaving town during the curfew was too risky, we had to wait until morning. I trusted Stefan at once. Tall, dark and trim, he wore glasses and impressed me with a special warmth and intelligence.

I woke up my sister. While Leila told Mama, I threw a few things into a knapsack. Mama begged me not to go. If I had a child I would understand, she said. I tried to explain that under the circumstances my presence might endanger them both. She concealed her anguish, embraced me in silence, and wrote a note to take along to my father.

No time for tears. Choked at the thought of being torn away from my mother and Leila, I wondered in panic when I would be able to see them again.

Stefan was spending the night on the living room couch. I threw my notes into my knapsack, wrapped in a sweater. If Stefan hadn't reminded me, I would have forgotten my camera. We boarded the first bus at sunrise to the outskirts of Zagreb. At an appointed spot on a road less travelled by the enemy, a comrade picked us up with a truck. We drove to the area above the town of Krapina, in the Zagorje region. I kept praying that my fellow student had been able to escape. I could hardly wait to embrace my Dad. But how would Mama and Leila fend for themselves, deprived of my help and burdened with the added worry about the two of us?

We had barely arrived when Bogdan greeted me with the news of my father's death. He had been shot last night while on patrol. His companions buried him right away. Bogdan, who has become the leader of the group, showed me no sympathy. He left me alone in my shock and grief.

Stefan's quiet presence was my only comfort.

I was unable to grasp how Bogdan had changed. I hardly recognized him with a full beard. Along with a piercing look, his manner is now curt and clipped. When I tried to learn more about Dad's death, he only shrugged.

I was stunned. Assigned a thin bed of hay in a shack with three young feminine freedom fighters, I wept inconsolably. During that grief-stricken night I longed for Victor more than ever. My feelings hadn't changed in five years of separation. On the contrary, they had grown deeper and stronger. I yearned for his tenderness, innocence, and compassion, knowing that he, like my Dad, would be lost to me forever.

I tried to calm down by thinking of my first impression of Victor. After my high school reunion in Munich I had decided to surprise Aunt Martha with a short visit in Stuttgart. My arrival interrupted an afternoon chamber concert. I sat down quietly among Martha's guests and listened to Mozart's B minor flute quartet. What a contrast to those meetings in Munich... On the train taking me to Stuttgart, I was still shaken by the hatred against the Jews by my former classmates.

I felt immediately drawn to the young flautist, to the sweep of his full lips, high forehead and Greek profile. Such looks and such a flawless performance. He played his part with closed eyes and I closed mine in turn, carried away by the music. After the concert, my aunt introduced us: "Tatyana, meet Victor, my friend Hannah's son."

As soon as our eyes met, I was struck by the deep connection between us. While greeting his mother, I heard Martha say, "And this is Sophie, Victor's bride. They just got married last month."

I stared at a shy young girl, trying to hide my shock.

The guests had just left when my aunt told me that Sophie was "expecting". Later that night, tossing and turning in bed, I couldn't stop thinking of Victor. Had he felt obligated to marry the girl because of his carelessness? Could Sophie have trapped him with her apparent helplessness and innocence?

But who was I to judge? I was appalled by my jealousy and troubled by the intensity of my feelings. Although I would never intrude on their lives, I was convinced Victor and I had known one another forever.

The next morning I went for a walk in a nearby public garden. I saw Victor on a bench calling my name. I had no idea that this chance encounter would change our fate. Sitting down beside him, I learned that he worked on the main floor of the Jewish department store across the street. This was his lunch hour. We talked for a few minutes before he had to go back to work. Reluctant to part, we stopped three times to wave at each other. When I thought we might never meet again, I felt alone in the world.

I spent my last day with Aunt Martha. It grew dark in midafternoon. As Martha busied herself in the kitchen, I packed my few belongings. Startled by a scream, I ran to check what was happening and saw shop windows shattered across the street. At the end of the block, the neighborhood synagogue was in flames.

My first thought was: *Victor! What has happened to Victor at that store?* I took the house keys and called out to Martha that I would be right back.

Glass was breaking everywhere. I ran into the public garden and from there across the street. Hoodlums in Nazi uniforms were swinging mallets and hammers, breaking the huge illuminated windows of the department store on the ground floor. I found an entrance at the rear, then followed a long dark hall, all the time in fear for Victor's life, aware that I loved him with a passion I had never known. Customers and employees were running through the aisles. Victor stared in horror at the shattering windows. Before he could grasp what was happening, I dragged him out through the hallway and the alley into the deserted public garden. Hand in hand, we ran back to Martha's.

Later, while she slept, we shared a few precious moments. I shall never forget his tender embrace and the touch of his lips on mine, before we tore ourselves away from one another.

All we can do is keep our courage burning through the night ahead…

7.

TATYANA

The death of a deer

Our group consisted of sixteen people, including myself. Assigned to stay with the women, I was to receive and transcribe reports by wireless. We worked in a shop of rusty tools. I was given a rifle. Ludmilla taught me how to shoot. She was a friendly loudmouth, good looking in a vulgar way. She never combed her unruly black hair. I feared her shrill laughter might be heard by the enemy. Every other night she would disappear from the shack and return bleary-eyed before dawn.

Bogdan continued to ignore or avoid me. He would come to our working place on his nightly rounds and listen to radio reports. With a peck on my cheek and a pat on the shoulder, he wished me a good night's sleep. I pulled away from him. Was he sarcastic, or trying to comfort me with this clumsy ritual?

One starlit night in August, I'd had enough of how he treated our fellow partisans. It was maddening that he claimed a large tent for himself and enjoyed all the privacy and luxuries he desired, while his comrades slept in abandoned sheds, under trees, or entrenched in camouflaged ditches. They wrapped themselves in canvas to keep out the cold and the rain. No one knew where he had found that tent. He alone had a cot. A leader's right, his haughty manner seemed to say. Since Dad was gone, I was worried about Mama and Leila and missed them more than ever. Stefan had left on some assignment, and I waited anxiously for his return.

One night I decided to face Bogdan and ask him about my father, but as soon as I entered his tent an inner voice warned me against it. I was about to remind him of his promise to find a hideout for my family when I noticed a shadow moving up and down on his cot. I fled in disgust at the sight of Ludmilla's black hair in a sliver of moonlight.

It was dawn when I heard her return to the shack. I took my rifle and went out. The fog was lifting early on sunny mornings. All of us took turns guarding our fort. Any movement by the enemy was to be reported. We were to shoot only in self-defense. Though it wasn't my turn for guard duty, I needed to get out. Grief-stricken and furious at Bogdan for lacking the slightest regard for others, I hid behind a tall tree in the woods and waited. The sun slanting between two firs blurred my sight. I thought of Dad out on his last watch. *Did he fall between two such trees? Oaks, firs, pines? Suppose he was caught between those very two firs?* I could see his wavy dark hair and the windswept face I had loved so much. His face reminded me of a clear landscape after the rain. His honest eyes looked straight into mine. Now I watched him stand like a sentinel on a planet that was being demolished.

The new regime was to be ruled by the enemy and the Bogdans of this world. If only I could understand what caused Bogdan's indifference and alienation. I thought he and Dad had been friends.

A shadow moved behind one of the trees. Leaves rustled. I lifted the rifle and took aim. Three shots resounded in the morning air. Something fell. I ran downhill blind with fear, startled by my own courage. And then I saw it—the deer. I shall never forget its eyes, full of pain and astonishment. The poor animal was still alive. I didn't know how to end its agony. Of all creatures, I had to kill a deer. It was as if I lost my innocence in this strange rite of passage.

I now understand the meaning of what I did. I *was* that deer. With each act of violence against another living being, we kill something of ourselves.

I closed my eyes. What I had done brought me back to the memory of Kristallnacht. I was aching with longing for Victor. Why did I have to be here without my father and with a man like Bogdan? I no longer felt safe. Something rustled in the forest behind me. I opened my eyes and jumped back when I saw Bogdan with a pistol in his right hand. I thought it was pointed at me. Was he trying to scare me? A moment later, he gave the poor animal the coup de grace.

He laughed as he slipped the weapon into his pocket. "You were great!" he exclaimed. "Now we can have a feast."

Still on my knees, I sobbed. A few steps from my gentle victim, I saw Bogdan's shiny black boots. He had probably taken them from some SS officer he killed. Shuddering at the sight, I couldn't bear looking at those thin, smiling lips as he pulled me up from the ground.

How could I ever have thought of him as my protector? Eyes can deceive, but the mouth cannot disguise. Never believe in the innocence of a 12-year-old boy. Watch the metamorphosis of those sweet lips as he grows into a man. He put his arm around me. Three other partisans and Ludmilla were watching the scene. I pushed him away.

"Don't ever touch me again!" I heard myself shout, then caught sight of Stefan who must have just come back and was watching us in silence. Bogdan looked from me to Ludmilla. I realized that he took my fury for jealousy. "That's what you get for being nice to the kid," he said. "Come on Ludmilla, let's go."

To my surprise, Ludmilla shook her head and stared at him in anger.

Bogdan shrugged. "Women!" Forcing a laugh, he returned to his tent.

"I had no idea you two were engaged," Ludmilla told me later. She had learned it from Stefan. And Stefan might have learned it from Dad, who probably heard it from Bogdan himself. It never occurred to her, Ludmilla told me, because Bogdan made such hateful remarks about Jews. "He claims to be a Communist," she whispered, "but he acts like a Nazi. Look how he's treated you! Sooner or later, he'll do the same to me."

That evening, I refused to eat the deer's meat. Ludmilla followed my example. Bogdan had roasted the animal on a makeshift spit. He held up forkfuls in front of our eyes and tried to push them into our mouths.

Stefan put a stop to his teasing. "Leave the girls alone."

"You aren't eating any yourself. Look at you delicate, fainthearted Jews!"

"Ludmilla isn't Jewish."

"Never mind. She has joined the club."

"And what club have you joined, Bogdan?"

"Watch your tongue! I'm the leader here, as you know."

"*Ja, mein Führer!*"

"Shut up, you filthy Jew."

I couldn't believe what I heard. Stefan threw himself on Bogdan. He wasn't strong, but deft and wiry. Ducking Bogdan's blows, he caught him off guard and threw him to the ground. Other comrades intervened, saying we had better things to do than fight each other. Stefan reeled back to us, fuming with rage. From the moment I met him, I could tell he was Jewish, even though his comrades knew him as Stefan Skalovski from his false identity card.

I found him after dark and told him that I had to get away from Bogdan.

"You are right," he said. "As soon as possible…" We looked at each other in silence.

"Could we join some other group of partisans?" I asked. But Stefan had his own plans. He was trained as a parachutist and had special connections in England, where he was to join the Allies. It was the perfect moment to head for Italy together, he said. Mussolini had been arrested. It would be no problem to cross the Italian border, since Marshal Badoglio was now in charge. If we managed to get to Trieste, he could find his way across the English Channel, while I might safely wait out the war in Italy.

A dangerous journey lay ahead, but the warm weather was on our side. We would pass through Kočevje, a partisan stronghold in the mountains, where I could be provided with false Italian papers. Once in Italy, I might settle in a major city like Milan or Venice. I told him I had spent three years of my childhood in Florence where my father had worked as an architect. My Italian was still very good. That would make matters easier, he said. It might even help me earn a living.

I could hardly wait to get away. Stefan would be ready to leave tomorrow, right after dark. During the next afternoon, I took advantage of being alone in the shack and quickly packed my knapsack. Ludmilla appeared unexpectedly, catching me in the act.

"I'm glad you're leaving," she said. She promised in a whisper that she would go to Bogdan's tent a bit sooner than usual. Her ruse would give me some time before he discovered my absence. "I hope you don't mind?" she added with a worried smile. "I mean…"

"You can have him. By the way, I was never engaged to him, though he did propose to me."

When I thanked her, she drew me to her in a quick embrace. "Break a leg," she whispered in a broken German, "and be careful…"

I remember that I had been anything but careful. How could I throw those dangerous notes into my knapsack? Suppose we got caught? Victor had been right to call me foolhardy for taking that picture of the SS officer in the park. Even among the partisans, everyone seemed suspicious of everyone else.

As planned, Stefan waited for me at the crest of the hill. Sure of his direction, he walked swiftly ahead of me. We meant to be out of reach before anyone noticed our absence. Under favorable circumstances, it would take us two weeks to reach Trieste. Stefan knew the route from some previous mission and was familiar with the territory.

I asked him how we would survive without food. Not to worry, he told me. He knew farmers who would help us with provisions, and he also had partisan friends along the way. We kept walking down slopes through woods and meadows, away from roads and paths, avoiding checkpoints and enemy patrols. Afraid that I might take a wrong step, and sprain an ankle or break a leg, Stefan took my arm to help me across boulders, ditches, and holes, while always being on the lookout for the enemy.

Carrying flashlights and rifles instead of provisions, we reached the first refuge of fellow partisans before dawn. Thirsty and exhausted, we were given water and some food. We spent the night in a stable surrounded by cows.

Walking at night and sleeping through parts of the day, we were passed from group to group. Fellow partisans helped us cross the Krapina River. I'll never forget the young and old faces of those poor, hardworking people. There were expressions of kindness and fear. I saw palms clutch with greed, others open with generosity. Stefan and I learned quickly how to read those hands and expressions.

Grief for my father, anguish about Mama and Leila, and fear of running into the enemy kept me silent. Stefan understood and respected my distress. One day I asked him how long he had known Bogdan. Stefan said he had met him and my dad in the early stages of the war. The partisans were just getting organized. He had liked my father at once, while Bogdan...

"While Bogdan...?"

"At first, he seemed pleasant enough, though I could sense his cruel streak and lust for power. One night, we all sat around a fire, involved in some political discussion. Bogdan took charge of the meeting. He always needed to be center stage and contradicted everything your father was saying. He tried to humiliate him in front of our comrades. Your dad's humanism was pure Jewish hogwash, Bogdan declared. We didn't need wishy-washy philosophers but men of steel to confront the enemy."

"My God, Stefan, I had no idea..."

"That did it for me. I can't stand fanatics, and he has become a fanatical anti-Semite. I was ready to jump on him. Most of our comrades were incensed, but your father—who was a mentor to us all—calmed everyone down and reminded us to save our strength for the fight against the enemy. But he never looked at Bogdan, nor ever spoke to him again."

"We all used to like Bogdan as kids," was all I could say. "The war must have driven him mad."

"The war brought out what's inside him. I remember the day he got that tent and the cot, and later those boots from a German officer..."

"How could he grab that tent for himself alone? It would shelter half a dozen people."

"Exactly. He took it as a trophy, after killing a few Nazis in their sleep during a surprise attack. Apparently, their guard had dozed off. He bragged about having done it alone. Right after, he proclaimed himself the leader of our group."

"Stefan, do you think it possible that Bogdan was the one who...?"

Stefan stopped. He looked at me gravely. "It's hard to believe," he said, hesitating, "but I do. I've heard more stories like this happening among partisans. What made you suspect?"

"I accidentally shot that deer and didn't know how to put it out of its misery. I was kneeling beside it in shock, then saw Bogdan with a pistol in his hand. He was pointing it at me. I froze... A moment later, he turned it on the animal."

"My God, Tatyana—you must have been terrified."

"I'd had some vague suspicion before, though it seemed too unlikely; but at that instant I knew."

Stefan pressed my hand warmly. "I'm so relieved... We got away just in time."

***

During a windy night, we crossed the Sava River near Videm in a boat with the help of two experienced partisans. A searchlight caught us in midstream. Bullets flew past the four of us. We jumped into the water and, after being carried downstream, managed to scramble ashore through the strong current unhurt. My camera disappeared with the capsized boat. The two partisans returned to their hideout, while Stefan and I headed for Dolenska. Dripping wet and still trembling, we were filled with gratitude for this narrow escape.

Stefan always knew how to calm me down or cheer me up with some funny tale. I don't know what I would have done without him. In Dolenska, we were taken in by a farmer's family. They provided us with food and blankets and hung our clothes to dry near an open fire. The next day, in Kočevje, headquarters for the partisans, I was given a false Italian identity card. Born in Trieste, my name was now Tatyana Danieli. Stefan helped me prepare a plausible story about my background.

"German," I suggested, "from my mother's side. This happens to be true. She always spoke German to me. I'm used to writing my notes in German. And I'll just pretend that my Italian father left us when I was 6 years old. We never heard from him again."

"You have it all figured out," Stefan said, laughing.

From Kočevje, it took us another week to cross the Julian Alps before getting to the Primorska seaside and, ultimately across the border to Trieste. I remembered those peaks from a childhood vacation. But now, even as we stopped to admire the glory of the landscape, I wasn't able to connect it with those early memories. My identity card would only serve me in Italy. Wary of the usual dangers, I ignored my blisters and sore muscles and prayed for our safe arrival in Italy.

Stefan had taken the same route before and knew more partisans who would help us find food and shelter. I dreaded his departure for England. How was I to go on alone without him?

He shook his head when I asked him to take me along to England. He couldn't expose me to such hazards. Besides, the Allies needed specific people for specific assignments.

Wasn't a photo journalist specific enough?

"You are remarkably specific, Tatyana."

His words and smile revealed how much he cared for me. I was uplifted and filled with gratitude. He was the best friend I had left in the world. I was about to tell him about my encounter with Victor, but then bit my tongue and was silent.

We moved on cautiously with growing trepidation. On reaching the border, he whispered some password to two friendly Italian guards who let us through without asking for our papers. Deeply relieved, we went on slowly in the direction of the sea.

8.

TASHKENT

Victor's hopes dwindled as soon as he arrived in Yangiyul. How could he be recruited with his poor knowledge of Polish? It would not only give him away, but also throw doubt on the document declaring that he had been released from the labor camp as a Pole. He might get arrested, since such documents could easily be bought. Everything could be bought, from ration marks to passports, to certificates from fictitious working places. Some Russian citizens acquired Polish identity papers with the intention of leaving the country.

Victor spent time at the bazaar, where rumors multiplied. He heard an old man whisper to another in Yiddish that two of his Russian relatives were permitted to leave the country with the Polish army. He followed the men from stall to stall and, after making sure no possible spy could hear him, whispered to the one who had shared the information that he, too, was related to a Polish officer.

"Is that so?" The red-bearded speaker clicked his tongue in disbelief.

"I heard you mention that relatives may leave with the army."

"Just a rumor," the man said curtly.

"Perhaps you can tell me where I could get a document to prove my…"

The red beard interrupted. "What document? How do I know? And who are you?"

"A brother."

"With a German accent?"

"A Jewish brother."

Once more, the old man looked at him with an air of mistrust.

"You don't look Jewish."

"I think he's telling the truth," the other man said. "Doesn't look Jewish, but has a good face."

"Don't trust a face."

The other man did not listen. He told Victor that all kinds of documents were sold at the bazaar. Such documents had been stolen from dead souls in labor camps or deportees from Polish territories and could only be obtained for exorbitant prices.

Victor thanked him and went on his way. Freedom was a commodity beyond his reach. *What next?* He decided to stay in this town for another two days, hoping to run into some good Samaritan with access to free false documents. He spent long hours at the bazaar, keeping his eyes and ears open for a possible lead.

He slept on the floor of a teahouse. Unable to afford roasted lamb on a stick, he began to share the Russian obsession with bread. A young Polish soldier put a small loaf into Victor's hands. Those lucky fellows were selling everything they could spare, using the money for vodka to celebrate their departure.

Taking his loaf to a teahouse, Victor remembered the saying of a Polish peasant woman: *As long as there is bread, there won't be hunger in the house.* Back in Bukhara, he had seen long lines forming in front of the place of distribution as soon as the loaves were brought to the collectives from the factory. There was only one factory baking bread for the entire city. The Soviets had declared Uzbekistan a cotton land because of its climate and no one was allowed to plant wheat or corn. The *Sovchosen* and *Kolchosen* collectives were forbidden to add anything else. Wheat was delivered from central Russia. The fear of not receiving enough bread made families hoard more than they needed which brought greater scarcity. The distribution of food grew more and more inadequate. Tremendous shortages occurred when people fled to the interior from the advancing German armies.

The ceaseless influx of refugees to Yangiyul caused the already exorbitant prices to double. The prospect of acquiring a valid document faded with Victor's dwindling money. His loneliness added to his dejection.

He decided to leave for Ashgabat, capital of Turkmenia. Only twenty-five miles from the Persian border, the city might serve him as a stepping stone into Tehran. It was rumored that a number of people had managed to cross the border. This filled him with fresh optimism. Once in Tehran, he hoped to obtain an exit permit and a visa from the American consulate.

He waited until dark. After making sure that one of the freight trains was leaving for Ashgabat, he climbed into a wagon and hid behind wooden crates. Fear of getting caught kept him awake all night. The train stopped at dawn before entering the city. Careful to remain unnoticed, he jumped down from the wagon and crossed numerous tracks between other trains, then followed the way to a deserted field. He lay down under a mulberry tree and immediately fell asleep. When he opened his eyes, the sun was high above scattered clouds.

Disheveled, craving a bath, he went into the city with the determined steps of a man who knew where he was going: chin up, hands folded behind his back. He stopped next to a man at a farmer's market who was whispering something to a woman behind a stall. Unable to understand her answer, Victor saw her point in the direction of the main street.

"It's a teahouse," he heard her say in Russian. "Right over there. Look for Pavel," she added, with a furtive glance at Victor.

The man left in the direction she had indicated. Victor bought a handful of dates, and then followed him at a safe distance.

The teahouse was right around the corner. Victor entered and sat down at its opposite end where the man was talking to a handsome turbaned Muslim. After a while, the man rose to leave. Victor feared the Muslim might walk out with him, but the man took some newspaper cuttings and rolled himself a few cigarettes. He stuck one into the corner of his mouth without lighting it and stared at the empty cup on his table.

Victor sat down beside him. "You must be Pavel," he said in Russian.

"Who sent you?" the man asked, lighting his cigarette.

"A farmer from the bazaar."

"Fjodor?"

Victor nodded.

"Going to Tehran?"

Victor nodded again. "How much?"

Pavel lifted his hands: "A thousand rubles."

"I have no money."

"Black market. I show you." He told Victor in his fragmented Russian that he couldn't have chosen a better time. The Allied conference was about to take place in Tehran. The city was full of American, English, and Russian military personnel. Fugitives, disguised as Polish soldiers, were driven across the border in military trucks. In all that confusion, they passed without fail.

It sounded too easy, except for the money. Victor dreaded dealing in black-market goods. Every stranger was a potential suspect and could fall into the hands of the secret police.

"Think about it," Pavel said. "Tell me tomorrow morning. I'll be here."

Victor spent the night on the podium of a different teahouse where he met another refugee, who warned him that Ashgabat was swarming with secret agents. They would gather people, take their money, give them uniforms, and drive them straight into jail. So much for contact with the West in Tehran.

Suppose Pavel was one of the secret police? People had begun noticing Victor wandering about the streets. Were they just staring at his worn-out coat, the dirty scarf, his toes sticking out of shoes filled with old newspaper? What made them single him out in this town crowded with poor vagrants?

Surely that melon-head with a harelip, smiling at him from the next table, must have followed him. Victor remembered seeing him yesterday, probably in some street. *Be alert, but don't panic*, he warned himself.

What foolish impulse had made him take flight from Bukhara? It was impossible to go back after his defection from the music school. No one was allowed to leave his place of work without special permission. Besides, Victor would be ashamed to knock at Benjamin's door.

Be a man, he told himself, dismissing his longing for the comfort he had exchanged for hunger and uncertainty. Why not go on to Tashkent, a beautiful city he had heard people praise again and again? Experienced at last in the art of train hopping, he decided to hold on to the money left in his pocket for a bit of food.

Soon after dark, he walked back toward the train station. Moving through the open countryside, he climbed onto a freight train leaving for Tashkent and, after careful exploration, concealed himself in the space between two wagons. Three hours later, just as the train began to move, he climbed into a wagon filled with cotton bales. From one stop to the next, he felt safe in his corner, hiding behind two crates. Whenever the train entered a station, he got off and hid under a wagon until any possible inspection was over. In spite of his fear, he went on to the end of his journey.

"A mama's boy," Walter had called him. "Never taking a chance, never doing what you really want to do. What sort of a Victor are you? Your name is a mockery. It's about time you stop hiding your head in the sand. Take a good look at yourself. I'm just warning you, so you won't break into pieces..."

Victor had been hurt and angry then, but the truth hit home. He had always looked for the easy way out. Comfort in robe and slippers, no conflict to destroy his well-being. If only Walter could see him now! Shaken by the rumbling of the train, he thought of the old adage that it was better to try and fail than not to try at all. He might have felt comfortably trapped in Bukhara, but most likely the trap would have turned into a prison for life: an inner prison in Benjamin's home, preventing him from finding Tatyana and making him lose his pride, his courage and his integrity. The dangerous road he had chosen would at least not be filled with regret.

He jumped from the train at dawn when it halted in a small town. A passenger train had stopped on the nearest track, giving Victor a chance to leave the station with alighting travelers. No one seemed to be paying attention to anyone else. People were loitering, bargaining, eating, drinking. Close to the station, a fight had just started between some Russian drunk and an Uzbek, while a number of men watched and cheered them on.

Victor bought some food, then hopped back on the train. It took hours before it began to move through the countryside. In the middle of the day, a deserted plain spread out from either side of the train, interrupted here and there by a river. At last small settlements came into view. Victor was struck by the unfamiliar sights he saw in this land. There were endless huts of clay, some two-storied with ladders on the outside. Those settlements appeared amid cultivated gardens with shady apricot or oriuk trees, surrounded by the water veins of a complex irrigation system. The train chugged on without a stop and arrived in Tashkent in mid-afternoon.

Shaking the stiffness from his limbs, Victor left the station. His walk down the street carried him past small bazaars at each corner. People occupied intersections, offering their wares. There was an unusual amount of traffic: cars, trams and pedestrians.

He peeked into a restaurant that reminded him of the finest he had seen in the West. As usual, the place was reserved exclusively for the aristocracy of party members sent around the country, such as high army officers, leaders of large concerns, and presidents of collectives.

It was Sunday. Large and small families strolled up and down the crowded streets. Victor stopped a stout, motherly Russian woman in a red kerchief and asked for directions to the central marketplace. She gave him a lecture about the city, explaining how it was divided into an old and a new section, then waited at his side with maternal concern, making sure he wouldn't climb into the wrong streetcar. There were two cars to a tram, both of them overcrowded. The fare was passed from hand to hand until it reached the conductor. He exchanged it for a ticket, which was returned to the passenger by the same route.

On the way to the bazaar, the tram passed through the new town: a garden city mostly built in colonial Western style, with low, widely spaced houses. As Victor had learned from the Russian woman, buildings were kept low because of the danger of earthquakes. Broad thoroughfares led crosswise in four directions. They rode past a theater, a movie house, and a concert shell facing a vast square. Imposing modern white stone buildings surrounded a large pleasure garden. Victor assumed they were seats of the state or the federal government.

Little by little, the Russian passengers got out in the new town. Now Victor found himself surrounded by Uzbeks. He alighted with a stream of natives and followed them to the bazaar. Again there was one market selling fresh produce, another dealing in commerce. People would crowd any stall offering something to eat. Driven by hunger, Victor made his way through the throng. Stopping at a table, he saw a small boy tearing a bag from a woman's shoulder with the skill of a seasoned thief. The child zigzagged through a forest of legs and darted off in the opposite direction. An elderly man tried to pursue him, but shoppers blocked his way and refused to be pushed aside. The woman screamed for her purse, her would-be rescuer kept shouting and pushing, a fight ensued, and in the midst of this confusion the boy vanished with his loot.

Sorry for the woman, yet amused by the spectacle, Victor felt tempted to try his own hand at stealing—perhaps just an apple or a few grapes. Didn't he have a moral right to steal tons of apples, since he, an innocent man being punished for being in the wrong place at the wrong time, had paid for them in advance with fourteen months of slave labor? Try to explain this to the authorities, if they catch you with an apple in your hand. No, it would be sheer folly—years in prison, or some gulag in Siberia....

There was more pushing and shoving in front of the stall. Ready to buy some grapes, Victor threw his coat from one arm over the other. As he was about to pull the last coins from a back pocket of his pants, the groping hand sent a message of disbelief to his brain: the pocket was gone. His finger traced a neat square of emptiness where it had been. The corner of his khaki shirt slipped through it like a soiled handkerchief, as though to wave goodbye to rubles, identity card, work permit, and letter from the American consulate.

He had ceased to exist.

Some people expressed sympathy. Others laughed at his predicament. Everyone agreed that he must immediately report the incident to the police. It might be wiser to ask for their help than to be arrested as a vagrant in the street.

No one was able to steer him in the right direction. At last, a kind old man explained how to get there. Lost after a long search, Victor found himself right in front of the station. Confronted with Uzbek policemen unable to understand any Russian, he felt less conspicuous, since Tashkent was crowded with people of different nationalities—people who had fled from the war zones or had been evacuated. After much misunderstanding, Victor managed to report his predicament in pantomime, wringing his hands in despair and showing his mutilated trousers. When he asked for some document showing that he was residing in Tashkent, the chief of police shook his head, insisting that Victor was not from Tashkent because he was unable to show any residence. Since he came from Bukhara, he must go back to Bukhara. Any proof of identity could only be issued in Bukhara.

How was he to return to Bukhara without a document? He might even be arrested as a spy. The chief kept shaking his head, reiterating that he must have a document, although he could not issue such a document here. Only the chief of police in Bukhara was authorized to do so. In short, Victor wasn't allowed to stay in Tashkent under any circumstances and ought to be grateful for not being arrested.

Victor headed back the long way to the station. He put on his coat to hide the tear in his pants. Every now and then, he hopped on the steps of a tram. Concealed by the crowd, he held on for a few stops and then jumped off again.

In front of the railway station, he saw an old man laboring under the weight of a heavy suitcase and a parcel on his back. He went up to him and stopped. "Can you help me?" the man asked in Russian. Victor took his baggage and followed him to a streetcar. The old man handed him two rubles. Thanking him for this generous tip, Victor hurried to the next food stall and bought himself something to eat. A hot soup and a couple of pancakes soothed the imperious rumblings of his stomach, although it was far from enough.

He wondered where he might spend the night. Perhaps one of those bums loitering around the railway station could direct him to a place that was free of charge. Turning to a black-bearded man sitting on the sidewalk with his back leaning against the gate, Victor asked if he knew of a place to sleep. The man kept humming while rhythmically beating his knuckles on a large tin can. His emaciated looks made it impossible to tell whether he was thirty or sixty years old. Seeing him pat the ground, Victor sat down beside him. "I'll show you," the man said in a broken Russian, continuing his humming and drumming.

Victor pulled the recorder from his coat pocket and began to play a tune in harmony with the stranger's rhythm. The man stopped humming. He stared at Victor with jaundiced eyes, dropped a couple of rubles and a few kopeks into his hat, and set it on the sidewalk. Victor played on. A small crowd gathered around them. Slowly, the hat filled with coins. Mesmerized, forgetting his predicament, Victor first blew anguish out of his *sopranino*, then filled it with melodies of another time, another world. His songs were of warmth and safety, filled with nostalgia for Tatyana.

He went on playing through the dusk, his face turned toward the rosy clouds in the sky. When he awoke from his trance, the crowds had dispersed. The drummer poked him in the ribs with an elbow, waving the full hat in front of his eyes.

"Let's eat," he indicated with a gesture.

They went to the bazaar to buy some food, then looked for the nearest teahouse. They unwrapped their treasures, ordered a pot of green tea, and shared their meal in silence. Victor longed for conversation. He asked the drummer a few polite questions. His name was Ivan. He spoke in monosyllables Victor barely understood, then gulped down his food, never looking at his companion. After the meal, Ivan guided him to an empty public bathhouse. Victor recognized it as a place where people were being deloused. He found himself surrounded by sinister-looking men stretched out on the dirty cement floor. Ivan had vanished with the rest of what Victor had earned for them both. More and more men entered the crowded room, some of them drunk, others singing and shouting. Soon Victor felt fingers crawling up and down his body, searching for money and valuables. *At least I don't need to worry about that*, he thought, clutching his recorder.

After a sleepless night, he left before dawn, anxious to get out of that den of misfits and thieves. Even at this early hour, the square was filled with civilians and military personnel. Shivering with cold, he loitered near and within the station as arriving passengers streamed through the area.

On the lookout for passengers in need of help with their baggage, he tried to keep at a safe distance from the police. As trains arrived and departed, Victor's competitors appropriated potential customers before he was able to spot them. Husky teenagers and agile professional drifters pushed him aside. Heavily loaded, they would follow the travelers to the nearest tram or all the way to their homes. Too destitute to warm himself even with a cup of tea, Victor was ready to give up, when he spotted a stout middle-aged woman panting under two clumsy parcels and a heavy sack.

No one tried to interfere as he offered her his help. The woman put down her load. She handed him a rope, told him to tie it to the sack, then placed the sack across his shoulder. He took one of her parcels and cradled it in his left arm. She preceded him across the square with the other. He could hear his competitors deriding him as he trailed after her like a dog on a leash. The sack was so heavy he had to put it down after a few steps. The effort of lifting it once more was beyond his power.

The woman turned around and stepped back. Walking closely behind him, she lightened the load with her empty arm. On and on they went, breathing heavily or halting for breath, block after endless block. At last she stopped in front of an old bungalow. Dropping his burden, Victor collapsed on the steps. The woman went inside and closed the door. The rope, untied from the sack, was still in his hand. His body was too weak to remember its need for food.

He heard a door open. The woman put a mug of soup with a sausage and a piece of bread into his hands. His stomach warmed as he ate and the warmth spread to his heart. At last he noticed the woman watching over him. "Thank you," he said, looking up at her. "You are very kind." She took the empty mug and put five rubles into his hand. Tears filled his eyes, tears of gratitude and exhaustion. He must stand up. Dizzily, he got to his feet.

"Keep it," she said, as he tried to give her the rope. "It may help you in the future."

He saw the compassion in her eyes. Waving goodbye as he moved down the steps, his smile was as faint as the sun passing behind a dark cloud.

Back at the station, his competitors were gone. In the course of the evening, three more people needed his help. His earnings allowed him the luxury of more bread and fruit and a night's sleep in a teahouse.

For the next three days, he was able to carry luggage with the help of the rope and find shelter for the night on a meadow beyond the station. Yet his strength continued to ebb. A red gash was etched in his shoulder. At least he had learned to get used to hunger and the need for a bath. Getting used to affliction was a key to a man's survival.

9.

HOSPITAL CARE

In the afternoon of his fourth day back in Tashkent, Victor could barely breathe. Waves of heat rose to his head. He keeled over in the crowded railway station. Minutes or hours later, he awoke in the ambulance driving him to the nearest state hospital. In spite of a high fever, he had to take a warm shower under a nurse's supervision. Cleansed at last, he was given a pair of pajamas and a folding bed with a real mattress. His ward consisted of a narrow hall with a long row of beds. The warmth and softness of the bed gave him a sense of well-being and security.

Too weak to pay attention to other patients, he fluctuated between cold shivers and high fever. He could not control the chattering of his teeth. The nurse brought him another blanket. It failed to warm him. He waited for the cold to subside, but a moment later threw off his covers. His throat felt parched. The nurse brought him a drink of water. He took a few sips, then fell back, exhausted.

Nightmares disrupted his fitful sleep. He was roughly awakened with a lukewarm bean soup that he could hardly swallow. The young patient to his right did not waste a minute before asking him for his leftovers, and Victor was hardly able to nod in agreement. But as soon as his appetite was restored, the scant hospital meal left him unsatisfied. His neighbor pulled impatiently at his pajama sleeve for a share of his meal when the old Russian in the bed to his left shouted at him to stop. "Can't you see the poor fellow is sick? He needs his food more than you do."

Victor thanked him with a smile.

"You're sponging off the state," the old man went on. "It's time you get out of here and look for work instead of complaining about your aching leg. And then he walks around all day, up and down the steps without any trouble." He went on, turning to Victor, "So he can beg for a bowl of soup from people who are too sick to eat their meals. And for that his leg is quite healthy...."

Those words were parried with wild insults. The young fellow jumped out of bed, ready to attack his adversary. Victor closed his eyes. He began to shake uncontrollably. A physician was called in to examine him. He concluded that the patient's symptoms pointed to malaria. His attacks were repeated every two or three days. Too weak to worry about his illness, Victor hoped to remain in bed as long as possible. During the third week, the fever subsided and the days grew longer. Like other convalescents, he could hardly wait for breakfast which consisted of hot water, one spoonful of sugar, and one hundred grams of bread. The bread was broken into a bowl, sprinkled with the sugar, and covered with warm water. Hoping to fill his stomach, Victor asked for another drink of water.

After breakfast, he would stare at the ceiling, avoiding his equally apathetic neighbors. Some of the men hid their heads under their blankets until it was time for lunch. They were brought a cup of broth with some rice or vegetables, followed by a scoop of overcooked oats. In Uzbekistan, potatoes were unavailable except for rare exceptions. Sent from Central Russia, they landed on the tables of the upper classes.

Bread was of utmost importance. At first, Victor tried to save crumbs from his dinner for the following day, but then he exchanged his bread for a handful of makhorka tobacco. That small chunk of bread would hardly satisfy his hunger, but tobacco curbed the appetite and made the days seem shorter. Smoking was prohibited by law, but the patients knew when doctors and nurses made their rounds. Victor bought an old newspaper, then learned how to roll those pungent cigarettes by copying his young neighbor. Privileged patients took advantage of poor fellows who constantly craved for a smoke. Victor followed their example, trying to reduce his dependency on the starvation diet of hospital meals by letting his bread go up in smoke.

He kept silent and withdrawn. His Russian was now fluent, but frustrated patients responded with insults to any polite remark. Once he asked a fellow for a tiny amount of tobacco, promising to pay for it with his bread ration the next morning, but was rudely rebuffed. "You filthy bastard!" the man screamed at him. "Go to hell and sleep with your own mother!"

Laughter from the other beds hit him like a dagger. Feeling the hatred of the mob, he understood its need for a scapegoat, if only to forget its own misery.

As soon as his two neighbors were sent home, the bed to Victor's right was occupied by a stocky youngster who was served three mouth-watering meals per day. He introduced himself as Grisha. Noticing that he sent back his food untouched, Victor reluctantly asked if he would pass his meals on to him.

"Of course," Grisha said with a condescending smile, handing him his full tin cup and plate. Victor tried to exchange the food for his small treasure of makhorka, but Grisha shook his head and said he only smoked the finest foreign cigarettes. Now the bland soups and mush Victor received at each meal were tainted with humiliation. Pretending a lack of appetite, he no longer accepted anything from this neighbor. Grisha took no notice, but went on boasting about being a highly respected member of the Communist Youth Party. He had just prepared himself to join the army, he added, when he was diagnosed with a rare blood disease. He had mistakenly landed in this miserable hospital, but would soon be transferred to the best one in town. His girlfriend prepared all his tasty meals and dropped them off each morning on her way to work. Victor told him he must be very grateful about his good luck.

"I'm entitled to it," Grisha said.

Victor ignored his brazen remark. "But why are only a few given such privileges?" he asked.

"Because the State is interested in supporting its leading and most useful officers."

"Doesn't the State support all people equally? And isn't everyone entitled to decent care?" Victor demanded to know.

"We can't support all those useless bums...especially in times of war," Grisha went on in his broken Russian. He was devouring large forkfuls of lamb. "And with its limited means, the State first needs to help its most deserving citizens. Now you see why I'll be sent to the finest hospital where only the best doctors will take care of me."

"But don't you believe that every citizen working for the State is useful?" Victor asked with an innocent air. It was more a statement than a question and he expected no answer.

The response came a couple of days later. "Do you know how well the State has been taking care of you?" Grisha asked, obviously looking down on him as one who belonged to the absolutely useless. "They've treated you for your fever. You have received the care of doctors. They gave you medicine. Don't you know that on entering a hospital, all citizens of Tashkent must bring their ration marks for bread? Only refugees like you receive a daily amount without those marks. And what do you do in return for all your privileges? Complain! Nothing but complain…"

"I haven't complained at all," Victor said firmly, remembering what the State had done for him in the past. Realizing that he was confronted with his first narcissistic Soviet citizen, he felt sure it would hardly take any time for Grisha to turn into an absolute tyrant.

On awakening a few days later, he was told to leave the hospital before noon.

10.

TATYANA

Hiding above ground

Venice, August 1943

Stefan left me with his friends in Trieste before continuing his journey to England. He would do everything in his power to give me his news, but I was concerned about his safety. How was he to reach me without a forwarding address? All I needed to do was send my new address in Venice to the friends in Trieste, he told me, and they would forward it to him. He bought me a railway ticket to Venice and slipped some money into my coat pocket, which I discovered during that lonely trip.

His friends in Trieste gave me a recommendation to a family in Venice, but it was of no help. They sent me to some other unknown people who had no use for me either, but were kind enough to put me up for the night. To my relief, their maid, who arrived in the morning, knew of a lady in need of a nanny. So I turned myself into a quiet German-Italian maiden, ready to take care of a little boy and a colicky baby. Had my employers known that their nanny was a Jewish partisan who had just crossed mountains and rivers with a rifle on her back, they might have thought better of giving me this employment.

But here I am, living in a *palazzo* on the Grand Canal. From the window of my room, I can see San Giorgio Maggiore. The *vaporetto* stops right below, at regular hours. Instead of enjoying this magical city, I feel utterly alone and bewildered. I can't stop mourning about my Dad and am worrying about Mama, Leila, and Stefan. As to Victor, I can only pray for a miracle.

During my months with the partisans, I tried to write in the evening, away from prying eyes. Thanks to the horrifying experience with Bogdan, I didn't feel safe with any strangers in our group. The notes about my escape with Stefan were written here, at night, after I got settled in the privacy of my room.

There is no park or public garden in our neighborhood. I'm following Signora Bardelli's instructions and taking the children to Campo Santo Stefano. From the table of an open-air café, I can watch 6-year-old Franco run around on his tricycle as I sit with the baby in its carriage or on my lap. Franco is a good-looking schemer with Titian curls and a mischievous smile. I am teaching him German, cleanliness, and to be less cruel to cats. He picks up a stray animal, holds it upside down by its hind legs, and drops it into the canal. I am trying to stop him by yelling at him in Italian. Though supposed to teach him German, I'm afraid of arousing attention in public and only speak German to him at home. I bathe him in a huge Roman tub, supervise his piano playing, and read to him at bedtime. In spite of his cruelty to cats, I have quickly grown to love him.

The baby took to me from the first moment. She screams when her mother tries to pick her up. My pretty *Signora* uses her as a toy. At a loss of what to do, she covers her infant with small Italian kisses. Peck, peck, peck. The baby turns blue from screaming, stretching out her arms for me. Sometimes her mother is torn between jealousy and the need for my help. Yet she is always kind to me, and any resentment is soon forgotten. She gave me elegant clothes she can't have worn more than once or twice.

Thinking of the misery, hunger, and worry I feel rising like a sea all over Europe, I restrict myself to wearing only one of her simpler dresses. So much for my peaceful life in Venice. I miss my camera. It would give me some comfort to take pictures of the many stunning sights. Yet its loss may save me from doing anything foolhardy...

I'm more than relieved to know that Mussolini is tucked away in a fortress and that Italy can breathe more freely under Marshal Badoglio. In spite of my grief and the uncertainty about what is happening at home, I must keep strong for any eventuality. If only I could hear from Mama and

Leila. There is no answer to my letters. Perhaps they never arrived, or were made illegible by Nazi censors. I'm fearing the worst.

September 1943

The Nazis have rescued Mussolini. Two weeks before the Allies landed in Calabria, the Germans set up a Republican Fascist government in Salò. After rescuing the Duce, they disarmed the Italian military. Sicily has been invaded by the Allies, and masses of fighters are dying on both sides. The rest of Italy is now under German command. The confusion has turned into chaos, fear is stronger than ever, and the new resistance is becoming more organized. Each day, the Nazis get more cruel and intense. I told the *Signora* that I don't want to teach German to Franco any longer and she agreed immediately.

Still no news from Stefan. I sent my address to his friends in Trieste, but there has been no response. I wrote notes to a cousin in Zagreb, asking about Mother and Leila, but again, no answer. One night my *Signora* treated me to Verdi's *Aïda* in the Fenice Theater. I dreaded going out alone at night, but dared not refuse her generous invitation. I sat in a loge alone, except for a blond young man in the second seat to my right. Steeped in troubled thoughts, I was unable to enjoy the music I had so loved in the past.

During the first intermission, the stranger, most likely a member of a wealthy Venetian family, turned to me with a few polite words. A blue-eyed northern Italian with regular features, he could pass for a German or Englishman. Explaining that he had shared this loge with the Bardelli family for several years, he asked whether I was one of their friends or relatives. He smiled at me warmly when I told him I was their children's nanny.

"Francesco da Verona," he introduced himself.

"Tatyana Danieli."

During the second intermission he wanted to know if I wasn't afraid of being out alone at night. I would hop into the *vaporetto*, I said, which practically took me back to the house. But the Germans, he whispered, were everywhere now, and they might stop me, so close to the curfew, or even a bit later...

Alarmed, I accepted his offer to see me home. Was he trying to pick me up, or concerned about my safety? Did he sense I was Jewish and in Venice illegally?

As we waited for the *vaporetto,* he asked if I was going to attend more operas in the future. I had no idea. Then he wanted to know if and when he could see me again, how long I had been in Venice, and if I liked my work.

I weighed my answers carefully. No, I hadn't been in Venice for long. I liked my work, was given one day off per fortnight, enjoyed the children, but felt restricted in my freedom.

"Sorry, *Signorina* Tatyana, I don't mean to seem inquisitive. I just want to make sure not to lose you—right after I found you."

The *vaporetto* chugged along past darkened patrician *palazzi.* Did I ever take the children out? Feeling safe in his presence, I told him we usually went to the Campo San Stefano.

"May I join you there the day after tomorrow?"

I was about to say, "It's a free country," but immediately checked myself, careful to give him permission by smiling and nodding.

On Monday morning, Francesco was waiting for me in the middle of the *campo.* He looked shorter than I remembered. I wondered why I had allowed him to meet me. I longed desperately for Victor. Francesco turned out to be so correct, so polite and conventional. Everything about him was so very so. But I felt deprived of adult company. The *Signora* was always out on some errand, meeting friends for tea or a game of bridge. As to Francesco, my position as a nursemaid added to my reticence and proud behavior. What could a man of an old and wealthy Venetian background want from a girl like me? And what was he doing at home, instead of being in the army or with the partisans?

After admiring the sleeping baby and exchanging a few words with Franco, he told me he was in charge of his late father's real estate company. Fortunately, it was well organized and left him plenty of time for interests closer to his heart.

"Such as?"

"Let's rather talk about you, *Signorina.* I can sense there are more pressing matters in your life than whatever my needs may be."

"Such as?"

"Such as finding you a more appropriate position. Some more interesting work, I mean, that gives you more freedom."

"Freedom is a commodity that has disappeared from the countries of Europe," I said, hoping to find out where he stood in the chaos of European politics and war.

Our conversation was kept in rhythm with the ball he and Franco tossed back and forth. My last words broke the ice. He had suspected at once that we were on the same side, he said. Not even his family knew that he had been dismissed as a pilot after a feigned nervous breakdown. He lived with his mother and sister, two old-fashioned Catholic women. Never doubting that his occasional bouts of melancholy were authentic, they made every effort to please him. I trusted he wasn't making any of this up to gain my confidence, but remained on my guard. Was I fluent in German, he asked, holding onto the ball Franco kept ogling like an attentive dog. I nodded, somewhat disconcerted, since I didn't want to reveal too much about my real background. Not to worry, he said, there were no politics involved. A friend of his was looking for an office worker, able to translate scientific articles from German into Italian.

"If you come back here with the children tomorrow, I'll let you know more." He turned to Franco. "I must go now." He tossed the ball in the boy's direction, kissed my hand, and kissed the baby's clenched fist. Hurrying along the path with the steps of a clumsy dancer, he kept waving back at us. His odd walk endeared him to me and made him more real. Yet I wondered why he was trying to change my life. No doubt he meant well, but was he doing this for selfish reasons, or out of a genuine desire to help me?

Stefan would have found it wiser if I stayed with the Bardellis. How I longed for a friend who could stand in for Stefan...

And Victor, dear Victor...he, too, would have warned me not to ask for trouble.

Francesco met me at the appointed hour. His friend expected to see me on my day off, first thing in the morning. Noticing my hesitation, he asked what was wrong. I did not mention my qualms, but said that I had no working permit. He promised to bring me one to sign on Wednesday morning, explaining he had a friend who was connected with the underground.

A few days later, armed with my permit, I went to a building behind Piazza San Marco. Though excited by the prospect of work that would restore my independence, I still seesawed between doubt and optimism. Ill at ease about leaving the Bardellis and the security of my lowly position, I realized how much I would miss the children. The work I was offered promised to be more interesting, but my freedom of movement might be fraught with new dangers.

I met my three fellow workers: Mario, the oldest; young Berto, who had been wounded in Africa; and Clara, a mousy woman of indefinable age. In the end, my love for freedom and adventure won out over my hesitation. I promised to start as soon as my *Signora* could find an adequate replacement.

Signora Bardelli reacted with dismay and anger when I told her of my plans. How sly of me, she reproached, to look for another job on my day off! One couldn't trust anybody these days. The children had grown more than fond of me. Didn't I have any feelings for them? I assured her that I would pay them regular visits and wait until she found the right new nanny, but she kept ranting and crying. My own mother never made me feel so guilty. Three days later, an agency sent her a young woman from Udine who corresponded to her qualifications. *Signora* Bardelli told me how well she understood my need to improve my situation and dismissed me with blessings, a kiss, and an embroidered blouse.

I found a furnished room in the vicinity of the old Jewish ghetto on the island of Giudecca. Apart from a chatty landlady and innumerable cats screaming for love and food, the place was unusually quiet. I sympathized with those hungry cats. They, too, were victimized by the war.

The former ghetto was a reminder of grim reality. I had breakfast in a small *latteria,* bought whatever bread, fruit, and cheese was still available on the farmer's market, and ate it on the Rialto Bridge during my lunch hour. After work, I would take a book to read and eat dinner in a *trattoria,* always on edge about some enemy raid.

Thanks to the help of my colleagues, I learned my tasks in less than a week. They consisted of office duties and translations of German articles into Italian. Mario and Berto turned out to be good comrades, but Clara was always morose. "She's one of Cinderella's nasty sisters," Mario whispered behind her back. Her brusque manner contrasted with the open and friendly behavior of most Italians I had met. It reminded me of our Yugoslavian moodiness. Since I, too, tend to get grouchy, I told our colleagues that I had heard about Clara's sick old mother, who had no one else in the world, and was entirely dependent on her daughter.

Perhaps she was jealous of me. In spite of my attempts, she never responded to my friendly gestures. I finally gave up. She didn't change her clothes and hardly ever seemed to wash her long, lackluster hair. Our office was permeated with the acrid smell of her perspiration.

Francesco's devotion lapped at me with the constancy of those agitated waters against ancient *palazzi*. He tried to see me almost every day. I allowed him no more than small tokens to prove his affection on a weekend, such as a war-weakened *caffé-latte* amid the pigeons in an open-air café on Piazza San Marco, or an ersatz ice cream cone during an early evening stroll. Opera tickets were out. When he invited me to *Tosca*, I told him I would be too embarrassed to share the loge with the Bardellis. In mid-January, I agreed to accompany him to a concert where we ran into my former employers. I was wearing a coat the *Signora* had passed on to me.

The next time I went to visit the children their mother questioned me about Francesco. I told her how we had met and that we had become good friends. She didn't believe in our friendship. She had known Francesco as long as she could remember. There was no finer person. His mother and sister were devout Catholics. She wanted to know about my own religious beliefs. I admitted that I never went to church. "A pity," she said. "However, if you play your cards right, Tatyana, you won't spoil your chances."

I did not intend to play any cards, right or wrong. While Francesco's courtship was growing more intense, my incapacity to requite his feelings began to oppress me. I would find excuses not to see him.

It was a grim winter. There was no heat in my room. The scarcity of food increased the chill in my bones. Yet nothing compared with the constant fear of some unknown terror. The enemy was ready to strike around any corner. If stopped in a raid, my false papers might no longer be of help with the entire Italian nation subjected to the harshest German surveillance.

Since I had no access to a radio, Francesco was my only connection with the outside world, but I realized that he didn't want to alarm me with bad news. When I asked if the partisan who had helped me get a false working permit might now provide me with a more convincing one, to my shock, he replied that the man had been arrested. Unfortunately, Francesco had no other close connection with the resistance.

One afternoon in mid-March, in the Café Rialto under the arcades on Piazza San Marco, the two of us watched the abduction of a man feeding pigeons in the rain. Even the birds fluttered away in fright. I must have grown pale because Francesco took my hand and pressed it.

"I'm not what I seem to be," I whispered after a long pause, my eyes on the now deserted square.

"I know. Why did it take you so long to trust me?"

"It wasn't that. Why involve you? That's the first rule for any partisan. The less you know, the better—in case of torture."

"You were a partisan?"

"For a short time. Until I fled from Yugoslavia to Italy."

"*Ma sei ebrea?*"

I nodded. "Yes, I'm Jewish."

"Oh, Tatyana! You might have been better off staying with the Bardellis. I helped you find that job because…well, I wanted to see you more often. That was unforgivably selfish."

"Don't say that. I could have said no. Thanks to you, I feel much more independent."

He took my hand again: "I have the ideal solution. Will you marry me?"

Before I could answer, he added that he would be the happiest man, if, once married, no one would search for my true identity and all my troubles would be over.

Or begin, I thought. I told him that I couldn't marry him just to save my life. To save my life mattered more than anything, he said. One day, I might even grow to love him. All at once, Victor's image hovered between us. When Francesco begged me to think it over, I could only shake my head and thank him for all his kindness.

The following Saturday he invited me to take the *vaporetto* to the Lido where he meant to introduce me to his best friends, Dora and Giuseppe Battista. He had spoken about me to them on several occasions and now had mentioned the danger I was facing. They responded by offering me a refuge in their home. We took an immediate liking to each other. When I expressed my hesitation, they would not hear of it and assured me that they had plenty of room. Dora asked me to move in at once. The Nazis were arresting people all over the city. It might be a good idea, however, to keep my place on Giudecca. By leaving a few belongings in my room, the landlady would assume I was coming back.

Immensely grateful, I accepted this courageous and generous offer, then let Francesco take me back to my room on Giudecca. To my relief, the landlady wasn't home. I packed a small

suitcase and left her a note, explaining that I was going to Milano for a few days.

Although the servants could be trusted, Dora was careful to introduce me as her favorite niece from Rome. I had come to join them on the Lido, she told them, to complete my studies.

The next morning I went to the office, since I needed to use a typewriter and dictionaries for the completion of my translation of a German article about recent discoveries. It would take me only a few more days. Though Dora urged me to give up my job, I reassured her that I felt safe among my colleagues. They knew nothing of my plight. It was much more convincing to finish my assignment. I would tell my colleagues that I was going to look for a job that would give me a chance to pursue my special interest in photography.

Just then I was reading Thomas Mann's *Death in Venice*. The passage about the plague that spread from Asia to Venice reminded me of the Nazi scourge infecting the world. Had Aschenbach listened to the advice of the English clerk and left before it was too late, his life might have been spared. He was too engrossed in his passionate pursuits to worry about his own survival. Or was he in love with death, as were so many of his compatriots? Young and careless, I, too, had not yet found my own best way to travel. But where could I find that way, since all maps were encircled by barbed wire and the future lay beyond the wall of war?

At the beginning of June, Francesco came to the Lido to tell me he had to leave on a business trip to Milano and would be back in about a week. Two days later, while Clara and Berto had left the office on an errand, I was sitting on the wide windowsill enjoying the warmth of the sun, when Mario stopped beside me and asked if I was Jewish. I stared in shock at his worried face, his yellow tie with the spot in the center, and his trembling hands. He told me that yesterday afternoon Clara and Berto had just gone home, when two Gestapo agents in civilian clothes appeared to ask a number of questions about me. He told them I was a fine worker and, as far as he knew, my papers were in perfect order.

I had never felt so frightened in my life. Someone must have denounced me. "We are surrounded by scum, ready to destroy anyone for a handful of *lire*," Mario said, urging me to leave immediately.

Instead of following his and Dora's sensible warning, I was just as heedless as Aschenbach. I told Mario my translation was almost completed. I would leave the office for good after dropping it off the day after tomorrow. When I begged him to meet me a few minutes before Berto's and Clara's arrival, and to set a broom beside the entrance to indicate he was alone, he reluctantly yielded to my request.

Two mornings later, I found the broom beside the entry, handed my work to Mario, and immediately turned round to leave, when two harmless-looking men in gray collided with me at the door.

11.

TATYANA

The black hole

Zagreb, 1945

O nce you fall into the black hole, it's just that: a black hole. The gates of hell closed behind me, and I found myself in the great beyond. What will surviving mothers tell their children? Silence about the past causes nothing but anguish, while words fill the mind with a horror too deep to grasp. There are no answers. The air is filled with questions hovering in limbo while the truth remains concealed in a fog of incomprehension.

In the abyss, all time translates into eternity. Before my sojourn in hell, things happened to me; but since my arrest, any former life no longer exists. I must have made it up in a dream, or someone told me a story about the person I was. Three months ago, I was brought back to Zagreb more dead than alive.

I'm no longer sure I want to resume the habit of recording my thoughts, although the mere act of writing may give me some inner peace. But how can I bear to describe the horrors of the camp? Some of them stand out vividly, others are vague or forgotten. If I sweep them under the rug, I may be haunted by nightmares as long as I live. Right now, my hand is trembling. It takes me hours to write a page. I'm still too weak to hold up a pen. In an attempt to start a new existence, or resume what we call a "normal" life, I'll try to record only a few personal events, leaving the rest to some black notebook. All I know is that we need to rise above the forces of evil which have already destroyed much of the world as we knew it.

Two weeks later.

To recapitulate: back in Venice the two nondescript agents in civilian clothes took me to an empty warehouse used as a temporary prison for women. There were about fifty or sixty women, more than half of them wearing yellow stars. I sat down on the cement floor among partisans, doctors, professors, teachers, and working girls—women of all ages. Though they were probably terrified, they hardly behaved like victims. Forgetting their own troubles, two doctors, three partisans, and a matronly professor quietly encouraged the rest of us. They assured us in whispers that the Allies had almost reached Paris and were fighting all over. The war couldn't last much longer. No matter where the Nazis were going to send us, we mustn't lose hope, for we would soon be back.

In spite of fear and uncertainty, most of us seemed to be encouraged. Yet my optimism was soon deflated by the worry of getting grilled by some SS man. I couldn't think of anyone who might have denounced me. My landlady was more than trustworthy, and I felt relieved for having held onto my place on Giudecca. She could prove in good faith that I was renting one of her rooms, should the Gestapo check out my identity and search for clues to any political association.

The official who finally called me from an adjacent room looked more like a stocky clerk than a harsh cross-examiner. "Are you Jewish?" was his first question, after assigning me a seat across from his desk. I firmly shook my head no. He held up my Italian identity card and told me that he had seen such phony documents before. Suddenly turning red with anger, he shouted that Italians spelled my name with an I instead of a Y. I gave him some plausible explanation, but he didn't listen.

"So you translated scientific articles in that office," he went on, "but I know you are a liar and a fake—because you filthy Jews are all disloyal and ready to betray your fatherland for your greedy schemes!"

He went to a corner cabinet, opened a drawer, and pulled out a few scraps of cloth, along with a black spool of yarn with a sewing needle. He threw them into my lap. His crazy words and hate-filled gestures were followed by a final command: "Get out and sew these on your clothes at once or you will be shot!"

Seeing that he meant to hit me, I rushed out as fast as I could. There was nothing I could do but sew the first of those ugly yellow stars on the summer dress I was wearing. It made me feel naked and exposed. Instead of the Star of David, it gaped at me as a symbol of death.

After a sleepless night on the cement floor, most of us were taken to a German gathering camp in the town of Carpi, in Romagna. We were to buy some food to hold us over for a journey of ten to fourteen days. Waiting my turn in line, I stood beside a young girl who was sobbing disconsolately. Fellow travelers, about to buy their provisions from the camp's kitchen, were too anxious to take notice of her. I found a handkerchief in the pocket of my cardigan and handed it to her. For a moment, she stopped weeping to thank me with a nod. I offered to buy her the same meager supplies made available to us. She thanked me again and quickly pulled some money from her purse.

"You are very kind," she managed to say in a poorly accented Italian. When I came back with her food and the change. I noticed her delicate features, framed by blond curls. She was deadly pale and her eyes were red from crying. She must have been about nineteen or twenty and reminded me of Leila.

"I don't understand German. Only a few of them speak Italian," she said unexpectedly.

"My mother is German," I explained, "so I can help you, but I'm Yugoslavian—from Zagreb."

"Me, too, from Belgrade." She seemed relieved by this revelation. "Svetlana", she introduced herself.

"Tatyana." I shook her ice-cold hand. "I could tell by your accent. But I didn't see you in Venice."

"Because I was sent here from Bologna," she explained in Serbo-Croatian. She had come to Bologna as an art student to learn the skill of art restoration.

We stepped outside for a breath of air. "But you mustn't take it so hard," I tried to comfort her. "I was told that we'll soon be back. The Allies are close to Paris and Italy will soon be free."

"That's not why." Her eyes filled again, and she had to take a deep breath before going on in a whisper: "They just killed my boyfriend, right in front of my eyes, then sent me here to be deported."

"Oh, my God!" I looked at her in shock.

"He was only twenty-two. They didn't even know he was an Italian partisan. But he lost his temper and kept yelling and cursing them when they came to arrest me."

She was trembling all over. I pressed her hand, feeling tears well up inside me. Reading between the lines of a letter from a friend in Belgrade, she had figured out that her widowed mother had been killed in a Yugoslavian concentration camp. I stared at her sweet young face, secretly vowing to help her in every way I could, while wondering in anguish about Mama and Leila.

From Carpi, a train would take us to Auschwitz within the next few days. Some of us had heard that name, but no one knew where it was or what to expect, some labor camp, possibly in Poland. I told Svetlana we ought to stay close, but since we couldn't trust the enemy, it was best to pretend we didn't have anything to do with each other.

Just before German soldiers pushed us into the train, I saw Francesco waving at me from a distance. He must have been notified of my arrest on his return from Milan. Someone might have told him about that gathering camp in Carpi. I suppose he had driven here, hoping to find me in time to beg or bribe some guard to help me escape. I hardly managed to wave back. He was probably still blaming himself for having enticed me to give up my safe position as a nanny. His grief only made matters worse.

At this moment, sustained by the courage of my fellow prisoners in Venice, I was still hopeful. But as soon as we were pushed and crowded like cattle—about fifty men, women, and children, old or young, healthy or sick—into each filthy boxcar reeking of urine and sweat, all prisoners seemed to fall into a collective shock, moaning, crying, or silent. Everything turned into the darkest night when the doors were locked from outside. A loudspeaker announced again and again that the train would leave hours later. We waited forever in deadly fear until the train began to move with a sudden jolt. I almost fell down. Someone groped for my hand and pulled me to the floor.

"It's me, Svetlana…"

She had found a small place and sat leaning against a wall. I didn't let go of her hand.

It was the eleventh day of June 1944. I shall never forget that date. Silently screaming for help, I took my final leave of Victor.

12.

A SCREAM IN THE NIGHT

When he left the hospital, Victor was clean-shaven. He wore new pants and a blue cotton sweater, courtesy of the State. Except for his old coat, he felt as good as new. The rope was still in the coat's left pocket and his recorder in the right. After a long confinement, the fresh air, cleanliness, a piece of bread and sunlight were like a promise for a better future. Hanging onto an over-crowded streetcar, he rode back to the railway station, ready to survive with renewed confidence as a baggage-*schlepper*.

As he entered the station, however, he had to sit down on a bench to rest. Too poor to buy his next meal, he knew that his strength could only be restored with some nourishing food.

A big woman alighted from a train, pulling down a heavy suitcase and what looked like a huge sack of rice. Before anyone noticed, Victor rushed to her side. He took out the rope, tied both pieces together, and tried to lift them onto his shoulder. Native porters pointed at him, doubling over with laughter. Everything was déjà vu: the mocking, his despair, the woman using her strong arms to lighten the weight of the sack on his shoulder, the constant bumping into people rushing out of the station. He could barely move. His neck stretched forward and his back bent painfully under the burden as they waited for the streetcar. When it finally arrived, there was no place to sit down. Trying not to keel over, he felt the sweat of weakness and effort as the woman kept talking to him in a language he did not understand. On reaching her building, she made him follow her into a ground-floor apartment where she gave him some rubles, a chunk of bread, and two apples. Thanking her with a gesture,

Victor went out and sat down, leaning his aching shoulder against the wall of the small building. He ate his bread, hoping to exchange the apples for something more substantial at the nearest bazaar. Half asleep, he rested with up-drawn knees among evening shadows. A woman came out of the house next door to hand him a bowl of hot bean soup. He opened his eyes and stared at the apparition, unable to thank her. He wept, slurping some of the tear-sprinkled soup.

Beware of self-pity, he admonished himself.

The good woman returned to pick up the plate. At last he managed to thank her. She wiped her eyes with the back of her hand, pressed his shoulder, and left. Then a man walked by in the dark, noticed the stranger, and chased him away with insults and curses. "Dirty thieves and vagrants!" Victor heard him shout. He pulled himself up with an old man's effort and began to walk back toward the station.

He had forgotten the apples. It meant losing his chance of selling them, and being able to afford sleeping in a teahouse. And the rubles—where had he dropped them? The tram wasn't crowded enough to allow him to hide inside without paying. Hanging onto an outside rod and hoping to remain unnoticed for a few stops, he waited as long as possible before jumping off and hobbling back to the station. Finding it over-crowded with soldiers and civilians, he left through a back door in search of a spot to bed down for the night, but found himself in a jungle of railroad tracks. If only he could volunteer as a soldier and go to the front.... Perhaps it was best to make an end to it all. Stepping over a rail, he moved toward the open countryside, expecting some train to grant him his wish at any moment.

How long must he wait? Should he close his eyes? Would the train kill him on the spot or tear him to shreds?

What had happened to his positive outlook and those encouraging words he had said to Rachel? Hadn't he asked her never to give up?

I shall hope for you, she had promised. And now he was too faint-hearted to live up to that hope.

What about the flaming torch of courage he and Tatyana had promised each other to carry as a pact against the hardships awaiting them in the future?

It was June 11, 1944. Almost five and a half years had passed since their unforgettable encounter in Stuttgart. What made him hope to ever see her again? His all-consuming nostalgia was all he had left to save his life for an impossible dream.

He thought of *Anna Karenina*. Was he too much of a coward to follow in her footsteps? Now the whistle of an incoming train made him jump out of the way. Puffing out smoke, the black monster of the locomotive appeared out of nowhere. There was a second whistle, mingling with a human scream. He could hear Tatyana's voice, desperately calling him for help. What was happening, and where was she?

Releasing its final breath of steam, the locomotive came to a shivering halt beside him. Though he tried to convince himself that the cry for help could be no more than another whistle, he was sure he had heard Tatyana's voice.

Thoroughly shaken, he moved back in the direction of the station, stumbling into a crowded garden in front of a building he hadn't noticed before. Families were stretched out on the ground as he sank down in the dark. He noticed a young couple trying to make room for him. The woman was in an advanced stage of pregnancy. She kept moaning as her husband folded his jacket under her head and covered her with a blanket. His attempts at making her more comfortable seemed to have the opposite effect. The woman writhed and whimpered to herself. Was she going into labor?

Filled with compassion, Victor tried to concentrate on the plight of others, when he heard a strident voice:

"You there, come here!"

The stern call was addressed to him by a soldier armed with rifle and bayonet. Victor knew at once that he was caught in a police raid. The N.K.V.D were looking for suspects, spies, deserters, and refugees without documents. A moment later, two soldiers marched him out of the garden into the street, where he was given a boisterous welcome by a group of men who had just been arrested. They addressed him with rough jokes he was unable to understand. The soldiers snapped at the men to shut up and ordered everyone to sit on the ground. The command was obeyed in sullen silence.

Hours passed. Although the days were getting warmer, the nights remained bitterly cold. Victor concentrated all his willpower on averting the chattering of his teeth and the trembling of his body. By the time he was ordered to follow one of the soldiers into a smoke-filled office, most of the captives had vanished, and he was facing a commissar with a pasty complexion. His beady eyes were mean and colorless. He stretched out a purple hand.

"Your papers!"

Victor tried to explain the theft of his wallet but was immediately interrupted.

"Where are you from?"

"Poland."

The interrogation was continued in Polish. Seeing Victor's blank look, the man shouted furiously: "You are an impostor!"

"I was already a refugee in Poland. An antifascist," Victor tried to explain in his poor Polish.

"A German spy, that's what you are. You ought to be shot."

Pulling something shiny from his pocket, the commissar took aim. Victor closed his eyes. *Now,* he thought, *now...*

He heard steps in the room, another angry voice, the scraping of a chair across the floorboards. Opening his eyes, he saw the commissar lighting a cigarette with the shiny object. Another agent drew up a chair beside him. Now the two of them began to cross-examine an adolescent boy in a fur coat. In the process, the second agent pulled bundles of money from one of the youngster's pockets. Finding pictures of the Russian and German fronts in the other, he studied them carefully. As he noticed Victor glancing at those pictures, he slapped his face. "Get out of here!" he shouted.

Once more, Victor was lost in the night.

Someone whispered in Russian, "Hey, you there, got some tobacco?" He discerned a young fellow in rags. Victor found some makhorka in his pocket and handed it over. "Do you know of a place to sleep?" he asked. Without answering, the youth drew him into a niche beyond the railway station and made him crawl through a hole into an empty stable. Victor sank to the ground and immediately passed out in sleep. A man with a shining miniature gun rose in a dream and threatened to kill him.

Don't shoot!" Victor moaned. Shots went right through him as he fell and turned into his father run down by a truck. With little Hannah in her arms, Sophie sank to the ground. A dead horse lay beside them on the moonlit plain. He was Bubachoff, killed by a falling tree, then Walter, shot in flight. He had turned into all the homeless, nameless, downtrodden creatures on this earth.

13.

TATYANA

Trial by fire

My connection with Svetlana had barely begun when I feared to have lost her. We had stayed close during the nightmare of that never-ending journey, finding some comfort in each other's company, but on arrival in a place called Birkenau, I was in a semi-conscious state and could hardly straighten my legs, get out of the train, or follow her through the throng of fellow travelers. As we were pushed into buses taking us to Auschwitz, she was nowhere to be seen. I feared the worst when I heard someone mention that a number of people had vanished in Birkenau.

On arrival in Auschwitz, men and women were called to gather in separate lines. Husbands and wives were immediately separated without being allowed to say goodbye; so were the old from the young and mothers from their children. The women were to wait in line again before being marched to the "sauna," a shower room, where we had to wash ourselves with no soap and get dry without towels. Rough female guards shaved our heads and privates, ending the ordeal by tattooing numbers on our left wrists. We were turned into animals, stripped of name and identity.

Next, we had to slip into striped prison garments. Shapeless, filthy, and full of tears, they reeked of sweat and disinfectants. More and more worried about Svetlana, I was too thirsty, exhausted, and depleted with humiliation to remember the dreadful details of that first day. We were told to tie our clothes into a bundle and leave them on the floor of the "sauna". They disappeared with our shoes, which were exchanged for worn-out clodhoppers that didn't fit.

After another long wait in line, we were given a spoon for our daily ration of watery pea soup and a chunk of stale bread. Thanks to our shorn heads and shapeless garments, we all looked alike. Even family members hardly recognized each other.

A young girl waiting in front of me turned her head in my direction. Staring in shock at her naked skull, I at last recognized Svetlana. I was deeply relieved, but reminded myself we had better act like strangers. Later, as we waited once more for the long nightly roll call, a guard stopped before us and ordered us to report for work together at five o'clock in the morning. This command was given with kicks and slaps. I was more astonished than hurt, unable to grasp how such hateful acts against innocent strangers had become gestures of habit for men turned into heartless automatons.

We were to sleep in a hut filled with rows of bunks, which rose in three tiers to the ceiling. Thanks to lack of space, each bunk had to be shared by two women. Svetlana and I were assigned one on the lowest tier. I could hardly believe that we were given a chance to share the insanity of this place. We would work and sleep side by side, pretending to dislike one another whenever we felt observed.

Those "beds" consisted of wooden boards covered with a thin sack of straw and two dirty blankets. In the great filth of the barracks, lice and fleas turned into a plague, along with the disgusting smell of unwashed straw sacks, which had been used by former inmates.

Trembling with cold at dawn the next morning, we were sent to a farm and ordered to carry heavy cuts of pork, beef, and other victuals, along with countless bottles of beer, to the homes of guards and SS officials. The sight of all that food increased our relentless hunger, but no housewife offered us as much as a piece of bread. Like beasts of burden, we walked hour after hour, dragging ourselves and the weight of those never-ending supplies. Too exhausted to sleep, we were terrified of what might happen from one day to the next. We were quick to learn that strong young people were cynically exploited until they collapsed. We could easily be replaced by other strong young people.

I would neither wish nor be able to describe the hunger, fear, and gruesome degradations we had to endure. Yet this was nothing compared with our showdown with death. When Svetlana told me her story, I had meant to lighten her grief by taking her under my wing. I had tried to comfort and cheer her up as much as I could. Under normal circumstances, our friendship would have grown by our mutual interest in art and photography, but no words could help us in our terror and exhaustion. A silent understanding of one another brought us closer from day to day.

At that cold summer's end, Svetlana grew more and more disheartened. I knew she was looking at the electrically charged barbed wire fence surrounding the camp. Before the Nazis decided to kill us, she said, she would rather make an end to this ordeal.

To avoid any possibility of escape, the prisoners were threatened with death if they didn't keep a distance of at least two feet from that fence. I told her that her boyfriend had tried to save her and wanted her to live. Her mother would have wished the same. We were young and a new life might still be waiting for us. While I tried to persuade her, I realized that my desire to save her was giving me a reason not to succumb to the enemy and to maintain my own courage.

It grew bitterly cold in November. To our relief, we were ordered inside. Our work was passed on to some male prisoners. We were given the task of carrying sacks filled with clothing to be cleaned and sorted out. To our dismay, we soon discovered that these were the pants and dresses of little boys and girls, and their underwear, shoes, coats, and toys. I could visualize a huge number of children who had used them with pride and pleasure. Feeling nausea rising to my throat, I saw tears running down Svetlana's face.

"Keep moving!" shouted one of the guards.

Trembling and weak-kneed, we carried sack after heavy sack to some shanty filled with mountains of children's clothing. Other inmates were sorting out and cleaning each small garment. I picked up a little girl's bonnet with a pink ribbon, trying to imagine it tied around a small, pretty face, then stared at a teddy bear who looked back at me with the saddest of eyes.

I remembered having seen only a few children when I arrived. They had soon vanished, with or without their mothers. Svetlana and I remained speechless for the rest of that day. I tossed on our hard wooden bunk that night while keeping an anxious watch over my friend. As I had feared and suspected, she rose from her side in the dark. I got up and followed her out the door. My misgivings were confirmed when I saw her move in the direction of the electric fence.

Calling her name in a whisper, I implored her to turn around. But as soon as she heard my voice, she began to run. I followed her, faster and faster. She had almost reached the fence when she lost her balance and fell, face down, to the frozen ground. Noticing that her arm was close enough to touch the barbed wire, I threw myself on top of her. She tried to shake me off, but I covered her with all my strength, grabbed her arm, and pulled it back. Breathing heavily, we struggled with each other, she trying to get hold of the fence, and I holding down her arm and trying to pull her away.

"If you touch it," I whispered, "you'll kill me too."

She stopped at once. "Oh, Tatyana, why don't you let me go?"

Shining in the light of the moon, her shaved head made me recall her golden curls. As I inhaled the acrid smell of her perspiration, I thought that our bodies, now almost skeletal in these prison garments, would be unrecognizable to anyone who had known us.

"I don't want you to leave me," I whispered, noticing that I, too, was bathed in my own sour sweat. I slowly got up and pulled her to her feet. "Let's hurry back, before the searchlights turn on us."

"I can't bear to go on."

"Yes, you can."

"No, I..."

"You will, Svetlana."

Supporting her in her reluctant steps, I spoke of the good things we might still enjoy if we survived. I spelled them out to her, quoting them like a schoolgirl, and not believing a word I said. This hurried, whispered conversation was one of the deepest horrors I have experienced. I couldn't get those children out of my heart. Their garments threatened to suffocate me in recurring nightmares.

As I would later find out, those clothes were distributed among children of Nazi families who knew, but pretended not to know, their origins.

***

Growing weaker each day, I began to despair along with most of the others in our hut. Though surrender was an act of cowardice and played into the hands of the enemy, I gave in to my helplessness.

Each night I lay beside Svetlana, exhausted, starving, and equally desperate. How could I find the strength to go on? The only way to preserve my integrity was to sustain others. It used to help me rise above my own weakness and hold on to my inner freedom. I knew that my desire to die meant choosing defeat. But how could I summon the strength of spirit to rise above my helplessness?

Just then, waking one night from an eerie dream, I heard a voice whispering in my ear: "Tatyana, my darling, take heart..."

I sat up, holding my breath. How could Victor have found me here in this hole? I must be hallucinating. Before I could respond, he was gone. I couldn't tell whether he was dead or alive. It hardly mattered, since our bond was enduring, beyond life and death.

His words filled me with fresh confidence. I found myself turning to the God in whom I no longer believed, imploring him to bring Victor back to me, while promising that I would never succumb to the enemy.

To my surprise, my prayer was answered. Victor came back once more, holding me close in that narrow bunk, whispering encouraging words into my ear. His touch reopened new hope and helped me embrace a world filled with a love that would heal us from all the terrible hate we must endure.

The next morning, still imbued with the warmth of his presence, I was able, at last, to forget my surroundings. They came back soon enough, but Victor had appeared to me in my weakness to comfort and save me from the underworld. As in a Chagall painting, I pictured us flying hand in hand over cities and oceans toward an island of peace and freedom. Although he was gone, he had helped me brace myself against final despair.

After the liberation, it took me some time to understand my delusion. No doubt I must have been mad, but I know that my longing for Victor's love has kept me from drowning. Madness or not, he restored me to life.

14.

THE THIEF'S APPRENTICE

Victor awoke from his nightmare at the first light of dawn. Someone shook him by the shoulder. He recognized the Mongolian face and stocky body of his rescuer of the previous night.

"I'm Misha," the young man said, squatting beside a goat, which had appeared out of nowhere. As Victor tried to explain his situation, Misha interrupted and volunteered that he was about to return to Alma Ata, his hometown.

"Would you like to come along?"

"Why not?" Victor said.

"Good. Meet you tonight at eight in front of the station." He was gone without waiting for an answer.

Victor reentered the station and looked at a map. Alma Ata was close to China. It might be another avenue of escape. But what would lie in store for him in China?

He was sick of his aimless wanderings around Tashkent. The sun was shining; the day had barely begun. He took a short walk, then sat down to rest on the steps of some bungalow when he heard a woman calling him from a window. She stepped out and asked in Russian whether he would help her move some rubbish out of her courtyard. Within an hour, the work was done. The woman gave him a thick bean soup with some smoked meat. She added a few rubles and a chunk of bread. In the afternoon, he repaired a few chairs for an old man. It earned him another plate of warm food and a few more rubles.

He walked back to the station at sunset. Would Misha keep his word? It was not quite seven thirty, but there he was, waiting for Victor.

They walked to the train yard and climbed into a freight train expected to leave for the east. Their crate-filled wagon was hardly a comfortable place for a long night's journey, but the pleasure of traveling with a companion made up for any discomfort. Victor shared his bread and meat with Misha, who told him how to behave in case of an arrest. "In a small town, always say that you just got there from the nearest city. You're looking for your evacuated family. Get it?"

Victor nodded.

"Remember, we don't know each other. No one likes to keep prisoners in a small place. The prisons are the shits, and so is the food. Most of the guards are Russians, sent to those boring towns for God knows what punishment. They're always angry, and who's there to get kicked? The prisoners, of course. Get it?"

Victor got it.

"That's not all. The policemen are native Uzbeks who have to swallow a lot from those assholes. So who's there to get kicked?" Misha squinted at Victor with his Mongolian eyes, then yawned like a contented cat. "Remember not to get stuck in a small place."

"Misha, since you are such an expert, do you know if it's possible to get into China from Alma Ata?"

"Possible, yes, but don't ask me how…it's not as close as you think. It's easier to get across the Afghan border from Termez."

The two of them took turns sleeping and keeping watch. Before dawn, they jumped off the train. It was hard to remain inconspicuous in a small station, but Misha managed to sneak across the rails unseen, dashing between the cars of freight trains with Victor at his heels.

The scenery reminded Victor of the countryside near Tashkent. They reached the bazaar of a small town and mingled with crowds who hardly distinguished themselves from the Uzbeks. Misha explained that they were *Tadshiks* from the Republic of the U.S.S.R. He pointed out how the women's hair was turned into skinny pigtails snaking down their backs.

Delighted to have found such an able guide and good companion, Victor enjoyed the sights without worrying about arrests or their next meal. Somehow Misha would know how to avoid the one and provide for the other. The unexpected windfall of such a companionship, the simple contact with a fellow human, turned out to be as precious and nourishing as bread. To share danger and food was a bliss he hoped to savor as long as possible.

But Misha was nervous. He had no desire to wait until evening for another freight train. He preferred to try the regular route. On reaching the station, they watched a passenger train overcrowded with soldiers and civilians. As it came to a stop, the small station teemed with people rushing out in search of water for their flasks, teapots, or empty jam jars. At the whistle of the locomotive, Victor and Misha mingled with the travelers who were getting back on the train. They were squeezed onto a platform among sweating and tired passengers.

Victor now understood Misha's fear of inspection. They dared not ask how soon the train was supposed to reach the next station. When it at last stopped, a number of people got out. Victor was about to move toward the exit with the throng, but Misha pulled him back. They waited until most of the passengers had alighted, then jumped off and sneaked across the tracks unseen.

"Didn't you notice the militia?" Misha hissed. "Idiot, idiot!" He entered the town way ahead of his mortified companion, then strolled toward the bazaar. Victor watched him approach shopping housewives and friendly women vendors from a short distance, begging them for food. He tried to follow Misha's example, stretching out his hand like a deaf-mute, afraid that his foreign accent might give him away. At last an elderly woman dropped a few coins into his open hand. It was hardly an initiation to turn him into a beggar, for begging and stealing was now a matter of honor or disgrace.

Angry at his clumsiness, Victor felt it was unfair to accept half of the begged-for or stolen goods from his resourceful companion. According to Misha, he could do nothing right. Perhaps he might help him more by distracting his targets with his recorder. He hadn't played in front of strangers since the night with Ivan, the tin can drummer.

It was growing dark. Victor blew his first notes, hoping for the attention of the vendors who were about to go home. This was the moment for Misha to grab whatever he could, while the farmers were turning their backs to fill baskets and crates. From a distance, Misha gave him an angry sign to stop. *I can never do right by him,* Victor thought helplessly.

He put his *sopranino* back into one pocket of his overcoat and stopped in front of a stall where the farmer had just turned his back, filling a crate with apples. The man was talking to a large woman when Victor scooped a handful of mulberries from another crate, dropped them into the other coat pocket, and backed away slowly. Pointing at him, the woman murmured something to the farmer. Victor started to run. The big fellow jumped across the table, caught up with him, and pulled him back by the collar of his coat. Yelling, cursing, and gesticulating, he dealt Victor a few painful blows, then kicked his behind with a muddy boot. Victor ducked out of his grip and ran. Satisfied to have given vent to his anger, the farmer stopped his pursuit and returned to his stall.

Victor hid around the corner of a house, waiting for Misha. The dropping of the mulberries into his pocket reminded him of a rainy winter afternoon back in Stuttgart. He had wandered about a department store in search of a present for his mother's birthday when he spotted a pair of leather gloves on an empty counter. Padded with fur, they were warm and soft to the touch. It was the perfect gift, for her hands were always cold in her threadbare mittens. Shocked at the price, he saw that the gift was way beyond a poor schoolboy's means. He had looked carefully around, making sure that no one was watching, then gently shook his wet umbrella until it opened just enough to push the gloves off the counter and let them drop in. His heart beating wildly, he continued to move about the store with the air of an interested customer.

His mother was overjoyed with his gift. Had she known about the theft, she would have made him return the gloves on the spot. Years later, however, he still remembered her delight without the slightest pang of guilt.

Walking back toward the train, Misha told Victor that he considered him a nitwit. "You could have gotten ten years of forced labor in Zing-Ata. For a handful of mulberries!" Misha slapped his head again and again. No words could give vent to his exasperation. But as soon as they were settled in an empty freight train, he offered Victor a share of his loot. He admitted that the incident with the mulberries had actually distracted the vendors long enough to fill his pocket unnoticed.

***

This finally convinced Victor to partake of the flat bread Misha pulled out from under his shirt, along with dates, figs and a ball of sheep cheese, which Misha explained was a specialty of the region.

For the next two nights, they traveled toward Alma Ata, interrupting their journey for Misha's daily foraging in towns or village bazaars. He made Victor promise not to help. His cooperation would only land them in jail. With Misha as sole provider, Victor felt like a kept woman.

Before they entered the station of Alma Ata, they jumped off the train. Misha needed to relieve himself and disappeared behind some bushes in an open field. Victor waited for a long time, but Misha vanished from his life as unexpectedly as he had entered it.

Still unable to grasp the finality of his defection, Victor crossed the open field and soon found himself in a suburb. There were apple orchards all over the area, which reminded him of Misha's explanation that *Alma-Ata* meant *Father of the Apple*. It was supposed to be one of the most beautiful cities in the U.S.S.R, a corner of paradise, which spelled hell to Victor. Had he been chosen by a cruel god, like Job? But figures like Job were legion in the Soviet Union, lost souls without the need of proving their faith to the Almighty. He went back to the field, bedded himself behind a bush, and immediately fell asleep.

The sun was high in the sky when he awoke. He went back to the suburb. Strolling through the streets, he looked for signs of activity behind the windows of bungalows. A woman was hanging wash in her yard. He stopped to ask if she could use his help. The woman shook her head. He must look a sight: unwashed, hair unkempt, his clothes in tatters. He had borrowed Misha's shaving knife and tried to rid his face of stubble, without soap.

"Can you spare some bread?" he asked casually. *That's much better*, he could hear Misha say. *A good thing I left you. It's time for you to learn and grow up.*

The woman disappeared in the house and returned with a chunk of old bread and two apples. He thanked her and went back to the field, where he tried to eat his bread as slowly as possible. He would hold onto the apples for another time. In the evening, he went back to the railway tracks, remembering that Misha had mentioned Termez, close to the Afghanistan border. He decided to take the first freight train in the direction of that city.

Back on the rails, he wondered why he never found any other homeless people riding in freight trains, but then recalled how Misha had alerted him to the severe punishment awaiting those who were caught.

Within a few days, stopping to beg for food in various towns and traveling by night, he arrived in Termez, determined to cross the Afghanistan border. Kabul was his goal. Once in Kabul, he would look for an American consulate. Although the letter from the consulate in Kuybyshev had been among the documents stolen from his pocket, he still hoped the Americans would be able to retrieve a copy.

15.

TATYANA

In purgatory

Zagreb, May 1945

Ironically, the illness threatening our lives at the end of the war has spared us. At the news of the German defeat, the remaining survivors of Auschwitz were taken out to be shot at random during their death march, while the sick, like Svetlana and myself, were left in the camp to die. I learned much later that, panic-stricken about the early arrival of the Soviet army, countless Nazi guards and officers exchanged their uniforms for civilian clothes and ran for their lives.

In December, Svetlana and I had been waiting for the Russians, hoping to be saved at last, yet worried by rumors about their brash behavior and utter indifference to what we had endured. They arrived in the camp sooner than anticipated, just before we were both sent to the so-called infirmary. In spite of my high fever, I was still conscious when a few Russian soldiers arrived. Uncouth, dirty, and profane, they showed no pity for any of us. Perhaps this was due to their own harrowing war experiences.

I can't remember what happened next. Diagnosed with tuberculosis, I was also afflicted with typhoid fever. I awoke on a stretcher, then was hoisted onto a wagon with Svetlana and two more Yugoslavian girls. I lost consciousness when we moved through some dreary countryside. Too sick to wonder what had happened to my friend, I awoke in a hospital in Trieste. At my urgent questioning, I was told that Svetlana had been sent back to Belgrade after a bad case of bronchitis.

Thanks to some American organization, or perhaps the Red Cross, I was taken to Zagreb after many detours. Our apartment had been occupied by strangers. The only relative I could find was Dad's cousin Eva. She and her two sons were the only survivors of our extended family. She took me in and nursed me like a long-lost daughter. When I asked what had happened to Mother and Leila, she told me reluctantly that they had died in a Yugoslavian concentration camp.

I felt as though I had died with them. The flow of my tears never seemed to stop. A survivor had told my cousin that Leila wasn't allowed to bury Mama when she collapsed near a quarry. Leila was shot a few days before the liberation.

Thanks to Eva's good care, my health gradually improved, but the grief grew stronger and deeper. Perhaps my tears helped me recover, for they opened the sluices of sorrow that had been kept in check for so long. Giving in to my mourning cleansed me of the constant control I had to enforce on myself in the camp. Now, as the last survivor of my family, I was unable to embrace my freedom. Yet the depths of such sorrow prevented me from turning to stone.

If hell had receded, the charged barbed wire remained coiled inside me. Was purgatory next? I craved justice; but justice turned out to be as arbitrary as oppression. Life deals blows at random. Tyrants perish to make room for new ones. People would be suppressed again and suffer. Who could ever stop that vicious circle? Is forgiveness the answer? Not for unspeakable atrocities. To forgive means to absolve, pardon, acquit. How can I do this without understanding the icy heart of the enemy? It took me weeks to write those few pages about horrors in the camp.

I still need to sort out this maze in spurts, then knot the thread where it was torn. The hardest part is to deal with the present moment and try to take the next step.

***

Two days later.

I have been informed that Auschwitz was closed on the 27th of January.

Just now, as I slowly recover, I see Eva's sons begin to chart their future goals. Yugoslavia. Marshal Tito. Their polished black boots mirror their standards. They honestly believe in their New Order. I can hardly blame them. They have not experienced my disillusionment. I watch them paint a rosy future awaiting us under our new leader. Their sermons reinforce my decision to leave Zagreb for good as soon as my health allows.

Knowing the futility of arguing against fanaticism, I prefer to ask cousin Josip if he had heard anything about Bogdan. The two of them were in third and fourth grade together.

"Why torture yourself, Tatyana? You probably know he's dead."

"I had no idea. I was just wondering."

"He turned into a monster," Josip said. "When the Germans caught him, he betrayed all his comrades."

"Sixteen of them," Todor said.

Josip nodded. "It didn't help him at all. The Nazis killed him in the end."

"I'm not surprised." Josip gave me a puzzled look. I asked if he had ever met a woman called Ludmilla. "She was a few years older than me and looked like a gypsy."

"Ludmilla...I'm not sure. But I think her name was among the sixteen—caught and killed, thanks to Bogdan."

Poor Ludmilla. I remember her kindness. And will I ever see Stefan again? I still wonder. If he is alive and has come back to Belgrade, he might try to find me. My cousins don't know him. He was the best person left in my world. I fear that he too might have perished. And Svetlana... how will we be able to get in touch with each other?

As to Victor...I need to close the door on my foolish hopes. How can he still be alive after all these years? His nocturnal visits to Auschwitz were the result of my constant nostalgia. Yet now, more alone than ever, my reasoning mind tells me he can no longer be alive. And if he were, he might no longer be the same...

I told Eva that I hope to return to Venice as soon as possible. But first I will look for help with the Red Cross or the American Jewish Committee in Trieste. It's time to free her of my long convalescence. Eva protested when I said I've been a burden to her long enough. I confessed to her that my other reason to leave Yugoslavia is the loss of my family and my loathing of any dictatorship. I asked her not to mention this to her sons who sincerely believe in Tito's integrity and idealism.

My dear cousin provided me with some food, Italian lire, and a train ticket to Trieste. I long to return to the Lido, but can't disturb or even face Dora and Giuseppe in my current condition. I'm deprived of health, hair, and shoes. My eyes are two dark circles in a skeletal face. Two years have passed since I first arrived in Venice. I'll stop in Trieste and look for a youth hostel near the railway station.

***

As soon as I arrived, I thought of Francesco da Verona's devotion and the grief he had shown at my departure for Auschwitz. The least I could do was to let him know that I'm still alive. I would pretend to be a friend of mine and tell him Tatyana had survived the *lager*. I remembered his number and found a phone in some café. Sweat was running down my back. After three rings, the familiar voice said, "*Pronto,*" at the other end.

I covered the mouthpiece with my hand and muffled my voice. "This is a friend of Tatyana's," I told him. "She went back to Yugoslavia and asked me to send you her regards."

A dead silence. Then the voice cried, "Tatyana! Where are you?"

"In Trieste. Am I such a bad actress? I just wanted to let you know that I'm still here."

"Oh my God! I…where can I find you?"

"I don't want you to see me. I have no hair. I have TB. You won't recognize me."

"Sick or well, hair or no hair, I will come and get you. Oh, Tatyana, it's hard to believe—I thought of you day and night. Tell me exactly where you are."

I sobbed the address into his ear.

"Say it again, more slowly. I can't hear you."

I took a deep breath, repeating the words. He would be there first thing in the morning.

Pity is written all over his face. Pity and love. I regret my foolish impulse to call him. He speaks in whispers, afraid that a loud word might harm me. He holds my arm on the way to breakfast, as though I am made of china and will break at the gentlest touch. He forces himself to eat lest I see his tears, but he is unable to hide them. At last, he weeps without shame. I try to comfort him. "It's all right, I'll be all right. So many of us got tuberculosis in the end. But the doctor in Zagreb assured me that I'm no longer contagious."

"What did those fiends do to you, my poor Tatyana? I wouldn't believe it if I didn't see it with my own eyes."

"How are the Battistas? Do they know...?"

"I called them right away. Dora is so excited. They can't wait to see you. We can take the noon train back to Venice."

His mother and sister were expecting me—ready to nurse me. They worried about his anguish on my behalf and were delighted about the good news.

"Francesco, I can't accept."

He swept my objection aside. First, he must get me a decent pair of shoes. How could anyone walk around in those awful old barges?

We stopped at a neighborhood shop, where I chose a pair of postwar platform monsters. They were the cheapest. He wouldn't hear of it and asked for the finest leather. I cried with happiness when I walked out with the most exquisite pair of handmade black leather pumps. "I'll sleep with them," I said, "and never take them off." For the first time I saw him smile. Later, on the train, he predicted that those shoes would carry me into a new life. For a moment, my gratitude came close to love.

In the *vaporetto* taking us to his home, Francesco whispered that I had never left. He would help me recover from an unimaginable nightmare.

As a portal was opened to an ancient *palazzo,* two women came down a wide wooden staircase. *Signora* da Verona is short, gray-haired and wiry. She reminds me of her son, except for the cold look in her steel-blue eyes. Unable to hide her shock, she murmured a formal welcome. Her daughter Sandra, a striking young woman, gave me a warm embrace. I could see myself through their eyes: a poor waif with hardly any hair, in elegant pumps and a shapeless dress. A door closed behind us. I felt trapped.

16.

PLUTOCRATS AND PROLETARIANS

Loitering at a bazaar in Termez, Victor felt no more conspicuous than the other ragged tramps. Some border police were there, but no one stopped him. A merchant stood behind his table, spooning soup from a cup. Victor pointed at some dried fruit and nuts one could obtain without coupons. "How far is Kabul?" he asked, putting the money on the table and explaining in Russian that he had relatives in Afghanistan he hadn't seen in years.

"I'm not sure," the merchant said. "Be careful," he whispered, adding a small loaf of bread to Victor's small provisions.

"But I have no ration marks left," Victor told him.

"Don't worry," the man answered in Russian, "just take the bread."

Victor thanked him, making sure no one was around to listen, and then asked where he might find a map of the city. The man raised his hands and shoulders to indicate he had no idea, adding that Victor ought to avoid any checkpoints at the border.

"But I'm not going anywhere," Victor said, laughing. He felt confident that the merchant was only trying to help, and yet, to make sure he wouldn't spy on him, he thanked him again for the bread and turned toward the center of the city.

Since he was unable to tell whether any freight or cargo trains were crossing the border, he waited until dark, settled down to sleep in a field, then started at dawn for the long march in the direction he hoped might lead to Kabul.

***

In the early dawn, the new moon threw a faint light on the road. Victor carefully avoided all border controls and found a small shelter under a bush. Shivering with cold, he stepped through some vacant spot into what he hoped was Afghanistan. Walking along a deserted plain, he paused for a brief rest. Peril seemed to lurk everywhere. Propelled by fear and his intense longing for freedom, he walked faster and faster. Gazing at faraway mountains, he guided himself by the rising sun. Unexpected heat made him slow his pace. A torn blister on his left heel forced him to stop. He took off his coat—a last relic of his mother's world. It had turned the color of lead. He sat down on a rock to finish his last morsel of bread.

Alone in the world. No living creature wherever he looked. Silence within silence.

"Don't stop," he admonished himself aloud, in German. "Just keep moving. Shake the kaleidoscope and the colors and shapes will change."

He took off his shoe and carried it in his hand, resuming the walk with a limp. At a turn in the road, something shimmered in the distance, slowly moving toward him. Was it a mirage, or a Fata Morgana? No, they're just men, he encouraged himself. Perhaps they would help him.

On coming closer, he distinguished four dark horses in the glare of the sun. Rifles were slung across the shoulders of the riders. Four Muslims in Turkish trousers and white shirts cut open at the chest rode the horses. The customary skullcaps sat on the backs of their heads. Victor waited. With a pounding heart, he was about to ask for directions when the first rider jumped down from his horse. The others began to gesticulate and shout at him in an unknown tongue. They looked like Uzbeks, but Uzbeks usually addressed white men in Russian. Victor tried sign language to show that he was lost, but they continued to shout, looking at him with fierce black eyes, pointing their rifles, ready to shoot. Victor raised both arms, shoe in hand, shouting in turn: "Kabul! Kabul! Kabul!"

He kept repeating the word, as though the name of that mysterious city would open Sesame for these four heavenly messengers who might carry him to his destination on their winged steeds.

Instead, the one who had jumped down now charged at him, searched his pockets, and pushed him brutally toward his sweat-covered horse. He tied one of Victor's arms to the saddle with his halter, then made him turn around in the direction of Termez. He jumped on his horse and the ride was resumed. Unable to keep up with the horses' pace, Victor feared being dragged through the dust to his death, as he had seen in American Western movies in Stuttgart. Mercifully, the rider slowed down, allowing him to ease his pace.

Where are they taking me? One shoe on, one off, he limped as fast as he could. They finally left the path and turned east, or west. Faint with thirst, fear, and exhaustion, Victor noticed that at last they were entering a town. A glimpse at the peaked military caps of guards in front of a small police station confirmed his impression that he was still in the Soviet Union.

The horseman untied Victor's arm. A police officer locked him into an empty room, where he lay down on the cement floor and fell asleep. Someone roused him with kicks and curses. Where was he? Two guards marched him out and made him climb into a truck. A few minutes later, he recognized the road from the previous night and knew he was back in Termez.

They drove him straight to jail and then locked him into a cell. Too exhausted to worry about his fate, he fell on the cot and continued to sleep. At dawn, a guard awoke him with a bowl of watery soup. He ate a chunk of stale black bread. An hour later, he was to meet with a police official for questioning.

Victor recalled Misha's warning. "I've been looking for my family," he heard himself explain. "I lost my wife and son during the evacuation."

"Liar! You were escaping to Kabul," the officer smirked. "Next, you'll tell me that your family was evacuated to Afghanistan, eh?"

Wishing to erase that grin, Victor realized how foolish he must sound.

"That's not true," he protested. "I thought those riders had come from Kabul. They misunderstood because they don't speak Russian. I had been unable to find a place to sleep in Termez, so I took to the road."

"Do you mean that you walked across the border to find a place to sleep? Where did you live before you came here?"

Victor remembered Misha's warning: "Always tell those pigs that you lived in Tashkent."

The official filled out some papers on his desk and ordered Victor to sign them. Victor was unable to decipher a single word. Was it a death sentence?

Once more in his cell, he paced from wall to wall until he grew dizzy. Changing direction, he moved diagonally from corner to corner. The window was too high to look out. There was nothing to do but lie on the barren cot. He fell asleep after dark, but again was shaken awake in the middle of the night. Soon he found himself marching to the station with a group of other prisoners. Ordered to climb into a passenger train, he learned that their particular wagon was reserved for the "habitual bums."

His traveling companions consisted of two middle-aged Russian tramps, two young boys and girls in rags, and an old invalid with a disheveled beard. Guarded by two policemen, they were given hot water—the policemen called it "tea"—and a piece of bread. Listening to the tramps' conversation, Victor gathered that they were being taken all the way back to Tashkent.

The young people appeared to be in excellent spirits. It turned out they had run away from reform school. The old invalid scratched at his lice, talking cheerfully about his adventures along the road, all over Mother Russia. Victor listened in silence.

More and more prisoners were added along the journey: vagabonds, deserters, petty thieves. The newcomers had to stand in the overcrowded compartment. In front of Victor, a tall man in a soldier's uniform kept staring at his feet. Making sure no one was looking, he pulled a pair of shoes from a small bundle and pushed them into Victor's hands. Victor pushed them back, suspecting stolen goods. The man, obviously anxious to get rid of a hot item, dug a hard fist into Victor's rib as he bent down and put the shoes under the bench beside his feet. His secretive gestures were quick, determined, and threatening.

Victor had no desire to arouse attention by starting a fight with this bully. He took off his torn felt boots stuffed with newspaper—a gift from the Soviet state. They dated back to the hospital in Tashkent. With a kick of his heels, he pushed them way under the seat, then slipped into the new shoes, which were made of synthetic material. He was delighted at their perfect fit, which made him forget his painful blister. He breathed with relief; no one seemed to have noticed.

The prisoners were counted as they alighted in Tashkent after the long journey, then ordered to stand in line. Policemen marched the group toward some unknown destination. One of them held a pistol in his hand, ready to shoot. With piercing blows from his whistle, he startled any bystander who got in the way. People dispersed like frightened birds. Others stopped to watch from a safe distance, looking on with compassion or cheering the prisoners with a few kind words. Victor was amused by the youngsters from the reformatory who waved back merrily and kept shouting until the policeman pointed his pistol in their direction.

At last the captives passed through a gate into a large courtyard surrounded by several barracks, where they were sorted out according to age, crime, and nationality. Victor and two other prisoners were taken through a door into one of the barracks. Someone pushed him into a dark room. Men of all ages were sitting or lying on the concrete floor. "Take off your shoes!" someone yelled at him.

His new shoes were caked with mud. He took them off and threw them into a corner, knowing he would never see them again.

As his eyes grew used to the dark, he saw that most of the men were asleep. Like snakes in an overcrowded cage, arms and legs were entangled in grotesque positions. Finding no space to lie down, Victor remained leaning against the wall near the entrance. He had no idea where he was. And who were these prisoners? Tramps? Refugees? Criminals? A tall silhouette emerged from the other room.

"Hey you, over there!" The call was addressed to him. Victor followed the voice and groped his way through the door. "Got money? Tobacco? Cigarettes? Are you married? From Tashkent?"

"*Niet*," Victor answered the questions, shaking his head. Getting used to the dark, he noticed that this room was far less crowded than the other. The tall fellow laughed out loud, called him a peasant, and gave him a friendly push that sent him reeling back into the crowded room. He fell across some sleeping bodies.

"Why don't you watch where you're going, you cursed devil!" one of them screamed at him in Russian, while another kicked and punched him furiously. Victor hit back at them in a rage until he had secured a tiny territory for himself. He heard someone applaud. Everything grew quiet until the door opened. A naked bulb was turned on and two guards entered, shouting, "Wake up, sit up, everybody!"

The guards started to count the prisoners in the overcrowded room. They came up with a large discrepancy in their numbers and started counting again, and again, coming up with various results. At last they settled on a number, turned off the light, and went out.

Four men were dominating the prisoners in both rooms. One of them, called Pjotr—the tall silhouette Victor had met the night before—called him into the larger room after a breakfast of hot water, mush, and bread. "Where you from?" he asked in a broken Russian.

"Poland."

"And why are you here?"

"I was arrested near the border of Afghanistan…"

"Ouch! That means at least five years in Zing-Ata."

"A camp, you mean? Is it a bad one?"

"Better than Karaganda." Searching through Victor's coat pockets, Piotr pulled out the *sopranino*. "What's this?"

"A piccolo recorder—a small flute."

"Play something for me."

Victor began with a Strauss waltz. Pjotr looked at him with admiration. A stubbly beard covered half of his gaunt face. Next, Victor played "La donna è mobile" from Verdi's *Rigoletto*. During the men's applause, Pjotr went into his corner, pulled out a small dried herring from under his comforter, and threw it at him. Victor caught it in midair, then gulped it down with a bite of bread he had saved from breakfast.

This exchange was repeated for several mornings, making Victor feel like a trained seal, to be rewarded with a herring for a potpourri of tunes. Once more, he was applauded by the "plutocrats", as the men occupying the more spacious room were called by the "proletarians", who now looked at Victor with envy and hostility. Thanks to Pjotr's protection, however, no one dared lay a hand on him.

"Hey, comrade, what's the matter, you devil? How was it in Poland?" Pjotr wanted to know. "Have you been to the big cities?"

Victor amused him with a few episodes from his past in Stuttgart, pretending they had happened in Polish cities. Pjotr wished to learn more about the theater, music, tasty dishes, and life in the west. Victor satisfied his curiosity as well as he could, recognizing that his tales were about the person he had once been: a young musician from another planet.

"You're a liar!" Pjotr exclaimed. "It sounds too good to be true. But, here…" and he handed him a couple of dates.

Most of the time, Victor sat brooding on his narrow space of cement. His hunger led him to escape into dreams about dishes his mother had prepared for him as a child. He invented a method to keep himself in bread. He had started a new habit of breaking his one daily slice into small morsels, concealing them in his empty trouser pockets. This gave him a small treat to look forward to at the end of the day. It took all his willpower not to devour the entire piece at breakfast, and he was pleased with himself for resisting the temptation. Some proletarians saw him fumbling in his pockets and asked what he was eating. "Look at the Pole," they shouted, "chewing his own lice!"

"They are delicious," Victor said. "Would you like to try some?"

To his regret, Pjotr was sent to Karaganda a few days later. Victor was sentenced to hard labor in Zing-Ata, just as Pjotr had predicted.

17.

TATYANA

My mother's maiden name

Venice, October 1945

The afternoon of my arrival at Francesco's home, Dora and Giuseppe Battista rushed over from the Lido to welcome me back. Dora brought me the first entries of my notes, which she had carefully concealed from prying eyes, since they were written in German during the war. I was sad for not being able to stay with her at the Lido. She showered me with gifts, among them a dark green winter coat and two lovely dresses. Anticipating that nothing would fit me, she had asked her seamstress to come over in the morning and take measurements for any alterations.

I ought to have been overwhelmed with joy and relief for the Da Veronas' kindness, but could only pay lip service to the gratitude I was supposed to feel. Exhausted from the journey, I managed to hide my apathy and incapacity of embracing a world in which I no longer belonged.

Francesco's sister Sandra admired my new shoes and asked where I had found them. I told her that Francesco bought them for me in Trieste.

I noticed her disapproving look. As she went out to check her mother's tea preparations and to gather everyone in the dining room, Dora held me close in a long and silent embrace. "Oh, Tatyana," she whispered, "when you didn't come back that day, I..." She was breathing hard, trying to control her sobs. We heard voices in the hall, and she quickly dried her eyes and whispered how sorry she was that I couldn't come back to stay with them, but Francesco had the right to claim me first. I could only press her hand to express that I felt the same way, moved by our special bond.

The Da Veronas assigned me a charming attic room with a splendid view over the Rialto and a stretch of the Adriatic Sea. It was hard to imagine a finer haven, but I longed to spend my convalescence in Dora's healing presence.

The next morning, ready to leave for his office, Francesco asked me why I had told Sandra he had bought me the shoes.

"She wanted to know where I got them. Was I supposed to keep it a secret?"

"Of course not."

"I didn't think there was anything wrong."

"Of course not," he said again. "I just need some privacy."

"I'm sorry, Francesco. I had no idea."

"Don't worry. You couldn't possibly know."

But I did worry. Was it money? Hardly, since Francesco had always been more than generous. Was Sandra jealous? When he was gone, I felt abandoned in that big house. Sandra was out doing charity work for orphaned Catholic children. Way down in the kitchen, *Signora* Da Verona supervised the cook. She was in full charge of the household. I offered my help, but she had no use for it. Everything was under control, or better, *her* control.

There was nothing for me to do but read or listen to music on the radio. All three Da Veronas were anxious about my recovery. They urged me to rest, to eat. Each time I entered a room, they were speaking in whispers. I felt like a caged bird, to be pampered and fattened till I would sing again. Even the maid took part in their solicitous instructions.

In the eyes of mother and daughter, I was Francesco's future wife. Too delicate to be mentioned, this fact was established by my presence in their home. Although I was no longer contagious, my condition remained precarious, and I could well understand their concern about their own safety. Restrained by my gratitude, I was too weak to stand up for myself.

Twice a day we would gather around the large oak table for the family meals. We ate in a genteel silence interspersed with polite remarks. I secretly watched Francesco. The breadwinner in this matriarchal *palazzo* was overshadowed by a despotic mother and a kind, critical, ever-watchful sister. Signora Da Verona carried the keys to all the cupboards around her waist: cupboards holding linen, dishes, tins of coffee, and other valuable goods. She was the guardian. Her children were to ask her for anything they needed.

Sandra's impeccable politeness was intimidating. In spite of her show of sympathy, I was afraid of breaking through the thin layer of her good manners. I would have liked to photograph her handsome face with the eyebrows raised. Perhaps she thought Francesco had committed an unforgivable act of rebellion by bringing me home. An ailing, destitute Jewish girl of foreign extraction who almost died in a concentration camp would be no asset to any family. Mother and daughter accepted me, because not to accept me meant to alienate their son and brother. Any resentment was stifled for the sake of his happiness.

What happiness? The remark about his need for privacy revealed his true feelings. Like me, he wanted out, but feared confrontation. Countless married Italian sons continued to live in the homes of their widowed mothers. I imagined us, confined together in that somber milieu, always committed to following its clockwork routine. I avoided being alone with him as much as possible and managed to keep the whole family at arm's length with my concern about their health.

As a partial surrender to the family's care for me, I didn't go out for the first six weeks. Haunted by the loss of my hair and fearing to be seen by the people I knew, I didn't mind waiting until I felt and looked human again. When the Battistas came to the house for regular visits, I kept a scarf on my head. By early September, my head was covered by a fine down. It looked like a feather cut, which was the rage of the moment. Having gained some weight, I began to recognize my old self, but still lacked the strength and desire to resume the life I had lost.

So here I am, back with my notes, a welcome occupation during these lonely hours. In need of fresh air and the sights of a liberated Venice, I decided to look up the Bardelli family and my colleagues at the office. Since Francesco and Sandra had already left for work, I told the *Signora* that I was going to visit some friends. She strongly objected to my outing, but I assured her that I felt much stronger and needed a change. She made me promise to be home for the midday meal.

I stopped on the way for a brief hello with the baker, the owner of the *latteria*, and a glass blower, all trustworthy people I used to meet on daily walks to the office.

Mrs. Bardelli burst into tears as soon as she saw me. "I couldn't get you out of my mind. My dear Tatyana, what a miracle to see you again! Francesco told me what happened. If only you had stayed with us! They would never have found you."

I looked at her in silence. She went on to chat about the children. Franco was in school, he would be sad to have missed me, but I must promise to come back soon. The baby no longer remembered me. She was a pretty little girl I would never have recognized. I took her into my arms. Holding her, I was filled with love and regret.

Later, I walked slowly through the narrow lanes. My hair would soon grow full again. I wore Dora's lovely clothes. Yet all this was camouflage to hide the skeleton beneath. My dead family kept me in thrall, as did the memories of the horror I had gone through. In spite of the cold day, I felt hot in Dora's green coat. I took it off and threw it over my arm. My cheeks were on fire. *Oh, not another fever!* I thought in panic. I looked at my watch. It was too late for a visit to the office. *I should have gone there first*, I thought. *Something's holding me back.* I knew that Berto and Mario would be happy to see me again. What made me hesitate?

I stopped in front of a shop window. Staring through a display of fine lace tablecloths, I kept seeing Clara's lifeless face.

That night I slept fitfully. I dreamt of Bogdan and of the comrades he had betrayed. He was shooting at what I thought were enemies in the woods. Coming closer, I recognized a family of deer. One by one, they fell dead to the ground. I tore the rifle from his hands.

"Enough!" I awoke, feeling choked with grief about my dad. It was as though he had paid with his life in order to save me. If Bogdan hadn't killed him, Dad and I would have stayed with our group of partisans and suffered their fate in the end.

It was past ten o'clock when I joined Signora da Verona for breakfast. "All dressed up? Going out again?" she asked. I nodded, taking a bite from a roll and a sip of coffee.

"It's raining hard, Tatyana. Perhaps you had better stay home. At least take an umbrella."

"*Signora,* please don't worry. I'll be all right."

Too preoccupied with what I was about to face, I forgot the umbrella and walked briskly to the office. It was tempting to spend the rest of the morning in the shelter of a café, but I told myself I must eradicate fear from my life. Drenched by the time I opened the door to the office, I ran my fingers through my wet hair.

Mario saw me first. He stared at me in shock.

"Yes, I'm back," I told him. "You aren't seeing a ghost."

Berto rushed to embrace me. No sign of Clara.

Mario watched me in silence, his face as wet as mine, though not from the rain. "Oh, Tatyana. I had never hoped to..."

"Where's Clara?"

The two men looked at each other. "She's no longer with us," Berto said. "Your friend Francesco was out of town at the time. As soon as he came back, he asked where he could find you, but we had no idea where those fiends had taken you."

"He did find me. Too late. Anyway, I'm staying with him and his family. They have all been very good to me."

Mario took my hand. "How wonderful to see you again! I hope you have time for lunch. Let's take her out, Berto, what do you say?"

"Sorry, I promised my friends to be back before one. Maybe some other time. What happened to Clara?"

Again, they both remained silent.

"She was the one, wasn't she?"

"How did you find out?"

"Just a guess. I still can't figure out how she knew that I..."

"One day I found her looking at your identity card," Mario explained. "I walked into the office after the break, while you had gone out for a moment. She murmured that you had left your purse. She had found it on the floor, and when she picked it up, your card fell out. It didn't sound plausible, but I gave it no further thought. A few days later, she asked casually if I knew that Schwartz was a Jewish name. I had no idea. She was merely wondering, she said, since that was your mother's maiden name on the card."

Berto shrugged. "It never crossed my mind that she might denounce you. Only much later, when I heard that she gave away other people, did I realize…"

Back in Kočejve, after our dangerous river crossing, I had forgotten to ask the partisan who forged my ID card to change my mother's Jewish maiden name.

"I knew Clara was jealous of you," Mario went on. "Of your youth and your beauty."

"She was dismissed right after the war," Berto said. "Disgraced and spat upon. She had denounced a number of people. For five thousand lire a head. Can you imagine?"

"Does she still live in that old building?" I used to help her carry documents to and from her place, and remembered the day she had introduced me to her invalid mother. Berto nodded.

On leaving the office, I assured them both that I would soon come back and join them for lunch.

18.

ZINGATA AND THE EVANGELIST

Another blow dealt him by some invisible judge. Where was his crime to fit the punishment? In the cellar of his helplessness, there was no wall to pound. To rage against injustice proved as futile as rebelling against death.

I suffer; therefore I am. Victor could not remember where he had read it. *But what is the purpose of my suffering, if it destroys me before I may learn its why and wherefore?*

Month after month, he worked slave-like in the cotton cleaning industrial plant near Tashkent. The camp consisted of several thousand men and women prisoners toiling in the textile branch. Assigned work in the industrial *combinat*, where seeds and hulls were separated from the fibers, Victor found himself hemmed in by bales of cotton to be processed in the spinning mill. The mountains of cotton snow invaded every cell in his body and entered his dreams. Cotton particles filled his eyes, his ears, his nostrils, his lungs.

Like a cottonseed, he had turned into a particle of those masses for whom the revolution had presumably been fought: enslaved men and women too exhausted to rebel against their fate.

He learned how to spin. Slowly turning his first clumsy attempts into a fine skill, he dreamed of Rumpelstiltskin helping him weave a magic carpet on which to fly out of this prison, out of reach of that invisible guard who held this immense country in his iron grasp, and whose name was never mentioned, except as "No.1".

No one was allowed to speak. It was a rule more strongly enforced here than in a Trappist cloister. Confined within such verbal isolation,

Victor felt his spirit turn as weak as his flesh. Plagued by fevers and night sweats, he began to spit blood. Perhaps it was the Reaper arriving in the guise of Rumpelstiltskin. In this gigantic network, one nameless slave would be replaced immediately by another. Victor saw himself as the lowest of all, no longer of use to anyone, including himself.

A medical examination confirmed a possible relapse of malaria. He was sent to a different part of the camp and put into a narrow hut with two other sick prisoners. A small wood stove gave out more smoke than heat. Stormy nights made the men shiver under threadbare blankets. The meager diet—diminished according to their uselessness—hardly added any warmth. And yet, the repose within the cocoon of his weakness was a welcome relief after the battles with those cotton bales.

Although the sick men were allowed to talk to each other, Victor's two Uzbek companions did not understand Russian. They were both recovering from pneumonia, and prayed on their knees to Allah, bowing and facing east. One of them was tall and skinny with tourmaline eyes, the other short and squat with a pockmarked complexion and the trickle of a beard. They never cursed or shouted. They smiled and bowed to Victor with distant benevolence.

Barely recovered after two weeks' convalescence, the two men were sent back to work. Now Victor was left alone in the hut. Thanks to the rest, his cough subsided. Once a day a guard brought him his ration of water and food, while every few days an attendant checked his fever. Medication was unavailable.

One morning a stranger came through the door, pulled the only rickety chair close to Victor's cot, and sat down beside him. A scrawny neck with a prominent Adam's apple was visible under a sparse yellow-gray beard. Spectacles sat on the bridge of his pointed nose. Wisps of gray hair fell over his wrinkled brow.

"I am here," he said in broken Russian, looking at Victor with large bumblebee eyes, "to help the sick."

"That's good of you."

The man smiled, then continued in German. "Your accent tells me you come from my homeland. What can I do for you, my son?"

"Are you a preacher?"

"Not really. Though…" He stopped, embracing his knees with gnarled-knuckled fingers.

"There's nothing you can do for me," Victor told him in German.

"Granted, there is nothing. But just being here might…"

"Might what?"

"You are not the first to greet me with mistrust. Because of my faith."

Victor did not respond.

"Where are you from? Southern Germany?"

"You have a good ear."

"*Ach, ja.* A good ear for inflections, and a good eye for a good heart. Your speech reveals your background, my friend, and your face tells me a story, a story of suffering, of strength in adversity, of a worthy soul."

"And what are you doing in this camp?" Victor was disturbed by the sight of a German, yet pleased to communicate in his mother tongue for the first time in years.

"Trying to help if I can, to comfort the sick. I was sent here with my wife and four daughters." The man pointed toward a window. "Our hut is right over there. You may come any time you feel strong enough to go out. Any time you wish to warm yourself at our stove, have some tea and bread."

Victor turned his head toward the window. "Thanks for your kind offer. But you still haven't told me what brought you to Zing-Ata."

"I was persecuted for religious reasons. Which is to say that God brought me here. For more than two generations, my German family has lived in the Ukraine. I was arrested for my activities as a man of faith. Though I'm nicknamed 'Evangelist', I'm not a preacher, just a simple carpenter. So I make myself useful by doing repairs and looking after the sick."

"And bringing a few sheep into the fold…"

"People are just as hungry for the bread of life, my friend, as they are for that other bread. Prisoners come to me by night to be close to God, to listen, to talk."

"Not to speak of the warmth of your hut, the tea, and that other bread, as you call it."

"That too, of course, that too. I don't blame them. You are a Doubting Thomas, but some day you will seek out God. How can you carry your cross without His help?"

"I carry no cross, Evangelist. Mine is a Star of David. You are a good man, no doubt, but please, don't preach to me. If your God exists, he has chosen for me to suffer, along with my people and millions of others. Should a miracle change my life for the better, my personal lot wouldn't alter any suffering for those other millions."

"What you are saying only proves the depth of your caring."

"You needn't be religious to care."

"But you must believe in something. I can hear the passion in your voice, the love..."

Victor propped himself up on his elbow. "Yes, I believe in matter turning into spirit. It's beyond our grasp. Our planet is a mere speck in the universe. We understand little, we have no answers. Only Hitler and Stalin have answers. Religions harp so much on humility, but then true believers claim to be the center of God's attention. Wouldn't you call that a blatant conceit? A man of faith owes God more respect than to assume that he should involve himself in our petty concerns. We are part of the universe, which minds its own business, and so must we. We aren't entitled to be rewarded for trying to improve the world."

Stunned by his own lofty speech, Victor wondered if the floodgates after his long exile and silence had opened in spite of himself.

The Evangelist pulled thoughtfully at his beard. "But we haven't come so far yet. The people need to be comforted in their suffering."

"How are we ever to grow up, if we keep asking for comfort like frightened children? Why not do what needs to be done for its own sake, without forcing our beliefs on others?"

Victor took a deep breath. "Sorry, here I'm starting to preach myself. But unless we finally make that choice and get rid of ideologies, including fascism and all the hoaxes that are passed for communism..."

"Shush...someone might hear you."

"So I get a life sentence. Do you think I'll survive even one more year in Zing--" Victor interrupted himself with a violent fit of coughing.

The passionate delivery of his first speech in years had excited him to a feverish pitch. His chest hurt. He broke into a sweat, gasping for breath.

The Evangelist rushed to his aid, wiping his forehead with a soiled blue-and-red-checkered handkerchief. "It's all my fault," he declared, holding Victor's head against his chest. "You must not exert yourself. I'll sit here until you fall asleep. Just breathe, very quietly."

Soothed by the old man's concern, Victor felt gratified for having been able to express his thoughts in his mother tongue to another fellow human. After a long silence, he assured him that their talk had actually done him a great deal of good.

He remembered his mother reading to him about Adam and Eve from the Bible. As a boy of thirteen, he had been fascinated by the story of Eve, the snake and the apple, but couldn't understand why God didn't want his creatures to eat from the Tree of Knowledge.

"Aren't you glad about everything I learn?" he had asked his mother.

"Of course I am."

"I don't understand. I mean, I don't understand God..."

"You aren't supposed to," his mother said.

The Evangelist came to see him each day. As soon as he could stand on his feet, Victor was sent back to work. Although he was allowed to remain in the hut at night, he could hardly regain his strength. Hunger, more than physical torture, was now an agony of the spirit. Yet he clung to life tenaciously, unable to think of anything but the next meal.

He loathed himself. As the days went by, he lost hope of ever seeing Tatyana again. What had made him keep his promise to carry a flaming rod through this endless night? Would *she* be able to gather such courage under dreadful circumstances? How would he ever be able to return to the west and find her-alive or dead?

In spite of his exhaustion after each day's hard labor, he managed to pay nightly visits to the Evangelist. Slipping across ice or sinking into deep snow in the scanty cotton-lined boots that had replaced the shoes he was forced to relinquish in prison, he dragged himself to the barracks, where the old man would read from the Bible. The hut was usually crowded with women and children. Though bored by the reading, Victor enjoyed the warmth and serenity of the Evangelist's voice. Compared to the rest of the camp, this hut was a shelter of love and peace. One of the old man's daughters would hand him a bowl of thin soup and a small piece of bread.

The lack of privacy gave the two men no opportunity to resume the discussion of their first encounter. Victor preferred it this way. He felt no desire to enter into those murky religious waters and shamelessly favored real bread over the Evangelist's "bread of life".

The old man told him one night that he agreed with whatever motive Victor had for his visits. "It hardly matters why you come, as long as you find anything to give you sustenance."

The sincerity of those words put Victor at ease.

The Evangelist folded his hands on his lap. "Do you realize that the war has been over for half a year?"

"I had no idea."

"Yes, and we weren't even told. Six months..." he repeated. "You must grow strong, my friend, for now we may soon be free."

The news meant little to Victor, who had been sentenced for life. He touched the old man's knee. "But I'm glad for you."

"Now things may change. They may let you go home."

"I have no home, nowhere to go."

"But you are young. You'll come with us, as soon as we go back to the collective farm. There is always room for one more."

Victor gave him a warm embrace. "You're like a father to me."

"A selfish father, who needs a good son. But more than anything, I pray that you may have a good life."

What kind of life? Victor wondered. What outer freedom could ever release him from inner captivity? Six and a half years had passed since his flight from Poland. What made him cling to life with such tenacity? For some reason, he was not free to die. Something would have to kill him. Like a falling star, the image of Tatyana flashed through his mind.

"Do you happen to know if the Germans invaded Yugoslavia?" he asked.

"I'm afraid so. The war spread all over. I can never forget how lucky we were to be spared the terrible fate of the Russian people in the war zone."

"And we never learned what really happened. No radio, no newspaper. No one seemed to know or care.

***

Weeks and months went by. War or peace, nothing changed in a prisoner's life, which was just as Victor had expected. He got sick, was sent back to work, fell ill again. One night, the Evangelist embraced him with the news that he and his family were free to go home within two weeks. In spite of signs to the contrary, he still hoped Victor would be allowed to join them.

The following morning, Victor could not get up for work. Shivering with fever, he was hardly aware of lying in a pool of sweat that changed from fire to ice and back to fire, just as during the days of his hospital stay in Tashkent. But now, with no nurse to take care of him and being of no use to the State, he would simply be left here to die.

In his delirium, night and day came and went. He was in a cave, cold and damp, trying to move, to find his way out, but the effort was too great. At last he fell into a torpor, from which he awoke days or weeks later. When he finally opened his eyes, the Evangelist was bending over him. The entire room seemed to be filled with his worried bumblebee eyes. Before lapsing back into darkness, Victor heard the old man say that he was waiting for him to get well, and repeated his promise to take him back to his village with the rest of the family.

As though he had never left his side, his friend was there when Victor awoke once more. He gave him some water and wiped the sweat off his face. There was little else he could do. As he repeated his promise, Victor indicated with a gesture that he was not going to recover.

The next time he opened his eyes, the Evangelist was holding his hand. Victor managed no more than a smile and a sigh, then dropped back into his no-man's-land. It was dusk when he had another glimpse at his narrow world. He felt weightless, almost disembodied.

"Victor, *mein Sohn,* let us pray," the Evangelist implored and, as the dying man remained silent, he begged him to speak the words after him, even if he did not believe in them. Too weak to resist, Victor obeyed.

"Our Father, who art in Heaven…"

The words had no more meaning to him than a poem parroted by a child. As he repeated them after the old man, he was hardly aware of his tears. They rose incessantly from the depths of his heart, then poured from his eyes, washing everything away—pain and fever, cold and loneliness, captivity and hunger. An instant later, he was drowning in a sea, helplessly sinking lower and lower.

This must be the end, he thought, touching the sandy ground under his feet. And, touching it, the gentle drop caused him to rise again, inch by inch, as he passed through layer and layer of restorative sleep, until a current carried him back to shore.

Waiting for him, Tatyana stood on the beach. She was waving at him. Able to breathe at last, he slept the sleep of a dying man about to come back to life.

***

It was dark in the hut, except for a small oil lamp shedding its feeble light across the woman who sat on a chair beside him. He recognized the Evangelist's wife. Her once rosy face looked haggard and anxious. The room was hot and humid. There were other cots, other people asleep on those cots.

"Where am I?" Victor tried to push back his blanket.

"Please, Victor," the woman said in German. "You are still weak."

"I feel much stronger. Who brought me here?"

"My husband and the girls. They carried you over on a stretcher."

"When was that?"

"About a week ago."

"Your husband…you all nursed me back to health?"

"There wasn't much we could do. Some warmth, a little food."

"How can I thank you? When are you going back to the Ukraine?"

The woman's face darkened. "The Evangelist…" She drew in her breath.

"Where is he?"

"He was punished, because—"

"Was he spending too much time with me?"

"He was neglecting his duties, so they sent him to work in the factory. But he came back sick after a couple of days. He's old; he isn't used to…"

"And where is he now?"

"Over there, on his cot. He caught the flu, alas. It turned into pneumonia."

"Thanks to me." Victor remembered seeing his friend bent over him again and again. While keeping his watch, he had probably stopped eating and sleeping, then had finally carried Victor here through ice and snow with the help of his daughters. And then he was punished for the crime of trying to save the life of a useless prisoner.

Still weak, Victor got to his feet and, with precarious steps, moved to the corner where the old man lay on a narrow cot. He looked like a shadow of his former self.

"You shouldn't get up." He could barely speak.

Victor found a chair and sat down beside him. "I feel much stronger. Thanks to you. And now it's your turn, because you took such good care of me."

The old man's skull looked almost transparent.

"Victor, my son, don't be foolish. People get sick in these camps. The Lord chooses mysterious ways of restoring some and taking others unto Him. If nothing else," he added with a weak smile, "you should have become a true believer. A miracle brought you back, even when I gave up hope."

Thanks to the needed rest and food that you all provided for me, Victor thought.

His health was slowly improving. Although he was still weary and weak, he went back to watch over his old friend often, talking to him softly, but most of the time the Evangelist was too tired to respond.

The next morning, a guard appeared to warn Victor that, sick or not, he must leave the camp within three days.

"And where am I to go?"

"That's your problem. Thank the stars for your good luck."

The Evangelist was pleased to hear about Victor's imminent release. He no longer spoke about his return to the Ukraine. "Thank the Lord, you are going to be free. All my prayers for you have been answered."

"I don't know where to go."

"Wherever she is, you'll find her."

"What do you mean?"

"I heard you mention her name three times, in your delirium."

"I did?"

"It wasn't quite clear when you whispered it for the first and second time. But then, when you came back after our prayer, you called 'Tatyana!' out loud, almost joyfully."

The night before his departure, he took care of the old man, deeply saddened that he was being forced to abandon him. "Getting out of this hell was my only wish," he explained, "and now I feel like a traitor. To be thrown out of here, when you need me most..."

"You are wrong, Victor. Nothing could make me happier than knowing that you'll be free."

"I would no longer be alive without you."

The old man shook his head and smiled. "Of course you would. It was that prayer and Tatyana..."

"Not the prayer, but your caring. For me, human love has infinitely more power."

"That may be so. Though prayer is another form of love."

"Then let me pray for you to get well soon, so you may leave for your village."

"But permission has been cancelled."

So that was it, Victor thought.

"It may be granted again," he said.

"True. But you must get out before they change their minds."

The old man spoke with difficulty, interrupting his words as he gasped for breath. Yet he seemed livelier than before. "At least your illness disqualifies you for slave labor," he said. "The State doesn't want to support sick prisoners." He had folded his hands on his breast. "You said you would pray for me." Then, as Victor nodded, "You will really do this? Even pray *with* me?"

"I will do anything for you, *Väterchen*."

"That's what they called me in my village—'*Little father*.' I want you to know I am a happy man. Thanks to you. *Ja, ja*, thanks to you."

Victor covered his hands with his own. "I don't know any prayers, but will make one up for you. Our Father, who art in Heaven," he began softly, and the Evangelist slowly repeated the words. A smile spread across his ashen face. "Give us this day our daily bread. Give us the bread of enlightenment, before we die of indigestion from that stale loaf we receive in these dreadful times. Give us back our sanity."

The sick man repeated Victor's words with great difficulty.

"Put an end to all slaughter and persecution. Please, Lord, let my friend go home to his good, fruitful labor. Help the wretched of this earth, the women and children, the hungry, the sick. For yours is the kingdom, the power, and the glory, forever and ever. Amen."

The old man had no longer been able to repeat the words after him. He nodded several times, sighed contentedly, and closed his eyes. His hands were once more folded across his chest. "Roles reversed, Victor. You are my priest."

Victor remained by his side. When the woman came to check on her husband, she found him in deep slumber.

"Let me watch over him," Victor said. "If you don't mind."

"Thank you. I could do with a bit of sleep."

He kept his watch through the night. At dawn, he went to fetch the patient a drink of water. Before setting the cup to his lips, Victor knew he was dead. He lay in the same position with an expression of deep contentment, eyes closed, hands folded on his breast.

As soon as she learned what had happened, the Evangelist's wife broke into tears and laments, and her daughters left their cots and embraced her, and then embraced one another and wept. Victor promised to help with the burial. He felt wondrously calm.

"You are so good to us," the woman cried. He took her into his arms. "He loved you like a son. That's what he said, didn't he, Marie, Irmgard, Gretl? He said it was the most wonderful miracle to see you restored."

***

Victor was unable to help with the burial. The guard appeared and chased him out. "Go to the office and get your things."

"This poor man just died. I want to help his family."

The guard yelled at him with a curse and pushed him out. Victor stumbled into the office, picked up his coat with the recorder in one pocket. His red scarf had faded to a dirty pink. The commander of the camp made him sign the dismissal papers that had his name written across the page. "Nameless Victor," last name first. Victor signed it in the same order, just as he was told.

19.

TATYANA

My Antagonist

As soon as I returned from my outing, I heard Sandra's angry voice. I was late for the midday meal. The three of them were gathered in the dining room, squabbling freely in my absence.

"She locks the coffee away from me," Sandra complained, "so I can't have a cup in the afternoon, or even invite a friend!"

"Coffee is too costly to be squandered," her mother said.

Francesco protested. "Mother, we can well afford it."

I took off my coat and waited. Though embarrassed to eavesdrop, it would be more indiscreet to join them at this moment.

"I am still in charge of this household." I could see the mother's thin, puckered lips, the look in those cold eyes. Francesco replied that no one disputed her authority, but that from now on he would buy Sandra all the coffee she wanted. End of discussion.

I chose that moment to come in. "You are late, child," the *Signora* said. "And look at you, soaked to the bone. You are going to catch your death."

I apologized for my tardiness. We ate in strained silence. I knew that Sandra was repressing her anger in my presence, anger at her mother, which perhaps camouflaged the general anger at my being there. If coffee was too costly, I was infinitely more expensive. Never had I felt so ill at ease, so alienated.

"I hope it's not too much for you," Francesco said. "I mean, going out so often."

"So often? Yesterday morning I left the house for the first time."

"I'm concerned about your health. Did you go to the office this morning?"

I nodded. "Mario and Berto send their greetings."

"And Clara?"

"She doesn't work there anymore."

It was all I could tell him in the presence of his mother and sister. He obviously had no idea about her dismissal, or anything else.

At last Maria came in to pour the coffee. "No, thank you," I said. Sandra gave me an inquisitive look. When Maria was about to fill her cup, she covered it with her hand and shook her head. Glancing at me, she broke into a friendly smile.

The ladies retired for the afternoon siesta. Francesco went back to the office. Before leaving, he urged me to take a rest.

"Later, perhaps. There's one more errand."

"What kind of errand?"

"I'll tell you later."

"Tatyana, you must take care of yourself."

"You sound like your mother."

"I do?" He seemed hurt, but then smiled at me, saying that he well understood my pique for being constantly reminded of my health. He was happy to see me getting stronger each day. "We need to make plans for the future. Let's talk somewhere alone. What about meeting me at the Florian café around five? Will that give you enough time for your mysterious errand?"

"Five is fine."

***

The rain had stopped. Mists rose from the Adriatic Sea with a wintry breeze. Brackish water splashed against the Venetian *palazzi*. After taking a boat to Campo San Marcuola, I moved slowly along back canals in that poor neighborhood, inhaling smells of rotting fish and garbage. The water was black, the houses huddled beneath a gloomy sky. The silence of that afternoon and the mists wafting over the canals were in tune with the grim nature of my errand.

There was still time to turn around. Why confront that despicable creature? It would serve no purpose, heal nothing. After rounding the corner of Calle de la Malvasia, I stopped abruptly. *It's no use.* What good would it do to hold my head high and confront the enemy? Yet I needed this confrontation.

I forced myself to go on until I reached the iron portal of the dilapidated ochre-colored house around the corner. Pushing against the heavy door, I stepped into the foyer. There was no elevator. Slowly, breathing heavily, I climbed the three flights to the apartment, then waited for my heartbeats to subside. No sound could be squeezed from that rusty bell. My rap at the door remained unanswered. I knocked again; no response. Almost relieved, I started to go down. At the rattling of a chain, I ran back up to the landing.

"Who's there?" The question was hostile.

"Clara, is that you?"

My low-key woman's voice did the trick. Her curiosity was aroused. She opened a sliver of the door.

"May I come in?" I said, before the shock of recognition had registered.

Without waiting for her answer, I stepped into the dim light of the vestibule. Clara's pasty complexion couldn't turn any paler. She gasped at the apparition that had come back from the grave to haunt her.

"Yes, I'm alive. You didn't expect to see me again, did you?" She stared at me in shock.

"I've been back in Venice for some time. Berto and Mario told me what happened to you."

Clara said nothing. She did not move.

"I know you wanted me dead." My knees gave. I had to brace myself against the jamb of the door.

"I never..." She lowered her eyes. Getting a hold on myself, I stood up straight and took in her sallow face. My antagonist. How pitiful she looked in her old paisley dress.

"I'm here to find out why you did it."

"Did what?" Her breathing was heavy, constrained.

I felt like a hunter in pursuit of prey. "Have me deported. For five thousand lire. Why? What did I ever do to you?"

She covered her face with both hands. "I don't know what came over me." She burst into tears. "My mother needed so much care; we were desperately poor. I had nothing against you,

Tatyana, honestly."

"So the five thousand lire must have been a tremendous help."

"Mother died three weeks after you left."

"I see. And after she died what excuse do you have for denouncing more people?"

I wanted to pull her hands from her face and make her look at me. Growing more irritated by her silence, I tried to elicit a response by throwing words at her, words that felt like earth and stones.

"It wasn't that miserable sum of money they paid you for every innocent person. And it wasn't because of your mother. You weren't even a fascist. Perhaps you were jealous of me. But that wouldn't make anyone go to such extremes. If we can't find a reason for such despicable acts, there isn't much hope for the world, is there?"

She said nothing.

"Is there? Speak to me!" I put my hands on her shoulders and shook her. "You aren't any better than the fiends who murdered millions of innocent people! Some of them were obeying orders. But you did it of your own free will. No remorse, Clara? Do you have no shame?"

"Oh, Tatyana, I'm so sorry! If only you knew how I've paid for what I've done! Forgive, please forgive me."

I was stunned. It was my turn to remain silent.

All at once she squatted down in front of me, pulling frantically at the hem of my coat, imploring me once more to forgive her.

"Don't. Let go."

But she kept tugging at my coat, meekly asking for absolution. I tore myself free and ran out.

20.

TATYANA

Something must be wrong with me

Written after my departure from Venice

I dashed through a narrow lane after leaving Clara, feeling the frenzied beats of my heart and sweat running down my back. A coughing fit made me bend over in pain. I stopped for breath and leaned against a wall. Small hammers beat in my temples. My cheeks were burning. I waited for the attack to subside. Moving along the cobblestones like an old woman, I wondered what foolish obsession had forced me to look up that wretched creature. Why did I go there, and what had I expected to find?

It was half past four. I needed to be alone, to think, to calm down. It was best to wait for Francesco in the Café Florian on Piazza San Marco. I sat down in the corner of a window seat in the almost empty café and ordered hot lemonade. As usual, people were feeding pigeons in the center of the *piazza*. The last time I had been here with Francesco, we had witnessed the arrest of that man feeding pigeons. On that dismal afternoon, Francesco had asked me to marry him. Now he might ask me once more. I still wasn't ready to answer. We were liberated. People were no longer arrested for feeding pigeons or being born. Life could go uphill once again for those who had the legs and the breath to climb.

Closing my eyes, I thought of Bogdan. Bitterness still held me captive. Warming my hands on the steaming glass of lemonade the waiter had brought me, I realized that by confronting Clara, I had buried her, along with Bogdan. This reminded me of the shame I felt for those guards in the camp, when forced to witness their brutality. They had thrown off any sense of humanity. If I had ever been able to forgive Bogdan or Clara, Bogdan would still have died unredeemed and Clara would never be able to forgive herself.

I could still feel her tugging at my coat. Was it possible that the thought of her regret could tug at my heart?

***

Francesco was just making his way through the crowd that had gathered in the café. I stood up to wave at him.

"At last!" He held me in a tight embrace. Sitting down beside me, he was unable to conceal his low spirits. I knew he suffered the frustrations of a captive. Thanks to the constant surveillance of his family, he could not establish a closer relationship with me. Though we were both trapped in that oppressive palazzo, I welcomed the circumstances that kept us apart. I was still in limbo and felt pressured by Francesco's unwavering courtship. My emotional recovery would even take longer than any relapse of my TB. No doubt Francesco was hoping that everything would fall into place as soon as I got well. He waved at a waiter and ordered an espresso.

I was still shaken by my encounter with Clara and told him about our confrontation. He waited anxiously for me to say more.

"She was the one who denounced me to the Gestapo."

"Oh, my God! It must have been an ordeal to face her."

"It was good that I did. It helps me understand that I need to face a number of things."

"Such as?"

"I can't go on accepting your family's hospitality. When I called you from Trieste, I just wanted you to know I was alive. I never expected you to take me into your home, but meant to get in touch with an American organization to find shelter. I was too weak to protest and stand up for myself."

"Tatyana, don't you remember that we sat at this very table when I proposed to you? It seems like yesterday. You said you weren't ready. I hope this is the ideal moment to give me your answer. Please don't protest before you hear what I have to say."

He paused for a moment. "I have decided to move, to find a new home for us—if you will marry me. There won't be any more problems in our way. What do you think?"

"I deeply appreciate your offer and what you have done for me," I said. "But I can't marry you."

"Because of your illness? I've waited so long. I can wait a little longer."

"You are so good to me, Francesco. But I must be honest with you. I can't…because I'm not in love with you."

He stared at me in such horror that I regretted not having used my illness as an excuse. Yet I was relieved that the truth was out. No more subterfuges. After a silence, he murmured that he admired my honesty and would never stop loving me.

I was about to thank him for his patience when I was overcome by a coughing fit. Hadn't the doctor said only two days before that I was on the road to recovery? My head was on fire. Francesco watched me in helpless concern. "We'd better go home and put you to bed. Just do me one favor. Promise to stay with us till you get well."

"How can I accept, under the circumstances? Please try to understand my pride. There's a saying that *pride goeth before the fall*. In my case, the fall came before the pride."

Something must be wrong with me, I kept thinking in the *vaporetto*, in spite of my rising fever. Any other woman would jump at the prospect of marrying a man of Francesco's caliber. Such a union ought to restore my balance, give me a new lease on life. Francesco had many desirable qualities. I could find no reason for rejecting him, except for my own lack of excitement.

His incapacity of asserting himself at home was disturbing to me, but I might be the one causing it. My presence disrupted the family's routine, stirring the stagnant canals of their lives. *Dear God,* I prayed, *don't let me relapse into my treacherous illness…*

Could it be that the thought of Victor was holding me back? How could he still be alive? Was it sheer madness to love him forever, beyond the grave?

It was. But I did.

Tossing in fever that night, I thought about my encounter with Clara. I sat up in bed in semi-slumber, listening to a voice that said, *Vengeance is a reversal of roles. It closes the door to the future.* By the time I came down for breakfast the next morning, Francesco and Sandra had left. Their mother was about to go out. She apologized for leaving me alone, but Francesco would soon be back. He seemed quite concerned about me. As usual, I told her not to worry.

Tomorrow Dora meant to pick me up and take me to the Lido. I had looked forward to our visit as a lifeboat. Opening my heart to her might help me clarify my confusing emotions.

Perhaps my fever was no more than a nasty cold. I would buy some aspirin, go back to bed, then come down for lunch.

Walking to the pharmacy was a struggle against the chill wind. I knew I must do all I could to get better, in order to earn my future keep. Wind and misery brought tears to my eyes. In the pharmacy, a couple of women waited ahead of me. I looked out the window, watching the people hurrying by.

Two men stopped in front of the store, talking animatedly. Their coats showed elegance particular to the upper class. Their hats were pulled over their eyes. With a shock I recognized Francesco. His mouth was moving and his gesturing hands accompanied words I couldn't hear. What made me feel that I was looking at a stranger? No one could have been more kind to me. Was I hard-hearted because of my inability to love him?

The two women were gone. Suddenly chilled, I clenched my teeth. "What will it be, *Signorina?*" I looked at the pharmacist, trying to remember what I had come to get. "But you are ill!"

"I just need some aspirin."

He hurried through a back door and returned with a glass of water. "Here, take these." He handed me two pills. I swallowed them, drank some water and took the small bottle he pushed into my hand. "Never mind," he said as I attempted to pay him. "Let me call a doctor."

"No, thank you, I'll manage; I must have caught a cold...live just down the street."

"Let me take you home." His worried round face bent over me. I felt his supporting hand on my elbow as I stumbled through the door. *This is my Italy,* I thought gratefully. *This is my kind of Italian.*

He hung a sign on the door that read: *Will be back in ten minutes.* He locked the door, took my arm, and slowly walked me down the cobblestones. We stopped in front of the house.

"I'm feeling much better," I said, taking the key from my purse. "Must be the aspirin. I don't know how to thank you."

Somehow I managed to climb the stairs to the attic room, where I fell on the bed. I don't know if I was raving in fever when the shadows bent over me—shadows of the Da Veronas, of Dora and Giuseppe. Was this Saturday morning? Had they come to take me to the Lido? And poor Francesco. Had I said *I can't marry you, you are a stranger and I'm sick*? Or had I dreamt the words, dreamt the shadows?

A man in a white coat said, "Sanatorium, as soon as possible."

Francesco sat by my bed. He took my hand, forcing a smile as he said, "Thank God, Tatyana, you are back. I was afraid I'd lost you."

"Francesco, you must let go of me and forget me. I bring you nothing but grief."

Had I said those words, or were they part of the blurred images rising and falling, then lifting like fog from my mind?

"Listen. I'll take you to a sanatorium near Sondrio. It's in the Alps, close to Switzerland, the very best. You'll get well there in no time, and then you go wherever you like."

"No, Francesco," I cried, "I can't accept. You have done so much for me already. Please call the Red Cross or the American Jewish Committee. They will take care of me."

He ignored my plea. He must provide me with the best care, he said, or he would be unable to live with himself, insisting that he wasn't doing this for me but for his own peace of mind.

21.

REAL BREAD
AND THE BREAD OF LIFE

Dismissed from Zing-Ata, Victor walked through the countryside in a daze. In mourning for the loss of his friend and unable to comfort the man's grief-stricken family, he could hardly think about his pressing need to apply for work. He was about to walk past a collective farm when he saw a young fellow repairing a fence. Victor asked the way to the director's office. The man pointed at a nearby bungalow.

A moment later, Victor surprised an old man sipping vodka from a half-empty bottle at his desk. The floor was scattered with debris and filthy papers, cigarette stubs and apple cores.

"What can I do for you?" the director asked in Russian, sounding surprisingly sober. Victor introduced himself, explaining that he was looking for some temporary work while recovering from a recent illness.

"Then you're still sick."

"Not really. I'm getting better every day. "

Instead of being chased away with curses, the director told him he was in luck.

"I'm looking for a guard to watch over a field of turnips," he explained. "Only two peasants are allowed to harvest them in the fall as fodder for the animals. You have to make sure no one steals them. You'll be paid for twelve hours' work, but need to keep watch around the clock."

"Suits me fine," Victor said. He followed the director to a nearby field, where he was to gather some brushwood and build himself a lean-to against an old mulberry tree.

"Make yourself at home," the Russian said.

Grateful for the man's friendly reception, the mild summer weather, and the easy assignment, Victor took to his shelter with the appreciation of a homeowner. An hour later, the director sent him a blanket for the night, a pot and pan to cook his meals over a fire, along with a cutting knife, two plates and cups, and a few more utensils.

Victor could hardly believe his good fortune. The job turned out to be more lucrative than he had expected. The field descended from a road in close proximity to the village district center for food and various goods, which were brought daily to the state farm from a nearby mining town. Each morning, as soon as the driver's appearance was announced by a neighing horse and a cloud of dust, Victor ran to the vending stall. Being the first to arrive, he kept away impatient buyers, while the merchandise was unloaded. This earned him the driver's friendship and some free bread, sugar, fat, and kindling wood. He stored his treasures in the branches of his tree, adding his own modest purchases and making sure no man or animal could reach them. He meant to barter whatever he could spare.

The warm summer air, the rest and simple food, the comfort of his blanket and the general peace surrounding him—all contributed to the improvement of his health. He considered the sanatorium of his mulberry tree the perfect place for his convalescence.

One night he was kept awake by a crying baby. Although there was no sign of human habitation in his neighborhood, he rose to follow the sound. Walking through the field, he caught sight of a family of hyenas in the full moonlight. He picked up a stick to chase them away, but the animals merely stared at him. Nor did they budge when he threw stones at them. At last, he frightened them away with loud shouts.

Shortly after sunset, three wolfdogs began appearing in the vicinity of his tree, attracted by the goods on its branches. They kept him awake, barking at the moon, wailing at the wide-open spaces. Victor was touched by their plight, which reminded him of his own. He wasn't afraid of the animals, but regretted not having enough food to spare. Every now and then, he left tidbits at a small distance from the tree, adding a few turnips. The animals would devour them quickly, then sit quietly and wait for more. Victor talked to them in German, apologizing for being so poor, for not having enough to eat for himself, and the wolf dogs listened to his voice with pointed ears. Later, as they wailed at the moon, he felt that they howled for him too.

One morning, he asked the truck driver if he had anything to spare for the dogs.

"What dogs?"

"There are three of them," Victor said. "They come to my tree every night."

"Do they look like wolves?"

"Yes. They're wolf dogs."

"You are crazy. Those are wolves! And you want to feed them?"

"They're very gentle."

The driver tapped his forehead, indicating that Victor was quite mad. "Not me. I throw no good food to the wolves."

That evening, Victor observed his friends more closely, and saw that the driver was right. He remained unperturbed. Knowing they were wolves changed nothing about his sense of kinship. He was amazed at himself. As a child, he had run to his mother in dread of the tiniest dog, the faintest bark.

I must be turning into another Saint Francis, he mocked himself. *Next I'll be giving sermons to the wolves. Saint Victor of Tashkent…*

What had caused him to turn fear into love? As he lay on his canvas at night and gazed at the stars above the latticework of his wooden tent, he knew that the change was part of some new inner peace.

How had this happened? He turned it over in his mind, unable to find an answer. Surrounded by hungry wolves, he leaned against the trunk of the mulberry tree and watched clouds drifting across a waning moon. He still remembered the Evangelist's prayer he was to repeat in his delirium. One night it came to him: with the clarity of his faith, the Evangelist had transmitted the serenity of his generous heart to his adopted son. In spite of his concern for his family, he had parted from the world with unquestioning acceptance.

"It doesn't matter why you are here," he had said, knowing that

Victor had come to his hut for warmth and bread--"as long as you find anything to give you sustenance."

Sustenance! Real bread and the bread of life. Victor was able to look at his loneliness and suffering with new eyes. Having partaken of the sustenance, he felt free to think of Tatyana, yearning to find her again at any price.

***

Harvest time meant the end of being a lifeguard for the turnips. Fall was in the air. As it grew colder each night, Victor did not mind leaving his solitary outpost in search of warmer grazing grounds. The director released him from his duties and sent him to a colleague at a nearby sheep and cattle farm. Thanks to his recommendation, the new foreman was open to hire him, but scrutinized him with hostile eyes, asking about Victor's experience with cattle. Victor confirmed his skill without much conviction.

"You don't look right for that work. You must be one of those *no-goodniks* of the *Intelligentsia*."

So that was it! The man was trying to mortify a *nogoodnik* by assigning him the most humble task.

"I've been in many trades," Victor said. "I can always learn a new one."

"You will take the cattle to pasture."

This was the last thing he had in mind. Assigned to sleep on a cot in the windowless cubicle of a peasant hut, he had to get up before dawn. A peasant took him to the corral and introduced him to a number of cows, oxen, and sheep. Before taking the animals out to pasture, he was to count their heads. Counting and recounting, he came up with different results each time, which reminded him of the prison guards who had been unable to add up the heads of convicts.

The peasant shouted at him to hurry up, then left him to his own devices. The animals flowed out one by one in a chorus of mooing and bleating. Victor followed them to the grassland, where they scattered in all directions. What was he to do? There was no one in sight. He ran after some cows, calling and coaxing. Sensing the inexperience of their new herdsman, the cows mooed with disdain and indifference.

The exasperated herdsman sat down helplessly in the grass. On sighting a cow about to fall into the creek at the meadow's border, he jumped up in panic and rushed to her side. Too late. The poor creature was lying on her back, ready to drown, legs thrashing about and head under water. Victor stepped into the creek and barely managed to lift her head. She snorted wildly, flailing and catching her breath. Drenched to the waist, he felt the water's sting like melting ice against his thighs and back. He heard sounds of men digging behind the bushes in an ad-joining field and called for help, still cradling the cow's head in his arms.

At last, a couple of farmers appeared with a rope. After repeated efforts, they pulled the animal to its feet. Embarrassed, Victor tried to express gratitude and regret, but was rebuffed with shouts and invectives as the men gathered the scattered herd. Why was their coaxing so much more effective than his? He shivered with cold; his drenched clothes clung to his body. He was running after a stubborn ox when two small boys emerged from nowhere and chased the animal back into the fold.

The farmers called out to the boys and told them something Victor did not understand. The men pointed at him, and the boys burst out laughing. The farmers returned to their field and the boys watched the herd. *They must be brothers*, Victor thought. Their close-set eyes and swarthy looks were almost identical. To judge by their coal-dusted faces, they might have come out of a mine. Neither of them spoke Russian.

After a while, Victor sat down in the meadow beside them. He took off his pants in the warm midday sun, wrung them out, and spread them on the grass to dry. Laughing at the sight of his ragged long underwear, the boys wouldn't stop until he pulled out his wet recorder and began to blow a tune. To his relief, the instrument wasn't damaged. The boys drew in their breaths and listened, spellbound. As soon as he stopped, the elder pulled the recorder out of his hands and blew on it forcefully. Unable to get any sound from it, he tried again and again, until Victor showed him how to cover the holes with the tips of his fingers and blow. The boy beamed in delight at his own first notes. His brother waited for his turn, produced a few feeble sounds, and gave the instrument back.

Now Victor was no longer a laughingstock. The boys had learned that a foolish herdsman could be good at a skill beyond their grasp. They strutted through the meadow after his long legs. Victor briskly played the recorder, and they danced to his tunes while they kept an eye on the herd. Ears pricked, the animals stood still, ruminating in rhythm with the music.

Later, Victor took out some of the last bread and cheese he had plucked from his mulberry tree. The boys shared the food and communicated with gestures, song, and laughter. In the late afternoon, just when Victor had pulled on his stiff, dry pants, three more boys appeared in the meadow. Victor played song after song with the five boys trailing behind in single file. He swayed ahead of them, singing in broken Russian, "I'm the Pied Piper of Tashkent, yes, dear comrades, your very own Pied Piper." The boys hummed along exuberantly out of tune. At sunset, they gathered the herd and drove it back to the corral. Victor counted sheep, cows, and oxen again, now assisted by his young cronies. They came up with different results as each drew a number in the air, and then tried many times more until they reached an agreement. "Tomorrow…" Victor inclined his head and raised six fingers to tell his companions that he expected them at that time in the morning. They smiled, repeated his gestures, and nodded.

There was no sign of the boys in the morning.

"I could use a dog," Victor said to the foreman. The man went into a shed and returned with a small mongrel. Victor managed to get the herd safely out to pasture. The dog kept everything under control as he ran and barked furiously.

By midafternoon, Victor lost hope of seeing the boys again. Disappointed and bored, he lay down in the meadow and fell asleep. He dreamt about a number of cows sitting on top of a fence, complaining in Russian about the shortage of bread and love. Stifled by their warm, heavy bodies that smelled of meat and milk, he looked for an opening in the fence that would let him slip through, unseen. Finding no gap, he hoisted himself onto a cow's back and dropped to the ground on the other side. Unlike the ox that morning, he flew over pastures and fields, farther and farther away from the barking mongrel at his heels.

As he opened his eyes, the sun was setting behind a chain of clouds. How had he survived all these years? He saw himself as a nameless man walking beside him as a shadow. He looked back at Russia as though he had left it behind: the eighteen months he had spent in Lvov, the endless time in the gulag by the river; in Bukhara, Tashkent, in the hospital, in prison, Zing-Ata. He followed scene after scene like a film in slow motion. The war had finally ended and it was time to move on. He could never belong to this country, but had no idea of how he could belong anywhere else. Was he destined to remain on this treadmill of chance events?

Remembering the Evangelist who had brought about his amazing recovery, he thought, *No, a thousand times no!*

22.

MEETING DASHA AND THE WANDERING JEW

Taking his dream for an omen, Victor jumped over the fence and fled from the farm after dark. For a while he followed a country road leading back in the direction of Tashkent. As soon as it grew dark, he went to sleep in a ditch, vowing no dog would ever chase him back into the corral.

At dawn, bright sunlight brought him to his feet. He found himself in front of rundown bungalows at the outskirts of the city, and he waited a while before knocking on doors and introducing himself as a craftsman prepared to do any work in return for food. After several fruitless attempts, a Russian woman showed him the broken ceiling of her parlor and provided him with a ladder and some rusty tools. He climbed the ladder and began to hammer at bulges, straightening and smoothing the surface, adding some fresh plaster she found in her shed. The ceiling needed painting, and the woman provided him with just enough paint to finish the work. He slept in a cubicle of a small barn and was awakened by the tongue of a cow licking the sole of his foot.

The woman invited him to share her meals. Her name was Dasha. Still youthful and attractive in her middle age, there was something touching in her sad smile and intelligent eyes. Victor learned that her husband and son had been killed in the battle of Stalingrad. She had taught school in Tashkent, but now took care of two grandchildren while her widowed daughter worked in the fields. Would Victor like to stay, she asked unexpectedly, perhaps marry the young woman and be a father to those poor children?

Victor was nonplussed. He had not met her daughter. She ate in a canteen and came home late at night. From the top of the ladder, he had once seen the children run through the room.

"I'm afraid that's not possible. I'm trying to return to the West as soon as I can. But I thank you for your trust."

"I understand. You need to go home. Though you are a stranger, you are one of us."

"That's kind of you to say. I've been an outsider for the longest time. Even back in the West, I may still feel in exile with a bit of longing for Mother Russia."

"I wonder why?" Dasha said.

"I'm not sure. Possibly because of its open spaces you call *prostor…*"

"I suppose you don't have such open spaces, our kind I mean, in the West?"

"It's a feeling you can't put into words," Victor said.

"That's true. But in spite of those spaces, our people are fated to suffer. You may have found much cruelty and confinement, but also much caring."

"You're right, Dasha. My people are suffering too. If it's any consolation, it may help us overcome prejudice and understand each other. Someday, I hope, things will get better—for all of us."

She shook her head. "Not now, not for a long time. There's too much fear and suspicion. But even if it takes fifty or a hundred years, there'll always be Mother Russia."

"Yes, your earth seems to absorb it all. This country will always haunt me. But I'm Jewish, and my people have no earth. We are homeless children, scattered all over. We share your wide open spaces, but our *prostor* is a landscape inside us, which may reach across the entire planet."

The woman gave him a strange look. "A Jew?" Perhaps she was trying to match what she had heard about Jews with the man facing her across the table. "I've been told that the Jews have the devil in them."

"The Jews? What about everyone else? You must have been told the opposite of your *prostor*."

"I don't understand."

"I mean, it doesn't go with your wide open spaces to judge people you don't know."

She lowered her eyes. "You are right."

"I like women." He looked at her warmly.

"What makes you say that?"

"Because you connect so quickly. Because you think with your hearts."

She blushed. "Perhaps suffering brings out the best or the worst in us."

"You remind me of a young Jewish girl I knew in Bukhara. That's the sort of thing she might have said."

"Do you know what happened to her?"

Victor shook his head. "She was surrounded by a loving family."

"And you had to leave. Couldn't settle down. Is that it?"

"Only part of it."

"Men. You always need to go on."

"Not always."

***

The ceiling had magically improved its appearance. On the third day, Victor took his leave from Dasha. She gave him some money for his labors and a chunk of bread with two sausages for the road.

"I hope you can go back home soon and have a good life," she said somewhat formally.

"And I wish you the best as well. We'll have to work hard to rebuild what we lost."

"Oh, that." She dismissed his words with a gesture. "In fifty years, perhaps…" She turned her head away. "Go now, go with God."

"Or the devil?" he quipped, immediately regretting those words. It was the wrong thing to say at their moment of parting.

He kept thinking of her as he looked for a bazaar, then stopped near a market, sat on a rock, and watched farmers unload their wares. A tall old man with a mane of silver hair stopped beside him. Setting down the sack he carried on his shoulders, he addressed Victor in Russian, asking if he was looking for work. Bright red lips shone like berries through the thicket of his full white beard.

Victor nodded. He noticed one blue glass eye, while the other, equally blue, sized him up with a mixture of kindness and cunning.

"Then come with me. I can use some help."

Victor leapt from his perch. "What kind of help?"

"Speak German?"

"Not much. But I understand."

"Want to go home…back to the *Reich*?"

"There's no going back. Only forward. To America."

"To America, no less! Then you must be a Wandering Jew, like me. Have a visa?"

"Not yet."

They left the marketplace and were heading for a canteen. If one didn't belong to some working place, his companion informed him, one might starve.

"Young man, what are you waiting for? Join the Poles. Get out of here! What about the Promised Land? Does that interest you?"

"It does, but…"

"Looking for some lost sweetheart, is that it? Stick with me." Victor remained silent. "You'll find a group in Tashkent that will take you along. In a while…ah, if only I were young, I'd join you."

"You still can. Why don't you?"

"My wife is dead. Three sons killed in the war. My future lies behind me."

Like Dasha's, Victor thought. *The suffering Russian Jew, despised by the suffering Russian.* "But you are still strong," he said. "Why not give it a try? Perhaps we can help each other."

The old man stopped and looked at him. "You really mean that, I can tell. My sons, blessed be their souls, would've left without me. 'You're too old,' they would have said, 'too weak to start again.'"

A guard stood at the door of the canteen. He grinned at the old man, who was pulling a few newspapers from his sack, and handed them to him.

"My assistant." The old man pointed at Victor.

"That's all right, *Ata* Jacob."

They entered the canteen. Father Jacob gave two newspapers to a big blond waitress. In exchange, she dished out two cups of bean soup and two slices of bread. It was hardly possible to get a meal without ration marks. After leaving the camp, Victor had found himself with only a few food stamps in his pocket, but thanks to the guard and the waitress's craving for makhorka, the old man was able to barter food for his newspapers.

"Would you like to go into business with me?" he asked, chewing his bread.

The rounding of a circle. *Ata* Benjamin, Rachel, and now Father Jacob. He had mentioned three sons. Was there a daughter?

"I thought you wanted me to get out of here," Victor said.

"Exactly. You make a living with me, you save some money, you pay your way out. Plan ahead, I told my sons, always plan ahead."

"A good point. What do you want me to do?"

"In the morning, we go to the station. People carry heavy sacks with agricultural products. We help them with the transport to Tashkent. In Tashkent, we make contacts for them to barter their goods for other goods they need to take back."

Victor nodded: "In other words, the black market."

"How else do you think people will survive?" *Ata* Jacob's good eye pierced through Victor like a sharp stem of makhorka through its newspaper wrapping.

"Anyway, in Tashkent you'll look for the big-bosomed women in the marketplace." Relishing Victor's astonishment, Jacob went on: "Well, they are big-bosomed to begin with, but they balloon." He demonstrated how with an all-embracing gesture, "with newspapers stuffed under their pretty blouses or shawls. Lucky newspapers!"

Victor followed in the old man's tracks. He helped him transport sacks of goods for the farmers to Tashkent, watching Jacob barter with the women in the marketplace. Thanks to years of shortage, news in print no longer existed, but the women had secretly collected bundles of old papers, which were much in demand for rolling cigarettes and kindling fires. They charged a few rubles for a bundle. Laughing at the old man's blunt jokes while unobtrusively filling his sack with the old papers, the women would top them with a loaf of bread. The Wandering Jew returned to the small town each afternoon, then sold those papers, or exchanged them for mush or soup.

It didn't take long for him to see that Victor wasn't cut out for haggling and bartering. They slept on the floor of a teahouse where the young man was kept awake by the old man's snoring.

On the fourth day, Victor was left on his own. *Ata* Jacob decided to look for more lucrative pastures. He promised to meet Victor in the evening for a meal at the canteen.

Victor waited for him in vain.

Lost without his companion, he concluded that it was easier to watch a herd of cows. One woman gave him three old newspapers for the price of two, adding loving looks and apples to the piece of bread she placed on top of his sack. Another one drew Victor to her stuffed bosom when no one was looking and filled his ear with sweet Uzbek words he didn't understand.

23.

TATYANA

Shipwrecked

Fall 1947

I don't know how I lived through the months that followed. Francesco drove me to this luxurious sanatorium, making sure I was well looked after. In my apathy, I was hardly aware of his doleful leave-taking. Transported into an enchanting landscape between Bergamo and the Rhaetian Alps, close to Bellinzona and the Swiss-Italian mountains, the memory of my new residence is blurred by doctors' visits, injections, and daily routines. I wasn't able to absorb much of my elegant surroundings.

Months passed. When Francesco came to see me a few weeks ago, I tried to comfort him about my poor condition. Instead of cheering me, his visit made matters worse. He promised to be back soon, wrote me awkward letters, and didn't understand that his devotion hit me like a reproach. I told him it might be better not to come, for it would cause him nothing but pain. To my surprise, he agreed. His letters turned into short notes. I lost track of time.

Then Sandra arrived unexpectedly. We had tea on my balcony. She said Francesco had fallen into a deep depression. He found no consolation in meeting a charming young woman. She asked me to release him, for the sake of his health, perhaps his life.

"But I did release him," I said. He obviously hadn't told her about his proposal and my rejection.

"My dear Tatyana, I can't tell you how much I appreciate your understanding." She paused. "Please don't mention my visit in your next letter."

"Don't worry. I'm sorry for all the trouble I caused Francesco and your family."

"You mustn't say that. We loved you."

"*Loved* me? You must be happy that it's all in the past."

"I didn't mean it that way."

"Yes, Sandra, you did. You have resented me ever since you found out that Francesco bought me those pretty shoes."

"That's not true! I have always felt a special love for the Israelite people. When you came to our house…you don't know how I wept for you that night!"

The word *Israelite* grated on my ear. But then I remembered why decent Italians used it out of respect, in reaction to our degradation. The sincerity of her tone made me regret my cutting remark.

"I'm sorry, Sandra. I don't mean to seem critical. You were all more than good to me. But it's hard to be the object of charity. I haven't learned to accept it gracefully."

She reached for my hand and held it. "I can see why Francesco loves you so much."

I offered her more tea and cake. She declined.

"I'll write him that the Red Cross is going to take care of me and ask him not to come back, since I'll be leaving in a short time."

She shook her head, wiping a tear from her cheek. "But Francesco wants to take care of you! At least until you can stand on your feet…"

"I'm standing on them right now. You must stop worrying about me."

"How can I help it?" She burst into sobs.

"Oh, Sandra, what a waste! We could have been friends all along. Real friends, I mean."

She got up to embrace me, averting her face. "I cared for you from the moment I saw you," she whispered, "and couldn't get over your terrible ordeal."

Her reticence was nothing but fear for her brother's sanity, she explained. He kept saying he was the cause of my tragedy and could never forgive himself for encouraging me to leave my safe job as a nanny. I promised her again to free him from his vow to save me.

"Thank you, my dear Tatyana. Francesco told me about your losses. You went through so much and are incredibly brave. Are you sure about the Red Cross?"

"Quite sure," I said.

***

In my letter to Francesco, I expressed my gratitude for all his caring and generosity. I would never forget what a wonderful friend he had been. There was no reason to blame himself for my deportation, since I had welcomed the opportunity of working in that office and had enjoyed the freedom it offered. I never stopped blaming myself for neglecting my safety, for failing to listen to Dora's advice and remain hidden on the Lido. I begged him to forgive and forget me. It was time to think of his own well-being. I felt confident that he would soon recover from the heartache I never meant to inflict and would find the happiness he deserved.

Posting the letter, I realized I was sending away the key to the last door connecting me to the world. I was too weak to move forward. Instead of feeling freed from a burden, I was more alone than ever, left without a tool to build a new life. Sleepless, I tried to comfort myself, as I had in the camp, by recalling the happy days of my childhood, but the tragedy of my family had turned those memories into lifeless matter. Traveling past violence and destruction through a wasteland of fever and loss, I felt that neither courage nor any superhuman effort was going to help me.

I withdrew from the world, expecting nature to finish what the Germans had meant to conclude. That night I sank lower and lower. The air thickened around me. I could hardly breathe. Closing my eyes, I gazed at an isolated universe within. Then I heard a voice, whispering: *"Have you forgotten our promise? What happened to your remarkable courage?"*

"What courage?" I cried, abruptly sitting up in bed, weeping.

***

Woods and meadows spread like a tranquil sea beneath my fourth-floor balcony when I opened its shuttered doors the next morning. The breathtaking view of valley and mountains in the bright morning sun did little to dispel the darkness inside me. I stepped out on the balcony and looked down. A fall would kill me on the spot. I recalled the night I had prevented Svetlana from touching the electric fence. Now I was ready to end my own life. I could imagine her looking at me reproachfully. "Tatyana, you fool," I heard her say, "are you forgetting what you told me? Now that we are free…"

Free? After Auschwitz, how can anyone ever feel free? Yet my horror at violence against any human being, including myself, made me quickly step back into my room. To this day, I haven't been able to get in touch with Svetlana. Perhaps she has settled in Belgrade or left for the United States. The prospect that we may never find each other again is now added to my misery.

***

The bell was ringing for breakfast, but I was in no mood to eat or face any fellow humans. After a while, a nurse came up to see if anything was wrong. I told her I had overslept and would come down later for lunch. As soon as she left, I packed my few belongings. It was best to leave after dark. I would go out by the back door and take a gentle walk through the woods until I collapsed. Dying along the way would be a gentle act of leave-taking—far better than a violent drop from my balcony.

Svetlana would have understood. At least I had been given a chance to support her in her most desperate moments. I hid my small suitcase in the closet, went back to bed, and fell asleep.

"Be down in a minute!" I called out groggily in response to a knock at my door. Unable to open my eyes, I was startled by a second knock. A maid came in to announce that a gentleman was here to see me.

I opened my eyes in panic. "What gentleman?"

"*Un signore molto simpatico.* A tall stranger, very friendly…speaks Italian with a funny accent."

I gasped. It couldn't be…how would Victor know I was here? I turned to the girl. "Tell him I'll be right down."

"But he's waiting behind the door, *Signorina!* Very anxious to see you."

I jumped out of bed, ran my fingers through my hair, and threw on a robe. "Please show him in." Breathing deeply, I tried to slow down the wild beats of my heart.

The clean-shaven Stefan Samuelson hardly reminded me of the young, bearded partisan Stefan Skalovski. I recognized the warm glimmer in his eyes. His presence lit up my room, and the life I had renounced. He drew me into his arms.

And then we wept.

***

Svetlana sent him to me. I could hardly believe she had saved me, in turn, from running against some invisible charged barbed wire.

"I ought to have taken you along on my way to England, instead of sending you to Venice," he said, "even though my journey proved to be extremely dangerous. It was impossible to contact you from London through ordinary channels."

At my request, we were served lunch on the balcony. I'm still trying to recall what he told me about his experiences during our long separation. A few weeks after his arrival in England, Stefan had joined an American team. During the fiercest period of the war, he was sent from London to German-occupied Rome. His task consisted of screening partisans for the Italian commandos. This meant taking great risks, for fascists constantly infiltrated their ranks. I remembered Stefan's uncommon intuition. One small misjudgment would have been enough to jeopardize his life.

He made that mistake when a particular partisan was to be sent on a special mission. Something about the man, the tone of his voice, the way he smiled or avoided looking into his eyes, reminded Stefan of Bogdan. Since everyone had relied on the partisan's perfect credentials, he ignored his misgivings.

Three days later, Stefan was arrested and about to be executed, but a partisan friend on the outside succeeded in bribing a guard, who helped him escape.

From a letter Svetlana sent me a few days after Stefan's appearance at the sanatorium, I learned that he had been presented with the Medal of

Honor from the Allies for heroic service and was given American citizenship at his request. Appointed assistant director for the American Jewish Committee in postwar Milan, he had never stopped searching for me. From police reports in Venice, he found my name among those arrested in 1944. Fearing my deportation, he looked up the lists of survivors from various camps but was unable to find me among them.

One month before our reunion, he went back to Yugoslavia. On his way to his home in Belgrade, he stopped in Zagreb, where he still remembered the location of our home. According to police records, all members of my family had vanished. Stefan lost hope of ever finding me again. Back in Belgrade, he learned how his own family had met with the same fate.

While helping displaced persons in Yugoslavia, he continued asking if anyone had seen me in one of the camps. Svetlana was among the survivors. Expecting the usual negative response, he was amazed to hear her describe our friendship and miraculous survival. After the liberation, we had been separated because of my critical illness. I had been taken to a different hospital in Trieste, while Svetlana was sent back to Belgrade, where she recovered from a high fever.

Before meeting Stefan, she thought she'd lost me for good. But I had told Svetlana about Francesco da Verona in the camp, and of my refusal to accept his first proposal. She had shaken her head at me for being such a romantic fool. Never mind my feelings, she would have married the man on the spot. What love could there be without life?

"Someday perhaps," she had remarked to Stefan, "Tatyana may marry some Francesco da Venezia in Verona..."

Having learned the name of my admirer, Stefan looked up his number in the Venetian telephone directory. Francesco's mother answered the call. Her son was ill, she said, but on hearing that the caller was a Yugoslavian friend of mine, she gave him my address, so Stefan drove here immediately, leaving word at his office about being called out of town on an emergency.

"I'm sorry to be in such a hurry," he said, "but I was dying to see you. Next time I'll make sure to come for a whole weekend."

We had finished our meal. A maid came in to remove the dishes, and we went back into my room.

"There almost wasn't a next time," I said.

He looked at me quickly. "What do you mean?"

"I had no energy left..."

"So I just arrived at a perfect moment." Stefan moved his chair close to mine, stroked my hair and kissed my cheek.

"Oh, Stefan. You and Svetlana were the last people left in my world. I was afraid I'd lost you both."

"It's even more amazing to find you alive." He took a deep breath. "You probably know that I was in love with you then—and still am."

"I was drawn to you, too, but couldn't..."

"Couldn't what?" Seeing me hesitate, he looked straight into my eyes. "I knew all along... that you were keeping some secret."

I was about to confide in him, I said, but feared he might judge me, or think of me as a childish dreamer.

"Tatyana, I would never judge you."

He bent over to hold me, and I responded with all the sorrow for my lost youth and the years of my unfulfilled dreams about Victor, who was most likely long dead. At last, I told Stefan of our brief encounter in Stuttgart.

"I have never mentioned him to anyone. The last time I heard about him was in a letter from my aunt about his mother's fatal heart attack and the family's deportation to Poland a few months before the Nazi invasion."

"So you are at the end of your rope, poor child." His voice was unsteady. "I know all your sorrows. Let's assume, at least, that shared sorrow is half a joy." He reached out to dry my eyes with a handkerchief. "Let me take you out of here to a convalescent home not far from Milano where I'm now working for the Allies. Or to some other, less fancy, but more pleasant sanatorium. What do you say?"

"I can't accept."

"This is no charity, Tatyana. It's your right and part of my job. You won't have to be grateful, or account to anyone. Just work on getting well."

"All right, I'll try."

"Do you still feel bitter about Bogdan?" he asked, stroking my hair.

"How can I help it? We both know he killed my father. In the end he betrayed all our comrades and then the Nazis killed him in turn."

"That's what I heard. I keep asking myself how we can deal with all that evil."

I told him about Clara's betrayal and our encounter, adding that I later sensed her sincere regret when she asked me to forgive her. "I could never forgive Bogdan, but perhaps Clara didn't realize what she was doing."

"Turning into a true Christian," Stefan said, smiling.

"I've been wondering if it isn't wiser to let go, for my own sanity. Without turning the other cheek. So we can look ahead and make a stop to these endless retaliations."

"I'm glad you've come to that conclusion. Because, historically, we are in the same boat."

"What do you mean?"

He explained to me that he was working on a plan for European recovery, which included Germany. "Especially Germany. If you were well, you could help me with your languages."

I remembered the packed suitcase in the closet and my decision to walk farther and farther away till I collapsed. "I might as well tell you," I said, trying to catch my breath. "After Auschwitz, the loss of my family, my illness, and the state of the world, I lost all hope. Just this morning I was ready to give up. If you had come tomorrow, you wouldn't have found me."

Taking my hands into his, Stefan spoke to me like a father: "Tatyana, you can't give up now. Not after what you faced in the camp. Svetlana told me how you comforted her after losing her boyfriend and her mother. You not only saved her life on several occasions, but you encouraged other women as much as you could. The few who survived will love you forever."

"It was nothing. My small chance to help gave me a reason for living. Now I'm wondering if I'll ever recover from this treacherous illness."

"Of course you will recover."

"I feel useless, no good to anyone."

Stefan shook his head. "That's Nazi talk. It's not for you to judge who's useless."

"You are right. Seeing you safe and well is giving me new hope."

"Svetlana will be so happy to hear that I found you."

"And I was afraid to have lost you both…"

"She has an aunt in Denver, Colorado who invited her to live with her. I hope she'll be able to join her as soon as possible."

Stefan embraced me on leaving and promised again to be back the following weekend.

24.

THE MIDWIFE

One early morning at the bazaar, a market woman was adding a few old newspapers to Victor's small purchase when a hand touched his shoulder. Turning around, he was confronted with a pudgy teddy bear of a man with round spectacles on his nose.

"Excuse me," the stranger whispered in a clear Russian, "I just wondered if you would sell me one of your papers?"

Victor looked at him in silence. Although he seemed friendly enough, he might be a secret police officer ready to arrest him for his daily acquisitions of old papers that he meant to sell later for twice the price. So many things were forbidden, and this might be one that could cause him to land in some other godforsaken camp.

"Do you speak Russian?" Victor nodded. "I have some makhorka and just need a page or two, to roll a few cigarettes."

Victor took out one of his papers and handed it to him.

"How much?"

"No charge."

"That's very kind of you. Let me offer you some tea. There's a *chaykhana* right around the corner where we can talk."

Perplexed, Victor paid the woman, who put a couple of plums into his hand. He thanked her with a warm smile. The stranger was waiting for him at a small distance, checking his watch.

They walked to the teahouse in silence. The Russian ordered a pot of black tea, then cut one page of his newspaper into several pieces with a pocketknife, dropped a small amount of tobacco on each, and rolled four cigarettes with nimble fingers.

"My wife is about to give birth," he said, lighting one cigarette for Victor and one for himself. "We have another little boy. There's no help around the house," he went on, blowing smoke through his nose. "You may not have noticed, but I have been watching you buying those newspapers on the market for the last two days. You don't seem to like what you're doing."

"Not particularly."

"Would you like to work for my family? Help with the chores, I mean, till the wife gets back her strength?"

"I would like that very much." Deeply relieved, Victor puffed a ring of smoke from pursed lips.

"The pay isn't much. I'm a poor tailor. But there'll be food and shelter. I have a good job at the factory sewing suits for local dignitaries. When I saw you, I thought…"

"I'll be happy to help out."

"Good, very good. But I must get back to work. Here's the address. We live in the old part of town." He wrote the name of the street and the house number in a corner of the newspaper. "By the way, my name is Igor Rokovsky." He shook Victor's hand. Before Victor could introduce himself, he rose and said, "My wife is at home—I told her I would talk to you. See you tonight."

***

As soon as Victor arrived at the small apartment building, a young boy opened the door. He craned his neck, looking up at the stranger.

"Is your mama home?" Victor asked.

"Mama! A man is here."

His mother, as tall as she was round, came out of the kitchen, drying hands on her apron. She was obviously in the last stage of pregnancy.

"Your husband asked me to work for you."

"Please come in. Then you agreed? I'm so glad!"

Victor nodded. He noticed her heavy breathing. The baby must be taking all the room inside her. He stood in the small hall, confused by this miraculous change of circumstance.

The boy pointed at the floor. "Sit down," he said. His face was a replica of his mother's.

Victor squatted beside him. "Is this better?"

"Now I'm big like you. What's your name?"

"Victor."

"Fantastic! I'm Viktor, too!"

"Then we are brothers."

The mother stood smiling as she watched. Her teeth were strong and healthy and her lovely pink cheeks reminded Victor of shining apples. Her black hair fell down her back in one thick braid. "He isn't used to tall men." She gestured toward her son. "My name is Sonja, Sonja Rokovsky."

"And I'm Viktor Rokovsky," the boy said proudly. "Viktor with a k. And you?"

"Victor Nameless. Victor with a c."

"That's not a name!"

"Viktor, don't be rude," his mother said.

"No, you are right," Victor turned to the boy. "I had another last name once, but lost it when I had to run away from my home."

"How did you lose it?"

"It must have dropped from my pocket."

"Mama...." The boy gave Sonja a worried look. "Will I lose my name too?"

"Don't worry." Victor tapped the boy's shoulder "You will always be a Rokovsky."

Viktor sighed with obvious relief.

"Please tell me what you want me to do?" Victor turned to Sonja, and she asked him timidly if he would take out the garbage and help her straighten their rooms.

"Of course. Viktor and I are strong men. We can do that in no time. Right, Viktor?"

The boy nodded eagerly. "I'm here," Victor went on, "because your dad told me your Mama needs to rest."

"Right, *Mamotchka*!" Viktor took his mother's hand and guided her to the bedroom. "You must lie down."

Sonja smiled. "You fellows are spoiling me!"

By the time the two Victors finished their chores, Sonja was back in the kitchen, ladling lamb, rice and cabbage onto three plates. Victor took bread, dates, and plums from his knapsack and put them into a bowl. They ate in silence. Victor reveled in every bite of the delicious home-cooked food.

"When is the baby due?" he asked, cleaning his plate with a piece of bread. The boy followed his example.

"In a week or two."

That's why her husband was anxious to find help, she explained, especially after the baby's birth. She was a bit worried because the hospital was at a good distance from their home, and there was no transportation. She hoped they would send an ambulance.

"You just concentrate on your baby. From now on, Viktor and I will take care of things. Right, Viktor?"

"Right!"

***

The two of them did all the chores around the house, which freed Sonja to weave baskets and help supplement the family's income. It was an art she had mastered and loved. Following her instructions, Victor learned to cook a few simple dishes. In rare moments of leisure, she taught him the fundamentals of her craft. In spite of her advanced pregnancy, she worked with a skill and speed he could hardly follow.

The 8-year-old boy never let Victor out of his sight. As soon as he came home from school, he was eager to accompany his friend to the farmers' market and help him choose vegetables and other products.

Victor showed his young namesake how to blow on his recorder and was amazed at how quickly he learned to play a clear tune. He took to the instrument with such enthusiasm that Victor gave him a daily lesson. In turn, Viktor read to him from a book in Cyrillic that Victor still had trouble deciphering.

On daily walks, the boy listened to fairytales his new friend remembered from his own childhood. Snow White was their favorite. They decided to be the seven little dwarves, surprising Sonja with unexpected tasks and repairs around their home. By the end of the week, Victor would buy her a bouquet of flowers or a small plant from his salary and pretend it was a gift from her son.

He slept in a niche off the kitchen, the only space for a narrow bed. He relished the warmth and was grateful for a roof over his head. Each night, as soon as Igor came home, Viktor greeted his father with a glowing demonstration of what he had learned. Sonja would praise Victor's work and the good influence he was having on their son. Her husband seemed pleased at first, but Victor soon noticed a growing resentment.

"I hope Viktor doesn't neglect his homework," was Igor's stern warning.

"On the contrary," Sonja declared, "Victor makes sure that he finishes that first."

***

Three weeks after his arrival, Sonja had grown ponderous and found it more and more difficult to breathe. One morning when Igor had left for work and Victor was doing his chores around the home, she felt the first labor pains. Since it was a Saturday, Victor left the boy with a neighbor, who promised to look after him and then rushed to the nearest telephone to call the hospital for an ambulance. There were none available. He was told roughly that the patient could surely wait a while since her labor had barely begun. Back at the house, he found Sonja writhing and moaning. "My water just broke. Please hurry and call them again. No, wait, just go to the neighbors and ask for their relative, the midwife."

The neighbor gave Victor the midwife's address. She lived around the corner of the teahouse. He ran to her ramshackle place as fast as he could. A toothless elderly woman opened the door to his impatient knocks. Sorry, she murmured, but her daughter was out on duty for the rest of the day.

He found another public telephone and tried to call the hospital again, but could not get connected. When he returned Sonja was in bed, screaming with pain, her hands clenched around the iron bars of the bedpost. "Wait, I'm going to boil some water," he said, prying her hands from the post. "Try to breathe deeply, slowly." But she clung to his arm with the ferocity of a wild cat. "Don't fret," he whispered. "I've had a baby once; let me get some sheets and towels."

"Then you know what to do?" Victor nodded yes and rose, gently removing Sonja's fingers from his arm. He rushed into the kitchen, put the kettle on the fire, washed his hands with the precious cake of soap the family reserved for weekly Sunday scrubbings, then gathered all the sheets and towels he could find.

I've had a baby once. He did not add that he had never assisted at a birth, but had only watched doctors in movies slapping babies' bottoms and holding them upside down.

Clearing the night table, he made room for a basin and remembered to fetch the soap from the kitchen. Mindful of the umbilical cord, he sterilized the kitchen scissors with a piece of burning newspaper. During these feverish activities, he wiped Sonja's brow as she cried out, the pains following one another more and more frequently. Holding her hand in his, he talked to her softly; telling her it wouldn't take long now. He was here to help.

She managed to smile in her moments of reprieve, her eyes full of gratitude and anguish. Suddenly, her pains grew intense, and she drew up her muscular legs and began to push down, breathing forcefully. Victor took a clean sheet, lifted her lower body, and spread it under her just in time for the baby's head to appear. She pushed again as she screamed, once, twice, and he cupped his hands to receive the baby's head as it emerged from its place of moist darkness, black-haired and slimy.

Now Sonja breathed with relief, pushing more gently with barely a whimper. The body followed quickly, and Victor held the little creature upside down by its slippery legs and slapped it gently, just as he had watched on screen. The baby cried out softly, then more heartily, to assert its existence.

"You have a fine little girl." Victor placed the infant on her mother's stomach. This was what the doctor had done with Sophie, right after little Hannah was born. He saw Sonja beaming at her small new creature, her eyes full of joy, relief, and gratitude. Victor felt himself choking up and quickly turned away to fetch water for the basin.

"What would I have done without you?" Sonja whispered, watching him pour the water and test it for warmth.

"You would've done just fine, all by yourself."

"Never. I would've died. You saved my life."

He gave her a drink of water, then warily took the baby into his hands to wash her, weeping softly to himself.

"Victor, you are crying. What is it? What happened to your baby?"

"It's so long ago."

"It was a girl, wasn't it? Did she die?"

"Never mind!" he shouted, drying his tears with the back of his hand. "Let's not talk about it. Not now."

"I'm so sorry."

A knock at the door. He felt he would choke with grief, but there was the umbilical cord to be cut, the door to be opened. He wrapped the baby into a soft clean towel, put her back on her mother's warm body, and went out to see who it was. A huge woman stood before him. She wore thick lenses and had a large black wart on her fleshy nose.

"I'm the midwife."

"It's all over."

She pushed him aside and made straight for the bedroom to investigate any possible damage done by this usurper. First, she pulled her own special scissors from her bag to cut the umbilical cord; next, she pushed down on Sonja's abdomen.

I forgot the placenta! Victor looked for a pail in the kitchen and presented it to the woman. Dropping the placenta into the bucket, she shook her head at the way Victor had wrapped the baby. She removed her from the mother, commanded Victor to bring her the items Sonja had set aside for the hospital, and began to swaddle the infant with such stern efficiency that Victor feared it might suffocate. The baby cried, and Sonja gave him an unhappy look. But the midwife, reminding Victor of an old painting of the prophet Jeremiah he had seen long ago in Stuttgart, put the newborn into the cradle next to her mother's bed and made for the kitchen.

"Take out the basin."

Victor removed the pan with the baby's bathwater from the small table and poured it out in the kitchen sink.

"I'm going to wash the mother," the midwife informed him. "Bring me a fresh sheet for the bed and then put up the water for tea. What are you waiting for?"

"You can at least say 'please'. I'm not your servant."

"Oh." She gave him a startled look. "All right. Please bring me a fresh sheet." She waddled back to the bedroom with the air of an insulted duck.

There was another knock at the door. The ambulance had arrived. "It's too late," Victor said. "The baby's here, and a midwife is taking care of her."

"Why didn't you call the hospital?" The driver walked away, cursing.

Little Viktor appeared on the threshold. "Where's Mommy? Is the baby here?"

"Yes. You have a tiny sister. And your mommy is fine."

"I wanted a brother. Can I see her?"

"Viktor!" The neighbor was calling from her door. "Come back!"

"Be a good boy. You may come home in a little while. I'll call you."

Reluctant, the child turned away. Victor went back inside to make the tea. When he brought the tray into the bedroom, the midwife was braiding Sonja's hair. Sonja cried out at the woman's rough tugs. She was propped up on two pillows, looking fresh and clean. Still pale with exhaustion, she was suffused with a particular radiance that Victor had once perceived on Sophie's face. Again, he was seized by a sorrow beyond his control, remembering his fear of taking his own fragile daughter into his arms. The memory of her once-dreaded arrival now overwhelmed him with love and awe. The miniature limbs, the tiny fist folding around his gigantic finger…their sweet baby, and Sophie transfigured into a goddess of creation.

He fled to the kitchen stifling his sobs, washed his face, and went back to pour the tea. Sonja watched each of his gestures with an expression of tender regard. He put the cup to her parched lips, and she drank avidly, her hand enveloping his. In his grief, he hardly noticed the change in her behavior. He ascribed it to the event they had just experienced together.

The midwife fed the baby some water from a bottle. Settling down with her own cup of tea, she sighed deeply. "I've worked hard and deserve a rest," her sigh seemed to say. Sonja and

Victor exchanged secret smiles. At Igor's arrival, the midwife was just walking out the door.

"I took care of everything," she said. "You have a healthy daughter."

Igor paid her and Victor went out to call the boy.

"Thank God the midwife came in time!" Igor embraced Sonja and took his daughter into his arms.

Sonja sighed. "No, she didn't. She gave herself big airs, but it was Victor who helped me all along. He saved my life."

Igor glanced at Victor, who had just come back with his son. Obviously vexed that a stranger had shared such shamelessly intimate moments with his wife while he had been away from home uninformed, he now put the baby into the cradle, trying to hide his pique. No one paid attention to little Viktor. He stood beside his father, watching his sister's fist in the palm of Igor's hand.

Igor looked at Victor. "Why didn't you send for me at the factory?"

"There was no time. Everything happened so fast."

"I told you he saved my life," Sonja said. "And you don't even thank him. You only think of your own petty concerns!"

Victor took the tray with the empty teacups and carried it out to the kitchen. Closing the door behind him, he noticed the loving look in Sonja's eyes.

He was followed by the sound of angry voices. Then saw little Viktor pulling at the sleeve of his shirt.

"Can Mommy send her back?"

"The baby?" The boy nodded. "I don't think so." Victor looked down at his sad little face. "I know why you want to send her back. You think she's just in the way. But soon you'll love her a little more every day and help your mommy take care of her, especially after I'm gone."

"When are you going?"

"Soon. I'll stay till your mama gets strong again."

"I don't want mama strong. I want you to stay with me."

***

Igor was given a few days' leave from the factory, and Victor kept out of the family's way. He cleaned, shopped, and cooked all the meals, but left the father in charge of his wife and children. It reestablished both Igor's role as head of the house and the friendly distance between Sonja and himself. Just as the baby took more and more to her mother's breast, Victor gradually weaned the boy from the bond that had grown between them. He told Igor how important it was for little Viktor to spend some time with him at this crucial moment, and Igor understood, eager to win back the affection he thought Victor had stolen from him. The boy began to follow in his father's footsteps, neglecting his friend.

Sonja was growing stronger. She resumed some of her tasks, weaving her baskets when the baby slept, preparing a few midday meals. She seemed amused and touched by the unusual concern her husband was showing her and told Victor that Igor had learned a great lesson from his example.

"See this little plant? He never brought me a plant or flower before. And he is always trying to make me comfortable now, putting a pillow behind my head when I nurse the baby and serving me tea in the afternoon the way you used to. Can you believe it? Igor serving me!"

Victor was pleased to see Sonja restored to her former self. The emotions that had threatened to engulf her were slowly and gently ebbing back. She was wiser for it, and richer. The love for her children and Igor and the memory of her special bond with Victor would now sustain her.

Though pleased to find harmony restored, Victor hovered between past and future. Only at night, alone on his cot, could he surrender to his sorrow and finally face the tragedy of his own losses. To this was now added the knowledge of the debacle of his people and millions of others. Each day, he learned more from the Polish refugees at the bazaar about the horrendous crimes the Nazis had committed. He was haunted by his dreams and oppressed by the memories of his endless, painful journey.

"Väterchen, what hope will you give me now? How can anyone do such abominable harm to his fellow humans? And how will I ever find Tatyana?"

"Be patient. The seed of hope will grow again," the Evangelist whispered in his dream.

"You planted it yourself, remember? Live from day to day, as you have learned to live from hand to mouth. Help those in need. There's endless need. Never close your heart to it."

***

One of the Poles he met at the bazaar invited him to join a group of refugees about to be repatriated. Within the next two weeks, a transport was to leave Tashkent for the Ukraine, or Upper Silesia. Prepared to leave, Victor worried about his documents. As though he had heard his cry for help, *Ata* Jacob—the Wandering Jew—appeared at the bazaar the next day.

"Victor, my friend, where have you been?" The old man embraced him.

"It's I who should ask *you* that question. You meant to meet me, but never showed up."

"Oh, that. I was here and there. So you deserted our trade."

Victor told him about his new life and his intention to move to the west. What documents would he need?

"Don't worry. I'll get you the right papers on the black market. It will cost you. Got some money?"

"A little."

"Tell your tailor to get you a nice suit. You look like a bum."

Victor laughed. "Are you going to come along, *Ata* Jacob?"

"I told you I'm too old. Besides, I'm a Russian, not a Pole."

That night, to his amazement, Igor presented Victor with a brown suit. Almost new, it had been given to him by a once trim and tall dignitary who had grown too fat for any alteration.

"I think it's going to fit you perfectly. Try it on."

"Igor, I can't accept it. Unless you let me buy it with my salary."

"Nonsense. I have no use for it. I'm much too short."

"You can sell it."

"Can't you accept a gift?" Igor said. "It's only fair, after all you've done for us."

Victor slipped into the pants, protesting that he hadn't done anything in particular. The trousers and jacket were a perfect fit. He went out to admire himself in the small kitchen mirror. Jacob was right. He had looked like a tramp for years.

"Now you are a real capitalist!" Igor exclaimed. "Sonja, come look!"

Sonja appeared in the kitchen with the baby in her arms, followed by Viktor. "Goodness, a film star!"

"A real capitalist!" Igor clapped his hands. "Don't eat too much when you go to the west, or you'll burst through the seams like that dignitary."

"A *capilatist*!" Viktor exclaimed.

"I don't know how to thank you."

"Now he needs a shirt," Sonja said.

"And a coat and a pair of shoes," Victor added, staring at his worn-out felt boots—a relic from the camp. "See what happens? Once you start as a *capilatist,* there'll be no end to your needs."

"You took my advice, eh!" Father Jacob greeted him the next day. "Lord, you work fast. Now you look like a real gentleman. People will think you're rich. Anyway, here are your papers."

After paying his debt, Victor found a few more rubles in his pocket and asked if they might buy him some secondhand shoes. Jacob guided him to the home of a black marketer, who fitted him with a pair of brown boots made of ersatz leather. Finding himself short three rubles, Victor gave them back, but Jacob put the money on the table. "It's time for another coat," he said. "Here, I brought you a nice one from my late son. Let me see if it fits."

"Everyone is spoiling me," Victor said gratefully. "It fits perfectly."

"I want you to make a good impression when you get out of the Soviet Union," Sonja told him the next day, admiring the new coat, then measuring a tan cotton shirt against Victor's shoulders. She had secretly sewn it at night, and it was ready just in time for his departure.

"Fine work." Igor looked at him with professional approval. "Only these boots are of inferior quality…"

Victor embraced Sonja in silence. "I feel guilty to leave you. It's still too soon for you."

"Don't worry. It's all under control. The neighbor promised to help with the baby, if necessary. But I'm fine now, I can manage."

"Someday, I may be back. Then Viktor will be so tall that I won't have to squat. Right, Viktor?"

The boy nodded. "Are you going to find your last name when you go back home?"

"I'll look for it. Though I'm not really going home." The child stared at him in dismay. "I'll try to find a new home and my old name. And I'll write to you about it when I do."

They were all up at dawn to share their last breakfast. Sonja prepared a few provisions for the journey. Victor slipped his recorder into Viktor's hand as he kissed him goodbye.

25.

TATYANA

Dante without Virgil

Summer 1947. Another sanatorium....

S tefan came back to pick me up. I had just closed my small suitcase and filled the old knapsack with my few possessions, among them my notes which would no longer be a threat to my safety.

Later, on the road to my new destination, I basked in the warmth of our friendship. We stopped for a meal in a cozy restaurant. I felt a new glimmer of hope, trying not to worry about another confinement, with its dreaded rules and restrictions.

Stefan planned to come back every weekend. I spent my days in anticipation of his next visit, grateful for our amazing reunion, his dedication, and encouragement. Not only was my illness in remission, but I had begun to hope for a visa because Stefan had provided me with an affidavit, thanks to the help of an American uncle. Dora and Giuseppe surprised me with a visit from Venice, bringing gifts and a note from Sandra with news about Francesco. I was delighted to see them and glad to learn about Francesco's recovery from a disease called Tatyana. He is now engaged to the woman he refused to see. A wedding has been planned. I wrote him a letter with all my best wishes and thanked him again for everything he had done for me, then added my expression of gratitude to his mother and Sandra.

I don't want to be pulled back into the painful past, but instead try to look ahead to a better future. Svetlana wrote me that she expects to leave for the States in the next few weeks. In her last letter, she urged me to also try for it. She hopes Stefan might be able to help me. I ought to join her in Denver.

We would not only be able to start a new life together, but recent medications and cures will soon make sanatoria obsolete. An operation to restore my collapsed lung might cure me in a short time. The National Jewish hospital is known for its slogan: "Those who enter do not pay. Those who can pay do not enter." She promises to look for the finest specialist to take care of me and make me as good as new.

Could there really be a network of human care awaiting me across the ocean? As soon as I put the wheels for my emigration in motion, all expectations were shattered by a fresh bout of illness: bronchitis, followed by pneumonia. It takes time to recover my strength. Stefan, dear soul, tries to pull me out of my apathy. What still holds me back is that endless longing for Victor. Stefan senses my reticence, in spite of the comfort I feel in his presence. I miss him sorely whenever he goes back to Milan, yet have never told him that for five days of each week I feel as lonely as ever, lost in a dark wood like Dante, without a Virgil at my side.

26.

DREAMS OF A NEW SILVER FLUTE

On the train taking him out of the Soviet Union, Victor thought of rebirth on the wings of music. Dreams of a silver flute to replace the one he had lost, eons ago, at the Polish border. Its limpid sounds were carrying him into the freedom of a new existence. The red scarf was dissolving like dust in the air. His future flute was wrapped in red velvet and bedded in a soft leather case. Floating through the sky, propelled and sustained by his music, he thought of Tatyana with infinite longing, then looked down from the heights across the great spaces of Mother Russia and saw little Viktor playing on his *sopranino*. Five small urchins followed in his footsteps, dancing to the tune.

PART THREE

27.

HEADING WEST

After a long journey, the small group of Polish refugees reached the western Ukraine. In a temporary camp at the outer edge of a small village, Polish and Jewish survivors waited for a transport to take them to Vienna, and later to Turin, Italy, where they would be gathered in some shelter for displaced persons. Protected by the American Red Cross, they isolated themselves from the hostile Ukrainian population.

A mild attack of his recurrent fever segregated Victor from his fellow travelers. He was given a room in an empty house close to the camp, formerly occupied by the Germans. At war's end, many German Ukrainians had fled at the approach of the Soviet armies. Now a number of their farms and homes were filled with refugees from different parts of Eastern Europe.

Victor was forced to go to sleep early, for the house lacked electricity, flashlights, or candles. Recovering in a matrimonial bed in that deserted place filled with German books, he remained oblivious to the outside world. Nothing but meals interrupted his hunger for knowledge, his involvement with fictitious worlds set against the background of stark reality. The books brought order to his life. Stranded without a past, present, or future, he found comfort in stories trying to convince him that life has a beginning, a middle, and an end.

Although his hunger pangs were gone, yearnings kept underground in the past, now rose to the surface with unexpected urgency. By immersing himself in these literary riches, he tried to push off dismal thoughts about the absence of music in his life. Looking back at years of deprivation without the simplest creature comfort, he still felt nurtured and molded by invisible hands: the hands of the Maker, as the Evangelist would have said.

I am tilled earth waiting. Waiting for what?

Day after day, he thought of his old friend. Freed at last from hunger and fear, he was still confined, wondering whether he might have to face another battle for survival. Two Polish brothers, Avram and Benjamin, and their sister Leah were trying to adopt him as a third brother, inviting him to join them in their dream of reaching Jerusalem.

Victor was touched by their faith in the future of a better world. How could it be otherwise, they said, after such horror? The brothers, with their curly black hair and dreamy eyes, seemed to have stepped out of a Murillo painting. They bore no resemblance to Leah, a slender girl with elongated features, a thin nose, and close-set eyes.

Each morning, Leah would bring him breakfast from the canteen around the corner: ersatz coffee, bread, margarine, and jam. As he got better and began to take his meals with the young trio, he told them about his intention to leave for the United States.

"You have relatives there?" Avram asked.

"My late wife's sister."

"But you need a new home, a country of your own."

Benjamin smiled. *"Cherchez la femme?"*

Victor shook his head, then added sadly, "Someone I lost ages ago."

Leah looked at him in shock. Always prone to laughter, she now grew subdued and downcast in his presence. Newly aware of her feelings, he hated to hurt this kind young girl, but thought it best to end an illusion before it took root.

***

Awake or dreaming, he heard a rustling noise in the middle of the night. Someone pulled back his blanket and slipped into bed beside him. He could feel soft, feminine hands touching his face, arms, and shoulders. Slowly, the hands wandered over his chest, touch turning to caress. Her fingers halted above his beating heart, as though listening to its fitful rhythms. He lay there immobilized, holding his breath as her lips wandered over his chest, his neck, and his face, slowly, haltingly, until they met his mouth in a lingering kiss.

He was trembling then, as he had trembled during his frequent fevers, growing hot and cold with desire that had been buried for so many years. Not a word was said or whispered, not a sound made on this bridal night of silent consummation. He could neither see nor hear his amorous assailant, yet had known her forever. Groping in blindness, he savored the silent flow of their intimacy until she vanished before dawn.

How could such a vivid dream be nothing but a mirage? Night after night, he whispered her name, hoping for her return, more hungry for her tenderness than he had ever been for bread. A voice warned him against foolish flights of fancy. What if he couldn't find this precious needle in a thousand haystacks? Suppose she was alive and married with children—thus reversing their former circumstance into an equally hopeless one? And yet he still believed in tendrils of new life growing from reveries.

***

The departure for Vienna filled him with anguish. His attempts to flee to the West were finally coming to fruition. Representatives of the American Jewish Committee had made arrangements for a comfortable journey. In Vienna, the travelers were taken to an inn near the railway station. Withdrawing to his room, Victor hoped to fall asleep at once, but was aroused by laughter, blasting music, and happy songs rising from the parlor. A knock at the door made him turn on the light and abruptly sit up in bed.

"Victor," Leah whispered shyly outside the closed door, "why don't you come down and join us?"

"Sorry, I'm too sleepy."

"So are we. But we are free at last and want to celebrate."

He opened the door. "Please, Leah, not here, not yet. Vienna is hardly the place for it. The Austrians were even worse than the Germans. I'll much rather join you later in Turin."

She must take me for a killjoy, he told himself. Longing for the return of his lover, he finally fell asleep, holding her close in another dream. In the morning, he dragged himself out of bed, groggy and sad. The mountains were shrouded in fog while the train passed through innumerable tunnels. He shivered as he listened to the songs of his companions, feeling the movement of the carriage wheels under his seat. Drifting once more into sleep, he found himself back in Tashkent, trudging behind the woman with the heavy sack. Now the mountains seemed to turn around him, slowly at first, then faster in a wild, windy dance. Little Viktor took his hand and said they must hurry; the baby was about to arrive.

"Here we are." Avram was tugging at his shoulder. Victor alighted from the train like a somnambulist as he entered Turin's dimly lit Porta Nuova station. A bus took the group to an old school building which had been turned into a shelter for displaced persons. After a satisfying dinner, the travelers were shown separate dormitories for men, women, and families. Each hall was lined with rows of narrow beds. Victor sank onto the bed assigned to him without taking off his clothes and immediately fell asleep.

The next morning each newcomer had to fill out a questionnaire for the American Committee. This was followed by a medical examination. To Victor's relief, the American physician explained that his recurring fever was not caused by malaria. Symptoms of his illness might have resembled it in the past, but there was no sign of severity or organ dysfunction. Yet Victor still needed a lot of rest for a full recovery.

"A convalescent home in San Remo just made room for a few displaced persons," the doctor told him. "I'll call the people in charge to make sure they follow my recommendations. Since I'm driving there in a few days, "I can take you along if you like."

***

Although the convalescent home was an improvement over the shelter in Turin, he remained indifferent to his new surroundings. He could barely exchange the necessary courtesies with patients and nurses, given his disorientation and scant knowledge of Italian. As his health improved, he strolled along the deserted shore, or spent hours in one of the empty boats on the beach, reading or studying this new language. During the years of captivity and travel, he had been driven by the desire to find freedom in the West. And now that he had finally come back, relief turned into disappointment.

Reading about the chaos and destruction of much of Europe's beauty and culture, he no longer belonged there, nor anywhere else in the world. Although he did not have to fight for each crumb of bread or fear arrest at each step, his life was not his own. Enforced idleness exhausted his mind as much as hard labor had depleted his body. He missed his music and the comfort of his recorder and remained in a void without purpose or meaning.

At his request, Sophie's sister sent him another affidavit to his new address. He had finally been able to thank her for her past efforts and to write her a letter explaining what had happened to Sophie and the baby. Lisa had guessed long ago that mother and child were no longer alive. Grieving for her sister, she could hardly imagine Victor's ordeal. Her letter stirred up feelings he had not faced in years.

How had he managed to survive his losses while suffering hunger, illness, captivity, and loneliness? There was no one left in his life. Still grieving for his mother, he no longer remembered the addresses of cousins, uncles, and aunts who had lived in other German cities. They had probably been deported, killed, or they had fled to unknown places. There was nothing left but the dream of finding Tatyana. She continued to stir his feelings with the same constancy that had kept him human. If she were alive, how would he ever find her? Yet he would always keep searching for her.

Many aspects of the war were like those of the Middle Ages: an era of similar barbarism, with cities turned into rubble, entire populations shifted, deported, enslaved, or repatriated against their will. The incessant sound of falling waves on the beach seemed to reiterate man's inhumanity. It made him think of Gustav Mahler's *Rückertlied*, reminding him that he was lost to the world.

He envisioned America beyond the horizon, across the great expanse of the Atlantic Ocean, and asked himself what kind of life might wait for him in that enormous, strident land. He felt like a gnarled tree, aching with solitude. Waves rolled up on the deserted shore, their ceaseless song deepening his desolation. Here and there, a seagull would dip into the gray expanse, discharging an outcry like those that never escaped his lips. Churning waves disrupted his troubled sleep. At last, he stopped going to the beach and barricaded himself behind the shuttered window of his room.

Each night Tatyana's image appeared to him in various guises. Suppose she was still alive but had changed beyond recognition? He wondered whether the 12-year-old boy who had wished to marry her was still in her life. If so, and if he wasn't Jewish, he might have saved her. He could hardly hope that she was back in Yugoslavia, still alone, still yearning for him as he yearned for her, year after endless year....

One afternoon, his Italian physician found him reading in the dark. "Is anything wrong?" he asked in a pure English, handing him a letter. He opened the shutters, scolding him for ruining his eyes.

Victor assured him that he had no complaints.

"Victor, don't play the martyr. Something is bothering you. The Allied Committee pays for the care of war victims." The doctor was pointing at the letter: "I want you to know that in addition, you are entitled to a small monthly sum for your personal expenses."

Victor returned the envelope. "It makes me feel like a beggar."

"Come on! You needn't be proud. American Jews are more than happy to help." He put the letter on the table and sat down to face him. "Perhaps you don't like it here?"

"It's not that. It's the sea."

"The sea?"

"I mean the noise of the waves. The closeness, the constant bouncing and rolling..."

"Would you rather move to the mountains? Have you ever been in Meran?"

Victor shook his head. Meran was a well-known resort in the now Italian Tyrol, the doctor explained. "Hitler handed it as a gift to Mussolini," he added with a grim smile. "The Tyrolians resent being incorporated into Italy, so most of the older people speak nothing but German. I can easily transfer you to a peaceful Italian convalescent home in the center of the town."

"Thank you, Doctor, but I don't think… It makes me feel like a prima donna."

"Don't be too hasty. You'll have to return to that shelter in Turin as soon as your health is restored."

"How much longer will I have to wait? I mean doing nothing. All I ask is to be useful."

"You must learn to be patient."

I've spent years learning to be patient, Victor thought. How could he explain that the prospect of moving to that secluded resort meant being hidden from Tatyana at the other end of the world?

28.

A NEW SENSE OF PURPOSE

Settled in Meran, it did not take long for Victor to improve his condition in the convalescent home for recovering Italian patients. Thanks to his intense studies of Italian during the spring and summer in San Remo, he was now able to make friends with Doctor Ferrari, his new physician, his nurse, and some fellow patients, as well as Mario, the chef, and the kitchen personnel. Their warmth and kindness was the perfect antidote to the harshness and incessant cursing he had experienced in the Soviet Union.

Set in the valley of the Alto Adige, with a view of distant mountains, Meran had long been a place for the rich and famous, as well as a refuge for artists and intellectuals. Victor explored the Gothic church and the Castello Principesco, a castle built between the fourteenth and fifteenth century by the Hapsburgs—all close to the convalescent home. Wandering through the old town, he discovered the Empress Elisabeth Park, where he sat down on a bench and absorbed the warmth of the sun.

Yet nothing—not even the stunning view of the distant Alps— helped him recognize the culture and nature of Europe. Each day, he learned more about the Nazi crimes, yet the utter devastation of German cities, including Stuttgart, gave him no sense of vindication. Pitying any innocent victim wherever he went, he felt that Germany had died for him with his mother.

Unable to remember certain masterpieces he had once cherished and known by heart, like Richard Strauss's *Alpine Symphony,* he wondered how much music he would need to recover, after years of nostalgia and tribulation. At age thirty, he considered himself as old as Methuselah and his hope of finding Tatyana was flickering like a dying match.

During a medical visit, Dr. Ferrari asked him about his music. They had talked about it before, but Victor had hardly mentioned his early career. Now he felt free to confess that he had been deprived of his music for more than eight years. At the doctor's request, he told him about his solo appearances as a 10-year-old flautist, his early compositions, and the harrowing piracy of his flute during the family's deportation to Poland.

"It would have been stolen anyway, sooner or later."

"My goodness, Victor, you must have gone through hell. It just occurs to me that the director of a music school, right here in the center of town, is a friend of mine. Would you like me to ask if he could lend you a flute and let you practice in one of the music rooms? Your health has improved, so you may get back to your playing."

"It sounds too good to be true."

"Maestro Belluni is an excellent violinist and teacher. I'll call him right away. Don't hesitate to tell him exactly what you need."

"I will," Victor promised. "I don't know how to thank you."

Two days later, he was called to the office of the music school where he met a corpulent middle-aged gentleman with horn-rimmed glasses. Facing him across a large desk covered with scores and musical literature, the maestro came right to the point. "Dr. Ferrari told me about your long exile in the Soviet Union. I can't imagine how I might have survived all that time without my violin. I will lend you a flute and you may practice whenever possible. But first, I would like to hear you play something for me as soon as you are ready."

"Of course, Maestro. I can't thank you enough for your generous offer. I would like to do something for you, or your school, in turn…"

"Do what?"

"You probably know that I have no working permit because I am stateless, but I would like to reciprocate your kindness and offer free tutoring to some of your youngest students."

"Tutoring? How?"

"Teach them composition, the flute, the piano."

"Well, let's give it a try. I don't understand what you mean by *composition*?"

"I loved to compose as a child and would like to experiment with youngsters of all ages who may be interested in learning how to write and play their own tunes."

"Sounds like an interesting experiment. Have you ever tried it before?"

"Not exactly. All I had in the Soviet Union was a tiny recorder that I always carried with me. I taught an 8-year-old friend of mine to play a few tunes. He couldn't get enough of it and began to blow his own melodies. They were more than charming. This inspired me to help him with a few simple theories, which we pretended to use like ingredients needed for baking a cake. That's how I started to teach myself as a boy, back in Stuttgart. My experience told me that kids love to improvise, and that it sometimes works like magic when they are allowed to do it on their own."

"Can you give me a demonstration on your recorder?"

"I'm afraid not. I left it with my friend in Tashkent. But I can do it on the flute."

"It sounds intriguing. As to the flute, I hope it won't take you too much time to resume your playing, after being forced to do nothing but manual labor for all these years."

Victor took a deep breath. "So do I. Though I'm a bit stiff, I try to remind myself that it's like riding a bicycle. One never forgets."

***

Maestro Belluni lent Victor a concert flute in the key of C and gave him access to the music library. With the use of a private room and a good instrument, Victor could practice three mornings a week, and was allowed to take the flute home whenever all of the rooms were occupied by students. His embouchure was quickly improving, but his once supple hands seemed to have lost their sensitive touch. He repeated simple passages over and over again, despairing of ever recapturing his once flawless playing. Frustration brought him almost to tears, but he was determined to improve his technique, which was as hard as felling trees and carrying logs to the river.

After a few weeks, he resolved to keep his promise and play for Maestro Belluni. Still dissatisfied with himself, he was surprised and relieved to learn that the director was genuinely impressed with his rendition of the adagio of Mozart's B minor flute quartet. It was the adagio he had played at Tatyana's arrival, and he still remembered every note by heart.

Soon after, the Maestro introduced him to the school's youngest students. Thinking of the five boys who had helped him keep the cows in their corral, Victor pretended again to be deaf to the spoken word and communicated exclusively through the sounds of music. Instead of hopping about like a tramp playing his *sopranino*, he made the children laugh at his pantomime of the Pied Piper of Tashkent, this time with the help of the flute, as he improvised songs in both German and Italian.

His success with this humorous approach to music, and his connection with the children he quickly grew to love, gave him a new sense of purpose. In turn, it took no time for the youngsters to love and trust him. On the other hand, the hard work of trying to regain control of his instrument robbed him of sleep. Resting in the privacy of his room after hours of work, he reminded himself to be grateful for the comforts he had missed for so long: the delicious meals consisting of a mixture of Italian and Austrian cuisine, the softness and warmth of his bed and downy comforter, the sympathy and appreciation of his doctor and of the inhabitants of his temporary home. At last, he no longer felt afraid to open his heart to others.

***

Walking through Meran one late November morning, he found himself at the entrance to a public park. He followed a path covered with carpets of autumn leaves, then climbed toward a large building at the top of a hill. Stepping onto a deserted terrace, he heard the sound of voices behind a closed-in veranda and gazed through one of its windows. A number of people were scattered around wooden tables, mostly men playing checkers or cards. Someone in a white smock, obviously a doctor, was talking to an elderly couple.

When he left the terrace and returned to the park, Victor caught sight of a dark-haired young woman looking out a window from the third floor of the large building. Feeling his gaze, she turned her head toward him. Before he could have a look at her face, she closed the window and withdrew from sight.

He crossed the park in the opposite direction. A middle-aged man in a loden coat and hat sat on the nearest bench. He pulled pieces of bread from a paper bag and threw them to some hungry birds at his feet. Smiling at Victor, he moved to make room for him.

"Is this a public garden?" Victor asked, after thanking him in German. "Or does it belong to the hotel?"

"What hotel?" The man brushed crumbs from his coat.

"The big building, over there."

"That's a sanatorium." He spoke with heavy Austrian inflections.

"Are you one of the patients?"

"What gives you that idea? Thank God, no! Those are displaced persons, nothing but scum. I can tell you are one of us, a real gentleman. What part of Germany are you from?"

Victor jumped to his feet. "You are wrong! I'm a displaced person myself. And a gentleman. That's why I'm not, and will never be one of you." Walking away, he saw the man pull his hat over his eyes and turn his back to him. In his outrage, Victor kept seeing the young woman at the window. His heart went out to her, as though she had been the object of that insult.

The next afternoon he returned to the park. To his relief, the man in the loden coat was nowhere to be seen. Victor settled on the nearest bench and pulled a collection of stories by Ernest Hemingway from his pocket. A weak sun shone through the trees. Chilled, he continued reading, writing down words he didn't understand. He meant to improve his English and Italian from day to day, while maintaining his fluent Russian. If he couldn't find enough work with his music, he might be able to survive as an interpreter or translator.

A cold wind forced him to get up and walk around the deserted park. The meager sun disappeared behind clouds. He hurried back to the convalescent home. That night he dreamt about the woman at the window. He hoped to get a look at her face, but the back of her head was always turned to him. Although he awoke on several occasions, he saw nothing but her short black hair, then fell asleep again to dream the same dream.

It was past ten o'clock when he rushed out of his room in the morning, thinking of the riders who had appeared out of nowhere to drag him back to Termez after his attempted escape to Kabul. There was probably no freedom in Afghanistan, and the woman at the window was nothing but another fatamorgana.

In spite of his doubts, he hurried once more through the deserted park, never catching his breath until he reached the terrace, determined to meet the dark-haired woman on the third floor.

29.

TWO LINES MEETING IN THE INFINITE

When he entered the spacious room from the veranda, he found it empty but for a few patients playing cards in a corner. In a niche at the opposite end, the dark-haired young woman sat writing in a notebook. Victor stopped. The entire room seemed to reverberate with the beat of his heart. He crossed the room and faced her across the round cherry wood table. Sensing a presence, she kept on writing and only looked up when he whispered her name.

"Tatyana…"

"Yes?"

He took a step back and was silent.

"Who are you?" she asked in German.

"Don't you recognize me?"

She stared at him for a long moment. "Oh, my God…" She paled. "Victor! I can't…"

Her features—the eyes, the Slavic cheekbones and generous lips, even a lock of hair falling over her brow—were as he had recalled them throughout his long odyssey. Yet something was different. She had grown delicate, almost fragile, and her once luminous eyes had lost their radiance.

"I must be seeing a ghost," he heard her say.

"Oh, Tatyana…" Held back by her reticence, he dared not embrace her.

Her eyes filled. She rubbed them, averting her head with a fit of coughs.

"But how did you find out I was here?" She was still catching her breath. "And what brings you to Meran?"

"I suppose you did. Well, I've been here for some time, but yesterday I climbed up this hill and saw you at a window on the third floor."

"That's more than a miracle." She gazed at him, shaking her head. "I can hardly believe that you are still alive."

"And you."

"Both of us tucked away in this town--of all places."

For a moment her smile, just like her melodious voice, broke through the silence. Then her face darkened. "But where's your family?"

"All gone."

"Oh no!" She covered her face with her hands.

He pulled up a chair and sat down beside her. He couldn't bear to speak of it, but she was waiting. He mentioned their deportation to Poland and his mother's death.

"Yes. Aunt Martha wrote me about it. It was the last time she heard from you, and I from her."

"The shock killed my mother. We hardly had time to bury her."

"I'm so sorry! What about Sophie and the baby?"

"Shot by the Nazis with many others during the invasion." He swallowed hard. "It happened while I tried to find us a hideout in the countryside, but it was too late. I ran east like a madman, toward the Soviet Union."

"So you were in Russia, alone…for how long?"

"All these years."

She stared at him in shock. "As a prisoner? In camps? How did you survive?"

He remained silent.

"The Nazis killed my whole family too," she said. "I found out that Aunt Martha was deported and never returned."

Victor envisioned himself back in the music room the moment Tatyana had appeared to him as a dream, and later in Martha's guest room, so long ago, where he and Tatyana had talked and briefly embraced on Kristallnacht. He could see the Nazis robbing Martha's grand piano, then pushing the poor woman into that bottomless pit reserved for God's chosen people.

"So here we are," Tatyana sighed. "After so much hell, so much grief. What does it all mean?"

"There'll never be an answer."

Just the two of us, he thought, *miraculously saved for each other…but who is she now? And who am I?* Unsure of her state of mind, he was afraid of any wrong word he might say.

She closed her notebook. The gesture caused the sleeve of her sweater to slide up and reveal a number tattooed inside her wrist.

"Auschwitz?"

She nodded.

"Oh, Tatyana." He choked, wishing to erase that monstrous symbol engraved in her skin. Sorrow dampened the ecstasy he had felt only a few moments before.

"I could no longer tell what you looked like," she said. "You were so young, barely 22, and have changed so much. Like pieces of a puzzle that no longer fit."

"Have I really changed that much?" Was she trying to distract him because she feared being questioned about her own past? Though anxious to learn what had happened to her, he dared not inquire.

"Not changed," she said, "but grown strong and mature. You seem to have outgrown that impetuous young fellow who played the flute like an angel and had little confidence in himself."

"Do you remember our promise about the courage we were going to need? I always remembered it in my darkest moments, and hoped it would do the same for you."

"It did support me, at first, even in that hell, but when hell turned into the afterworld, all fires died. I didn't find the strength to rekindle it." She took a deep breath. "Much later, I found a sliver of hope, but lost it again."

Aware of how little he knew her, he looked at her sadly. "Oh, Tatyana—though no one can grasp all that horror—you have survived. It's not like you to give up. Not now."

"The more I think about it, the more I feel that everything we believed was a delusion."

He glanced at her notebook. "If you're writing it all down, I hope it will set you free."

"I wish." She looked at her watch. Before he could ask if she was expecting someone, she wanted to know if he had been in a war zone.

"No, never. I was lucky to spend half of those years in Uzbekistan and some other eastern provinces."

"But how? Were you in prisons or camps? Doing forced labor?"

"All of it. When I first got to Lemberg with a group of refugees, the Soviets turned the city into the temporary capital of the Ukraine. All fugitives had to declare their identity on arrival. The official was unable to spell or pronounce my last name, so he kept ranting and cursing and finally changed it to 'Nameless'. For all these years, I drifted in the nowhere as Victor *Nameless*."

Just as it had happened with the Evangelist, speaking German in Tatyana's unexpected presence eased his age-long apprehension to communicate in his mother tongue. She no longer glanced at her watch as he described the tragicomic moments during his long stay in Lemberg, then listened intently to the tale of his first encounter with Bubachoff and was shocked by his abrupt deportation to a distant labor camp.

"But it saved my life," he explained. "Because it happened a few days before the arrival of German troops in Lemberg."

"That's hard to believe. It's just as my illness saved me from the death march at the end of the war. I was carried out of the camp unconscious, and then taken back to Zagreb by some organization I can't remember. Through many detours and weeks of waiting, endless waiting."

She started at the ring of the bell summoning the patients to lunch. Victor gazed at her in amazement at the miracle of their survival, their incredible reunion, and the price they had almost been forced to pay with their lives. When the bell rang once more, she took her notebook, saying she had to go. The sanatorium imposed strict rules on the patients.

He held her back for another moment: "Remember when you felt we might never meet again? You were right, Tatyana, except for one thing. We forgot to hope for a miracle."

"I believe that you did; I mean remember to hope."

"Perhaps I did. But now the miracle has happened." Victor said. "And we are merging at this place, this time--like two lines meeting in the infinite."

"To think that we knew each other for only three days."

"Three days and a thousand years," he reminded her softly, pulling back the chair for her as she got up to leave. He admired her slim figure in a pale blue sweater and black skirt. She did not respond to his last remark. "May I see you again, in a couple of days?"

She thought for a moment. "All right. Let's meet here, the day after tomorrow, at eleven?" Shaking his hand to avoid an embrace, she said goodbye and hurried out the door.

Victor descended the path, wondering whether he had deluded himself all along. Though Tatyana hadn't forgotten him, her feelings seemed subdued. Did the love sustaining him through years of captivity remain unrequited? Yet it was *she* who had risked her life for him on *Kristallnacht*; *she* who suggested they think of one another, carrying the burning torch of their courage through the dark. Hadn't she admitted that it sustained her in hell? Or had terror and suffering turned all her hope to ashes?

How foolish to expect her to be the same Tatyana. She had said so herself. They had known each other for only three days. Other men must have been in her life and were possibly added to her many losses. Perhaps she was in love right now, debating how to convey this to him as gently as possible.

In spite of the cold wind, Victor broke into a sweat. At the convalescent home, he was late for lunch. He told Mario he wasn't hungry and went straight to his room. After calming down, he tried memorizing Italian irregular verbs, but Tatyana's face rose from each page, preventing him from concentrating on his studies.

How naive of him to envision a first encounter as a moment of pure joy without any obstacle in their way. Ignorant of the nature of her illness, he was afraid to ask what kept her captive in that sanatorium. He paced his room, then went for a walk in the park, trying to understand her aloofness. That night he realized how their long separation ran like a river between them, from then until now. But hadn't he found her after barely reaching the West? And hadn't he sworn to himself that nothing else mattered? His euphoria was dampened by a deep concern for her health, as well as some secret that might cause her to keep him at arm's length.

For the next few weeks, Victor and Tatyana met whenever his schedule at the music school allowed it. He would have preferred to share their weekends, but Tatyana told him about her doctor's urgent advice to reserve those days for a total rest. On a clear day, they would stroll through the park or stop in the center of town till it was time to be back for her lunch. Careful not to show his desire to take her into his arms, Victor hoped to make her feel at ease in his company by offering friendship and support. Afraid of intruding on her privacy by asking about her condition, he had to be satisfied with her assurance that she was no longer contagious. His questions might only increase her anguish about the fragile state of her health. She never tired of hearing about his Russian odyssey and the amazing reunion with Bubachoff. She was especially moved by the Maestro's death.

He described Bukhara, the music school, the colorful bazaars, and the meeting with Benjamin, but did not mention Rachel, or why he left Bukhara for the unlikely chance of finding freedom and Tatyana in the West.

You and the West were one, he would have liked to confess, but was too unsure of her feelings to say it. Sitting at her table during a snow-filled morning, he spoke of his clandestine journeys on freight trains, and the theft of his trouser pocket with all his documents and last rubles. She burst into laughter, then tried to conceal her tears.

"Oh, Tatyana, I didn't mean to upset you! It was actually quite funny."

"I know," she sobbed, laughing again, then wiped her eyes with a handkerchief. A few patients, playing cards at another table, looked up to watch what they took for a lovers' quarrel. He never mentioned his hunger and pain, his recurring illness and aloneness, but tried to amuse her with the story of his failure to change into a more successful thief under Misha's tutelage.

"You make it all sound like some comic adventure. But what was it really like?"

"I'd rather hear something about you."

"I was wondering why you haven't asked."

"I was afraid to pry," he said. "I could tell you didn't want to be reminded."

"That's right, I didn't. But then I thought you didn't care."

"Is that what you thought?" He was stung. "You don't want me to ask any questions, but are insulted if I don't. You want to know everything about me, but never breathe a word about yourself."

"Like a typical woman," she said, laughing. "I still have to work things out. Doctors and friends keep patronizing me, but I don't want you to join in their song, you least of all."

"I can't help feeling that you are holding something back."

She evaded his questioning look.

"As if you were trying to avoid me," he went on. "Each time I come here, you are writing in this black notebook."

"Oh, that. You were right; it's about Auschwitz. The stuff I need to exorcise. Every page takes me ages to write. I'm still at the beginning. It never seems to move on. Stuff I don't want anyone to read."

"You are more than brave to face it again."

"I'm not sure. Writing it down doesn't help me grasp all that horror."

Seeing him look at her in dismay, she added more softly, "But I write notes about my life before and after the camp. Forgive me if I'd rather not talk about that black book."

"I understand. If you prefer to leave me in the dark about your past," he said, "I won't try to turn on the light."

"What do you want to know?"

"Anything you want to tell me."

"I still have a collapsed lung, but right now I'm in remission. The doctors are baffled. In case of a relapse, I'll never be able to move to the States."

"I suppose you don't want to go back to Yugoslavia."

"I was there. And left again."

She told him about Eva's kindness and her two cousins who believed in Tito's New Order.

"Those words made me sick. I need a private place, free to leave my life in a clutter if I wish, without anyone's disapproval."

"I completely agree. We both went through hell, but your hell was much worse. Now you need to get better every day, and I want nothing more than to help you find that private place."

She did not respond. Victor wondered whether he had said something to displease her. "You have seen that I'm nameless too," she went on after a pause. "We were just numbers." Her eyes lit up in defiance. "Nameless of the world unite! Someday we'll carve our real names in stone."

She told him they might have changed roles. "I used to be too positive for my own good, while you, Victor, seem to have come back from Russia full of optimism about a new life. Forgive my confusion. After all these years, I no longer know who I am. So how can I tell who *you* are?"

"All I can say is that we were deeply connected. But now you seem to scrutinize me all the time. Are you testing me for some reason?"

"Perhaps I am."

***

During their next outing, Victor invited her to join him for a session at the music school. He introduced her to his young pupils and serenaded her with a sonata for piano and flute that he had composed as a teenager and still remembered by heart. Glancing at her as she listened, fully absorbed, among his gifted children, he was overcome with joy for his change of fortune. Here he was, close to her at last, once more absorbed in his music, able to teach, play, conduct, and compose.

The recital was followed by songs composed and enacted by the children. In the end, Victor entertained them with examples of certain ingredients necessary to musical creations, just as he had intended. "Now we have mixed butter, sugar, flour and eggs," he said. "What else do we need?"

In no time, the children added exotic musical spices to his recipe.

On their way back to the sanatorium, Tatyana expressed her

admiration for the rapport he had developed with his students. He informed her that Maestro Belluni had invited him to join his quartet as a guest artist for a chamber concert in the Gothic parish church in mid-May.

"That's wonderful news."

"I may choose any piece I want. Would you like to come?"

"I'll think about it," she teased him with an impish smile. "That's five months from now, so I'll have plenty of time to decide. If I'm still here, that is…"

30.

MISS SINGER MUST NOT BE DISTURBED

On several occasions, Victor had tried to invite her for lunch in town, but the rules would not allow it. She was expected to keep her regular hours: one o'clock for the midday meal, followed by rest. Once a week, however, weather allowing, she could finally skip this routine. On one particular Tuesday it snowed for a while, but then the air grew clear and the wind died down. This gave them a chance to stop for lunch at a charming inn.

"I hope you won't catch cold after walking through the snow," Victor said.

"Don't worry, I have sturdy boots. But look at you! Dressed like a gentleman, except for those awful cardboard slippers, or whatever they call them in Russian. Why didn't our saviors at the American Committee provide you with a decent pair of shoes, so that you won't get sick?"

"I'm used to getting wet feet. Russian winters were infinitely worse. I got these on the black market in Tashkent. They are much more elegant than the ones I used before, and they walked me into freedom."

"But not through the snow!"

"Through snow and ice, into freedom from fear and hunger, and without the threat of prisons or camps. I'm so grateful for all the care I'm getting here and, above all, for being with you."

"I'm afraid I'm more of a hindrance than a help."

"Tatyana, don't...don't ever say that."

On entering the restaurant, she whispered that it was much too elegant. Nothing was elegant enough for her, Victor said. "I love your green winter coat and your fine taste in clothes."

"Oh, that's my friend Dora's taste. She sends me beautiful things from Venice."

A hostess guided them to a corner table. As soon as they had settled down side by side, Victor picked up the menu. "Let me treat you to a *Kaiserschmarren*," he offered.

"Oh, I love *Kaiserschmarren*! Haven't had any since I was in my teens."

He signaled to the waiter, who took their order, then asked if they would like it with apple or cranberry sauce.

"Cranberry, please," Tatyana said.

As soon as the waiter was gone, Victor remarked that she still hadn't told him anything about her life, her childhood, and everything else.

"My childhood was carefree and happy. I think it gave me the strength to survive."

"In the camp, you mean? Remembering the good times?"

"Exactly. Though Dante said in his *Inferno,* 'There is no greater pain than to remember happy times in misery.' It was the opposite for me. I escaped into the best moments of the past. That's what saved me, at first. Though not now, not anymore."

"And why not?"

"Because dreadful memories stand like armed soldiers at the border of those happy ones. I'd like to get rid of them, but can't. Not yet."

He reached for her hand. Their eyes met. He saw her blush as she quickly withdrew from his touch.

"Tatyana, you must help me."

"Help you, how?"

The waiter arrived with plates full of golden shredded pancakes with raisins, which he sprinkled with powdered sugar. "*Guten Appetit, die Herrschaften.*" He set down two bowls of cranberry sauce before hurrying to the next table.

"That obsequious, bombastic language!" Victor whispered. "*Herrschaften!* I can't stand that word. Calling us persons of high standing because we are here to order a meal."

"You said I must help you." Tatyana put down her fork.

"Help me understand you. So I can lighten what ails you."

"As I told you, I can't understand myself."

Noticing his distress at her reticence, she added, "If I did, I would be the first to help myself, but I want you to know how much I appreciate your caring. And this wonderful meal!"

"Let's do it again, soon."

"If you promise to save your money for a new pair of shoes."

"I'd much rather save it for a flute."

"At least you have one for the time being. Is that what you are going to do in America? Play the flute?"

"It's my dream to earn a living in an orchestra, play chamber music, maybe even compose. If that's asking too much, I may find work as a music teacher or use my languages in any possible way."

"I'm sure your dream will come true. Everything else may be just temporary. You will heal so much pain with your music."

"What about you? Any plans for the future?"

She shrugged. "After all my studies, I can't tell if my health will ever allow me to…"

"It will. You've made tremendous strides, and we both are here, together again, eating *Kaiserschmarren* against all odds. I couldn't ask for more."

They finished their meal in silence.

"I'm amazed at your courage and your positive outlook," she said. "After all you went through. You, too, must have felt like dying on various occasions."

"I did. If I got back on my feet, it was because of my longing to find you and my love for life, music, and freedom. All things that matter to me most, combined and connected as one.

But there was one time when everything seemed to be coming to an end for me. "He stopped, taking a deep breath. "I've been meaning to ask you, but was afraid."

"Ask me what?"

"Perhaps we'd better not. Not right now."

"Ask me what?"

"It happened one night, on June 11, 1944. I'll never forget that date. I was at my wits' end, near the railway station in Tashkent, literally ready to throw myself in front of a moving train, like Anna Karenina. But I lacked her courage, and the whistle of that train made me jump back, just in time. Soon after, I heard a second whistle which sounded more like a desperate human scream, and for a moment I felt sure that it was you, calling me for help."

"That was the day of my deportation to Auschwitz. It's true, I was crying for your help without making a sound. I felt sure you would never see me again."

"Then I definitely heard your cry. But when I jumped back, I was sure that in some mysterious way it was you who had saved me instead."

Tatyana had grown pale. "I think it's time to go back." She put on her gloves.

Perturbed, Victor called for the waiter, who thanked him profusely for his tip. Slowly, they headed back to the park. He took her arm as they made their way through the snow, berating himself for having reminded her of that terrible day.

He hoped to take her mind off the subject. "You told me you are in remission. Isn't that a good sign?"

"Yes, though it may change. It's only fair to let you know. You must stop worrying about me."

"On the contrary. Now I have all the more reason to care for you."

She remained silent, withdrawn. "Please go now," she said as they reached the gate of the sanatorium. "I need to be alone."

"Tatyana, I'm sorry. Are you all right? Perhaps I shouldn't have mentioned that terrible day."

She did not respond.

"Would you like me to come back in the morning?" he asked. Trying to hide her tears, she turned away and hurried toward the veranda. He walked down the path, distressed by his foolish assumption that she requited his love.

Endless reserves of whirling flakes drifted from the clouds and spread a white blanket over the distant mountains. In the morning, Victor paced his room as he had once paced the prison cell in Termez. He finally dressed and went to the dining room for breakfast, but could only swallow a cup of coffee. He tried studying, but was incapable of absorbing any word in any language. It was snowing incessantly, but at half past one he felt imprisoned in his room and walked out. A white quilt covered the landscape. The wet snow soaked through his socks.

Hadn't he waited long enough? It was time to tell Tatyana how he felt, even at the risk of losing her. The façade of an easy comradeship had allowed him to see her on a regular basis, but now her possible rejection meant a final sentence from life itself, a sentence he must be prepared to face.

He forced himself to open the front door to the sanatorium and ask for Tatyana, only to be told that this was the hour of rest. Miss Singer must not be disturbed.

He sat down in the foyer and waited. After a while, he went back to the desk and asked when the hour of repose would be over. That depended on the patient, the clerk informed him. He sat down again, but got up after a moment to have a look at the large dining room, wondering at which table Tatyana took her meals.

After finding the men's room, he squeezed out his socks, then dried his feet and torn shoes with toilet paper. He remembered that there had never been anything like toilet paper to wipe drenched *cardboard slippers* in the Soviet Union. Back in the foyer, a group of patients came down the wide oaken staircase. It was three o'clock. Victor allowed another twenty minutes before asking the clerk to let Miss Singer know he was waiting for her.

The clerk sent up a busboy. He came back to say Miss Singer was not well and could not come down or receive any visitor. When did she fall ill, Victor wanted to know, but the clerk only shrugged. Victor stormed out of the building. "Why are you doing this to me?" Heading down the path against a rising wind, he hurried back to the convalescent home. He was wet, chilled, and bewildered. Yesterday Tatyana had shown concern about his shoes, and today he had climbed through the deep snow to see her. Didn't she realize how much she meant to him?

He took a hot bath, still seeking to explain her refusal to see him. Why had she turned away from him as soon as he said that this was all the more reason to care for her? She had admitted to having called him for help on that terrible day of her deportation. Wasn't that a declaration of love? On the other hand, suppose someone had hurt her so deeply, perhaps that mysterious protector in her childhood, that she had stopped trusting any man?

He understood that his Russian odyssey hadn't included such sorrows and unforseeable hurdles. Deprived of compass or map, he had been faced with a journey through wide-open territories, at the mercy of cruel events and the feverish demands of his heart. If only he could help her face the future with the courage and confidence she had shown him on Kristallnacht. He would never understand how citizens of what had once been a cultured homeland he loved and admired, could stoop to such atrocities. He cried with rage and pity for its victims. Not wishing to remind Tatyana of her own suffering, he had not spoken to her of his intense and bitter feelings.

Would she be able to recapture that vital spark he had treasured for so many years? He could sense that she tried hard to overcome her difficulty to embrace a so-called normal life again. No doubt, she was aware of her new depth and maturity. If only she would open herself to the power of his love. What made him confident that he might be able to help her heal better than any doctor or sanatorium?

31.

TATYANA

I don't recognize myself

After burying an unattainable dream I had pursued for almost nine years, an ironic twist of fate has resurrected it, and left me stranded in the maze of a new reality. If Stefan hadn't come to that sanatorium near Sondrio when I was about to end my life, Victor would never have found me. A few weeks after getting settled in Meran thanks to Stefan, the lost love of my life appeared out of the blue before me...

During our ride to Meran, Stefan asked me to marry him. I told this to Svetlana in a letter, and she wrote me back immediately: as the wife of a new American citizen and war hero I could count on getting a visa for the United States. She was delighted at the prospect of seeing me again in Denver, where she was going to help me find the best medical care.

Victor could hardly still be alive, and my rational mind embraced the chance of sharing my future with Stefan. Yet I asked him to wait until his work in Milan would end, explaining my reluctance because of concern for my health. I deeply appreciated his offer, but would only join him as an equal instead of a sick, dependent wife. This was true. I did hope to get well before making a final decision. Yet the deeper truth was my perennial yearning for Victor.

Svetlana scolded me for my hesitation—just as she had when I told her of my refusal to find safety in a marriage with Francesco. This time she was right. How could I refuse such an offer? Stefan was obviously taken aback by my reaction. It made no sense even to me, because I might turn into an equal, if my surgery was going to be successful.

But how could I give up years of endless longing for Victor? Suppose a miracle brought him back into my life? I couldn't stop waiting for him, not after my incredible hallucination in Auschwitz.

In the end, I explained to Stefan that I still needed to make absolutely sure that I wasn't contagious. He accepted my wishes with remarkable patience. Since I had begged him to keep me company on my lonely weekends, he had rented a room where we used to meet on Saturdays and Sundays. We played games of chess, took rides to Bolzano and resorts in the Dolomites, went to concerts and films, even restaurants my doctor gradually allowed me to visit as long as I got back by nine o'clock sharp.

Then Victor appeared. My cupboard, bare after so much loss and loneliness, was suddenly overflowing with riches. Instead of basking in the love of two outstanding men, I found myself in a state of utter confusion. I didn't know where to turn, how to act. Since I had immediately informed Stefan of Victor's return, I expected him to help me solve my dilemma with some good advice. Obviously shocked by this turn of events, he listened in silence, then said the choice was entirely in my hands. He added that it would only be fair to Victor if he stopped coming to Meran, for his presence mustn't influence my decision. He wanted me to be sure of my feelings.

No doubt, Stefan's reaction was selfless and high-minded, but I thought he would fight for my love. Now I was troubled by what I interpreted as an easy withdrawal.

At my request, he reluctantly agreed to come back on weekends, at least till I learned more about Victor because we both might have changed a great deal. At the same time he urged me to tell Victor the truth about our complex situation.

What I failed to explain to Stefan was my gratitude to him for saving my life on several occasions. Did I fear to lose his friendship? How could I bear to make him suffer? Was I motivated by loyalty or cowardice. Was I stalling for time as I worried about Victor's reaction to my special friendship with Stefan? The longer I wait, the harder it will be to explain my odd behavior.

I'm despicable, ashamed to confess the real reason for my procrastination, even to myself. When Victor asked me to meet him on Saturdays or Sundays, I told him that, according to my doctor, I needed a complete rest on weekends. Thanks to this lie, I missed the opportunity to tell him the truth. And now, after continued visits with Stefan, I'm even more frightened to face Victor's reaction. Thanks to my reluctance, he may grow jealous and refuse to believe in my innocence. Stefan, on the other hand, may wonder whether I'm just waiting for what is best for me; but this, too, is far from explaining my bewildering behavior.

Out of concern for Stefan, I find myself acting like a shrew to Victor and may be driving him away from me. In the end, I may lose them both.

***

Some weeks have passed since my last entry. On Saturdays, I still join Stefan in the *pensione*, where he spends the night. He no longer asks whether I've told Victor about him, knowing that I would speak up if I had. I can tell he is more and more concerned, perhaps even wondering about my sanity—perhaps blaming my madness on Auschwitz. It's true--the camp has turned my sanity upside down. My confusion makes me more reticent in Victor's presence, and aware of Stefan's growing doubts. Poor as he is, Victor frequently brings me flowers, chocolates, or an interesting book, while Stefan is oblivious to such thoughtful gestures. But I mustn't criticize or compare.

I don't recognize myself. A few days ago, Victor asked if I knew someone who could help me get into the United States. Instead of using his question to tell him the truth, I shook my head and said that wasn't likely—not if my TB flares up again. In any case, I told him that he must stop worrying about me. "But that's all the more reason to care for you," he said. Those words caused me to reject him. In my struggle for health and independence, I have begun to abhor being cared for like a helpless child.

What's the reason for my deceitful silence? It has spoiled everything for all of us. Victor asked to see me the next day, but I refused. He had walked through the heavy snow in his flimsy shoes to pay me a visit, but

I couldn't face him. I wept all night, deeply worried about him. I know he has suffered immensely. He has grown and matured without losing his innocence and open-heartedness—qualities I used to cherish. Perhaps my reticence keeps him from revealing the depth of his feelings. Even so, I am touched by his efforts to cheer me in his loving way, and have to hold myself back from a desperate longing to throw my arms around him.

I'm afraid he will never forgive me for not telling him about Stefan. Even if he should understand, how could he cope with my new and conflicted soul?

32.

PUTTING THE CARDS ON THE TABLE

Dear Tatyana,

I just came to the sanatorium to see you, but was informed that you were ill and didn't want any visitors. I can't help wondering whether your response was a refusal to see me, for whatever reason, or if you are blaming me for taking you out in the cold.

Since you keep me in suspense, I need to speak up and clear the air. Each time I close my eyes, I see your face. My world grew small during those years in that far, alien land. It turned me into more than an exile, banishing me from everything, including my real self. I've not mentioned this, since I didn't want to burden you with my lonely devastation and, to speak frankly, my almost fatal despair. I meant to let go of the past and rejoice in our miraculous encounter. Our meeting can't be dismissed as mere coincidence. Fate has brought us together once more, I feel sure, for some special purpose and meaning.

Now I wonder what keeps you from letting me know where I stand. You are warm and friendly one day and withdrawn the next... so much so that I'm afraid my words may chase you away for good. Tatyana, we were united over distant lands in our kindred spirits, our pain and aloneness. My only support during those years was the vague possibility of seeing you again. I think of those years as a test to prove that I am worthy of you. You have become the center of my being. I can no longer imagine life without you. Afraid to reveal my true feelings, I pretended to be no more than a friend. And all the time I really wanted to take you into my arms and hold you tenderly, kiss your eyes and sweet face to make you forget all the horror of the past.

I have been living from moment to moment, longing to build a good and fruitful life at your side. Though my world has grown larger than ever, I still have nothing to offer you but the refuge of my love. Please tell me honestly how you feel. I can no longer bear to wait alone in the dark.

- Victor

After another wakeful night, he went to the sanatorium, careful not to crumple the letter in his pocket. The sun had come out. Finding the thoroughfares swept clean, he decided to take the road instead of the snow-filled path through the park. He was expected to teach at eleven o'clock and meant to deliver the letter at the desk and leave. But as he entered the building, he saw Tatyana coming down the steps.

She greeted him with a happy smile. "I'm so glad you came back. I was afraid you'd never want to see me again."

"Why on earth..."

"I was so harsh with you Victor. I meant to call you and apologize. All I know is the name of your convalescent home. I don't have the phone number."

"Then you are feeling better?"

She explained that she had been extremely tired and in fear of a cold. Colds could be treacherous in her condition. But the rest had been of great help.

"Tatyana, I was afraid you might be seriously ill. And thought you didn't want to see me anymore, because..." He stopped, breathless, looking straight at her.

"Let's talk in *our* room," she whispered.

"Sorry, but I'm expected to teach in ten minutes..." He handed her the letter.

"It looks ominous."

"I may come back tomorrow."

The envelope trembled in her hand. "May or will?" she asked, as Victor was rushing out the door.

In the late afternoon, a messenger brought him her answer to his letter. There was no address on the envelope, only his name written in miniature characters, clear and softly rounded. He held it for a long moment in anguish without opening it.

Dear Victor,

Have you ever stepped out of the darkness into the blinding light? Your letter…I can't describe what it means to me. Your courage and honesty put me to shame. I must finally tell you that I have failed to live up to your shining example. I would rather tell you what has happened in person, for I'm worried about your reaction, afraid you may turn away from me, you, who are standing before me like a spirit from a better world.

Ever since your return, I have been in a daze. In my anguish, I held back and shrank from your touch. Only now, after receiving your letter, I understand that part of my behavior stemmed from the fear of being torn from you again. Since I lost my whole family and most of my friends, any close attachment threatens me with yet another loss. I'm not able to trust my own life again, at least not yet.

In this sanatorium, I'm always forced to follow rules, scrutinized by watchful eyes, and faced with the uncertainty about my health. Your assurance that my illness would make you take even more care of me only made matters worse. How could I burden you in this way and deprive you of the security you so clearly deserve? You mustn't waver, but return to your music and rebuild your life. Your love sustains me, but your dream of a life together must wait until I can face the future with you as an equal. First, I need to get well and strong.

If you think that I'm rude and difficult, I apologize. My behavior wasn't caused by you, though I must confess that you are the reason for the frightening dilemma in which I now find myself. Though you were always patient and considerate, you seemed equally withdrawn from me. Convinced that your feelings were no longer the same, I've held back for many reasons. But I won't leave you in the dark any longer. If you come by tomorrow afternoon, I promise to put all my cards on the table.

> *Please don't judge me too harshly,*
>
> *-Tatyana*

He devoured her words, reading them again and again. The first part of her letter struck him as an almost magical response. In spite of an unpredictable future, love might still overcome any hurdle, if only Tatyana could recover her health and with it her shattered trust. But what about the mysterious hint of a "frightening dilemma"? Her odd contradictions alarmed him, and he prepared himself for some dreadful revelation.

Unable to wait until the next afternoon, he went straight to the sanatorium. As he looked for her in the veranda after the hour of rest, he found her sitting in a corner, eyes closed, her face turned to the sun. A few patients playing cards stole glances in their direction. Feeling his presence, Tatyana looked up at him with a start. He sat down beside her in silence.

"You read my letter."

"On tenterhooks…"

"I know." She hesitated. "Have you any idea how I waited for you all these years? Only a few months ago I gave up, believing that you could no longer be alive."

She took a deep breath. "Let me start somewhere else. In the late summer of '43, a partisan friend helped me escape from Yugoslavia to Italy. As soon as we arrived in Trieste, he left for England to join the Allies. We had no contact for four years, but Stefan found me in another sanatorium last summer, just when I had decided to make an end to it all."

She stopped, noticing Victor's shock at this disclosure.

"You mean?"

She nodded. "I wouldn't have been alive if he had arrived the next day. It was a miracle, not as unlikely as your finding me here in Meran, but it saved my life. And it happened only a few weeks before you appeared so unexpectedly."

"What an incredible story."

"Especially since our stories are completely interwoven. If Stefan hadn't found me, you would never have found me either. He had saved my life on several occasions during our flight to Italy and is one of the two best friends I have left in the world. I immediately told him about your return, and he insisted that I let you know the truth about us right away, but I just couldn't do it. I was too frightened to hurt you, or worse, to lose you for good."

Was she trying to lessen the impact of this news? *Perhaps I ought to thank him for saving your life,* Victor thought bitterly. "The truth about you," he repeated. "So you were, or still are lovers," he managed to say. "Ever since your escape from Yugoslavia."

"No, never!" she exclaimed. "We were just comrades. He works for the Americans in Milan and has come here on weekends."

"When you told me that the doctor wanted you to take a complete rest."

She lowered her head. "I knew you would judge me."

"You are wrong, Tatyana. It all comes to me as a shock, but I'm not blaming you." He was choking on his words. "Fate has played nasty tricks on us. In your letter, you told me how you waited for me all these years, just as I waited for you. I was married, but you were free and had every right to love anyone you chose. But why did you wait so long to tell me the truth?"

"I just told you the truth. He was not and is not my lover. I found excuses not to marry him, while I begged him in my loneliness to come back on the weekends. I made you both suffer. I didn't know how you had grown and changed in all these years, and wanted to make sure that our dream was real. But the longer I waited, the more I worried. I lacked the courage to hurt either one of you; I'm unable to understand it myself. How can you forgive my cowardice?"

"But you were the most courageous person I ever met!" Victor protested. The card players looked up from their game to watch them with brash curiosity.

"Weeks before your arrival," she went on in a whisper, "Stefan asked me to marry him. As his wife, I would have no trouble leaving for the States and getting the best medical care. But I asked him to wait. As soon as I told him about your arrival, he offered to withdraw. He wanted me to choose between the two of you without any influence on his part. I had to be absolutely sure of my feelings, he said, and thought it unfair to you if he went on seeing me before I made my final decision."

"That was decent of him." Tatyana looked at him quickly. "I mean it, without any irony."

"I should have listened to him," Tatyana went on. "But I begged him not to leave me alone in my dilemma, so he continued coming back on weekends. My odd request only made matters worse. Though he never mentioned it, I could feel Stefan's growing suspicion about my truthfulness, just as you have expressed your doubts about me."

Victor took a quick breath. "You are the most amazing..." He looked at her in silence. "But why haven't you listened to your heart, as you did in the past?"

"Because that's what I've done all my life. And look where it's gotten me!"

"But it's the only signpost we always need to follow."

"There's no *always*. Auschwitz has been a monstrous lesson. My life has been thrown upside down. I must learn to use what's left of my reason instead of depending on my foolish heart."

"You are keeping me in suspense. All I need to know is what your foolish heart is telling you," he said softly, putting a hand on her shoulder and drawing her close.

"And if I do, will you forgive me?"

"There's nothing to forgive."

"Then I can only say that my foolish heart is about to burst because I love you so much."

33.

TATYANA

"The door will always be open for you..."

A weight has fallen off my shoulders. Since I confessed my love to Victor, everything else fell into place. We needed a refuge from prying eyes, but only the snow-covered park offered us a touch of privacy. We stole sporadic kisses under a tree, and tore apart at the sight of any strangers. A weak sun hardly protected us from the cold. Now and then, snow dropped from the branches on our heads or shoulders, but love made us forget any discomfort, except for the frustration of thwarted desire.

As last Saturday approached, the dread of Stefan's visit hung more heavily over me than any snow. I hoped to make matters less painful with a quick and honest statement about my decision.

We met at the *pensione* at the usual time. It was ironic that Stefan offered me the first bouquet he has ever given me. Red roses. Thanking him, I avoided his embrace and went to ask the landlady for a vase. When I entered the bathroom to pour water into the large jug she had given me, Stefan followed me from our sitting room. I said I had something important to tell him. One glance at his image in the mirror revealed he knew what it was. As in a film in slow motion, the water spilled over the edge of the jug.

"It's about your decision." His voice was toneless. I turned to face him. He had grown pale. "What else could I expect after your almost ten-year-old dream?"

"Stefan..."

"Mine lasted only for four."

"Oh, Stefan, that's not the issue."

"Then what is?"

"You know that I couldn't tell if and how much he had changed after all these years."

"And now you think you can?"

I didn't care for his aggressive tone, but would have given anything to spare him the pain.

"You kept me dangling, and have possibly been lovers all along." He took the jug from my hands, set it on the counter, pulled out the roses, and threw them furiously into a wastebasket.

I followed him into the hallway, listening to my own angry voice. "We have never been lovers."

He turned to look at me. It was too dark to see his face. "Don't lie to me."

"I've never lied to you. But you don't seem to trust me anymore. You, of all people."

"What do you mean?"

"I thought you were my best friend. No matter what, I'll always be grateful for all you have..."

"I don't need your gratitude. I asked you to marry me and offered you a new life in the States, and all you did was ask me to wait. The truth is you were waiting for Victor."

"I thought he could no longer be alive, but hoped for a miracle. I told you I was torn because I felt very close to you. I can't stand to be a sickly, helpless wife to anyone. You understood my need for independence. I'm sorry for all the turmoil I caused you and hate myself for hurting either one of you."

"In other words, it's now my turn to get more troubled and confused. I'll just drive back to Milan."

"Are you telling me you no longer care to be my friend?"

He did not respond. "I need to pay the landlady," he said, "tell her I won't be back. Unless you want to keep this place for you and..." He stopped abruptly.

I ignored his caustic remark. "You said the choice was in my hands. I understand your disappointment Stefan, but what have I done to make you so angry?"

"Nothing."

I was choking, unable to tell him that I would always care for him. As he kept standing in the dark hall, isolated in cold silence, I blamed myself bitterly for having caused him such pain. And now there was nothing I could do but leave him there in his grief.

In tears, I murmured, "The door will always be open for you," aware that I was just closing it softly behind me.

I was devastated, remembering how he had comforted me at my father's death, stood up against Bogdan, and then guided me out of harm's way from Yugoslavia to Italy. From the moment we met, he was ready to protect me. And now he might never want to see me again.

Not wanting to trouble Victor with my heartache, I barely mentioned Stefan's angry response. Victor felt sorry for him, but could hardly hide his own happiness. He told me not to blame Stefan for what he might have said to me in anger. His hurt at my rejection might have intensified his jealousy. "If I were in his place," he remarked, "I would go berserk."

He hasn't asked anything more about Stefan and our dismal encounter. I appreciate his tactful silence and don't want to upset him with the intensity of my grief and remorse. This painful experience is lowering my self-confidence. Had Stefan discovered something unworthy about me, something I refuse to admit to myself? But what good is our personal striving for improvement when innocent people have been killed by the millions?

***

As if he had heard my regret, I received this letter from Stefan:

Dear Tatyana,

I need to tell you how mortified I feel about my abominable behavior. I can't expect your forgiveness, though I hardly remember anything I did or said to you in my pain and anger. My bitterness was not directed at you, but at the deadly blow of my loss. In spite of my sadness, I loved every moment in your company. Although I expected your decision, its impact was too much to bear. Let me assure you that you are the dearest person I have ever known.

How could I be so insensitive, after learning from Svetlana that you tried to save her life again and again, while risking your own? No one knows better than I how hard you are trying to overcome all that horror and find your way back into the light.

Thank you for leaving the door open for me. Of course I want to remain your friend for the rest of my life. All we have left in this world are the people we love. What else is there to live for? I'm aware of the difficulties facing you and Victor and want to assist you as much as I can. If it's all right with you, I will meet you in a little while to find out how I may ease matters for both of you in any way. Please let me know if you are able to forgive me. I am anxiously waiting for your answer. With my warmest wishes, as ever,

- Stefan

I wrote back at once to tell him that there was nothing to forgive. It was I who needed to apologize for my dark moods and confusion. "I'm so happy to know that you are still my friend and can't thank you enough for your generous offer to help us."

When I showed Stefan's letter to Victor, we were resting on a bench in the public garden. I could feel how my relief was transmitted to him.

"Now I understand how hard it must have been for you to give him up for me," he said.

"Victor, you know I would give up anyone for you."

"You say that now." He gave me an impish smile. "But you *have* been worried for weeks about whether I've changed and matured in all these years."

"Well, have you?"

He laughed. "That's for you to discover."

I told him that I had not only learned a great deal about him, but was discovering how strong he had grown in the hard years of his wandering, lost and forgotten, through endless realms of the Soviet Union. Now we were both discovering the huge gap between dream and reality. Our separate dreams had always remained pure and harmonious, but reality is always filled with new obstacles and challenges.

"And you don't find that exciting?"

"Compelling, overwhelming, and startling." I kissed him after each word. "I only hope that I won't disappoint you."

"You couldn't if you tried. Our love is real and infinite, anything but a dream. It will never be finite. If it were, we wouldn't have waited for each other the way we did—beyond life and death," he added, holding me close.

"That's why I feel that it makes us grow every day," I said. "After all our wandering and suffering in the past, it seems to have turned into an odyssey of love."

***

Two weeks later, I came down the steps after my nap when I heard the sounds of a flute rising from the veranda room. For a moment, I assumed Victor had come by to visit me after leaving the music school. Finding the room empty, he was probably waiting for my arrival by playing a few tunes. But on opening the door, I was faced with a crowd at the various tables, laughing and listening, while others were dancing in the center of the floor. Victor was playing the flute, moving among them to the rhythm of a waltz by Johann Strauss. While his looks have matured, his fine features remain unchanged, and his dark blue eyes are more soulful than ever.

I watched the lively scene from a corner of the room. An oblique ray of sunshine passed through the glass doors of the veranda. Victor closed his eyes. As he reopened them I watched in awe, for he seemed to be radiating the sun's warmth with the sounds of his music and his whole being. I could see the joyous effect he was having on his audience, which consisted of survivors and refugees filled with the bitterness of recent tragedies. As soon as he stopped playing, they rose from their seats and applauded along with the dancers.

Their reaction was an homage to his presence as well as to his music.

His caring for others hasn't changed since our encounter in Stuttgart. In those ominous days, I had wished to save his life at any cost. Now this new Victor arouses my constant, passionate longing to be in his arms. I could tell that he was filled with a genuine belief in all the good and the positive this new life might yet have to offer. I wanted him, wanted this new Victor more than ever before.

Catching sight of me, he rushed to embrace me in front of everyone. A few couples surrounded us to congratulate me on my "wonderful fiancé". But Victor protested, saying it was the other way around.

"When are you getting married?" a woman with a strong Yiddish accent who had often seen him with me asked.

"As soon as she'll have me," Victor responded in German with an amusing Yiddish slant.

The woman smiled broadly, revealing a missing tooth: "*Mazel tov!*" she exclaimed, clapping her hands.

I have never felt so happy.

34.

A VICIOUS CIRCLE

During the third week of February, Victor received a letter from the American Committee stating that, according to his physician, he was now restored to health. Dr. Ferrari asked to see him in his office and congratulated him on this good news. Victor was to go back to Turin and wait for his American visa which wouldn't take long to arrive.

"Why can't I wait right here?"

"I'm afraid that's not for me to decide. You are now in the hands of the Americans."

After a moment's hesitation, Victor told Dr. Ferrari about Tatyana, the state of her health, and his fear of being forced to leave Europe without her.

"How much longer does she have to stay in the sanatorium?"

Victor had no idea. She survived Auschwitz, he said, but hadn't completely recovered from her TB.

Dr. Ferrari looked at the folder containing Victor's records. "You're taking much on your shoulders, after the hell you went through in the Soviet Union."

"Her hell was worse. Now she needs an X-ray for a clean bill of health, or she won't be able to move to America. In the meantime, my late wife's sister is sending us affidavits."

Tatyana was right, he thought. *Life gives us mere snippets of happiness...*

Two hours later, he faced Tatyana in their favorite cafe. "You are so limpid," she said. " Like a glass-bottom boat. I can look right through you

255

and watch all the wonderful corals and tropical fish inside you."

Finding her in a joyous mood, he dared not upset her with his news.

"Even in the gloomiest moments, just the thought of you, dead or alive, gave me some strength," she went on. "And now you've brought the sun back into my life. You picked up what I lost, like a charm that fell from my neck. Though now I'm not sure I still want it."

"Because you couldn't bear losing it again?" She nodded. Victor reached for her hand and held it firmly in his. "Suppose I fasten the clasp so well that you will never lose it?"

"I can only make myself responsible for that."

"I want you to hold me responsible, too." He hesitated before going on. "Unfortunately, I have no control over outer circumstances."

"What's wrong?"

"I have to go back to that shelter in Turin. It may be just for a little while."

"How long?"

"I don't know. I've asked Sophie's sister for a second affidavit. Then we may wait together for our visas to arrive."

"What visas? Oh, Victor, you must leave for the States, be free. I can't join you. They won't let me in."

"But you are in remission. As soon as I come back from Turin, we'll get married. And then we won't let anyone separate us ever again."

"My darling..." Tatyana hid her face in her hands, trembling all over.

He drew her close. "Look. Once married, we'll get our visas together and leave for the States. I promise I won't go without you."

"Suppose you get your visa in Turin and are forced to leave right away? If you don't, you may ruin your only chance."

"The Americans have a phrase, 'We'll cross that bridge when we come to it.' So let's wait and see."

"And if there's no bridge?"

"Tatyana, let's promise each other never to give up." His anguish was deeper than he cared to admit. He recalled the dreamer he had once been, the belief that had helped him survive starvation, prison, illness, and labor camps. Would the candor that had helped him overcome all that horror pull them through this new predicament?

For their last two days together, they walked hand in hand through the town, finding refuge in public gardens, cafés, and a cinema. There was no private shelter for their love. Victor expressed his outrage at the curtailment of freedom imposed on survivors, even years after the war's end. His compulsory return to Turin struck him as a singular cruelty. In the Soviet Union, everyone was forced to work. Now he felt equally violated. What good did the improvement of their lives, the care they and others received from this committee or that, do for any of them? Their hands remained tied. Freedom was a farce in this huge postwar ghetto.

He didn't tell her how much he feared their separation. In a little while she would be alone, facing that black notebook she was trying to complete. Svetlana had written about her imminent departure for Denver. She had repeated her promise to find the best surgeon to take care of her friend. What if Tatyana wasn't able to enter the United States? Her plight reminded Victor of the day his pocket was cut out of his trousers. The chief of police had insisted he go back to Bukhara for a document proving his identity. But how could he go to Bukhara for a new document without the old one?

Now he and Tatyana were caught in a similar vicious circle. Their last day together turned into a pilgrimage of leave-taking. They ate a plate of spaghetti in a *trattoria,* swallowing pasta and tears while bravely smiling at each other.

"I called Stefan and asked him to look you up as soon as possible," she said. "Since he works for the Americans and offered us his assistance, I told him you are fluent in Russian and speak several languages. Perhaps he can use you as a translator. He promised to look into it."

"That's embarrassing. How am I going to face him?"

"Don't worry. If it weren't for me, you two might be close friends."

Victor sighed. "By the way, I have a present for you, but left it in my room. I thought I might as well show you where I lived and dreamed about you every day."

"But I'm not supposed to…"

"Who cares? I'll leave a message at the sanatorium and tell them I'll take you back later in a taxi."

"Is this how you lure women into your cave?"

"Yes. Every Monday, Wednesday, and Friday."

"I can't believe there was no woman in your life. A man like you, in all these years."

"I was too hungry, too weak. Too wrapped up in the thought of you."

"So was I. I lived like a nun."

"And I as a monk. Waiting."

It was the hour of siesta. On entering his room Tatyana was out of breath, trembling with cold. Victor made her sit on the bed and covered her with the customary down quilt featured on every German or Austrian bed. He told her to close her eyes, then took a package from the table and put it into her hands. She couldn't tear the wrapping fast enough. "A camera, oh Victor, you didn't, you shouldn't, a Zeiss. Better than the one I lost in that river!"

Victor sat down on the bed beside her. "It will keep you out of mischief while I'm gone. There are enough rolls of film to get you back into practice. I'm a man who thinks ahead. I need a woman to support me in America."

"But how did you guess?"

"Guess what?"

"That photography was my first love, not for reportage, but…"

"I just knew."

"This is much too generous."

"Don't worry. Dr. Ferrari is driving to Turin in the late afternoon and offered me a ride. The Americans sent money for the trip, so I can use it to buy a pair of shoes in Turin."

"You must have spent all your money for me. Oh, Victor, the camera will be like a part of you for me to hold while you're gone."

She got up, took off her sweater and skirt, slipped into bed, and covered herself with the quilt. Still hesitating, he half undressed and lay down beside her. She put her arms around him.

Their kisses tasted of salt and eternity.

He fondled her gently, fearful that the excitement of lovemaking might be as harmful to her as an opulent meal to a starving man, mindful that it should be allotted gradually after such abstinence, hunger, and loneliness. He continued undressing her, then took off the rest of his own clothes and covered her face and body with kisses. For a fleeting moment he thought of Sophie, a spirit from another life.

"Let me know what you'd like me to do," he whispered. For an answer, she caressed and kissed him hungrily, arousing his passion. When he entered her, she cried out with pleasure. He could not distinguish his heartbeat from hers as they clung to each other. Alone at last in each other's arms, they were like two orphans dying for love.

"You are so lovely, so warm," he whispered. "Somehow I feel that everything will work out for us."

"If only you could come back as soon as possible," Tatyana whispered. "But how and when?"

"Sooner than you think. And then I'll get a new flute and serenade you every Monday, Wednesday, and Friday."

During the ride to the sanatorium, he held her close for a final moment. Sick at heart, he imagined her running up to her room, falling on her bed, and sobbing disconsolately.

35.

THE BLIND MAN WATCHES
THE LAME ONE DANCE

In Turin, Victor found a small number of displaced persons in the old school building. During the day, all inmates were allowed to leave the shelter. Food was plentiful and well prepared, and their barren rooms were kept meticulously clean.

Victor and Tatyana wrote each other every day, but he could feel her dark moods in spite of her efforts to be cheerful. Reminded of his isolation in the Soviet Union, he agonized over the loneliness she must have endured before and after the hell of the camp and was now forced to endure again. He was amazed at how their lives had always been intertwined by the longing for one another. What horrors was she now confiding to that black notebook? If only this would free her from the nightmares holding her captive. He dreaded the disastrous effect of that notebook, although her fortitude to confront the darkest days of her past might give her relief in the future.

During walks through the baroque streets of Turin, Victor moved through arcades of the new Via Roma, its elegant shops defying the postwar scarcity of materials. In old Via Roma, he found a modest pair of leather shoes and a quiet café. Settled in a corner with his first postwar cappuccino, he wrote Tatyana about the walks he was taking through the city or across the Po River. How, on leaving the river, he would hike uphill to the Monte dei Cappuccini, where the chocolate-colored habits of the monks must have inspired the name of those delicious coffee drinks. In clear weather, the view from the hill spread to the wide boulevards below, stretching toward the mountains in perfect symmetry, while snow-capped Monte Rosa grew visible in the distance.

One day he received a letter that broke through Tatyana's repeated efforts at cheerfulness:

My dearest Victor,

My eyes are red from too much crying. I miss you more than I ever imagined. You are all things to me, all losses reincarnated into this wonderful, hopeless love. Why did I find you so late, only to lose you again? I hope you aren't wilting away in that shelter and that you are as strong and serene as your letters try to make me believe. I would go to the end of the world for you, but feel useless, unable to do anything, for you or myself. Is this a new trial, another test? If it doesn't come to an end, it will be the end of us. And then I would rather die.

Her despair filled him with rage against the obstacles in their way. Worried what might happen to her if he left her alone, he was ready to rush back to Meran. But the next day brought him a different message:

Please forget my unhappy letter. My misery was caused by the awful memories that I had hoped to send downriver in the black notebook. But now I feel better. After facing the past, I'm able to breathe again. Even my lungs feel the difference. To confront that past was a dangerous undertaking. To my great relief, your camera served as an antidote. I can hardly express what my first photographs mean to me. Freedom and independence. Thanks again for your wonderful gift! Now I keep praying for some miracle that will soon reunite us.

In a postscript, she added that Stefan would pay Victor a visit on Sunday.

***

He was unable to sleep. What could he expect from such an encounter? He vacillated between hope and pride. Hope that their meeting wouldn't turn into an embarrassing experience, and pride, as he prepared to brace himself against any humiliating charity.

Stefan arrived in his blue Fiat at noon. He was taller and darker than Victor had expected. The warmth and firmness of his handshake and his sonorous voice made Victor immediately feel at ease, and his first impression matched the image Tatyana had evoked in the descriptions of her friend. He had come for just a few hours, Stefan told him, since he needed to be back in Milan for the evening.

"I appreciate all the more that you rushed here to meet me," Victor said. Stefan drove to a restaurant near Piazza Castello. As soon as they were settled at a quiet table, he told Victor that he had found Tatyana in good spirits. "What a great idea to give her that camera!"

"When did you see her?"

"Just briefly, the other day. She showed me some excellent portraits of fellow patients and said you had played the flute for them. They have accepted you both and now are eager to pose for her."

Struck by jealousy, Victor thought it unfair that Stefan should be the first to have seen her photographs. "She didn't tell me anything about those pictures."

"But she gave me a glowing report," Stefan said. "Your gift was a miracle."

"There's so little I can do for her. We're trapped. She's there and I'm here. A Russian proverb says the blind man watches the lame one dance."

Stefan smiled, assuring Victor that he would no longer be a blind man. "She's like you, an outstanding translator. Speaks three languages like a native and is fluent in French. I told her we might have a job for her."

"Do you think she has the energy?"

"Not yet. Anyway, she recommended you instead, knowing that Russian, English, German, and now even Italian are especially important to what's happening. She told me that you are fluent in all four."

The waiter was ready to take their orders. Stefan suggested a dish of roasted duck with German red cabbage. He chose a special red wine of the Piedmont region. The delicious meal reminded Victor of the cabbage rolls he had shared with Bubachoff. Stefan listened with special sympathy to the story of the two friends' reunion in the labor camp, their love of music and the Maestro's untimely death.

"I can't imagine how much you too must have suffered," he said.

In the silence that followed at the end of dinner, Stefan pulled a document from his briefcase and handed it to him.

Victor glanced at it in disbelief: "Am I officially allowed to work?"

"Yes, temporarily. The job won't pay much, but it's better than lingering here."

"Better? It's too good to believe!" Victor exclaimed. "What sort of work do you expect me to do?"

"Mostly writing, translating letters, interpreting. Nothing too exciting. You may start in a couple of weeks. I happened to see a 'room for rent' sign in walking distance from my office and will let you know if it's clean and reasonable."

"How can I thank you?" Victor asked. He needed some time to absorb this amazing turn of events. "I just had some other good news from my late wife's sister in New York," he went on. "She confirmed that new affidavits are on the way, and that our visas are soon going to follow."

Stefan looked straight at him. "I assume you'll soon get married."

"It's the only way to…" Victor was relieved to be interrupted by the waiter who brought them their after-dinner coffee and *spumante*.

"I'm glad for you both. Let's drink to Tatyana's health."

They clinked glasses. Victor was amazed at the comfort he felt in the presence of the man he had considered his rival.

"It's hard to believe what she, what you both, went through," Stefan went on. "I asked Tatyana to let us read her black notebook when she's done with it, but she thinks the world is already filled with too much horror, and that you and I know enough about concentration camps. I told her we need to preserve such personal documents for a number of reasons."

"You may be right," Victor said. "To be on guard against such evil may prevent a repetition in the future. But it may cause vicious people anywhere to mimic it for their murderous purposes."

"Everything is a two-edged sword. But the truth must be known.

Did she tell you about her friend Svetlana?"

Victor nodded. "On several occasions. They keep writing to each other."

"I suppose Tatyana didn't mention that she saved Svetlana's life again and again. Svetlana told me how the two half-starved girls had been forced to carry heavy loads of food from dawn to dusk; food intended for the families of guards and SS men. No German housewife ever took pity on them. One evening, lining up for the usual roll call—it must have been a couple of months before the end of the war—Svetlana was about to collapse. Tatyana put her arm around her and made her stand up straight. The SS commander ordered her to let go of her friend. If Svetlana passed out, she would be shot right there."

Stefan stopped for a moment to pour more *spumante* into Victor's glass.

"I had heard that prisoners were strictly forbidden to talk to a guard or official," he went on. "But Tatyana looked straight at the enemy and told him in her perfect German that Svetlana was all right and would be back for work in the morning. Svetlana told me in great excitement how the officer pointed his gun at Tatyana, ready to shoot, but then changed his mind and asked if she was German. 'My mother is,' she answered. He turned to a guard: 'I thought these two were Yugoslavian prisoners.' The guard confirmed it. The SS man looked at Tatyana and asked if she spoke any other language. 'Italian,' she said. 'Be in my office at nine in the morning,' he commanded, then went on with his inspection."

"And then…?" Victor asked anxiously.

"The next morning, Tatyana found him poring over some papers on his desk. 'So you lived in Venice,' he said. 'Do you know how to type?' She nodded, and he ordered her to come to his office three mornings a week. She was to translate and type letters to his Italian mistress, love letters, which he meticulously copied over in longhand. After a short time, he demanded she compose those letters directly. '*Mia amata* Caterina,' she wrote, 'my beloved Caterina, every day without you is a day without sunshine,' or some such kitsch. She was afraid to run out of ideas for her compositions—like Scheherazade—and then be killed on the spot. The brute depended on her skills. A married man, he threatened to *exterminate* her at once if she breathed a word about those letters to anyone. To 'strengthen her mind for the task,' he always gave her a piece of bread and a sausage for lunch. She ate only half of it, hiding the rest for Svetlana."

Stefan stopped for a moment. "Svetlana has told me that nothing impressed her as much as Tatyana's capacity to share that precious sausage," he went on. "The prisoners were starved, and the temptation of devouring that bread and meat on the spot must have been irresistible. But Tatyana never took as much as a bite from the half she saved."

Victor was deeply moved. He remembered the ordeal of his own endless hunger and was more impressed than ever by Tatyana's fortitude and dedication to others.

"What about her TB?" he asked after a silence. "Didn't it just happen weeks before war's end?"

"Exactly. Svetlana followed her to the so-called infirmary with a mysterious fever. She told me that Tatyana's 'benefactor' would surely have killed them both had the Russians not arrived weeks earlier than expected. I found out that at war's end, during the Auschwitz inmates' famous death march, the sick and dying were left to their fate."

"How amazing," Victor remarked, "that Tatyana was saved because of her critical illness, while I happened to be deported from Lemberg to a gulag, exactly two days before the Nazis invaded the city."

36.

THE GABLED ROOM

Milan was still cold and wet in March, but Victor cherished his unexpected freedom and usefulness. He moved into the room Stefan had found for him. From a cubicle close to Stefan's office, he corresponded three times a week with public officials in the Soviet Union, Italy, the United States, and West Germany. Quick to learn about daily transactions and postwar issues, he was earning a modest salary for the first time in years, while tutoring his young students on Wednesday mornings and practicing his music whenever and wherever he could.

Tatyana had written him a loving letter, stating how happy she was to hear the good news about his encounter with Stefan and his work and freedom. Since Victor had been able to leave the convalescent home, she hoped he would now be able to come to Meran on weekends. She could hardly wait to see him. Though amazed and delighted about his growing friendship with Stefan, she was sad to be unable to join them. Victor promised to come as soon as he learned to handle all the tasks expected of him. It would take about three weeks before he could plan a longed-for visit to Meran.

Mario, his friend and chef at the home, had once told him that his brother owned a house in the vicinity of the sanatorium and would occasionally let a couple of its rooms. Victor called him to ask if the place was still available. Mario called him right back. "You're in luck," he said. "You can have a room with a small kitchen. It's more than reasonable at this time of year. Just go up two flights. The key is in the lock, the bed will be ready, and you are welcome to try it."

It was close to midnight when Victor finally arrived in Meran. Relieved to find the last taxi at this late hour, he followed Mario's directions and immediately went to sleep in a charming room under a gabled roof. In the morning, after breakfast with Mario, he took a cab to the sanatorium.

Tatyana was waiting for him at "their" table. She looked radiant in a light green dress. "I can't believe you're really here," she whispered. They were reluctant to embrace in front of a group of patients, who interrupted their games to wave their welcome to Victor. Moving from table to table, Victor shook hands with them one by one.

He told Tatyana that he wanted to show her a lovely room in the neighborhood, but wanted to make sure she liked it. A taxi was waiting outside. They could look at the place together right now.

"Together," she repeated, "what a lovely word."

This was the young and carefree Tatyana Victor remembered from the days they had first met. He waited for her to fetch her coat, then helped her get settled in the rear of the cab. Calling out the address to the driver, he closed the partition between the front and back seats.

Their eyes met in a silent embrace. He put his arms around her and held her close until they arrived. When the cab stopped and he paid the driver, the man smirked at him through his Bismarck moustache. Hand in hand, they skipped along a short path that wound through a wintry garden to the entrance, then climbed the stairs to the gabled room. There was no one in sight when Victor unlocked the door.

"I slept here last night," he said. "If you don't like it, we'll move to another place."

Tatyana looked around absentmindedly. "But I love it!" she exclaimed. "Our first home."

"You are my home."

He took her coat and threw it over a chair. "My dearest Tatyana," he whispered, drawing her to him, "how did I ever manage to live without you?"

They fell on the bed he had made up so carefully that morning. During his absence, their longing for one another had grown to be unlike anything they had known in their life.

Later, a deep satisfaction spread through Victor's whole being, as though Tatyana's blood were coursing through his veins. For a long time they remained silent in a close embrace. When Victor opened his eyes to kiss her, he saw tears rolling down her temple.

"What's wrong, my love?"

"Nothing's wrong."

"But you are crying."

"For joy." She propped herself on her elbows and looked down on him, smiling.

"Then you are happy?"

"Yes, terribly happy. You may find it odd, but I'm happy and sad at the same time. I mean, sad about any good turn for the better."

They had a late lunch in a neighborhood café. He told her about his work and how much everything promised to improve. They could finally look forward to their weekends. He hoped she would often weep for no reason but happiness in the future. "Besides," he went on, "I am always with you. I can hear your thoughts, even feel your heartbeat in the distance."

"And I yours. But then I miss you all the more. Even when you are with me, right now, I miss you."

"So do I."

She remembered on their way home that she would need a spare key for their room so that she could prepare dinner on Friday afternoon. "Be sure to catch the early bus."

"I'll try my best," he said, laughing. "I had no idea you were so domestic. Though we mustn't waste time, because…by the way, are you a good cook?"

"A dreadful one. But I've a whole week to learn, before you come back. The chef will teach me. We are on great terms."

"Will the doctor allow you to stay with me?"

"Yes, at last. I might even be discharged since I'm much better. At least for now."

"I can hardly wait. I didn't tell you that Stefan wants us to join him in San Francisco, right after you get cured in Denver. Before anything else, he told me to try for an audition with the symphony."

"I'm so glad you two seem to be kindred spirits."

"If it weren't for you, we could be the best of friends."

"Don't worry, I won't stand in your way. Oh, but Victor..." He could read the worry in her smile, "I'm afraid America will still lock me out."

"I'll find you a key."

"Here you go again--Victor Nameless, the eternal optimist."

He sensed a change of mood in her remark. It wasn't the first time she rejected his genuine desire to cheer her up. Why was she always ready to give support to others, he said, but refused to accept any help?

"I appreciate your good intentions, but need to restore my independence. I'm never allowed to fend for myself. After years in sanatoriums, I still feel like a prisoner, always forced to ask permission for this or that. Life changes, and I need to be free to grow and change along with it in my own way."

"That's exactly what I want for you, too."

"Sometimes, it's just that sometimes I feel helpless and angry at myself. I've always been moody, and now it's getting worse, like being in a constant state of alarm. I'm afraid that your love for me may die because of my short temper. Maybe you feel duty-bound by my illness but won't admit it."

"Duty-bound...?"

"Oh, Victor, it would be more helpful and give me more hope if you left as soon as your visa arrives."

"Tatyana, stop. Let's not go there."

She laughed, shaking her head. "But that's exactly what I want for you, to go there, to America, ahead of me. I can't stand destroying your future because of my nightmares.

Stefan told you about that monster in the camp who kept threatening to kill me if I breathed a word to anyone about his love letters. He repeated those threats before the end of the war and tried to force me to sign a paper stating that he had saved my life on several occasions. When I refused, he pointed his pistol at me again, so I asked him how he expected me to tell the Allies that he had saved me if I was dead."

"Good God, Tatyana, you took quite a chance!"

"Not really. I knew he was scared to death. By that time, I had learned what a coward he really was."

"Do you remember his name?"

"Yes, and Stefan was trying to take him to court. But no one has cared to react at all."

Victor frowned. "I can't leave you here, alone with all that."

"Sometimes you remind me of Francesco. Playing my savior."

"Poor Francesco. I felt sorry for him, but am so relieved you didn't marry him."

"We never had a humorous moment together. Nothing even remotely funny." Tatyana shook her head. "I couldn't have lived like that."

"Perhaps you think that I, too, am not remotely funny."

"For heaven's sake, Victor. You make me laugh every time I think of those loving market women with their newspaper bosoms. And that midwife who reminded you of the prophet Jeremiah. Your humor, your patience. It must have taken superhuman strength to hold on to your real self."

"Remember our torch? There was not much to hold on to but my longing to find you."

"How odd you should say that. Because you were the last thought I held on to. You who saved me at my worst moment in the camp."

"I don't understand."

"I was desperate, starving, too weak to hope or fight for my inner freedom when I heard you whisper in my ear one night, in the bunk I shared with Svetlana. You held me close and told me to take heart, restoring my courage at the most critical moment."

"What made you wait so long to tell me?"

"I was afraid you would think I lost my mind. You may believe I was hallucinating, but am sure that you and my madness saved my life."

"Perhaps it was telepathy," he said, deeply moved. "For you must have felt how I constantly dreamed of finding you again. Is it possible that we actually survived for each other?"

***

The following Friday, a rosy-cheeked Tatyana embraced Victor in great excitement. She was preparing her first meal of salad and *spaghetti alla carbonara*. The chef at the sanatorium had shown her how to fry cloves of garlic, crisp bacon and break it into small pieces, then add some chopped ham. With his chin on her shoulder, Victor watched her add some butter and parsley to the finished dish, beat in two eggs, and divide two portions on preheated plates, covering each dish with flakes of parmesan cheese.

After dinner, Tatyana showed him her photographs. She had taken pictures of many patients and roamed all over town, catching characters in shops, streets, or alleys. Stunned and pleased with her success, Victor asked why she hadn't shared her news with him sooner. She explained that she had asked Stefan not to breathe a word to Victor about her good luck because she wanted to surprise him on his next visit. "I used to think we had nothing in common," she said, as he contemplated the pictures of her fellow patients. "The camera taught me a lesson in humility. It obviously saw more than I did. Look at the eyes of this woman, the defeat."

Victor saw young faces turned prematurely old, men and women expressing thwarted hope and despair. Gazing inward, they seemed to be isolated in a self-imposed exile or an unbearable past. Only a few of them were smiling with confidence.

"We know nothing about others till we look at them closely," Tatyana said. "Without judgment. That's what these patients taught me. It's the only way to understand and record what they went through and how much they are still suffering. Thanks to you, my darling, and your camera, I have found this special world that means so much to me."

He looked at her work in amazement. It revealed the characters of her models, just as her own depth of character was mirrored in them. He was excited to discover a new maturity and unexpected artistry emanating from her stunning portraits.

"Each of these people has a story to tell," she went on vivaciously. "I just clicked at the instant of a heartfelt disclosure. Thanks to your camera, I recovered some independence after all that terrible stagnation. The good news is that a friend of Stefan's owns a gallery in town and is interested in my work. He has just sold a couple of my portraits."

***

During the weekends that followed, the most ordinary routines, such as shopping for food, preparing simple meals, walking on the hills on sunny afternoons, and, above all, their passionate nights of love, blended into one easy harmony. Even the weekly separation became part of that cycle. It intensified their longing for one another, rewarding them at each reunion with a happiness they had no longer hoped to find.

A letter from Svetlana announced her imminent departure for the United States. She hoped the two of them would soon follow her to Denver. She could hardly wait to be reunited with Tatyana and meet the wonderful Victor.

"It sounds too good to be true," Tatyana said. "Denver! When will you marry me?"

Victor gave her a radiant smile. "You propose to me only because you want to be with Svetlana."

"Am I that transparent?"

"Like a glass-bottomed boat. What sort of wedding do you want?"

"A private one. Just for the two of us, in Milano. Don't even tell Stefan. Then let's ask Dora and Giuseppe to come for a visit from Venice. I can hardly wait for you to meet them. If only I had listened to Dora and stayed with her at the Lido. She would have saved me. You were right when you told me, back in Stuttgart, that I was foolhardy. I've never forgiven myself for being such a foolhardy fool."

***

Awaiting Tatyana's final medical check-up before her dismissal from the sanatorium, Victor rented a larger room with a matrimonial bed, cooking facilities, and a shower that grew cold after the first two minutes. Would married life in such close quarters cause her new stress?

In the morning before his concert, Victor rehearsed Mozart's Flute Quartet No.1 in D for a last time. No longer used to appearing in public, his stage fright grew out of proportion when he entered the church in the early afternoon. The place was filled to capacity. A peek through the curtain revealed Dr. Ferrari, Mario, and a number of patients from his former convalescent home, as well as their friends from the sanatorium.

The flute quartet was the last on the program. As soon as he lost himself in the music, Victor's fear dissolved, and his hands grew as steady as the beats of his heart. The sounds of the flute began to rise, transporting him into a realm far from all other concerns. As the music flowed through him effortlessly, he felt like a mere conveyor of heavenly sounds transmitted to him by some divine interpreter.

The stormy applause, followed by a standing ovation, left him in a daze. Listening to Maestro Belluni and his colleagues' praise for his outstanding performance, Victor lowered his head, overcome with grief.

Dr. Ferrari invited all the players and Tatyana to dinner in a nearby restaurant. Victor would have preferred to be tucked away in the gabled room, hiding from all and especially Tatyana's all-seeing eyes. She had just whispered to him that, although this was only the third time she had heard him play, she could now foretell the full measure of his future achievements.

How could Mozart's music and a moment's success cause him to face all the darkness of the past, instead of allowing him to find joy in the moment? Had the horror, brutality, and indifference, along with his pain, hunger, and loneliness, assailed him more than he had ever admitted to himself? He could see how giving in to his despair would have caused him to die. But why stare at tragedy in his moment of triumph?

He forced himself to eat, to smile, to give his friends the impression that he was still lost in happiness and love for Mozart's exquisite music. On leaving the restaurant, he shook hands with everyone, thanking Maestro Belluni and the doctor for all their help, promising to keep in touch, perhaps to return to Meran in some distant future.

Back in the gabled room for a final night, Tatyana put her arms around him. He wept in silence for all the losses he had suffered.

"I'm sorry," he sobbed, "I just…"

"Don't be sorry, my darling. I'm so glad that you are finally coming to terms. You have needed this for the longest time."

***

Returning to Milano the next morning, Victor felt exhausted, yet relieved of the burden he had carried on his shoulders for years. Two days later, Tatyana surprised him in the late afternoon with a knock at the door. She had been dismissed from the sanatorium, and one of the doctors had an appointment in the city and offered to drive her all the way to Victor's new home. When Victor apologized for the ramshackle room, she told him not to worry. It reminded her of her place on Giudecca, in Venice. "Besides, it's only temporary."

He told her it might still take a while before the arrival of their visas.

"So we wait a little longer. You're teaching me to be more patient."

"But I want to offer you at least a lovely room."

"Room is in the smallest hut for a truly loving pair," Tatyana quoted. "I'm so happy just to be with you, to be out of that sanatorium. I thought it would never happen."

The next day, after the morning's work, Victor couldn't wait to get back to her for lunch and the welcome Italian afternoon *siesta*. Five days of longing to see her in Meran had merely turned into a few hours. Another day passed, and he found the room transformed. The landlady had given Tatyana two colorful cushions for their bed, a red and white checkered tablecloth, and some ceramic plates and cups. He brought her a bouquet of yellow tea roses and she surprised him with a light summer meal.

Stefan had lent him a bicycle. The ride to the office took him only six minutes. He didn't like to leave her alone in that stuffy room, in this noisy neighborhood. The heat was stifling. Tatyana didn't tell him how much time she spent outdoors on her photography. To her, each hour seemed to pass within five minutes. She was exhilarated by her new life in the big city.

37.

TATYANA

A very private wedding

Milano, June 24, 1948

I invited Dora and Giuseppe to join us at our wedding, asking whether Giuseppe would like to be Victor's best man. Dora promptly expressed her delight at the prospect of sharing our special day and meeting the mysterious Victor, while Giuseppe was honored to be chosen. I know Dora has always felt like a mother to me, and now she asked my permission to treat us to a special meal. She was going to reserve a table in a charming restaurant. "For five people, since I'm sure you'll want your friend Stefan to join us."

Dora and Giuseppe had met Stefan last year in Meran. Since our joyous occasion might cause him nothing but pain, I told Victor I didn't have the heart to invite him.

"But he definitely wants to be included," Victor said. "When I mentioned our plans, he wanted to treat us to lunch. I believe he's done a lot of soul searching. He fully understands how we both longed to be reunited after all these years."

"He has obviously grown to like you."

"Does that make you feel uncomfortable?"

"A little. But if that's the way he feels, we need to include him, especially after Dora's request."

Dora and I embraced each other as soon as she and Giuseppe knocked at our door. After meeting Victor for the first time, she took me aside and whispered her approval. At last I was rewarded, she said, for all my waiting. The two of them treated us and Stefan to an exquisite meal and brought me some lovely gifts: an elegant black pantsuit, a light blue silk scarf, and a soft leather purse.

I couldn't stem my tears. As I murmured an excuse and rushed to lock myself in the restroom, Dora must have taken those tears for a sign of gratitude. Though delighted to be among such good friends, to witness Stefan's selfless love and, above all, my deepening bond with Victor, I was shaken with grief for my parents and Leila. I missed them more than ever for being unable to take part in my happiness. I could hardly believe in my own good fortune. It was like a dance that only Victor and I were now able to share: our mutual losses, like steps alternating between singular happiness and deep sorrow.

After washing my face, I opened the purse I had grabbed in my turmoil and found a large white envelope with my name on it. Inside was a card signed by Dora and Giuseppe:

"*To our dearest Tatyana and to Victor, with our love and wishes for a long and happy life together…*"

There was a smaller envelope in a side pocket of the purse, stuffed with hundred-dollar bills. I counted up to ten. Like a thief, I quickly put back the envelope and closed the purse. Dora knocked at the door before I could recover from my shock and asked me what was wrong.

"I'm overwhelmed. You are far too generous."

"Not at all. Giuseppe and I decided you two will need something to hold you over till you can make a living in the New World."

"But you already gave me so many lovely presents."

Dora dabbed at my cheeks with a handkerchief. I told her about the camera that Victor had given me, and how it had changed my life, adding that he was still mourning the loss of his silver flute. Would she mind if I used part of that money to surprise him with a new instrument?

"Mind? I'd be delighted!"

"Oh, Dora, he'll cherish it more than anything else. See these cheap brass rings we just bought each other for the occasion? Now the flute and the camera he gave me will take the place of precious wedding bands and remind us of you every day."

She took my arm as we went back to join the men. They gave me worried looks. I apologized for my hurried disappearance. Victor pulled a check from his wallet and handed it to me. "Look what Stefan gave us for a wedding present."

"It's nothing but a bonus for the outstanding work Victor has done for me," Stefan explained. I thanked him, overjoyed about the love of our friends. Before thanking Giuseppe, I kept five of the bills in my bag and gave Victor the envelope with the rest of the Battista's lavish gift.

***

Through Stefan's connections, I found the perfect flute. He secretly drove me to the home of a retired flautist from the orchestra of La Scala who needed to sell one of his exquisite instruments. Of shining silver, the flute was covered by a red velvet cover and ensconced in a finely carved wooden box.

"I have to pinch myself," Victor said with the happiest smile when he found the flute on his dinner napkin. "My God, this is a gift from heaven." He slowly lifted the instrument to his lips and then put it down again. "Where on earth did you find it?" He ran his fingers up and down its length, testing every hole. "It's a dream from a forgotten world."

I told him that the flute was half of Dora's and Giuseppe's present to us, so I could turn my share into a wedding gift.

"My dearest, I'm quite mortified...I have nothing for you but..."

"*Kaiserschmarren*," I finished the sentence for him. "What about the camera? We gave each other the two most important gifts besides..."

"Love?"

"And I know how to make it now."

"Love?"

"No, silly, *Kaiserschmarren*. The chef at the sanatorium gave me a great recipe."

"I, too, have a whole book full of delicious recipes." Victor put his arms around me, whirling me in a dance through the narrow space of our room.

38.

UP IN HEAVEN,
DOWN IN HELL

During the last week of September, Stefan asked Victor to join him in the Galleria for a drink after work.

"Tatyana looks much better," he said. "I haven't seen her so well and happy in ages. This makes me feel worse, for I have to tell you that our offices are about to close. There is no more need for translations. It's not just losing your job. Your visas are about to arrive, and I'm worried about her X-rays."

Victor looked at him in dismay. "But she's in remission…"

"I'm afraid that may not be enough. Her condition seems unpredictable. In any case, I've made arrangements for your continuing support with the Jewish Committee, including your passages to Denver."

Victor was grateful for the lack of pity in Stefan's matter-of-fact delivery of the report. He asked about Stefan's own plans. He meant to join a center for world peace in San Francisco, Stefan said, and was interested in working for a future holocaust museum in Washington or California.

"As you know, your work permit was only temporary," he went on, pouring more wine into their glasses. "Should Tatyana be unable to join you when the visas arrive, it will be best if you leave ahead of her to prepare for her arrival and even her operation, with Svetlana's help. In the meantime, I may be able to help you find some temporary work in Denver."

"I appreciate your offer, but we may be stranded here for a long time. And I have no intention of leaving her."

"It may not take long. As you know from Svetlana's last letter to

Tatyana, she has found a highly recommended surgeon who will take care of her in that Jewish hospital."

Shocked by the news and too embarrassed to mention that Tatyana had never told him about that letter, Victor felt a surge of anger at what seemed to be an intentional omission.

"You had better join forces with that surgeon as soon as possible," Stefan recommended with unexpected urgency. "He may help you in more ways than one. I'll send him a glowing letter about your special contribution to our postwar efforts with the Allies."

"I appreciate the thought, Stefan, but I won't leave her here alone."

"She could go back to the sanatorium for a while."

"Remember what happened when she left for Venice?" Victor tried to catch his breath. "You expected her to be safe and she landed in hell. Those sanatoria have made her feel like a prisoner."

"Victor, the war is over. Things are improving."

"Not for millions. And not for us. Not yet."

***

Arriving home that night, Victor found Tatyana upset because he had forgotten to let her know he would be late for dinner. She always feared some accident on his bike in the heavy evening traffic. Instead of apologizing, he reported Stefan's news. "I understand you showed him a letter from Svetlana," he said, "but never mentioned this to me."

"There was nothing to tell." She filled their plates and set them on the table. "Since you always refuse to leave without me."

"You must have talked it over with Stefan."

"What of it?" she asked irritably.

"You two must have discussed it in secret."

"Suppose we did talk it over."

"Behind my back."

"We met behind your back to pick up your flute. It's no use discussing this with you because you are too stubborn to listen."

"Today he advised me to go ahead without you as soon as our visas arrive." He stared at the dinner without seeing it. "I can't make this out. He suggested that you might go back to the sanatorium while waiting for your chance to join me in Denver. I always thought he cared so much for you."

"He does care. For both of us."

"And you obviously don't mind risking another separation from me."

"That's not the point."

"Then what is?"

"Oh Victor, when will you ever understand that I don't want to keep you from getting back to your music?" She took hold of her chair and then sat down at the table. "You need to finally be free after your endless deprivations."

"Don't we all?"

"But now I'm the one holding you back."

"Stop repeating yourself. You have never held me back."

"I can see how disappointed you are because you are no longer able to work."

"And I suppose your bad moods are connected to your writing in that black book," he said to his own surprise. "What are you planning to do with it?"

"Nothing. Stefan wanted me to preserve it as an historical document, but I threw it in the fire."

"You did what?"

"It was an act of cleansing. Instead of helping me, it pulled me back into that hell."

"I thought you meant to bear witness. Stefan will be upset!"

"There are plenty of other witnesses. The world knows, and the world has done nothing."

Victor went to the window, still worried about a possible secret motive for her insistence of sending him away.

"Neither you nor Stefan can share my horror of having to remember those monsters all over again," she said dismally. "I'll never forget how they degraded us. Their foul language. They made me feel ashamed of the human race." Victor turned around to look at her. "To be exposed to such insanity," she went on, "such hatred. No one can imagine my relief when the flames devoured that notebook."

He sat down beside her. "All right, Tatyana, I understand. But we can't go on like this. You are up in heaven one day, back in hell the next. Perhaps, after all, you are sorry that you did not marry Stefan."

"I can't believe what you are saying."

"He's leaving any day now. If I let you go, he could still take you with him."

Tatyana gave him an angry look. "Thank you for pointing it out to me."

"What makes you so eager to send me ahead? Perhaps you didn't think Stefan would leave so soon, and hoped…"

"Hoped for what? That he would wait for me?"

"Yes, and maybe…"

"After all the friendship and loyalty he showed you…"

"Tatyana, I have no work and no future. You might have regrets. Stefan could give you a good and peaceful life."

"I can't believe…"

"What am I to do? Go for auditions in different cities?"

"Another one of your brilliant fantasies. Maybe you expect to play first flute at La Scala. Without a work permit."

He picked up a fork and tightened his fist around it. "So you don't think I play well enough?"

"Don't do this, Victor."

"I can always make a hatful of money with the beggars in the street."

"You know I didn't mean that. You just can't get an orchestra job as a stateless refugee. Not in Europe. Not at this time."

"Neither can you. But here you are, starting to sell your portraits and about to make a living for both of us. Look who's turned out to be a burden to whom."

He threw the fork to the floor.

Trembling, Tatyana pushed herself away from the table. "Since my bit of success is such a blow to your self-esteem, why not go ahead as soon as the visas arrive?"

"So you really want me to leave."

"Don't you understand that staying here without work will destroy you? It may destroy us both."

"And leaving you behind without knowing how and when you'll be able to join me will not destroy me?"

Here they were, fighting with each other instead of raging against fate. Feeling trapped and exasperated, Victor picked up his overcoat and rushed out the door.

"Victor! Come back!"

Deaf to her call, oblivious of the chill autumn wind, he walked through the dark streets, hands jammed into the pockets of his overcoat, smarting over his suspicions. And yet, hadn't he always felt sure of Tatyana's selflessness and loyalty? Perhaps he ought to question his own jealousy and anger.

He recalled the desperate letter she had sent to him in Turin and realized that she must dread a separation as much as he did. *She's trying to liberate me. If I stay, I'll remain trapped by the restrictions imposed on stateless persons in Europe. She may just want me to be free.*

As he walked on, taking deep breaths, it grew clear to him that she wasn't hiding any other secret motive. Stefan was not a factor. Tatyana was still ready to risk her life for him. In spite of her mood swings, she was more than ever the soul mate he had always adored. And she was still fighting her demons.

This insight confirmed that he needed to listen to her conflicting emotions more carefully. Hadn't friends and colleagues pointed out to him in the past that he had the perfect pitch of a true musician? His modesty had never allowed him to inflate his self-importance. And where was it now, this pitch? Knowing what she had endured, he was fully in tune with her fluctuating moods. She was one of the singular beings who had overcome the most terrifying hardships to preserve her inner freedom. He would never blame her if she had lost her courage under such circumstances, but loved her all the more for not succumbing to despair.

Caught in an icy wind and anxious to join her at home, he realized that he was lost. After wandering through unfamiliar streets for another hour, he found an open bar, where he ordered a glass of wine and asked for directions to Via Manzoni. To his relief, the bar's owner was about to close his shop and offered him a ride home.

At one o'clock, he turned the key in the door. Tatyana jumped out of bed and threw herself into his arms. "Oh, Victor, I was afraid you would never come back."

"And where did you think I would go?" he asked, covering her with kisses. "My dearest Tatyana, I can't tell you how sorry I am."

"Me too," she murmured. "Let's forgive each other tomorrow."

They sank into bed in a close embrace and immediately fell asleep.

39.

JENNIE AND ROBIN

Stefan left Europe in a cheerful mood, expressing his hope that Victor and Tatyana would soon be able to join him in San Francisco. Victor did not tell him about his fear of another exile or odyssey. This time as a penniless stranger in New York, forced to make his way through another unknown landscape. He also remained silent about his worries over Tatyana's permit to enter the United States and her pending operation in Denver. He spent his days practicing his music and preparing himself for a job in some faraway orchestra.

In one of his recurring dreams, the two of them were climbing a dusty mountain path, tired, thirsty and confused about their final destination. Their feet were bleeding. Stopping to rest, Victor took the flute from his knapsack and played her a tune. Tatyana drank the tune like water from a mountain spring. The music restored her strength. They resumed their climb when three riders appeared on the horizon. Or was it another fatamorgana, like the mirage he had imagined on his aborted flight to Kabul? As the riders came closer in the sweltering sun, Victor recognized three American cowboys. They stopped, then pointed their rifles, ready to shoot.

Victor threw up his arms, shouting, "Denver! Denver! Denver!"

They laughed at him and demanded to see Tatyana's X-rays. He pulled a document from his pack, but they shook their heads without looking at it, shouting that Denver would never open its doors to her. They cursed and spat, then lifted their rifles to strike them. Throwing nooses around their necks, they dragged them all the way to Termez.

He awoke in anguish. His nightmares returned in different guises, rekindling his fearful memories of Tashkent, prison cells, and camps. When would they ever overcome the obstacles denying them freedom and a new life?

He was pleased, on the other hand, about Tatyana's growing success with her photography. Stefan's friend was selling more and more of her work in his gallery. On especially fruitful days, they would dine in a small *trattoria*. One Saturday night in October, they had to share a table with another couple in the small restaurant: a handsome Englishman with a blond mustache and an attractive brunette who welcomed them in Italian with a strong Slavic accent. Victor and Tatyana learned that the young couple had just been married and planned to move to Australia by the end of December.

"We were also just married and are waiting to leave for the United States," Victor said. Continuing their conversation in English, the husband, Robin Scott, volunteered that he hoped to find work as an engineer in Sydney. His wife had escaped from her native Prague to England where she had worked in the Czech underground.

After a last perilous journey to France, Jennie had met Robin in London at the end of the war. She explained that she had secretly traveled back and forth to the Continent, bringing Jewish children to England with the help of nuns and priests who had hidden them in convents.

The young woman blushed as they looked at her with admiration. Her regal bearing ran counter to her unpretentious manner. The two couples took to each other like long lost friends. When Jennie learned of Tatyana's work, she asked to see her photographs, and Tatyana invited the young couple to their home for coffee.

Following that visit, they met twice a week for dinner. Jennie, inspired by Tatyana's work, was toying with the idea of taking up photography in Sydney. One day she joined her, walking the cobblestoned streets, carrying her own camera and watching Tatyana talk in her fluent Italian to bums, beggars, and stray cats hiding below parked cars. In the restaurant later that evening, Jennie related their escapade to Robin and Victor.

Robin took Tatyana's hand. "I wish you two could come to Australia with us."

Tatyana sighed. "I may be stuck here indefinitely, thanks to my condition."

"So, what are you going to do?" Robin asked, perturbed.

"I want Victor to go ahead to America without me."

Victor looked at her. "Please, don't…"

After a silence, Jennie intervened. "Come to our place tomorrow afternoon. And Victor, will you bring your flute? We'd love to hear you play."

***

The visas arrived a week later. Victor and Tatyana were to make an appointment at the American consulate. Everything promised to go according to plan. At the end, one of the clerks at the consulate handed Victor the papers to be filled out by the American physician who had been appointed to do their check-ups and take their X-rays.

It had been raining for several days, and the next morning Tatyana felt tired and chilled. Victor took her temperature. She had a slight fever.

"It's just a cold," she said, coughing. That night water ran noisily down the gutters in the street, and the wind whipped against barren trees, rattling the shutters of the windows. Tatyana's fever was gone in the morning, but she felt thoroughly chilled.

"Let's postpone the X-rays for a few days," Victor suggested.

By evening, she developed a sore throat, but insisted on keeping the appointment.

"I'll take a chance with the X-ray," she said. "I won't wait another day. We may be lucky."

But the following day, her cough got worse. Victor went out in the pouring rain to get more medication at the pharmacy. While the pharmacist was filling the prescription, Victor reached for his wallet and unwittingly pulled out the document he was to present to the American physician. Tatyana had signed it already. He stared at it in dismay, remembering the shock he had felt in Tashkent at the discovery of his mutilated trouser pocket.

They won't let her go, a voice rose inside him.

When the pharmacist returned, Victor shoved the pills into his pocket along with the document, put three thousand lire on the counter and, without waiting for his change, ran back into the storm.

Instead of going straight home, he rushed to the Scotts' apartment building and up the three flights of stairs to their flat.

Jennie opened the door. "Victor! What's wrong?"

He followed her into the sitting room. Too breathless to speak, he waved at Robin who was just coming in from the hallway.

"Let me take your coat," Jennie said. "You are drenched."

"I have come to…" Victor stopped, at a loss as to what to say.

Robin and Jennie asked him to sit down. They faced him on the sofa, waiting for him to say more.

The visas have finally arrived."

"At last!" Jennie said. "That's wonderful news."

"Unfortunately, Tatyana has a sore throat, but she is adamant to leave as soon as possible. We still need checkups and X-rays. That may ruin everything."

"Can't you just postpone it, at least for a week?" Jennie asked.

"She doesn't want to waste any more time and believes that a sore throat won't affect the X-ray."

"She's probably right," Robin said.

Jenny disagreed. "I think she's taking a big risk. She might ruin her chances and never get another one. Why can't she see that? Would you like me to talk to her? I feel close to her, like a sister. No, wait a minute. I have a better idea. Suppose I go to the doctor with you, pretending to be Tatyana? With my looks and my Slavic English accent, I could easily pass for Yugoslavian."

"Be careful," Robin warned. "Suppose you get caught?"

"I think Robin is right," Victor said.

Jennie frowned. "How would they find out? It's such a far-fetched idea. The doctor will never think of such a prank."

"Maybe so. But Jennie, really I…" Victor put his hand on her arm to make her stop. Jennie smiled at him. "Let's consider it done," she said.

Victor looked at Robin. "But you disagree. I really appreciate your good intentions," he said to Jennie, "but…"

"Jennie always does what she wants," Robin told him. "It's all right with me."

"Victor, you must trust me. I pretended to be the Protestant mother of a number of Jewish children and managed to smuggle them out, right under the Nazis' noses."

"Yes, she was amazing," Robin confirmed.

"But don't tell Tatyana till after it's done," Jennie went on. "Can you find an excuse to come back this afternoon and bring me the rest of the documents?"

"I have one right here." Victor pulled out the medical document from his coat pocket. As he hesitated, she took it out of his hand.

"Good," she said, scanning it. "Tatyana has signed it already. Her writing looks easy to copy."

"Jennie, I don't think..." Victor murmured. "It's not only risky to break the law, but wrong."

"Not if it saves your lives, after all this agony." Jennie declared. "Let me call the consulate and practice being Tatyana. This must be the number." She pointed at the document.

Before Victor could protest, she picked up the phone from a small table next to the couch and waited for the person in charge. Introducing herself as Tatyana, she asked for the earliest medical appointment "for myself and my husband."

"Wednesday morning, at eleven. Thank you very much," she said and hung up. "Day after tomorrow," she told Victor.

"Won't that be too soon?" Victor asked.

Robin assured him. "Fresh fish are good fish, the Germans say. Victor, it's not Tatyana who is going!"

"But be sure not to breathe a word to her," Jennie warned again. "Let's surprise her!"

Back home, Victor found it hard to control his agitation. Tatyana was still in bed. "What took you so long?" she asked. "Did anything happen?"

"I ran into Robin Scott."

"And what did you talk about?"

He shrugged. "Nothing. Australia."

Afraid of Tatyana's disapproval, he waited on her with false cheerfulness, feeding her cough syrup and hot cups of tea. Later, he serenaded her with passages of César Franck's sonata that he had transcribed for the flute, and then read her a story by Chekov in English translation.

The promise of a pizza was a good excuse for leaving her once more. He hurried back to the Scotts to let them examine the rest of the documents.

"Look." Jennie showed him a separate page filled with Tatyana's falsified signatures. "I've been practicing."

"And I have been calling her Tatyana all day," Robin told him. "Tatyana here, Tatyana there, Tatyana *su*, Tatyana *giù*."

"I don't think we should go through with this plan," Victor said again. "When I came to see you this morning, I just needed to pour out my heart."

"Oh, Victor, I can't believe you and Tatyana are such good Germans with your respect for all this disgusting bureaucracy that threatens to destroy your lives."

"What if we go through with your plan and get caught? It could destroy us all."

***

Tatyana sat up in bed when Victor returned with the pizza. She looked at him with feverish eyes. "I've been thinking," she said. "We might as well go to the consulate in a couple of days and get rid of this anguish."

His hands were shaking as he brought her a hot slice of pizza.

"Victor, what's going on? You were nervous when you came home this morning, and now you seem anxious. And what took you so long to buy a pizza?"

"I stopped for a cup of coffee."

"You can't fool me." Tatyana pushed the tray away. "Tell me the truth."

"I just…" He lowered his head. "There's nothing to tell."

"Yes, there is. You might as well let me know."

He took a deep breath. "This morning I went to the Scotts," he admitted to his own surprise."

"The Scotts, what for?"

"I needed to talk to someone. Jennie offered to help, but then she said…"

"Said what?"

"That she would go to the consulate in your place, pretend to be my wife and take *your* X-rays."

"For heaven's sake, doesn't she know that's criminal? How could you even think of doing it?"

"I was at my wits' end. And she was so eager to help us. She successfully smuggled Jewish children out of convents right in front of those Nazis. She believes that a minor transgression is all right if it saves our lives."

"She means well, but she must be out of her mind."

"You should've seen her generosity and enthusiasm."

"I know. But she might have ruined all our lives. Her silly scheme could be easily detected, and we might have been sent to prison. It could even have ruined the Scotts' chance to leave for Australia, not to speak of closing all American doors on us for good."

"Isn't that just a bit melodramatic?"

"Melodramatic!" Tatyana jumped out of bed. "Suppose Jennie's X-rays are compared with my latest one from the sanatorium? Dr. Forst has proof of my collapsed lung and Jennie's is healthy, probably perfectly clear. The consulate's doctor might already have a copy of mine."

"That's farfetched," Victor murmured, but she kept shaking her head. "She was utterly convinced that she would save our lives," he went on, "even called the consulate to make an appointment in your name, and was told that we could come on Wednesday. I was in a daze, too desperate to think of the consequences."

Abashed, he admitted to himself that his lack of resistance was based on Jennie's desire to help. "Tatyana," he pleaded, "Let's wait a few more days. Your cough might be gone by the end of the week."

"Wednesday, Victor. We might as well keep Jennie's appointment."

40.

ON A ROLLER COASTER

As soon as they arrived at the consulate, they asked for fresh papers. After filling them out, they had to wait in a hallway for nearly two hours as others, expecting the doctor's verdict, were called ahead of them. Their anguish increased with each crawling minute. At last, a nurse had them sit down in the doctor's office, where they waited on tenterhooks for another half hour.

A young man in a white coat finally hurried into the office, introducing himself as Dr. Murray. He held a large manila envelope in his hand, saying he had received a report about Tatyana's health and an X-ray from Dr. Forst in Meran. It included her deportation to Auschwitz and her long siege with tuberculosis.

Tatyana and Victor exchanged quick glances.

"What an ordeal!" the doctor exclaimed. "I served as a medic in the U.S. Army and couldn't believe what I saw in Dachau."

"Auschwitz was by far the worst," Victor said.

"How can human beings from a civilized nation stoop to such crimes?" Dr. Murray went on. "It's hard to believe that an entire nation can feel such hatred against people who have never done anyone the slightest harm."

Turning to Tatyana, he told her that he was glad to learn she was in remission. "See this small dark spot?" He was pointing at an X-ray he had pulled from the manila envelope. "It means nothing, most likely," he added with a smile that struck her as more apologetic than comforting. "But I must ask you to come back in a few days for another try, just to make sure. Will a week from tomorrow work for you?"

They were silent and subdued on the ride home. Tatyana's cough was on the wane, but she felt weak and went straight to bed. Victor brought her a cup of tea, then sat down at the table with a downcast air.

"The doctor seemed torn between duty and compassion," she said. "I believe he would have liked to open the gates for me, but his conscience wouldn't let him."

She could tell by his bent shoulders and the way one hand wrung the other that Victor was in turmoil. "His dilemma is understandable," she went on. "He is obviously kind and caring, but also responsible."

"Though he looks too young for a full-fledged physician, I can't shake the feeling that in spite of his youth you found him more mature than…."

"More mature than you?" she finished the sentence for him. "Oh, darling, no!" Understanding how devastating these last few days must have been for him, she felt sorry to have blamed him for accepting Jennie's foolish scheme. "You all meant so well," she said. "It was an act of love, but now you know better. You forgot everything else in your desire to help me. And here I am, scolding you and my brave friend, instead of showing my gratitude."

"You pulled me out of that department store on Kristallnacht," he said, "All I wanted was to take you into America through another back door."

"And I'm still wondering how you managed to survive all these years without losing your innocence."

"I had loneliness as my hiding place in plain daylight."

"There's more to it. Your kindness appeals to people wherever you go. You may not know this, but I believe you survived because of the power of your gentleness."

He laughed. "I don't think it had anything to do with your romantic idea."

"Then what do you think it was?"

"Being careful not to reveal my German or Jewish origins, except to people I could trust. If the wrong ones had ever found out, they would have destroyed me on the spot."

"That may be true," she said, "but there is more to it. I'm amazed about the way you accepted your suffering with infinite patience, and how you show love to others wherever you go."

"That's because you are my shining example—bearing the torch. You helped me test my capacity to accept and deal with whatever life held in store for me."

Waiting for another week was a new source of worry. In a silent agreement, they took walks in clear weather, read to each other when it rained, joined Jennie and Robin for dinner at the restaurant, watched a couple of Italian and American films. At night, they held each other close when unable to sleep, or on waking from nightmares. He knew she was haunted by that *small dark spot*, which kept growing larger and larger in dismal dreams. "*It means nothing, most likely,*" the doctor had said, and they tried in vain to find comfort in those words.

The night before the appointment, Tatyana was back in the camp remembering how all life had turned into a dance of utter dissolution. No living being should be subjected to such sadism of madmen in love with death—their own and that of others. After her ardent longing for freedom, her liberation had cast her into a wasteland of grief. Her losses, her illness, and the long sojourns in those sanatoria had made it hard to pursue the passionate dream she had hoped to turn into a meaningful purpose. She still had to learn how to overcome her bouts of dejection. If tomorrow that black spot wasn't erased from her life, Victor would refuse to leave without her and be forced to sacrifice his future for an indefinite period of stagnation.

Listening to his quiet breathing, she was aware of his dedication to her well-being and felt deeply grateful for his understanding of her short-tempered ways. All at once, she saw that most of their arguments were caused by love. The irony of it did not escape her. Hadn't their quarrels occurred each time one was trying to rescue the other?

She remembered the nights of her hallucination in the camp, and how her love for Viktor had widened into love for all innocent and suffering humanity. More convinced than ever that a worldwide caring was desperately needed as an antidote to war, hate and prejudice, she wondered if mankind would ever be able to embrace peace and harmony.

The nurse took a new X-ray of Tatyana as soon as they arrived at the consulate. Doctor Murray appeared a few minutes later. Solemn and reserved, he seemed much older, no longer the smiling young American. They watched in anguish as he removed a number of papers from his folder. After a moment's hesitation, he put a final stamp on their documents.

"Tatyana, may I call you Tatyana?"

"Of course."

He pushed the papers across his desk. "You are clear."

"Oh, my God," Tatyana murmured. "Do you mean...?"

"Clear to go, yes. I urge you, however, to go straight to Denver. This is still serious." He turned to Victor after an awkward pause. "I spoke once more with Dr. Forst. He gave me a report about the events of your lives, and your long years of separation. He said that you have admirers at the sanatorium who believe that both your experiences border on the legendary."

Tatyana looked at him, incredulous. "Dr. Forst told you all this? But he was always so strict--hardly ever said a personal word to me."

Doctor Murray smiled. "He told me that you are an exceptional young woman."

She burst into tears. "Forgive me, I can hardly believe.... You have saved our lives!"

The doctor pushed the papers back into the large yellow envelope and gave it to Victor. "I really didn't," he murmured, obviously embarrassed. He got up to give her his good wishes. "I hope you will have a successful operation," he said, patting her shoulder, then shook Victor's hand, wishing them both the best for a new life in the States.

"Thank you for all your kindness," Victor said warmly. "Tatyana needs time to believe in a change of fortune," he explained.

"I can well understand. How can anyone blame her?"

"It's wonderful, as well as frightening, to start all over again." There was a tremor in Victor's voice. "Free at last!" he added happily.

Those last three words were addressed to Tatyana.

Before taking a bottle of *spumante* and a bouquet of sunflowers to the Scotts, they sent telegrams to Stefan, Sophie's sister, and Svetlana.

"It's clear that the doctor took a special liking to you," Victor said in the cab. "But I'm still puzzled. Everything happened so fast. Remember how he showed us that X-ray with the dark spot? He didn't mention it again and just gave you the green light."

"I believe he didn't have the heart to separate us again—not after learning from Dr. Forst what happened to us in the past.

"You are absolutely right!" Victor exclaimed. "But why did he urge us to go straight to Denver? Was it concern about your health?"

"Most likely, though we'll never find out."

"I meant to ask him why we had to be in such a hurry," Victor said, "but something stopped me. I suspect that he took a major chance to help us."

After sharing their good news with Jennie and Robin, Robin filled their glasses. "Let's drink to your happy future."

"And yours," they said in one breath. "We may finally take life into our hands," Victor declared in a tearful voice.

"Victor finds it hard to believe in a change of fortune," Tatyana said softly. Bursting into sudden laughter, he gave her an impish smile.

"I just remembered a most wretched night in Tashkent," he explained. "It's one of the Harper's songs by Goethe:

'*Who never ate his bread with tears,*
Who never wept upon his bed.
In grievous night,
Will never get to know you—heavenly might!'"

He stopped for a sip of *spumante*. "Forgive my poor translation. But those words made me aware that my plight was much worse than Goethe's. He was lucky to have a bed to sleep on and bread to eat with his tears which is much better than eating tears without bread."

"At least you haven't lost your sense of humor," Jennie said, laughing, as she poured more of the liquid gold for everyone.

"I just had a dream. No, it was really a vision," Victor told Tatyana the next morning. "I was back in Zing-Ata. The entire camp was filled with cotton bales. Squeezed between two bales, I looked up and saw the Evangelist. He wore a white garment and slowly rose through a whirl of cotton snowflakes toward a gaping hole in the ceiling. He looked down at me and gave me a sign to join him. I began to float upward while he kept whispering, 'We will heal each other.' Then the two of us passed through the hole in the ceiling and flew into the vault of a star-studded sky."

"How odd you should say that." Tatyana murmured. "I have a similar vision about healing and changing the world. The amount of money spent for thousands of years on wars and destruction is beyond belief. Nature would provide our whole planet with enough food and material for a fraction of that cost. People would no longer have to die of hunger and disease. But human beings seem unable, or unwilling, to stop killing each other."

"Because billions of people have billions of different individual opinions," Victor interjected. "And billions are kept ignorant and prejudiced."

Are you saying that it will never change?"

"I never say never."

"Anyway," she went on after a pause, "I hope you and your Evangelist won't forget to take me along on your journey."

"I'll try to remember." Victor sealed his answer with a kiss.

She sat up in bed, fully awake: "You were always right," she said softly.

"Right-about what?'

"About helping each other. And I'm so happy to know that before anything else, you will soon be able to get back to your music without having to tear yourself away from me. I still can't believe it."

"What else do you have to tell me?"

"I may as well let you know how scared I was that you might finally listen to me and leave me here alone."

"I know. I always knew."

"Well, I...."

"Tatyana, are you sure that you want to leave now, in the cold of winter?"

"Quite sure. Fresh air and the sea can only do me good."

He sighed with relief. To postpone a meeting with the American surgeon who might restore her to good health could pose a greater risk than crossing the Atlantic Ocean in December. At last, Victor was able to fully sympathize with her need for self-reliance. Ready to free himself of his anguish for her, he was going to stand by her with hands tied by love that does not interfere.

41.

A VALEDICTION

His hat turned upside down at a small distance from his feet, an old man is fiddling in the piazza in front of La Scala. He almost sounds as bad as Ivan, the tin can drummer. Victor stops on his way, pulls out his flute, and starts to blow life into the old man's sorry attempt. Now the gouty fingers take a firmer grip on the bow. It is Violetta's song from Verdi's *Traviata*. His performance turns from consumptive whimper into steady lament. Aroused by the flautist's verve and the gathering crowd, he tries to compete with his unknown benefactor. Now the coins drop into his hat. Standing tall, he coaxes his pitiful violin to rise beyond its tinny sounds.

Three tunes later, after the generous applause of the listeners, the hat is full. The old man pours the money into a cloth bag. Warily, Victor beds his flute in its case. Waving goodbye to the old man, who bows to the audience, he thinks, *Ata Giuseppe, Ata Mario, or whatever your name, here is the rounding of a circle. Along with my valediction, I give thanks for the chance of our being able, at last, to leave this ravaged continent.*

42.

REMEMBER HOW I LOST MY LAST NAME?

Dear Viktor,

It seems such a long time since I left Tashkent. I hope you and your family are well. I have learned how to write better in Cyrillic, so you will be able to read this letter.

By now, you must have learned a lot in school. I'm sure you are a good student. Are you still playing the recorder? And do you remember our fairy tales and outings to the bazaar?

I have been in Italy for a long time. Remember how I lost my last name? Well, I finally found it again. I have also found a princess in my own fairy tale. It happened like this: I was walking up a hill through the trees toward a big house, and there I saw her, looking out of a window. She was very beautiful and very sad, but when I asked her to take my hand and sail with me across the ocean to America, she smiled happily. A bad ogre made her sick, and now we hope that a good medicine man will make her well again in a city called Denver. In a couple of days, we shall leave with a big ship from Genoa.

My princess gave me a flute of pure silver. It has a heavenly sound. I wish I could show it to you. Someday I hope to see you again, and then I will play it for you. I practice every day. It makes me think of you, and of how hard you tried to get better on the recorder. This gives me an idea. Each time we play, we can be together in our thoughts, even if we can't see each other.

Please give my warmest wishes to your dear parents, and a kiss to your little sister.

A big hug from your friend

- Victor

P.S. My last name is on the back of this letter. I shall send you my address from America.

Acknowledgements

I am grateful for the publishing services and guidance from Howard VanEs and his team at Let's Write Books, Inc.

Special thanks to my daughter Eva Mautner, artist and painter (eva.mautner-Instagram), for her creative input in the cover design and the practicalities of the final stages of bringing the book into the world.

A special gratitude to my friend and editor Renate Stendhal, for her firm belief in telling this story of the Holocaust that might have been lost like so many others if there wasn't a writer's voice to tell it. Renate worked with me on several drafts to the completion of the novel.

And to my virtual assistant, Daniella Granados, for her competent help and uplifting spirit.

Thanks to the early readers of the manuscript, Tom Solinger and Joe Cohen.

I am grateful to my daughter Daria Cohen for her consistent and loving support.

Many thanks to my grandson Ari, who always rescued me when my computer rebelled and disobeyed.

My deepest appreciation to my dear friend Helen, for always listening and believing in me.

And to ALL who helped to support me along the way—thank you for being there.

Author's Note

I was born in Chemnitz, Germany, and began to write poems and stories at age nine. I have never stopped since.

My father, having read *Mein Kampf,* saw the writing on the wall and decided to sacrifice his highly successful factory for freedom and poverty. In the spring of 1933, our family fled to Turin, Italy.

In spite of the loss of our home and my childhood, I grew to love the new country's beauty, people, and language. In 1938, after five years in school, Mussolini's "racial" laws forced my family to move to Holland. I was fluent in Italian and French at age sixteen, and now had to add another language. Lonely in this unknown country, I taught Italian and French to young children and made friends with neighbors and fellow refugees. Daily new threats against the Jews worsened our collective nightmare.

In 1942, I was twenty years old and married a German refugee friend. As soon as we had signed our names in the presence of the judge, we received a Nazi command to appear at the train station—which meant deportation to a concentration camp. Always in fear of death and worried about one another, my family fled to Brussels, where we found hideouts thanks to personal connections. A terrifying encounter with the German secret police forced us to flee again—first to occupied and non-occupied France, back and forth, trying to find a way to Switzerland, our last resort. After countless setbacks, we were finally able to crawl under a barbed wire fence into the countryside near Geneva. It was a miracle, for the Swiss had just opened their borders to fugitives, but for only six weeks.

Years later, I told the story of this harrowing flight to freedom in my partially autobiographical novel, *Lovers and Fugitives* (1985). I'll always remember a wooden panel on the wall of our rental in The Hague with the inscription *Alles zal reg ko (All will be well).* Those Dutch words had sustained me with hope and courage for the future.

In 1946, my family left for New York, and a new chapter in my life began. I worked in an elegant fur store on Madison Avenue, had my first child, and used every free moment to improve my English. It would take countless years before I would be able to write a book in another new language.

In 1953, after an amicable divorce, I pioneered to San Francisco with my six-year-old son. I began writing my first novel in English, *Out of a Season* (1968), the story of a mother and daughter who were both in love with a charming Italian nobleman. The following year, I married a member of the San Francisco Symphony, an outstanding violinist who was also an orchestra conductor and magician. A few years after giving birth to our two daughters, I began studying creative writing at San Francisco State University. It was the time of the Beat Generation, an occasion to meet poets and artists. At the university, some English professors were famous writers who befriended and consistently inspired me to keep writing.

***

At the end of the last century, I was invited, together with other survivors, to return to Chemnitz. It was my first visit to Germany since my childhood. I was unexpectedly touched and amazed by the sympathy of the many inhabitants who came to meet me. One by one, strangers entrusted me with their own tales about their suffering during the war, sometimes confiding personal secrets.

Many young Germans expressed their horror about the terrible cruelty of their parents or grandparents. When I rang the bell to our family's former apartment, the lady of the house was immediately welcoming and then invited me for dinner a few days later. I could hardly wait to write about places and connections that had seemed long forgotten. My memoir, *The Good Place* (2006), which I translated, first appeared in German, and it was published simultaneously as a series in the largest regional newspaper of Saxony.

At age ninety-seven, I enjoy Qigong, walking, reading, and playing chess with my sixteen-year-old grandson and listening to his wisdom. If time and health will allow, my hope is to complete a potpourri of short stories and excerpts of two more unpublished novels.

Victor Nameless is based on the true, almost unbelievable odyssey of a German Jewish friend during WWII. His experiences as a refugee in the Soviet Union and postwar Italy moved me deeply and gave me the inspiration to write an ever-widening story about courage and love. I stopped and started again and again, for many interesting characters were still elusive—until one night a dream appeared, revealing what I needed to finish the book. It was another miracle late in my life.

www.ingramcontent.com/pod-product-compliance
Lightning Source LLC
Chambersburg PA
CBHW072058020726
47501CB00003B/628